Maureen de l

Born in Shanghai, and interned in a Japanese POW camp as a young child during World War II, Maureen de la Harpe has spent most of her life in Zimbabwe. She was educated in Salisbury (now Harare), and at Rhodes University in South Africa, and lived on a farm in a remote area of the Zimbabwean bush for ten years, before settling with her family in Harare, where she worked mainly in journalism and publishing.

A freelance journalist, writer and public relations consultant, now living in the hills east of Perth, Western Australia, she has three adult children. Her ties with Africa are as strong as ever.

This is her second book. Her first *Msasa Morning* traced her years on an African farm.

MAUREEN DE LA HARPE

ELEPHANT ROAD

Published by Maureen de la Harpe
P O Box 1330, Midland, Perth, Western Australia 6936

© Copyright Maureen de la Harpe 2000

The author asserts the moral right to be identified as the author of this work

ISBN 0-646-39284-0

Printed in Perth, Western Australia
by the Western Australian Museum.
Cover printed by CJ King & Company, Perth, Western Australia.

All rights reserved. No part of this publication may be reproduced, stored in a retrieval system, or transmitted, in any form or by any means, electronic, mechanical, photocopying, recording or otherwise, without the prior permission of the publisher.

This book is sold subject to the condition that it shall not, by way of trade or otherwise, be lent, re-sold, hired out or otherwise circulated without the publishers's prior consent in any form of binding or cover other than that in which it is published and without a similar condition including this condition being imposed on the subsequent purchaser.

*To all who continue the fight to preserve
the wild places of Africa*

"I speak of Africa and golden joys."

Henry IV (Pt 2)
William Shakespeare

AUTHOR'S NOTE

As *Elephant Road* is set in the 1890s and 1950s, old geographic and place names are used throughout: e.g. Salisbury for Harare, Rhodesia for Zimbabwe; and imperial measures are used in place of metric.

Although the idea for the plot was inspired by the very real achievements of English nurses Rose Blennerhassett and Lucy Sleeman, who walked from Portuguese East Africa to the interior of Southern Africa in the early 1890s to start a hospital in the new colony of Rhodesia, this is a work of fiction. All characters are fictitious, except for the obvious public figures whose names appear from time to time.

ACKNOWLEDGEMENTS

Scores of people, too numerous to list here, helped with my research by giving me access to books, research material, their memories, and in a variety of other ways. They know who they are and I thank them. But I would like to make special mention of Tim and Di Tanser in Harare, and Rhona Barker in Perth for the wealth of historic material loaned to me; and also to the Rhodesian Association of Western Australia, for access to its library.

The following works were especially rich sources of background information: *Adventures in Mashonaland*, by Rose Blennerhassett and Lucy Sleeman (Books of Rhodesia); *Kariba*, by Frank Clements; *The Shadow of the Dam*, by David Howarth (Collins); *A Scantling of Time*, by Tony Tanser (Pioneer Head); and *Never a Dull Moment*, by JHR Savory (Stocks Publishing Co).

For the stunning cover picture, I have to thank Mike Coppinger for permission to use a photo from his co-authored book *Zambezi: River of Africa*.

In Zimbabwe, Dr Colin Saunders gave generously of his time to check the manuscript for authenticity of flora and fauna and other elements of bush life. And here in Western Australia, Rusty Whitington took on the thankless task of proof-reading.

Special thanks to dear friends Don and Grace Watson – for always having a bed for me in Harare, and before that, on Nyamfuta.

Finally, but most importantly, I thank my lovely family – the whole extended clan – for their support, practical help and encouragement in a host of ways.

PROLOGUE

Although mountainous clouds had been gathering over the escarpment all afternoon, the storm arrived almost without warning. Musa was repairing a reed fishtrap on the river bank, when lightning flared, thunder grumbled across the sky, and the first gusts of wind stirred the sultry air, sending leaves scudding over the sand.

The clouds advanced rapidly, and the wind carried the sweet, fresh smell of rain. At the water's edge, kingfishers swooped, a dikkop called plaintively, and a troop of impala drank nervously before skittering back into the cover of the trees.

Musa replaced the trap, and clambered up the bank. The sun had sunk behind the mountains across the water, and it was almost dark, but lightning flashes etched each blade of grass as he followed the track skirting the bank.

The first heavy drops plopped into the dust, and within seconds, river and forest were obliterated behind a dense curtain of rain. By the time he reached the low granite kopje overlooking the water, he could see no more than a few feet ahead.

On top of the kopje loomed a cave, but he could not take shelter there. It was a sacred place – the tomb of an ancestral chief, its entrance guarded by a giant mahogany, the domain of the chief's spirit, which lingered after death to watch over his people. Only the tribal diviner had the right to enter the cave; but an overhanging rock, still warm from the sun, jutted at the foot of the outcrop, and he huddled beneath it, hugging his arms against the icy spears of rain.

Lightning crackled, a roar of thunder shook the ground beneath him, and a massive branch hurtled past his head, dislodging a hail of stones. Water sluiced down from the rocks, branches crashed to the ground, and above his head the old tree creaked and groaned. Cowering against the rock, he covered his ears with his hands.

The storm ended as abruptly as it had begun. It was dark now, and as Musa emerged from his shelter, blue forks of lightning still flickered in the north and steam swirled upwards from streaming rivulets of water. The dust that had puffed in small clouds from his feet a short while ago oozed muddily between his toes as he slowly climbed up to the cave to inspect the damage.

He expected to see the giant mahogany battered by the assault of the storm but, although one side of its massive trunk was blackened and charred, and two great limbs lay on the ground, it still cast its umbrella of shadow over the surrounding rocks and tangled vines.

With the loss of branches, part of the lower trunk was visible, and a small, pale object, lit by a watery moon, glimmered from a hollow. Approaching cautiously, Musa withdrew a leather bag, so well protected it was not even damp.

Squatting at the foot of the tree, he opened the bag and took out a worn, leather-bound book. Puzzled, he riffled through the pages, and something fluttered out. When the moon emerged briefly from behind a cloud, he saw that it was a picture – of two white women, in strange enveloping garments.

Musa could not read, and he assumed these objects must be the property of the old chief; they must have been placed in the hollow trunk at the time of his burial. But how much longer would the tree stand after the battering of the storm, he wondered. As he replaced the book, he saw that there was something else in the bag, but he merely glanced at it briefly for it was familiar to him – and he was growing uneasy, and anxious to leave the sacred place.

Seeking a safer niche for the bag, he approached the rough stone wall that barred the dark entrance to the cave. It was well inside the shelter of overhanging rocks, and he stepped over it, and laid the bag on a narrow ledge, where it would be well protected from the elements. Something scrabbled softly from the dank interior, and he swiftly withdrew.

As he regained the track he sighed heavily, for he had much on his mind, and the discovery of the bag was an unwanted complication. He was returning to his kraal from an indaba, a meeting with the District Commissioner, who had told the gathering of headmen that the white men were building a wall across the river. When it was finished, the water would spread across the valley to form a giant lake that would make electricity. He himself had seen the uses of electricity when he had gone briefly to work in Salisbury to earn money to pay the government's two-pound-a-year tax. Electricity made light and moved machines, and it was clear vast quantities were needed for such a city as Salisbury.

New land had been found for his people, the DC told them, land where they could build new homes and plant their crops. The government would help by building roads, stores, schools for the children, and clinics for the sick.

For three days, the headmen had argued in the shade of the large thatched indaba shelter, turning the subject over and over, examining it from all angles. Some refused to believe what they had been told, and returned to their kraals determined to continue as before. Others grudgingly accepted the inevitable: if it was true the river was going to rise and flood their homes, there was nothing to be done but to obey.

But was it true? How could it be possible to stop the great river from flowing as it had done for many many moons? Would not the god of the river send a flood that would smash the wall and sweep away the white men?

What should he tell his people? If the DC spoke truly, and his people had to leave their homes, what of the relics of the old chief, relics of which he was the guardian? Would the chief's spirit, along with countless ancestral spirits that inhabited the forest, come and live with the people in their new homes?

He knew it was up to him to decide, but he was an old man, and tired, and in his heart he was sure of only one thing: he did not want to leave his ancestral land beside the broad, shining river that was as much a part of his life as the blood running through his veins. Perhaps, he concluded, it would be wise to consult the sikatonga *– the diviner – on this matter.*

From the heart of the valley reverberated the low, deep-throated cough of a lion, and he quickened his pace, hurrying towards the glow of a small fire flickering through the trees from his kraal.

PART ONE

1
1957

The aircraft descended through layers of cloud, and the land below, that had been no more than an umber carpet of folds and ridges threaded by strands of silver, resolved into wooded hills and valleys, half in shadow, half in sunlight.

Since their departure from London on an overcast morning four days ago, they had landed, refuelled and taken off four times on the southward flight over the African continent. And each time Elizabeth Pendennis peered through the window, she had been aware only of a vast, purple-brown expanse. Barely a suggestion of human habitation interrupted its wrinkled surface: at night, an occasional sprinkling of lights on an immensity of blackness, soon left behind. Only when the aircraft was descending to land did the anonymous mass form itself into recognisable shapes – roofs, airport buildings, small pockets of civilisation adrift in an ocean of brown nothingness which she found infinitely awesome, hugely daunting.

Now, as the aircraft approached Salisbury, she could make out individual trees, clusters of circular thatched roofs, ploughed lands, a flash of water, a ribbon of road, granite rocks heaped haphazardly. Sunlight glanced off metal rooftops, an avenue of trees with red flowers passed immediately below, and then the aircraft was skimming above the runway, with sheds and a small terminal building swinging into view on the right. Several large aircraft loomed on the tarmac, then smaller ones painted in bright frivolous colours. With a thud and a rush of sound, the wheels touched down.

Emerging from the cabin, disorientated by the sudden descent from air to earth, she was instantly struck by the quality of the light. After the soft, diffused sunlight of home, it had a startling clarity and richness; the sky, as she followed the other passengers across the tarmac, arched wide and high and deep blue overhead, the clouds were towering battlements of cumulus with dark shadows below and snowy crests above. Black men in overalls walked toward the aircraft and two white men in uniforms passed her, speaking in the clipped accents that immediately reminded her of her uncle.

He was waiting as she emerged from Customs – a tall, stooped figure with thinning white hair and skin burnt a leathery mahogany – accompanied by a gnome-like African with a wisp of beard and a face almost as lined as his own.

A kiss, a warm hug, the rough feel of tweed, and the comfortable smell of tobacco enveloped her.

"How's my girl? Was it very tiring? Stupid question. This is my right hand – Julius."

His companion grinned and nodded, displaying tobacco-stained teeth, as he took her cases from the porter.

She took her uncle's arm and they moved towards the entrance. "It was a fine journey, Uncle Nicky, but I can't believe I'm really here. So warm and sunny – you call this winter?"

"Wait till I get you out of Salisbury and on to the farm, it's even better. Air like champagne, makes you want to climb mountains – if you don't have a dickey heart," he grumbled.

She squeezed his arm, happy to be reunited with her favourite relative. "You look wonderful. How are things on the farm?"

"Not bad. Didn't get enough rain, and prices could be better. Wouldn't be a farmer if I didn't have something to complain about, would I?"

A noisy group moved past them, gesticulating and chattering loudly in Italian, and a figure detached itself and touched her sleeve. "Lizi."

"Mario." She was pleased to have a chance to say goodbye to her irrepressible companion of the past four evenings. They had met on the first night stopover in the hotel in Tripoli, where the young Italian had attached himself to her at dinner. Drawing her out of her disorientated, withdrawn mood, he had broken through her reserve, made her laugh at his fractured English, and charmed her with his Latin courtesy.

"Uncle Nicky, meet Mario Pallivera, he looked after me on the flight. Mario – my uncle Nicholas Hamilton – well, great uncle, really. Mario has come to work on the new dam on the Zambezi," she informed Nicholas.

"Kariba?" Nicholas looked with interest at the sturdy, square-jawed young Italian, who exuded an almost tangible vitality.

"Yes, is very exciting for me – my first time in Africa." He turned to her. "Lizi, you give me telephone number, please? Maybe I can see you when I come to town."

"Of course," and she looked inquiringly at Nicholas, who took out his wallet and withdrew a business card.

"*Benissimo*, thank you. Enjoy Africa, Lizi." His eyes were warm and intense as he pressed her hand. "*Ciao*. Goodbye, Signor Hamilton."

Nicholas raised a quizzical eyebrow as he took her arm and guided her towards the glass doors and out into a sunlight so dazzling she had to shield her eyes for a few moments. "He must be good if he's with the Kariba team – they've been hand-picked for that project."

He halted beside a battered Land Rover, veteran of thousands of miles of dust-blown corrugated roads. "You go in front with Julius, you'll have a better view – not that there's much to see in town."

The drive to the city, through wide streets bordered by flowering trees, took only a few minutes. The traffic was light: mainly African men on bicycles, and noisy, diesel-belching buses painted in maroon and cream. Nicholas drew from his shirt pocket a yellow packet of Flag cigarettes, the brand she had never seen him without on visits to England. "I've taken a couple of rooms at Meikles, so you can rest this afternoon, while I do a few things. Then we can head out to the farm this evening, nice and leisurely. How does that sound?"

"Wonderful – give my soul a chance to catch up with my body. I feel as though I left it in London. How far is it to the farm?"

"Only about an hour," Nicholas inhaled with the unalloyed pleasure of the true addict as the Land Rover rattled along a broad avenue of white buildings flanked by umbrella-topped flamboyant trees. The city had a relaxed, small-town feel; she glimpsed a few modern, high-rise buildings, but most reflected the colonial architecture of the early 1900s.

Julius drew up in front of a stately ivory-walled hotel encircled by cool, pillared verandahs. Tables, chairs and potted palms were set out on the pavement, and two stone lions guarded the entrance.

In the cool, high-ceilinged foyer, a porter in starched white uniform and maroon fez carried her bags upstairs to a room overlooking a square, where a fountain was set in clipped lawns shaded by jacaranda trees. Red and gold cannas stood in military rows, flower-sellers hawked their wares on the corner pavement, and black figures sprawled on the grass.

"What d'you feel like? Tea, lunch, stiff gin?" asked Nicholas.

She ran her fingers through her hair. "A cup of tea, a sandwich, a nap, and I'll be ready for anything."

"Spoken like a true Englishwoman. We'll have a snack, then I'll leave you. Got to see my accountant before I blow the season's profits at the races."

At a table in the small hotel garden below her room, Nicholas poured tea into thick white china cups, and handed her a platter of sandwiches decorated with shredded lettuce. For himself, he had ordered a gin and tonic.

The tea tasted different, pleasant but different. As she brought him up to date with family news, plump turtledoves pecked for crumbs around their feet, and passers-by called greetings to her uncle. She felt suddenly detached, as though she was listening to herself. I was with them only a few days ago, she reflected, but already it seems a long time, as though I've left that world behind.

The thought made her uncomfortable and she turned from it, studying her uncle as he talked, thinking that he looked like a gnarled, well-polished walking stick. Although his shoulders were bent into a slight but permanent stoop, his arms leathered by years under the African sun, and his hand shook slightly when he lifted his glass, the blue eyes – paler than of old – were still keen and lively.

Her disembodied feeling crystallised into an overwhelming tiredness and, as though her voice had betrayed her, he was quick to notice. "Another cuppa? No?

Then I'll take you up and leave you to snooze. You'll have plenty of time to see the town next time we come in from the farm."

"Good." She stood up, feeling a little dizzy. "What's that pretty park over there?"

"Cecil Square, after Rhodes – fellow who gave this country its name. It's where the original fort was built." He looked at his watch. "It's quarter past one. How about if I wake you at five?"

Outside her door, he pecked her cheek and was gone. She kicked off her shoes, wriggled out of her dress and took a flowered cotton wrap from her suitcase. She had bought it a week ago in London, attracted by the exotic blue-green pattern of birds and flowers, thinking: this will be just right for Rhodesia.

Despite the warm sunlight outside, it was cool in the room as she stood before the dressing-table mirror looking at her reflection. The dark mane of shoulder-length hair, tipped with chestnut glints, had been cut in London before she left, and badly needed a wash. She was pale, and her eyes stared back at her ironically – dark brown like her hair, but with gold flecks in certain lights. Now they looked strained. Peaky – that was the word her mother had used. "You look peaky, darling, hope that African sun perks you up."

She turned away from the mirror and slid between cool sheets. I'm in Africa, she said to herself experimentally. She had said the same words every day for the last four days, and still it didn't seem real. I'm in Africa. Everything was too normal, and she could hear a cricket commentary, in an English voice, on a radio somewhere in the hotel.

And yet... the voices outside – chattering, laughing voices – were not English voices; doves called, but they were not English doves, they cooed with a different rhythm. And although the room was furnished in an almost Victorian style, it was not an English room. It smelt of mosquito spray, dust, and a spicy floor polish that reminded her of something she couldn't quite place.

Before drifting into sleep, her thoughts turned inexorably and painfully to Alex. She wondered if he would be taking the boat out on the river this weekend.

She woke abruptly and stared in confusion at the white ceiling fan overhead, until she heard Nicholas' voice at the door. After another cup of tea they packed the Land Rover and, with Julius at the wheel, drove out of the city, through broad leafy avenues lined with hibiscus hedges. Within minutes, the suburbs gave way to open countryside where silver grass rippled in the late afternoon sunlight, and ploughed and furrowed soil, rich and brown, extended to a horizon of smoke-blue hills.

Nicholas pointed out landmarks, regaling her with pithy portraits of the landowners whose farms bordered the route. As most of the homesteads were set well back from the road, all she could see were rooftops amid clumps of trees, and lines of blue gums leaning over tin-roofed farm buildings.

The gently rolling landscape became more rugged, the crimson sun glinted on granite kopjes, and the wide tarred road was reduced to two narrow strips of tar. When a car approached, Julius swung the wheel over to the left so that the vehicle's right-hand wheels clung precariously to a single strip. A small antelope bounded across the road, but the only other animals in sight were well-fed cattle and horses in fenced paddocks. Occasionally, a whitewashed store loomed into view on the roadside, its tin roof emblazoned with a Coca Cola sign.

The sun dipped behind the hills and it was suddenly colder. Julius turned off the strips on to a dirt road punctuated by long, juddering stretches of corrugation. "We're in the reserve now – African land," Nicholas told her. Clouds of red dust swirled in their wake as they passed women with baskets balanced easily on their heads; a man with several skinny mongrels at his heels, who raised a hand in greeting; a family group, the man in front, followed by a woman and gaggle of children. Circular huts with thatched roofs and mud walls clustered in clearings, a small boy herded horned cattle into a fenced enclosure, and the fragrance of wood-smoke drifted into the vehicle.

It was getting dark, and as Julius switched on the headlights, speckled nightjars fluttered up from the ground ahead, trailing long tail feathers. The vehicle turned on to another dirt road. "On the farm now," said Nicholas, and Liz glimpsed a hand-painted sign on a plough disc: *Mushana Farm, N. Hamilton*. Ahead, a small grey hare, trapped in the headlights, bounded up the track from one side to the other. The Land Rover jolted over deep ruts and down into a narrow drift across a dry river bed, jouncing from side to side, flinging her back against the seat. "Julius, remind me to get the grader onto it next week," said Nicholas placidly, drawing on his cigarette.

The road circled a sheet of water, glimmering pewter in the gathering darkness. "Stocked with bream," Nicholas told her. "I'll take you fishing." The outline of a building loomed up, the spreading silhouettes of tall trees, and then they were rounding a corner and coming to a halt.

A door opened, spilling light on to the dark earth, and four dogs hurtled out, colliding with one another before flinging themselves against the Land Rover in a frenzy of welcome.

"Down!" roared Nicholas. "Get down, you bloody animals. All right, all right," and he petted each in turn. Satisfied, they bounced enthusiastically towards Liz.

An African in a white uniform and apron called a greeting as he came forward to help Julius with the luggage.

"*Kanjan*, Samuel? *Zonke ena mushi*? Everything all right?" asked Nicholas, rubbing his back as he slowly straightened.

"Ya. *Zonke ena mushi*. Evening, madam."

"This is Samuel, my cook," said her uncle. "Been with me nearly twenty years."

Samuel grinned, saluted and picked up her cases. The dogs continued to lavish attention on her, and Nicholas shouted until they sank into the dust, wriggling on their stomachs and smiling ingratiatingly.

He took her arm. "This way – through the kitchen. I don't have a front door."

The kitchen was vast and shabby, with pine cupboards, a table scrubbed almost white, an enormous old fridge that rumbled and grunted, a wood stove, and shelves lined with pots, bottles, and gas lamps. The dogs skidded across the black cement floor, almost knocking Nicholas over.

Beyond was a large room furnished with solid, comfortable furniture upholstered in faded chintz. Rugs and animal skins were scattered on the polished wooden floor; antelope horns, and an eclectic mix of paintings, prints, maps and photographs hung on the walls. In the muted lamplight, Liz saw well-stocked bookcases and, in the far wall, a massive stone fireplace. A heavy teak desk was piled with papers, files, a globe of the world; stone steps led to a dining alcove with a fine mahogany sideboard and a table set for a meal.

"Lovely." She looked around, feeling instantly at home, and her eyes stopped at a cluster of photographs on a bookcase. She went closer. "You and Felicity, James and Sally, Mum and Dad," she murmured. "And this is you too, isn't it?" She pointed to a faded print of a young man standing in a garden. He was half turned, smiling at a woman with blonde hair, wearing a high-necked blouse and a long slim skirt.

"Me and Clarissa – your grandmother. Taken – my God – it must nearly sixty years ago."

She picked up the photograph and looked closer. "I've only seen one photo of her, and it was terribly faded." Her grandmother was laughing at the camera, one hand raised to brush away a strand of hair. "Mum doesn't look a bit like her, nor do I," she remarked.

She set the picture down and followed Nicholas down steps and along a passage. He opened a door at the end. "I've put you in the smaller spare room because it has the best view."

The room was furnished with a bed covered in a woven bedspread, an easy chair, a table with a bowl of roses and daisies, and rough-weave curtains drawn across a window and glass doors – "That leads into the garden," said her uncle. He opened another door, revealing a huge, ancient, claw-footed bath with slightly chipped enamel. "Why don't you have a relaxing soak before dinner?" He yawned. "God, it's good to be home – hate going into the city." He patted her arm, and the dogs panted out behind him.

She ran a bath, unpacked a few night things, but decided to leave the rest till next morning, preferring to savour the pleasure of at last being here in this place she had visualised so often. Opening the window, she was assailed by sounds – crickets, frogs, a nightbird's fluting call, African voices from the back of the house, the muffled hum of an engine.

The bath water, faintly tinged with brown, was deliciously hot, and as she lay, watching the steam mist the mirror over the hand-basin, she reflected that the bathroom was bigger than the bedroom of her London flat. The walls were painted in cream enamel, and the ceiling needed a new coat of paint, but there were thick white towels on a rail, a capacious cane basket for laundry, and a cane chair in one corner.

When she found her way back to the sittingroom, Nicholas was pouring drinks at a cabinet on which a tray was set with a jug of water and an ice bucket. "Sherry?"

She nodded, prowling around the room, pausing to stare at a massive set of spiralling horns mounted on the wall above the fireplace. "Kudu," said Nicholas, handing her a glass. She noticed for the first time that he had a slight limp.

Settling in a deep armchair by the fireplace, she set her glass down on a table heaped with old issues of The Field, Country Life, the Rhodesian Farmer, and a book on the birds of Southern Africa. Nicholas sat down opposite her, pushing a dog out of the way with his foot.

Her eyes were drawn back to the photograph of Nicholas and her grandmother. "You've got her diary, haven't you? Mum mentioned it."

"Yes. Your mother gave it to me a few years ago – a publisher in Johannesburg was interested in turning it into a book. Then he got cancer, and nothing came of it. You can take it back with you."

"It was the one she kept when she came to Africa, wasn't it? I saw it once, years ago, but I was just a kid – I wasn't terribly interested. Could I see it sometime?"

"I'll get it out after supper. Let's go and eat."

Later, over coffee, he handed her the diary – it wasn't really a diary, just a black, leather-bound notebook her grandmother had used for the purpose. Although its pages were ivory with age, the forward-slanting handwriting was quite legible.

She skimmed through the closely-written pages. The early entries began in 1891, and were headed *At sea*; later entries had exotic names: *Pungwe River, Somewhere in Portuguese East Africa, Umtali*. Sometimes she had written every day, sometimes missed weeks or months. The final entry was written in England in 1895.

"What a marvellous record," she murmured, "no wonder someone wanted to publish it."

"Yes, well, you're a journalist, dear. Have a look and see what you think. Some publisher might still find it worthwhile, though it would have to be edited, there's some very personal stuff in there. The fellow I gave it to, he was a friend, I knew I could trust him. There are a lot of gaps that need researching, but you might enjoy that."

"I'd love it, it's right up my street. Was this her only diary?"

"As far as I know."

She looked at the photograph on the bookcase beside her, attracted by the candid, confident expression in her grandmother's eyes. "She looks as though she knew what she wanted," she said, a little wistfully.

"She did, most of the time. No one knows what they want all the time." He looked at her shrewdly and reached for his cigarettes. "Now, tell me what you have in mind. All I know is that you've come out for a holiday, but might consider getting a job for a few months. Is that right?"

She put the diary down. "Yes. I'd like to get a temporary job, to give me the chance to have a look around. I've heard so many of your stories over the years, I thought it was time I came and discovered my roots."

"Roots?" He peered at her through a cloud of smoke. "That sort of decision is usually prompted by some sort of crisis – or turning point."

"Well..."

"Well?"

She flushed and pleated the fabric of her skirt between her fingers. "Let's just say I needed to get out of England for a while, and this seemed like a good place to come."

"Fair enough," his voice was brisk and cheerful, "have to see who we can introduce you to."

"No, thank you, Uncle Nicky," she said firmly. "I just want to take it easy for a couple of weeks, then get to know this part of Africa."

"That can be arranged." Nicholas eased himself out of his armchair, went to the drinks cabinet and opened a bottle of brandy. "Nightcap, dear? No? I'll have to drink on my own – my nightly ritual. See that?" He pointed to a large fish, with jagged teeth, mounted on a length of polished wood. "That's a tiger fish, caught it down on the Zambezi, close to where your Italian friend will be working on the new dam at Kariba. Those corals are from Portuguese East Africa."

"That's where my grandmother got off the ship, isn't it?"

"That's right. I used to go fishing there."

She smiled at him. "You're a real old Africa hand, aren't you? I bet you don't consider yourself an Englishman any more."

"Oh, I'm still loyal to the old country, if it came to another war or anything like that – which God forbid. Couldn't live there though, not after this climate. Before I forget, that's a generator you can hear. When we turn in, I switch it off from my bedroom, so the lights will go out. Samuel has put a gas lamp and candles in your room, so you can read."

"Thanks," she yawned, and uncurled her legs from beneath her. "I think I'll turn in right now, if you don't mind."

"Good to have you here," he said gruffly, as she stooped to kiss his forehead. He looked tired too, and his hand shook as he raised it to her cheek.

Later, with the lamp hissing on the table beside her, and the whistle of a nightbird drifting through the open window, she plumped pillows behind her shoulders, and opened the diary.

2
1891

The damp, early-morning mist, that had shrouded the boat in a clammy blanket since they had climbed aboard, was at last beginning to dissolve; and Clarissa Hamilton saw to her relief that, in a sudden flurry of activity, Captain Edgar was preparing to cast off from their moorings.

Once the two black deckhands had clambered on board, there was barely room for her and Emma, and they would have to stand all day within yards of the belching boiler. "I hate to think what it's going to be like when the sun comes up," murmured Emma, nervously checking their luggage for the tenth time.

"Never mind, at least we're finally moving." Clarissa slapped at a mosquito, conscious of the knot of apprehension forming in her stomach as the steam launch chugged sluggishly away from the bank. This is the third time we have set off in a boat and I have had this feeling each time, she reflected. Southampton, Cape Town, now here. You'd think I'd be getting used to it.

She waved to the handful of men on the bank, and watched without regret as the prow swung upstream, away from the port of Beira and its pervasive smell of swamp, into the surging green waters of the river.

Lifting her face to a breeze from the west, she caught a new scent – dust and grass mingled with a strange, rich sweetness. A tingle of expectation flooded through her and she gripped the rails, glancing instinctively towards Emma, who was twisting a loose strand of hair around her index finger as she always did when she was nervous.

The launch puffed laboriously through the last wisps of mist, and Captain Edgar frowned in concentration as he negotiated the shifting shoals and invisible sandbanks which, he told them, made the river and the waters of the port a dangerous obstacle course.

The way ahead was a maze of small islands through which the little craft made slow progress, but the knot in her stomach was beginning to ease a little as she leaned on the rail, watching the prow cut a creamy swathe through the water past a shoreline of deep green foliage.

A loud bellow erupted from beyond the starboard bow, and several glistening grey mounds suddenly surfaced, each displaying a pair of round ears and two large nostrils. A barrage of grunts emerged from the small flotilla, and she reached instinctively for Emma's hand.

"Hippo?" she gasped.

"Always here, whenever we pass this way," said Edgar placidly, as the leading set of ears and nostrils advanced steadily towards the boat. "One of them can be quite cheeky…"

As he spoke, the ears submerged, and a gigantic head exploded into view no more than a few feet from the hull. Clarissa clutched at the rail and stared dumbly into cavernous pink jaws armed with huge tusk-like teeth. Emma screamed, Edgar swore and swung hard on the wheel. The head vanished, the water swirled and bubbled, and a heavy thud against the hull flung Clarissa hard against her companion, hurling them both to the deck.

"Hang on!" shouted Edgar, as the vessel lurched to port and slewed about in the roiling water.

As swiftly as it had begun, the attack ended, and the water ceased churning.

"Went clean underneath. Damn and blast," raged Edgar, "where's the bugger now? Pardon me, ladies, but it's time someone put a bullet through his head. Might just do it myself on the way back. You all right?"

Clarissa nodded, pulling herself upright and rubbing her shoulder, and Emma scrambled shakily to her feet. Their assailant had re-emerged behind the craft, and the herd settled once more into a cluster of shiny, rocklike mounds. Clarissa stared, fearful – and, at the same time – fascinated. But that's Africa, or what we've seen so far, she thought. The few times they had made landfall on the voyage up the east coast of the continent, she had been enthralled by its rugged grandeur, awed by the ferocity of its storms, and stricken by the sight of wide-eyed children with stick-like limbs and distended stomachs.

She glanced at Emma, who was laughing shakily, and knew she was thinking: what have we let ourselves in for? It was hardly surprising they were attuned to each other's thoughts. They had not been separated since their departure from Southampton six months ago, on a grey day which now seemed a world and a lifetime away. But the small, cold stone that hardened once again in the pit of her stomach was the same she had felt that morning as the shores of England receded behind a shifting veil of mist and rain.

After weeks of turbulent seas punctuated by rare days of calm and tropical sunshine, their storm-battered vessel had reached the Cape of Good Hope and dropped anchor in the cloud-capped shadow of Table Mountain. But, even as they had disembarked to catch the coach that would carry them north to their nursing posts in a large Johannesburg hospital, a message had prompted a change of plan.

A tiny outpost in a new British settlement north of the Limpopo River, needed nurses urgently. Would Miss Hamilton and Miss Clarke be interested?

"Definitely," said Clarissa, without any real idea of where the Limpopo was – she only knew it sounded exciting. Emma – less enthusiastic – had eventually been won over by the argument that Johannesburg had an abundant supply of nurses.

"As long as we're in darkest Africa, I suppose we should see the darkest bits," she said with reluctant resignation.

Within a matter of hours, they had committed themselves to nurse for two years in Umtali, a small settlement in a region called Mashonaland, under the supervision of the local bishop. "If we're working for the Anglican Church, it will be all right," Clarissa had reasoned, conscious of Emma's hesitancy.

Finding berths on a northbound vessel, they had exchanged the icy grey seas of the Atlantic for the warmer, aquamarine waters of the Indian Ocean. Their fellow passengers were a motley assortment of prospectors, traders, explorers and hunters, the younger sons of the English landed gentry, rubbing shoulders with roughnecks and itinerants from America, Australia and Europe.

All were fired by the prospect of making their fortunes in the new settlement. If the reports were true, Mashonaland offered the promise of a second Witwatersrand, where men were becoming millionaires overnight. It could prove even richer in gold-bearing reefs, argued the more optimistic. After all, legends of gold had been emerging from the African interior for centuries; and some of the wilder stories linked the region with the biblical land of Ophir, where the treasures of Solomon and Sheba lay buried.

Dazzled but wary at this talk of immeasurable wealth, Clarissa and Emma had disembarked in Beira, the Portuguese port at the mouth of the Pungwe River, where a small settlement huddled on a narrow spit of sand, with malarial swamps on one side and the anchorage on the other. A few tents, some shabby, tin-roofed shacks, and a cluster of thatched mud huts occupied by sickly and disgruntled Portuguese soldiers – that was Beira.

The two women were impatient to reach their destination, more so when the locals told them, with bleak satisfaction, that the port was one of the unhealthiest places in the sub-continent, harbouring a strain of malaria even deadlier than in the interior.

But a message from the bishop warned them not to leave until he sent word: the road to Umtali was not yet ready to carry wagons. They waited for a week, and then another and another. There had been some compensations. Despite its bleak and depressing surroundings, the small harbour bustled with Portuguese and British shipping and outrigger canoes manned by native fishermen; and in a frontier port where white women were a rarity, they had been showered with attention and hospitality.

After three weeks, they had had enough. Clarissa heard that the English doctor appointed to the new hospital was due to leave for Umtali from Mpandas, a small outpost a few miles upriver. If they went to Mpandas to meet him, they could travel overland together. "Let's go," she said immediately.

"You're mad," she was told. "The place is alive with lion, elephant, buffalo. You'll be weeks on the road, and if the lion don't get you, malaria will."

Clarissa was adamant. They had come here to work, not sit on their thumbs in Beira, and the knowledge that their destination was the newest outpost of Victoria's empire, established by the legendary Cecil Rhodes himself, lent an extra dimension of romance and urgency to their expedition.

Now, as the breeze carried elusive scents of that unknown hinterland, a rising excitement replaced her earlier fears. A white stork rose, heavy-winged, from a fringe of reeds on a sandbank, and a huge reptilian form slid, with barely a ripple, into the water.

"Ugly brutes," said Edgar succinctly, removing the ancient pipe that seemed permanently clamped between his teeth. "You'll see plenty of those. Saw a native taken along here. Fellow was on the bank fishing, and this gigantic croc came from nowhere, grabbed him by the leg, dragged him under."

"Couldn't you do anything – shoot it?" asked Emma with a shudder.

"Took a few potshots, but the brute never surfaced again. Neither did the black, poor sod."

The two women exchanged glances. At the wheel, Edgar studied them covertly, listening to their exclamations with a mixture of amusement and concern. Well, they might as well be aware of the dangers. In their neat, high-necked white shirts, long fawn skirts, and sturdy brown laced boots, they looked as though they would be more at home in a cottage in Devon, like the comfortable one in which he had left his own wife (with guilty pangs of relief) a year and a half ago.

Although both wore broad-brimmed hats, their creamy complexions were already faintly tanned and dusted by a sprinkling of freckles. The strands of hair that had escaped from beneath Miss Hamilton's hat were the same colour as the sun-bleached grass of the African savannah, and they framed a face which, while not beautiful, was one of the liveliest Edgar had seen. It must be the clear, grey-green eyes that invested it with a sense of vitality uncommon in this God-forsaken hole, where the climate sapped the energy from your body and the optimism from your soul. She was slightly taller than her companion, whose wide expressive mouth and dark eyes were framed by a mass of light brown hair drawn back into a knot on her neck.

There was little doubt Miss Hamilton was the decision-maker of the pair, and she was probably going to have to make a tough one tomorrow, reflected Edgar. The launch was headed upriver to Mpandas, where they expected to travel onward with the doctor. But he had the distinct impression that the road was still nowhere near ready. What was that bloody God-botherer thinking of, allowing them to set out on a two-hundred mile journey on a barely-passable track, even if it was in the company of a white man?

As the sun glanced off the water, dazzling the eyes, the sky and the marshy shoreline fringed with reeds were a-flutter with birds. A few Clarissa recognised from the English countryside, but most were unfamiliar – ebony and white ibis, dazzling kingfishers, storks with crimson bills banded in black. Hippos plunged into the water as the boat passed, sending a carpet of waterlilies bobbing, and small white birds pecked about in the gaping jaws of crocodiles basking on white sandbanks. The launch chugged past islands where ragged thatched huts were perched on stilts, and black men fished from dugout canoes.

But, as the sun climbed higher, movement along the shore slowed imperceptibly, and by midday the breeze had dropped and the life of the river had been stilled by the intense heat that shimmered off the water. Clarissa's shirt clung damply to her back, and as she licked parched lips she realised she had unthinkingly drained the last drops from her water bottle. Noticing her discomfort, Edgar withdrew from a locker an almost-full bottle of claret. "Have a drink."

Wiping the perspiration from her face with a handkerchief, she declined, knowing it would only maker her thirstier. Emma offered her own bottle and she sipped guiltily, longing to tilt the contents down her throat.

From the locker, Edgar produced a bag containing three small oranges. "What about one of these, then?"

The cool golden flesh was wonderfully refreshing to her dry throat, and as she savoured the fruit slowly, sucking out every last drop of juice before tossing the skin overboard, she recalled how her father would put one in each pocket before they went hiking in the beech woods near home.

When Emma's water ran out, they tried sipping river water from a ladle produced by the captain, but although it moistened their throats, the taste was putrid with rotting vegetation. The two black men, raking ash from the boiler and flinging it overboard, where it hissed and smoked in the glittering water, seemed impervious to the heat, but Clarissa noticed that Edgar took regular swigs from the claret bottle. Leaning back on the narrow bench behind her, she closed her eyes against the dazzle of sky and water.

Late in the afternoon a breeze rippled in from the sea to cool their burning faces, the sun dropped behind a hill, and the river bank came to life again. Antelope with graceful, lyre-shaped horns stepped delicately through the reeds to drink, a buffalo lunged into the shallows, and Clarissa smiled at the antics of a family of warthog wallowing in the mud.

"They are so ugly...." Emma was saying when, on the shore ahead, silhouetted figures appeared on the horizon.

"Portuguese military camp," Edgar muttered with a frown. Across the water drifted the beat of drums, and the voice of a man shouting unintelligibly. A rifle shot rang out.

Edgar shouted, "Get down!" and the two women scrambled unceremoniously behind the wheelhouse with the deckhands.

"English!" shouted Edgar, his face ruddy and perspiring. "We have permission to go to Mpandas. Permission from Portuguese Consul – Colonel Machado!"

The swarthy figure on the riverbank shouted and gestured furiously, his meaning all too clear. Behind him, the khaki-clad soldiers stood stiff and motionless, their weapons fixed unwaveringly on the launch. The drums continued to throb across the water.

"Colonel Machado!" shouted Edgar again, but the drumming continued, and abruptly he changed tactics and lowered his voice. "English ladies!" he announcing placatingly. "English nurses – hospital!" And he beckoned Clarissa and Emma forward.

Clarissa looked at him doubtfully, but he nodded urgently. "Just show yourselves, they won't attack women."

Hesitantly, she emerged from the behind the wheelhouse, followed by Emma. "English nurses!" shouted Edgar. Emma lifted her hand in tentative greeting.

The effect was almost comical: the stout commander instantly drew himself up to his modest height, bowed several times so deeply he almost fell over, and barked an order. The drumming stopped, the firearms were slowly lowered, the officer bowed again, his shouted apologies floating across the water.

Edgar wiped his face with a large dirty handkerchief, and grinned. "If he could, he would have kissed your hands. Bored to tears and just aching for a scrap."

"But why?" asked Emma, as the vessel slowly picked up speed.

"Didn't you hear? They're a touch jumpy. One of their forts has just been overrun by about forty British South Africa Police – Rhodes' men. Just this side of the border, at Massekesse. You'll be passing through it.

"Damn cheeky," he chuckled, uncorking the claret bottle. "The Portuguese lost a lot of face, because they had much greater numbers, but the police fooled them into thinking they had more men than they did. Here, have some."

"But why did Mr Rhodes' men attack the fort?" Clarissa accepted the claret bottle gratefully. Perhaps the red liquid would quiet her still-thudding heart.

"There's a dispute about who has rights over the region," Edgar continued. "Rhodes wants a corridor to the sea from Mashonaland." He paused. "But you don't want to bother your heads with politics."

"Indeed, we do," Clarissa said firmly, passing the bottle to Emma. "If we're going to work in Umtali, we need to know what's going on." It's a wonder he didn't say 'your pretty heads', she thought resentfully.

"Well, Rhodes wanted his men to take the fort, keep going and march right through to Beira. But London didn't want trouble, so they have agreed this is Portuguese territory, up to the mountains where you are headed. Rhodes is fit to be tied."

"I see," but she was still confused. "But the Portuguese officers in Beira were so kind and helpful."

"Who wouldn't be – to two charming young ladies?" Edgar rejoined gallantly, turning his attention to the river on which night was falling rapidly.

The craft steamed steadily into a warm velvet darkness in which scents and sounds became sharper and more acute. Clarissa was at once conscious of the sweet smell of decaying vegetation, the pungency of Edgar's pipe, the smoke from the boiler. A few faint stars pricked the sky, and the moon rose, pale and cool after the ferocity of the sun. She leaned against Emma, and after a while her eyelids drooped.

When she awoke, a thick mist had obliterated the stars and she was cold.

"You can see why we have to get to Mpandas tonight," the captain was saying to Emma. "You can't sleep on the river, it gets damn chilly and damp – begging your pardon, ladies."

As Clarissa yawned and smoothed her hair, a shout drifted across the water. Edgar barked instructions to the deckhands and steered the vessel towards a cluster of flickering lights. Out of the blackness loomed a rough wooden jetty and the silhouetted forms of men, some carrying lamps.

"That you, Edgar?" shouted a strong English voice.

"Mr Philips!" replied the captain.

The prow bumped against the jetty, and hands reached out to catch ropes and make the boat fast.

"Your servant, ladies." Yellow lantern light glowed on a ruddy bearded face, and Edgar introduced Jerome Philips, British vice-consul at Mpandas. Clarissa's legs were weak and stiff from their confined position, and she stumbled as she clambered down, clutching one of the hands that reached out to help her.

It was strange to stand on firm ground again, and impossible to see beyond the flickering lanterns illuminating the faces of the small group, but she could hear the almost deafening chorus of a million frogs from the darkness, and smell the same rotten, swampy smell that had pervaded the air of Beira.

"This way, ladies," urged Philips, and they lifted their skirts and followed him along a muddy track through a narrow canyon of towering reeds, up a bank and into a large clearing in which they could just discern a few huts, several tents and a great deal of equipment – spades, barrows, timber, wire – strewn in untidy heaps.

The vice-consul led them to a thatched hut, and Clarissa stooped to enter through the low doorway. Philips' lamp illuminated two rough timber stretchers supported on poles hammered into the ground. Mattresses of straw were covered by karosses of animal hide.

"Not the Grosvenor," his voice was apologetic as he set the lamp down on a packing case, "but you're the first ladies we have entertained here."

"It's perfectly fine, thank you" said Clarissa politely; behind her, Emma nodded tiredly.

"If you'd like to leave your things here, I have some refreshment for you..."

Seated on a circle of upturned packing cases in a small hut that served Philips as an office, they were handed large enamel mugs of sweet, steaming coffee. He introduced them to Ted McLean, a burly red-headed man in charge of the crew building the road to Mashonaland.

His words confirmed Clarissa's fears. "Yes, we've started clearing the bush, you can get through on foot, but it's not ready for a wagon, it's just a track. Definitely not designed for ladies to use."

"He's right," said Philips seriously. "You are welcome here, but your proposal is madness, and I have sent a message to the bishop telling him I would advise you to go straight back to Beira."

Clarissa stared at him, appalled. "We're not turning back now."

"But it's far too dangerous. Do you know how far it is? It will take you at least three weeks – if everything goes smoothly, which it never does. The country is crawling with lion, we lost a man to snakebite last week. I have half a dozen down with malaria...."

Exchanging glances with Emma, whose eyes were widening with alarm, Clarissa suddenly felt too tired to argue. "I can't think about it now," she said. "We'll work something out tomorrow. But, after all the delays, we can hardly sit around here waiting for a road to be built. The hospital needs the supplies we have brought as much as it needs our services."

"As you wish," said Edgar soothingly as he drew on his pipe. "The doctor should be here in a day or two, and you can discuss it with him. We'll make a plan."

"Yes." She smiled at him gratefully. We'll make a plan: it was a phrase she had heard many times since setting foot on the African continent, and now it had a comforting sound. Whenever a problem arose, and someone mentioned those words, a plan had materialised, and seemingly intractable obstacles had been overcome. Perhaps it would happen again.

"We'd like to stay here until the doctor comes, if that is all right?" she asked Philips.

"Of course," his voice was a little stiff, "but my advice stands."

All I want at this moment is sleep, she thought wearily, enjoying the warmth from the coffee seeping into her body. But first they were served with a watery soup accompanied by a stodgy, porridgy substance that Edgar called sadza, made from ground maize kernels. When at last they were escorted back to their hut, a man brought a bucket of warm water for them to wash in. Still in their rumpled travelling clothes, they subsided on the stretchers, too tired to do more than curl up on the soft karosses, and wrap themselves in their blankets. It was cold.

Clarissa was swimming on the edge of sleep when an eerie, gibbering howl broke the silence, setting her scalp prickling.

"What was that?" Emma's voice quavered. The sound came again, rising to a falsetto whoop, so close it seemed just outside their hut. "What is it?" she wailed.

"I don't know," Clarissa shivered as she felt for the matches Philips had left on the packing case. With difficulty she lit the lamp, and its glow flickered on two small black forms scuttling through the shadows at the top of the wall.

"I don't know what's outside," she said slowly, "but there are rats in here."

"Where?" Emma was on the verge of tears.

"Right there." She lifted the lamp. "Huge ones."

They stared into the long, dancing shadows, listening to small, scuffling sounds from the roof.

"I can't sleep here," Emma's tone was adamant.

"Yes, you can. You have to." The eerie gibbering came again. "Would you rather be outside – with that?" Emma said nothing.

Beginning to feel she was part of a confused dream, Clarissa lay down and shut her eyes. She felt as though the floor was moving beneath her, as if she was back on the water, so she opened them and stared into the blackness, remembering suddenly the old blue eiderdown she liked to cuddle into on winter nights at home. Don't, she told herself fiercely, rolling on to her side, pulling her blankets closely about her shoulders. It'll be better in the morning.

By day, Mpandas was even less prepossessing than it had appeared in the dark. Huts and tents were scattered haphazardly around the clearing, interspersed with road-building equipment, lengths of corrugated iron, and tiers of wooden boxes. Rubbish was heaped in negligent piles, and beyond the small encampment the wooden jetty extended into a stagnant channel swarming with mosquitoes.

The clearing was surrounded by head-high grass out of which towered the slender, yellow-green trunks of trees which Clarissa thought curiously beautiful. But the men called them fever trees and said they were a fitting symbol of the place.

"Anyway, we're not staying here any longer than we have to. Even if it means finding our own way to Umtali," said Clarissa decisively, after they had been given a tour of the camp by Ted McLean.

When they called on Philips in his hut, however, the situation brightened. He was deep in conversation with a portly, middle-aged man with a receding hairline and a broad girth. It was George Copeland, the doctor who was to accompany them to Umtali.

"Just got in," he told them. "Been hunting in the south. I believe the road's not ready, but I'm for pushing on. Dammed shame to expect you to go on foot, but if you are determined to do so, let us endure the trip together," he declared in a fatherly voice. As he tended to puff and pant in the steadily rising temperature, Clarissa wondered how much help he would be. Still, I suppose it's useful to have a man with you in Africa, she reflected, no matter what his condition.

"The bishop wanted us to wait in Beira," she glanced at Philips, who had preserved a dignified silence, "but we got so fed up we decided to come here and see for ourselves."

"Just as well. Never knew such a place for rumours, very few of which ever bear any relation to the facts. It appears the road is as much a figment of the imagination as the gold nuggets that are supposed to be lying around waiting to be picked up in Mashonaland," Copeland said dryly, wiping his forehead.

Philips interposed, "These ladies know my views. I am totally against them going any further. It's too dangerous, the track is too rough, it's too far to walk...."

"Not at all," interposed Clarissa. "We are both good walkers, and looking forward to it."

"It will not be easy," Copeland's voice was bland, "but, as I said, if you are determined to go...." He changed the subject quickly. "Now, if you will excuse me, I promised to have a look at the malaria patients."

"Can we help?" offered Clarissa.

"Thank you, m'dear," he huffed. "I may well call on your services. And after morning surgery, perhaps we can sit down together and make some plans."

Philips stared after him, then turned to Clarissa and shrugged resignedly. "If you can't be persuaded not to go, you'll need porters," he said decisively. "I know a native who would make a good personal servant. He seems to know the score around here, so he can probably recruit porters, which would solve one problem for you."

"Do we need a servant?" asked Emma.

"Absolutely. This chap's intelligent – bit of a smart-Alec, but he's a good tracker, can cook well and speaks a fair bit of English. Used to work for a butterfly collector – quite a cultured fellow, and Mukwasi likes to do things with flair. He's been working here, but he's keen to go back to Mashonaland. I'll send him over."

They thanked him, and went in search of Copeland who was in a nearby tent, tending two white men on stretchers, one weak but conscious, the other sweating and delirious. In a separate hut, half a dozen black men with grey faces and sunken eyes shivered and sweated on blankets on the ground. While Copeland dosed them with quinine, Clarissa and Emma brought water, straightened their blankets, and swept the mud floor.

When they returned to their hut, a tall, angular African of about thirty was standing outside. He wore a dark blue sarong, white shirt and cap, his legs were long and skinny, his features more Nilotic than negroid, and his eyes lively and intelligent.

"I am Mukwasi," he told them, "I myself can cook, can wash. I find porters, can go to Umtali with the madams." He smiled with self assurance.

He came from Mashonaland, which he had left some years earlier to join an expedition into the interior, "to Zambezi."

"The Zambezi River?" Clarissa asked, and he nodded. From there he had made his way south to Mafeking where he had joined the naturalist.

"Myself I help him. The *bwana*, he sick," and he indicated his heart. "He too tiresome, so I catch butterflies."

Clarissa suppressed a grin at his eccentric English, and asked whether he knew the way to Umtali.

"Ya, I know it too well."

She consulted Copeland. "If Philips recommends him, and he can get us porters and keep them under control, by all means take him on," advised the doctor. "Porters can be a devil of a problem, get fed up and make a run for it after a couple of days."

"Well, it seems almost too easy," she said doubtfully, after the negotiations had been completed, and she watched Mukwasi's lanky form wend between the mounds of rubbish, his sarong flapping around grasshopper-like legs.

"Don't complain. We're overdue for something to go right," Emma reminded her.

They had another visitor – a burly, bearded young giant with coarse black hair and a swarthy complexion. In travel-stained jacket and heavily-patched drill trousers, he paused awkwardly in the doorway of the hut, thrust out a large hand, and introduced himself in a broad, guttural accent: "Hennie van Heerden."

He was an elephant hunter, passing through the road camp on his way to Beira with a load of ivory, he told them. "I heard you was going to Umtali," he said, taking from his pocket a large folded sheet of paper. "Might be some help," he muttered gruffly as he handed it to Clarissa.

It was a hand-drawn map of their intended route through Portuguese territory to the settlement of Umtali. Though crudely sketched, it was marked with camp sites, rivers, villages, Portuguese outposts and prominent natural features. She studied it, with Emma peering over her shoulder: he had even punctuated the route with laconic warnings – *Bamboo, Mountains, Swamps*. While his handwriting was that of a child, and his spelling eccentric to say the least, the details were quite clear.

"This is wonderful," she murmured.

"Lion," read Emma apprehensively. "Is it safe to go that way?"

"*Ag*, there's lions all over," said the hunter casually, "near Sarmento is the worst. You just don't walk after dark, and you keep a fire going all night. You got a gun?"

"Yes," Clarissa pointed to the Holland propped against the wall.

"*Lekker*. Know how to use it?"

She nodded. "I used to shoot pheasant with my brother in England."

"Pheasant?" He regarded her doubtfully.

"How long do you think it will take us?" asked Emma.

"Should be two weeks, if you have no problems." With a stubby finger, he guided them through the route, pointing out where they would have to cross the

Pungwe by canoe, where they could expect to get accommodation from the Portuguese.

Clarissa folded the map carefully and put it away in a leather pouch, a present from her brother Nicholas on the eve of her departure.

"Have you done the trip often?" she asked the young giant.

"This is the second time," he replied, his accent reminding her of many she had heard during their few days in the Cape of Good Hope. "You be all right, just watch the sun for direction, so you don't end up walking round in circles – that's one way of going off your *kop*. Stick to the main track, and make sure you always carry water. There's plenty around just now."

"You think we can do it?" Emma queried anxiously.

"*Ja*, for sure. People always think women are weak, but I seen Boer women trek hundreds of miles," he assured them.

They were the first words of encouragement Clarissa had heard, and her heart lifted. "Thank you very much for your help," she extended her hand.

He shuffled in embarrassment. "*Ja*, well, *totsiens* then. Good luck," he took her hand. "I'll look out for you on my way back to Fort Salisbury."

By evening, Mukwasi had returned with the news that he had recruited twelve porters who would arrive the following morning.

"You'll need mealie-meal for them," said Philips. "We can give you some from our stores. Copeland can bag you some impala en route. If you keep them supplied with meat every few days, they'll stick with you."

"Thank you. We would never have been ready so quickly without your help."

"Don't know why I'm doing it," he said sternly. "Never forgive myself if anything happens to you. Better give me your family's address in England before you leave," he added gruffly, and his words frightened her more than all his dire warnings.

She lifted her chin defiantly, but when she returned to the hut she said hesitantly, "Emma, what do you really think? Are we being crazy? Should we go back to Beira?"

"You're not getting cold feet – I thought you were so keen?" Emma's voice was sharp.

"Well, I am, but…..only if you are happy with the idea," she added quickly.

Her friend looked at her in silence for a long moment, and Clarissa's doubts and fears crowded in on her. Then Emma sighed and grinned. "We can't go back there. And we certainly can't stay here. So there's no alternative, Florence Nightingale. We go to Umtali."

3

Clarissa Hamilton's father Richard was descended from an old family with roots deep in the fertile soil of Buckinghamshire. The family had lived for generations on land granted by a grateful Charles II in recognition for loyalty displayed to his own father by one Edward James Hamilton, who fought alongside Charles I during the Civil War.

More than three centuries later, Richard Hamilton extended the family land holdings by marrying Anne Caldwell, the only surviving offspring of a prominent military family. Through the death, by smallpox, of two unmarried brothers, Anne inherited a portion of the family estate which, combined with the Hamilton lands, ensured that both Clarissa's older brother Denis, and younger brother Nicholas, would one day come into comfortable inheritances.

Her parents were intelligent and open-minded, and Clarissa – in contrast with most young girls of her era – received a comprehensive education, which included exposure to new and controversial ideas of the day. Dinner table discussions ranged from the rights and wrongs of British rule in India, and conflict with the Boers in South Africa, to women's suffrage and Darwinian theory (Richard was an ardent amateur naturalist). His wife, in the best traditions of *noblesse oblige*, was very conscious of her duty to the welfare of those less fortunate than herself. She knew every member of the families who lived and worked on Elderbrook and, applying the knowledge of medicinal herbs passed on by her own mother, regularly visited the sick and elderly, both on the estate and in the nearby village.

Her two younger children often accompanied her. While bustling, efficient Anne tended a feverish child, Nicholas and Clarissa played with the local children and, in time, formed a close friendship with Robbie Jeffares, the eldest son of Richard Hamilton's overseer.

Clarissa adored the soft-spoken boy, who seemed to know as much about the natural world as her father, and it was with Robbie that she and Nicholas rambled through the countryside, peering into a fox's lair, catching glow worms on summer nights, or lying on their stomachs tickling trout in the stream that meandered through Elderbrook.

Though agile as the deer they tracked together, Robbie was not strong, and was sometimes unable to join Clarissa and Nicholas on their rambles. "It's his chest again," his mother would tell them, her thin face drawn, eyes preoccupied. As the months passed, the intervals between his bouts of illness became shorter until one grey November day when Anne Hamilton told them gravely that Robbie had scarlet fever. Although she visited the cottage daily, Clarissa and Nicholas were barred for fear of infection, and so it was with a sharp sense of shock that they learned, a few days later, of Robbie's death.

The shabby cottage by the willows was shuttered against the world as his family mourned their loss. But, in response to Clarissa's pleas to be allowed to say goodbye to her friend, her parents took her and Nicholas to the funeral in the village church. Holding fast to her mother's hand as she watched the small, light coffin lowered into the hard cold earth her playmate had loved so well, Clarissa faced real loss for the first time in her young life. Living close to nature, she was accustomed to the sight of young lambs which had succumbed to late frosts, or stillborn calves lying limp in the straw of the byre, but this was different. Her sense of desolation was profound, she was quiet and withdrawn for many weeks, and the incident left an indelible imprint upon her childhood, germinating a seed that grew over the years.

In the ensuing months, Anne Hamilton noticed her daughter's increased devotion to the task of accompanying her on her 'rounds', and a growing interest in her cornucopia of herbs. Several years later, through Richard's sister Kitty, who lived in London, Clarissa was introduced to a doctor friend with a busy practice, who nevertheless found time to set up a small weekly clinic – funded by charity – in the East End. Desperate for an extra pair of hands, he invited the fifteen-year-old to help him during her visits to Kitty in Kensington. Although concerned at the dangers of exposure to contagious diseases, her parents did not stop her, partly because Anne guessed that her daughter's voluntary work helped ease an unspoken sense of guilt about her relatively privileged and sheltered life.

The other profound influence on her childhood came from her mother's brother Chas, whose infrequent visits were occasions for family celebration. With his booming laugh and snapping eyes, Chas breezed in and out of their lives on a tide of energy, regaling them with a fund of hair-raising stories about his exploits on the gold and diamond fields of South Africa, where his prospecting had met with modest success.

In the evenings, when the family was seated around the heavy, smoke-blackened stone fireplace, Clarissa listened raptly as he puffed on his beloved cheroots and launched into colourful anecdotes. A couple of glasses of port seldom failed to lend a lyrical quality to Chas' recollections, and his words painted vivid canvases in the young girl's mind. Hunting elephant, following the blood-stained spoor of wounded buffalo with his Hottentot tracker; wild nights in the rowdy, ramshackle tent-towns around the Big Hole at Kimberley; and – always – the lure of wealth beckoning from the tailings of a prospecting pan.

Chas enjoyed his money, it trickled through his fingers as easily as the dust of the goldfields, and the day came when his Chelsea home was one of the few assets that remained of his South African days. He had never married, although Clarissa occasionally heard her aunt speak to her mother in lowered tones about 'unsuitable companions'. Although recurrent malaria had forced him to abandon his mining operations, the insistent spell of the African *veld* still ensnared him, and it was this fascination that he transmitted to Clarissa as she listened in the firelight, while the rain battered the windows of the old house.

As she approached adulthood, her aspirations were strengthened by the exploits of the legendary Florence Nightingale. Before the Crimean War, nursing had been looked upon as a haphazard and inexpert vocation followed by women of dubious background, with little education and – all too often – scant compassion. As a result of the war heroine's influence, it became a respectable profession, one of the few open to independent-minded women rebelling against the strictures of a society which expected them to find fulfilment within the confines of marriage and motherhood.

Spurred by the romance of the Nightingale legend, and acutely aware that disease spread more readily into labourers' cottages than in the homes of the wealthy, Clarissa pursued her ambition with a single-mindedness that surprised her family. "Robbie should not have died," she declared on one occasion, "children aren't supposed to die – and I'm going to do something about it."

Several training institutions had been set up for nurses, and at eighteen Clarissa entered Blacksley House in Reading – with the blessing of Richard and Anne, and despite the outspoken consternation of close relatives. At Blacksley she met Emma Clarke, eldest daughter of a doctor with a practice in the Cotswolds. They became close friends, graduating together and taking posts at a new hospital established in London's East End through the generosity of a wealthy philanthropist.

It was unglamorous, demanding work – mentally and physically – but they were healthy, energetic and brimming with idealism. Together they threw themselves into the back-breaking routine, confronting the sights, sounds and pervasive smells of their bleak surroundings with an almost missionary zeal. It was fun, too, exploring London together, but in time the work began to take a toll. After two years Clarissa suffered a severe attack of influenza that left her with a painful, insistent cough. During her long, slow convalescence she was warned by the family doctor to leave the dank, soot-laden air of London for a healthier climate.

Quite by chance (though later she called it fate) she heard through a friend that nurses were being recruited for a hospital in the South African gold-mining city of Johannesburg, and hesitated only long enough to ask Emma to accompany her, before sending off her application.

Where Clarissa was independent, practical and impulsive, Emma was timid, a dreamer, more inclined to follow than lead. Left to herself, she would never have conceived the idea of abandoning her familiar surroundings for a mining town in Africa; but Clarissa's eloquence and enthusiasm somehow transformed an otherwise terrifying prospect into an opportunity not to be missed. And although Emma was the more timid, her shyness concealed a core of strength as well as the sense of fun that had attracted Clarissa. Mule-headed, her father called her, but it was that determination that enabled her, in the face of family opposition, to stand by her decision.

Neither doubted that the expanding empire over which their aging queen presided was the greatest in the world, or that they would be bringing to a primitive, heathen continent the undoubted benefits of centuries of English civilisation. "Besides," exulted Clarissa, "think what an adventure it will be."

When she broke the news to her parents, they were at once appalled and overcome with pride. Indulgent, easygoing Richard was not too difficult to win over, but her strong-willed mother presented a more formidable obstacle.

"For how long?" she asked with her direct blue gaze.

"If we are accepted, probably two years."

"Two years!"

"That's not long, mother. Uncle Chas was there for ten."

"And look at him. His health has been completely ruined."

"...And I'll be with Emma so we can take care of each other. Don't look like that, we'll be all right."

"But you've been so ill. I won't let you go, you're not strong enough."

"I'm fine, but I won't be if I keep on working in London."

"There's plenty of nursing you can do around here. I'll make inquiries, we can find something. You don't have to go to Africa of all places," her mother said decisively.

"I know there is work here. But I've been here all my life. I love it, but it's dull. I want to see the world, do something different. I'll come back, don't worry. It's only two years."

"What about Edward?" Her mother was clutching at straws, but Clarissa wrinkled her nose at the mention of Edward Hayworth, son of a neighbouring landowner, and a persistent visitor over the past six months.

"What about him? You know I wouldn't marry him, even if I stayed here. He's dull too."

The arguments raged on, but Clarissa was adamant. In despair, Anne wrote to her brother, who came down from London the following week.

"We don't want to stop her if it's what she really wants," confided Anne, her forehead creased with worry.

"Yes, you do, that's exactly what you want," Chas contradicted her.

"Well, but.... Chas, I'm so frightened that if she goes, we'll never see her again. Talk to her, at least make sure she knows what she's getting into. She has no idea – you've filled her mind with all your romantic rubbish."

"So it's all my fault," he grumbled. "I wasn't to know she was going to get a hare-brained idea like this."

"So you agree it's foolish and dangerous? We have to stop her, and you've got to help me. Richard is hopeless."

Chas sighed, and stared out of the window over the peaceful, snow-mantled landscape. "Yes, Anne, we should stop her if we want to be sure she will be safe. Yes, she will face danger. Yes, it's a wild, uncivilised place, and I would be lying if I said otherwise.

"If she goes, and she's sensible – and lucky – she'll have an experience she will never forget as long as she lives. But she'd undoubtedly be far better off staying in Bucks and marrying some good, steady Englishman who will only risk her health by giving her a baby every other year. I'll talk to her," he said abruptly.

With characteristic frankness, he did not mince his words, and Clarissa listened in silence. When he had finished, she looked directly into his eyes and asked, "Would you go if you were me?"

"That's not a fair question, Lissa," he protested. "You know what I'd say. I'm talking about you. Your skills are just as desperately needed here as in Africa. Marry young Wheatsworth or Cornfield or whatever his name is, and forget about this idea."

"I thought you'd be on my side," she reproached him.

"I am on your side. Look, my girl, when I say that life is cheap out there, I mean cheaper than in the most wretched and miserable London slum. I've lost a dozen friends through one thing or another – strong, healthy men. Some of them didn't last more than a few months. It's no place..."

"For a woman. I've heard all that. Thank you for trying, Uncle Chas, but it won't work. And don't worry."

Now, as she sat with Emma in a damp, evil-smelling hut crawling with rats and insects, in the sweltering heat of Mpandas, she recalled those words, spoken with such blithe arrogance on that snow-bright morning. She was about to embark on an expedition her uncle would certainly have disapproved of; her mother would have blanched at the mere idea. And it seemed as though every white man in the camp, save Copeland perhaps, and Hennie van Heerden, were opposed to their expedition and had taken them aside over the past two days to urge them to return to Beira until the road was ready and they could travel by wagon.

She was tired of arguing, and wanted to get going before the doubts and fears that nibbled away at the edges of her mind had time to grow stronger. I came for excitement, she told herself. To nurse too, of course, but really, if I'm honest, because I felt I was missing out on life, back in England. Yes, girl, you asked for this.

"Disease, wild animals, heat, floods, savage natives – that's what Uncle Chas warned me about," she told Emma as they checked their supplies. "Let's see. We have quinine for malaria, a gun and ammunition for wild animals – and savage natives. Beads, calico, blankets and wire for trading with the less savage ones. The weather I can do nothing about."

"Do you have a churning feeling in your stomach?" Emma was staring at the medicine box as though the magnitude of the prospect ahead was just beginning to dawn on her.

"I've had it all day. But I have something for that, too." And she rummaged in a packing case and withdrew a small bottle of French brandy. "Mr Philips gave it to me this morning – for medicinal purposes and churning stomachs. But I don't think we should open it just yet. I have a feeling we're going to need every drop."

Emma's eyes gleamed. "Just a nip."

Clarissa passed her the bottle, which she was tilting to her lips when she became aware of Philips standing in the doorway. Flushing, she hastily lowered the bottle, but Clarissa only grinned at him and reached for it herself.

"Collywobbles," she told him. "You see how useful your gift is."

"Collywobbles? I should think so," he said grimly. "You haven't even had time to acclimatise yourselves, get used to the heat." He looked seriously at Clarissa. "Look. Why not..."

"We're not changing our minds, Mr Philips," Clarissa interrupted him. "Just a touch of nerves, that's all. We're really both quite tough, you know, and very strong."

He shook his head, and perched on the edge of a box, folding his arms. She consulted her list once more, ticking off the supplies they had bought in Durban on their journey north, with money sent by the bishop. Along with trade goods, they carried blankets, coffee, tea, tins of bully beef, tinned milk, biscuits, lamps, paraffin, matches, candles, soap, pots and pans, a kettle, canvas water containers, as well as medical supplies for the new hospital.

"Mosquito nets?" noted Philips. Despite his disapproval, he had already contributed generously towards their supplies from his own stores, and Clarissa suspected that secretly he would have liked to be going with them.

"That was an idea from a doctor on the boat," she explained. "He said there's new evidence that it's mosquitoes – not vapours from swamps – that cause malaria. When we were held up in Durban, we bought the netting and he showed us how to make them. See," she stood up and demonstrated, "there are tapes so we can tie it to a tree or, if there aren't any trees around, he made us each a collapsible wooden frame." She stared thoughtfully at the flimsy construction: "Now we're going to have a chance to try them out."

A small party of road-builders and camp officials assembled on the edge of the encampment to cheer the expedition on its way. Copeland strutted about, giving last-minute orders to Mukwasi and his cohort of recruits, while Clarissa checked boxes. One of the road engineers, Frank Harrison, a sturdy blond Irishman who was clearly infatuated with Emma, presented her with a scrap of paper scrawled with useful words and phrases in the local dialect: "Make fire," she read slowly, twisting an errant strand of hair nervously, "boil water, go away, hurry, put out the fire, kill the snake."

While she blushed her thanks, Philips took Clarissa aside and pressed into her hands a small brass compass in a worn leather case. "It could be useful," he said, as he showed her how to use it.

She took his hand, changed her mind and kissed his cheek impulsively: "Thank you for your help. I hope we see you again, perhaps on our way back to England in a couple of years."

He smiled, and patted her shoulder. "There might even be a road by then. A lot can happen in Africa in two years. Be careful now, and God speed. Sure you won't change your mind?"

She shook her head. "Not a chance."

The road builders offered snippets of advice. "Keep your eyes skinned for snakes around midday, ma'am," warned a strapping fellow, stripped to the waist and wearing a tattered felt hat. "Them puff adders like to lie in the sun, sometimes they don't wake fast enough to get out of your way."

Copeland shouldered his Martini Henry rifle, the porters picked up their boxes and fell into a rough line, and the two women checked their water bottles one last time. Mukwasi took the lead, striding down a track that led west into an ocean of head-high grass bordering the swamp.

A ragged cheer rose from the gathering, and the porters broke into a rhythmic chant that, to Clarissa, lent a touch of much-needed ceremony to their straggling departure. Her heart lifted, her pulse quickened, and if the tightness in the pit of her stomach did not dissolve immediately, at least it eased a little.

Although the sun was already slipping down the western sky, its heat was still fierce, and they walked slowly, glad of their broad-brimmed hats. Both women wore long skirts, khaki cotton shirts buttoned at the wrist, and soft leather boots custom-made, at the insistence of Clarissa's father, by his London boot-maker.

The track from Mpandas had been cleared to a wagon-width for the first mile or so, but it soon tapered to a narrow path winding through dense, damp grass that drenched their skirts, causing the hems to cling about their ankles. They looked enviously at Copeland's sturdy legs, encased in twill trousers tucked neatly into leather boots.

An abandoned wagon lay on its side, timber faded and paint peeling. Tramping through grass that often towered several feet over their heads, completely obscuring the landscape, was tiring and monotonous, and Clarissa was glad when the track wound downhill, the grass thinned and they entered the stippled shadows of riverine forest. They did not intend to walk far on their first day, having agreed to spend the night at a village only a few miles from Mpandas.

One of the porters shouted, and Copeland instinctively reached for the rifle slung from his shoulder as a blurred shape darted across the track into the undergrowth. "Wild pig," he muttered in disappointment.

The track meandered back to the river they had so recently left, and led to a palisade of bamboo surrounding a cluster of thatched, mud-walled huts on stilts, similar to those they had seen on the launch trip from Beira. Naked children with runny noses, playing amongst a gaggle of scrawny hens, interrupted their game to stare at the approaching column.

The doctor consulted Mukwasi, his portly figure in sharp contrast to the black man's lanky height. "This is where we take to the water," Copeland told Clarissa, "provided the canoes are here."

From the huts emerged bare-breasted women who joined the open-mouthed children to stare at the cavalcade and shout greetings to the porters. On the river's edge two dugout canoes were drawn up, one occupied by a skinny old man in a dirty loincloth.

"They look very small," Emma said doubtfully, while Clarissa scanned the bank warily for crocodiles. After a few rapid words with the old man, Mukwasi announced that the dugouts (he called them *makoros*) would take himself and the three white people across first, and then return for the porters and their loads.

"What do we pay him?" asked Clarissa.

"*Limbo*," said Mukwasi, removing a length of blue and white calico from the box of trade goods carried by the leading porter. The old man received it impassively, and signalled to another to take the second canoe out. Mukwasi climbed in with the doctor, leaving Clarissa and Emma to travel with the old man.

The craft was small, it lurched alarmingly and shipped water if one of them changed position even slightly. Although the river here was narrower than downstream, the current was strong. A flock of Egyptian geese rose noisily from the bank and flew into the setting sun; crimson streaks in the western sky were mirrored in the water, and a small black moorhen paddled into the reeds. The sight of it conjured in Clarissa's mind such a vivid picture of the brook at home that she felt a quick stab of homesickness.

On the opposite bank, a group of men struggled with a large, whiskered fish on the water's edge. As the craft approached, a spear slashed downwards, the fish stopped flapping and was flung into a reed basket.

The fishermen led them up the bank into a small kraal surrounded by towering bamboos and palm trees. Half a dozen women and a scattering of children watched their arrival in silence, and a tall wizened man with watery eyes and a grizzled beard leaned on an intricately carved stick outside a large mud hut. He greeted them warily, but Mukwasi spoke persuasively, and he finally nodded.

They were allotted a clearing beyond the huts near a clump of banana trees, beside a straggly patch of maize. While the doctor strode off to inspect the surroundings with a knowledgeable air, Mukwasi collected wood and kindling, lit a fire, set a pot of water to boil, and rummaged in the food box. As Clarissa unpacked her bedding, she watched him with satisfaction: the English butterfly-collector had obviously trained him well.

After a mug of coffee, Emma suggested bathing in the river, but the doctor shook his head vehemently: "Swarming with crocs. Just saw a couple." So Mukwasi fetched a bucket of water, and the women retreated behind the maize patch, where they stripped off their clothes, and draped them over a nearby shrub. Naked in the starlight, they doused their limbs with water and washed away the dust of the track. The evening air was cool and refreshing, but the insistent whine of mosquitoes forced them to dress hurriedly.

When they returned to the camp, the river still smouldered in the sun's crimson afterglow, and the porters squatted around their own fire, rolling cigarettes, and preparing their meal in blackened pots. Clarissa was suddenly conscious of an overwhelming sense of isolation. The arrival of night highlighted the fact that, apart from the doctor, they were surrounded by an alien people with whom they could barely communicate, and she felt an illogical yearning for the chaotic companionship of the disorderly road camp at Mpandas, with its motley crew of workers, officials and passing travellers.

A couple of days ago, you couldn't wait to get out of there, she told herself crossly as she strode away from the camp to stare across the river at fires glimmering on the far bank. She stood in silence, listening to the night sounds, then turned resolutely back.

Mukwasi and Copeland were feeding armfuls of wood on to the fire, sending crimson sparks leaping into the night air, and once she had opened tins of soup and corned beef, and Emma had set them to heat, her spirits lifted. The smell of roasting mealie cobs rose from the coals, and they ate hungrily in the flickering firelight. Mukwasi had retreated to the porters' fire, from where they could hear his voice raised authoritatively.

"I think," Clarissa rummaged in one of the bags, "as this is our first night on the road, we should treat ourselves," and Copeland's eyes glinted as she waved the brandy bottle.

"Could do with a nip," he agreed, "feeling a bit off-colour."

Emma looked quickly at the beads of perspiration on his florid face. "You're not feverish?"

"Just a touch of the sun. Nothing a good night's sleep won't put right." He poured a small amount of brandy into their coffee mugs before splashing a generous tot into his own.

The liquid burned their throats, its spreading warmth inducing a comforting sense of euphoria. Splashes and grunts floated up from the river, and from beyond the maize patch emerged a more sinister sound – the whoops and cackles that had startled them on their first night in Mpandas.

Clarissa shivered and hugged her mug for warmth and comfort, "Sounds like the hounds of hell. Is that a hyena?" she asked Mukwasi, as he fed logs on to the fire.

"Ya," he agreed, and Copeland nodded.

"One of the most treacherous animals in the bush," he told him, "it's all right," – as their eyes widened – "they won't come too near a fire."

He watched in amusement as the two women dragged their bedrolls as close to the flames as possible before unrolling their blankets and erecting their mosquito nets. Mukwasi stoked up the fire before lying down on the opposite side of it, and pulling his blanket over his head. Taking his rifle, Copeland disappeared into the dark to patrol the perimeter of the camp before settling down.

The night was very quiet as the two women climbed into their nests of blankets to lie and stare into the leaping flames of the fire. We've made a good start, thought Clarissa. She recalled the doctor's remark about not feeling well: probably nothing but a touch of sun, she reassured herself quickly.

The ground was hard, despite the piles of grass Mukwasi had heaped underneath their folded blankets, and as she wriggled to find a comfortable position on the unyielding earth, she could hear Emma twisting and turning restlessly. Finally, she found it most comfortable to lie on her back, comforting too to stare up at the starry river of the Milky Way, and pick out the constellations a sailor had shown her during the journey from the Cape: the sweeping curve of Scorpio with its jewelled tail, Virgo, and the glittering Southern Cross.

Sometime during the night, she woke with a start, and for a brief, panic-stricken moment, had no idea where she was. Her heart pounded, and then she saw the crimson embers of the dying fire, and remembered she was in Africa. The darkness appeared endless, it seemed to extend to the furthest reaches of the universe, and as she lay listening, she heard the cry of an animal – in pain or close to death. It seemed in that moment to be the most lonely and agonising sound she had ever heard. Drawing her blankets close about her shoulders, she looked across at the hump of Emma's body for comfort, but it did not help. She shut her eyes, and the darkness closed around her.

4

Dawn on a river in Africa. As the morning star fades, a rustle and a splash set off peepings, twitterings and flutterings, and a long low whistle from the reeds. A fine mist drifts on the water, and apricot streaks in the eastern sky gild the feathers of a goliath heron, motionless as a bronze sculpture. A waterbuck dips its regal head to drink, and a jackal barks once to mark the hour for the creatures of the night to withdraw and leave the world to the newly-minted day.

Clarissa opened her eyes and was immediately wide awake. It had been so ever since her arrival on this continent: no slow surfacing through layers of sleep, no temptation to sink back into warm oblivion. It was as though every cell was instantly alert and acutely aware of its surroundings.

Always, this was the best time of the day. As a child, she had been as familiar with the beech woods and streams surrounding her home as with her own bedroom. Her nature-loving father had encouraged his children in their rambling, and overruled their mother more than once to allow them to camp at night by the stream. Among her warmest memories were recollections of snuggling down in a tent in summer twilights, and waking early, to run barefoot through the damp grass with Nicholas to fish for breakfast trout.

A tousled strand of dark hair emerging from a disorderly pile of blankets told her Emma was still asleep. The fire was out, but porters were moving beneath the dark banana fronds that rustled in the light breeze. Crawling out of her mosquito net, she walked down to the water's edge. A jacana stepped fastidiously across a carpet of lily-pads, like a fashion-conscious lady determined to keep her shoes dry. A large baboon squatted at the bend in the river: "Good morning," Clarissa said, and he scratched his belly thoughtfully.

The fears of the night had evaporated. Today is going to be good, she decided, her pulse quickening at the thought of the unknown land waiting to be explored.

Emma's cocoon of blankets was stirring when she returned to the camp. "That was the worst night of my life," her muffled voice grumbled. "First ants, then mosquitoes. I don't know how they got inside the net, but they did. Then some wild animal snuffling around. I nearly woke you I was so scared. My body is not designed for sleeping on the ground." She lifted her net and peered out through a tangle of hair.

Mukwasi laid twigs and wood on the warm ashes of the fire, and blew it into renewed life. As Clarissa set a pot of water to boil, Copeland groaned and sat up, holding his head.

"Good morning, doctor," she said cautiously.

He groaned again. "Morning," he mumbled, revealing a face twice as ruddy as it had been the previous evening. "I'm going down with malaria," he announced abruptly.

"Malaria?" Her heart dropped, and she stared at him, aghast.

"'Fraid so. I know the symptoms all too well." He pulled a blanket about his slumped shoulders, and Clarissa felt his forehead. It was burning, and his face was beaded with sweat.

"I woke in the night with the sweats, and I've got a splitting headache. I'm afraid there's no doubt. Damnation," he growled.

Emma made coffee and handed him a mug. They drank in silence.

"We'll have to take you back – you can't be sick here, and we haven't come far," said Clarissa at last. "Don't you agree, Emma?"

Her friend nodded. "Could you make it on foot?"

"I've been lying here wondering what's best," he sighed. "Yes, it's probably the only thing to do. I can walk now, but if I get worse and we're further from Mpandas..."

"That's out of the question."

"I'm sorry." He looked so wretched and embarrassed that although she cursed inwardly, Clarissa's heart went out to him.

"You mustn't worry – we'll only lose a day. We'll take you back to the road camp, and then find our own way. We have Mukwasi, so we'll be fine."

"But you couldn't think of travelling on your own," he spluttered.

"Of course we can. We'll be fine," she repeated.

"You don't know what this country is like," he protested. "How would you protect yourselves from lion.... elephants... unfriendly blacks. What if you get lost?"

"I can handle a gun," said Clarissa firmly, conscious that he was in no condition to impose his will on her. "We have a map, and a compass, and Mukwasi knows the way."

Copeland shook his head wearily. "These blacks'll say whatever they think you want to hear. You can't rely on what they tell you."

Emma had been listening in silence. Now she spoke up. "People are going up and down this trail all the time. I don't think there's much chance of getting lost."

Weakened by his outburst, the doctor was silent for a few moments, head bowed, sipping his coffee. "If you insist – and I have to make it clear that I don't approve," he said stiffly, "I certainly won't delay you any further. I can walk back alone."

"But suppose you collapse on the way? You must let us come," Clarissa urged. But he would not be budged, and they finally bowed to his decision. In his present state of mind, the thought of being escorted back to Mpandas would be the final insult.

While quick to reject Emma's suggestion of allowing two porters to carry him on an improvised stretcher, he accepted the offer of a man to carry his belongings. They pressed him no further, and Mukwasi was dispatched to summon a *makoro*.

Emma helped the doctor to pack, and they walked down to the river with him. Puffing and panting, wiping his face with a large handkerchief, he made a great show of offering sage, last minute advice, "Tell them in Umtali that I'll be only a few days behind you. And keep a fire going at night," he urged, clambering clumsily into the dugout, the porter behind him.

They watched in uneasy silence as the small craft slid away from the shore. Already the heat was building up, and the sun beat down on the water. On the far bank, Copeland lifted his hat in a final salute, turned and struggled slowly up the bank, followed by the porter. He looked a lonely, dejected figure, and Clarissa felt a pang of guilt.

"We should have gone with him. D'you think he'll be all right? Suppose he does collapse?"

"He can send the porter on to Mpandas for Philips – he's not witless. Besides, I believe he would rather collapse than be escorted back by two women. That would have been the last straw. Don't forget, we are needed in Umtali," said Emma, being practical. "Worry about us. We're on our own now." She chewed her lower lip.

"Yes. One thing," Clarissa mused, "we'll go faster without him. He was a bit of a plodder, although he was probably already feeling sick, poor man."

They packed in silence, and with quickening pulse Clarissa told Mukwasi to assemble the porters. Philips had warned her they were not accustomed to taking orders from women, and she had been careful to communicate with them through Mukwasi. They seemed compliant enough now as they set off, chanting, in an orderly column.

The doctor's departure had delayed them, and the sun was hot on their backs as they picked up the track leading west from the river. The terrain was flat and scattered with tall grass, bamboo groves and banana trees; the damp grass soaked their skirts again, but the stiffness in their legs eased once they had covered the first mile.

Mukwasi led the way and the porters brought up the rear. Clarissa and Emma stayed close together, feeling the need for mutual support. Although the doctor's presence had not engendered an overwhelming sense of confidence, his sudden absence left a void that made them nervous.

After half an hour of plodding through long grass and slapping at mosquitoes that seemed twenty times worse than the previous day, Clarissa began to relax and take an interest in her surroundings. They paused to examine the shell of another abandoned wagon, lying on its side, incongruous and oddly pathetic, with peeling paintwork and two wheels suspended in mid-air. Nearby, the skeletons of oxen had been picked white by lion or hyena.

"The road may not be finished but the track has certainly been used. Why don't people use horses?" grumbled Emma, limping slightly as she nursed the start of a blister.

"Because of horse sickness and tsetse flies." Clarissa had asked the same question herself a couple of days ago. "This whole area is tsetse country."

"Tsetse?"

"A fly that carries a disease that's fatal to horses and cattle. It is so bad that the only horses you can rely on are ones that have survived and built up immunity."

After several miles the brown river, coiling back on itself like a giant python, gleamed through the trees. "Where is the *makoro*?" Clarissa asked.

"No *makoro*," Mukwasi spread his hands, palms upward. "Only little water. We walk."

"Walk? What about crocodiles?" Uneasily, her eyes flickered up and down the shoreline, fringed by dense, fluffy papyrus.

"We go quick. You shoot first – make noise," Mukwasi passed her the Holland. Dubiously, she fired in the air twice, upstream and downstream. With a beating of wings, a flock of whistling duck erupted into the sky, and a heron rose like a grey wraith from the reeds.

Mukwasi waded carefully into the water, testing its depth with his spear. By midstream, it was halfway up his chest.

"We can't do that," reasoned Emma. "He's about two feet taller than us. And I can't swim."

He retraced his steps, eyes darting rapidly from left to right to scan the smooth surface of the water.

"Mukwasi, we can't walk. Too deep," and Clarissa mimed a comparison of their heights.

"Ya, but the porters, they can carry the madams."

"Carry us?" Emma clutched her skirt about her.

"Is better," he insisted, as the porters descended the bank, chattering noisily. He summoned Manwera, the tall, bearded, natural spokesman of the group, who looked consideringly at Clarissa and Emma, sizing up their weight, and nodded.

"Better I go first. Madam shoot again," Mukwasi instructed, and after Clarissa had obliged, he set off, his pack balanced easily on his head, the Holland on his shoulder. The porters dropped their burdens and eased their sweating backs.

Clarissa followed his progress tensely, and sighed with relief as he waded out on the opposite bank and turned to wave them on.

"I'm not sure I wouldn't rather try to wade across," Emma murmured.

"The current is too strong," said Clarissa shortly; she was equally reluctant about the notion of being transported across the water like a package. But Manwera, clad only in a loin cloth, was already crouching and gesturing towards his muscular ebony back.

"You go first," she directed hastily. "I'll cover you."

"Coward." With as much dignity as she could muster, Emma gathered her skirt, took hold of her carrier's shoulders and straddled his back. Grasping her legs, he stood up and waded into the water as easily as though she weighed nothing at all. The remaining porters followed, with the exception of one man who stayed behind to carry Clarissa.

A kingfisher hovered over the shallows and, upstream, a troop of zebra trotted to the water's edge. Hoisting herself on to the porter's narrow back, Clarissa clutched his shoulders, and he grunted and straightened.

The cool air rising from the water was refreshing, and she wished fleetingly that she was a good swimmer instead of a splasher, as Nicholas had once called her. Her carrier was not sure-footed; he stumbled twice, and her heart jumped each time.

They were more than halfway when, glancing upriver, she saw it. A small dark object skimming the surface, approaching very fast. She stiffened and cried out, the porter gasped and lunged forward in panic. "Look out!" she screamed. He stumbled, lost his balance and plunged headlong, dragging her down with him. But before she went under, she had just enough time to see a small twig, trailing strands of water weed, sail smoothly past.

Emma burst out laughing; Mukwasi lowered the Holland and grinned broadly, and the men yelled with delight at the unceremonious dunking of the white woman. The spluttering porter looked apprehensively at Clarissa as she surfaced: her hat had stayed in place, but her hair had lost its pins and hung in dripping strands about her face, and her shirt clung to her body. She was laughing helplessly as she trod water.

"Go, go, I can manage," she gasped, waving him on. "If we haven't summoned every croc within miles by now, we never will."

"If your mother could see you," Emma shook her head in mock severity as she emerged, shaking herself like a dog, her long skirt clinging heavily about her legs. The unexpected dunking had given her a surging sense of well-being.

They walked through a blackened, fire-ravaged plain that extended to the horizon. Not a leaf or blade of grass remained, not an animal or bird stirred, no sound broke the eerie silence save their feet crunching on the charred undergrowth. The contrast between the lifeless landscape and the bush behind them, with its rustling grasses, quivering leaves and fluttering wings, was so striking it was like stepping into another world. The track evaporated and Clarissa looked questioningly at Mukwasi, but he marched confidently towards the northwest. The hem of her skirt was black with ash, and though walking was easier than in long grass, the heat was doubly oppressive and slowed their progress.

Clarissa's layers of undergarments, which in England had provided welcome warmth against the chill, were already proclaiming their unsuitability in this southern clime. Tomorrow I'll walk without a corset or petticoat, she decided. If only I had a pair of breeches, they would be far better for being carried across rivers. Besides, who is there to see, she argued, as though placating her mother. Only some natives who must think we dress ridiculously anyway.

She stumbled over sharp, charred tussocks of grass, wiping the sweat from her face; her feet were beginning to swell, blisters were developing, and she wondered how the porters could walk for days without any footwear at all. Detaching the bottle from her belt, she gulped mouthfuls of warm water. Heeding Philips' instructions, they had boiled up a quantity the previous evening, some for their bottles, the balance to be decanted into canvas bags. She was drinking copiously. "Must ration it more carefully," she muttered to herself.

"What?" Emma's face was scarlet and dripping with perspiration.

"We mustn't finish our water too quickly. The porters don't seem to need any at all."

But it was too hot to talk, and they lapsed into silence as the wasteland stretched into infinity, its ugliness a depressant on their spirits. Clarissa was alarmed at how tired her legs felt already: since her illness, her reserves of energy were easily sapped, and now she focused on walking steadily, conserving her strength.

In the early afternoon, they halted to rest in the meagre shade of a skeletal tree. But it was an inhospitable place, and after munching on biscuits, washed down by their rapidly dwindling water, they moved on through the pervasive silence. The heat had washed all colour from the sky, dust devils spun and swayed in the haze, and even the porters had stopped chattering.

The desolate blackened ruins of a small *kraal* loomed ahead. Staring at the remains of mud walls and a scattering of broken clay pots, Emma shivered, "I hope the people got away in time."

A distant belt of gold signalled the end of the fire-blackened landscape. The track led into thick sand, and after half an hour of painfully slow progress that left their legs weak and shaky, gave way to long grass and a water-logged *vlei*. They passed clusters of huts, from which the occupants invariably emerged to stand in open-mouthed silence as the column filed past.

Clarissa ran her tongue over parched lips as she consulted the map. "We should reach a small village soon. I had hoped to get further, but I don't think I can walk for much longer. What about you?"

"I've got a sore head, sore feet, and I'm exhausted." Emma slapped at a mosquito. "What I would like is a sparkling waterfall that I can stand under for half an hour, but at this moment, I'd happily stop right here. Is there water at this village?"

"I don't know, but we should get to Sarmento tomorrow, and it is by the river."

"Will Sarmento have beds, I wonder," Emma murmured wistfully.

The sun was low when they reached the *kraal*. It was larger than others they had passed through, but its almost treeless setting, close to a swamp, was infinitely dreary. The occupants were friendly enough, however, and once Mukwasi had presented a bolt of calico and trade beads to the headman, he was quick to produce a scraggy fowl and a small clay pot of fresh eggs. Emma's eyes brightened.

They made camp beside a few lank and straggly palms. The seemingly tireless Mukwasi gathered firewood, and once a pot of coffee had been brewed and he had plucked the fowl and expertly fashioned a rough spit, the smell of roasting flesh had a remarkably refreshing effect.

Emma plucked blackjacks from the folds of her skirt and Clarissa went in search of water. She was directed to a small, evil-looking pool fringed by untidy palms, where she washed her face, hands and aching feet, returning to the fire to find a heap of bananas had been added to their evening meal.

Two women approached. One was quite young, the other – much older, with pendulous breasts – carried a clay pot which she shyly presented to Clarissa. Smiling her thanks, she peered at the small charred brown objects within. "They look like grasshoppers," she said dubiously.

Mukwasi nodded vigorously. "Ya. Very good. You eat." He sampled one, and made appreciative noises.

Suppressing an unbidden image of soft squashy bodies, she popped one quickly into her mouth, shut her eyes and chewed rapidly. The taste was surprisingly good.

"Nice and crisp," she pronounced, turning to thank the women, but their eyes were fixed on Emma, who was unpinning her hair to wash it in a bucket of water. As the dark tresses cascaded down her back, they gasped and began to giggle.

"What's wrong?" Emma asked. "Why are they laughing?"

"It's your hair."

"What's wrong with my hair?" she grumbled, "I know it's dirty ...."

"I don't think they've seen long hair before." The younger woman reached out and tentatively touched Clarissa's head. She nodded, miming that she too had hair that fell down her back – unlike their own, which was cropped close to their heads. The women clapped their hands in amazement and departed, still giggling.

How simple life really is, Clarissa thought later, as she lay by the fire, easing her aching limbs into a more comfortable position. A few blankets on the ground, a chicken, a mug of coffee, swamp water to wash in. What more does one need? She thought of her aunt's Kensington house, where every surface was draped in lace coverings and cluttered with pictures, ornaments, candlesticks. Dear Aunt Kitty.....

During the night she was woken several times by a low, echoing roar that set prickles of fear crawling through her scalp. Mukwasi woke too, and crawled to the fire to throw on more logs.

In the morning, she was rolling up her bedding when he approached with an oddly blank expression on his normally mobile face.

"Excuse, madam," he gestured to a woman behind him, carrying a small bundle wrapped in cotton fabric. The woman approached hesitantly. As she laid the bundle down on Clarissa's blanket and carefully unwrapped it, her face wore the same blank, impassive expression.

Inside was the limp body of a very young child, no more than a year old. But its face and most of its trunk and arms had been so badly burned that it was almost unrecognisable. The eyes, barely visible, were open, but they stared past her, unseeing.

"How did it happen?" she gasped. Behind her, she heard Emma's indrawn breath, her murmured, "I'll get the box."

As Mukwasi's translated, Clarissa struggled to employ a device she had used in the London hospital, when sights and smells and overwhelming emotions threatened to engulf her. It was a matter of closing off a certain door in her mind; once she had done that, she was able do what had to be done capably and objectively.

It seemed the child – a little girl – whose only expression of pain was a small mewing sound, had rolled into the embers of a fire kept burning in the family hut during the night.

Emma returned silently with the box of medical supplies, and as Clarissa's eyes met hers, she shook her head imperceptibly. Together they set to work beneath the watching eyes of Mukwasi and the woman. The mass of glistening, bubbling flesh was still embedded with ash and debris, and it was necessary to remove as much as possible before they could apply the ointment they carried for the treatment of burns.

Although Clarissa braced herself for the expected screams of agony, it seemed the child had already moved into a realm beyond pain – it made no sound save the pitiful mewling. As she worked, she had the feeling she was performing some necessary but pointless ritual. Because it did not seem possible the tiny form could survive for much longer. And who would want it to, she thought involuntarily, as she dabbed ineffectually at the flesh of the frail arm with a piece of liniment soaked in ointment.

No one spoke. And when – after what seemed hours – the unspeakable task was accomplished, and the child was wrapped in clean fabric, the woman accepted the bundle in silence, with downcast eyes.

Later, as they picked up the track beyond the village, Clarissa's hands began shaking, and she clasped them tightly, walking fast. The suffering of children always did that to her. Mukwasi drew abreast of her. Without looking at her, and wearing the same unfathomable expression as earlier, he said slowly, "This child – can it be better some time?"

Clarissa gestured helplessly and shook her head. "No, Mukwasi, I don't think so. She is too small, you see, and the burns are too bad."

He was silent, then nodded, lengthening his stride as he moved ahead of her down the track. She watched him with a feeling of hopelessness. So much for white man's medicine.

The ground sloped upwards, and although the grass was still shoulder-high, the track was easier to follow, and the familiar bananas and palm groves were interspersed with larger spreading trees with almost European silhouettes. But that was the only similarity. At home, almost every acre was fenced, hedged, cultivated, or built upon. Here, except for the track, with its imprint of a thousand feet, there was little evidence that humans had passed this way; and the scattered *kraals*, with their inevitable patches of maize or millet, were like small enclaves encircled by an encroaching tide of bush that constantly threatened to engulf them.

By the time the sun had reached its zenith, they had emerged onto a vast savannah that rose towards a distant horizon of smoky hills. The air was so clear she could see for miles across a sea of grass afloat with animals. Plump zebra grazed in massed congregations, pausing to snort, head-butt skittishly, or kick up their heels. Ungainly wildebeest tossed shaggy manes, fleets of impala floated dolphin-like through copper grass, and timid hartebeest paused to stare at the bobbing heads of the porters. Overhead, the sky was alive with wings, and the trees swarmed with gold-and-black weaver birds. White egrets perched on flat-topped acacias, and an eagle soared in wide circles, a minuscule speck in the blue dome of sky.

"It's not what I expected," Emma commented. "I thought it would be jungle, very green, with vines, and tropical flowers."

"But it's beautiful."

True to her decision the previous day, Clarissa had shed stays and petticoat, Emma following suit, and they walked with an unfamiliar sense of freedom. Both kept their shirtsleeves tightly buttoned at the wrists and neck, however, and Clarissa still yearned to exchange her voluminous skirt for a pair of men's breeches.

Two black men approached, carrying spears and followed by a pack of thin, scraggy mongrels. "For hunting," explained Mukwasi. The hunters stopped to let them pass, staring in silence at the women, but exchanging greetings with Mukwasi and the porters.

Drenched with perspiration, they paused in the shade of a giant fig tree to sip water, eat dry biscuits and the hard-boiled eggs they had cooked the previous night, and watch the ceaseless coming and going of birds in the quivering green leaves overhead.

The heat rose from the plain in glittering waves, and their blistered feet pounded the dust more slowly as they walked directly into the sun's rays on a track that seemed to run before them to infinity. When it wound down to meet the river once more, Clarissa sighed with relief. Sarmento, which – according to Philips – was one of the main Portuguese outposts on the Pungwe, must be close. But they passed countless small isolated *kraals* before – in the late afternoon – a party of men fishing from dugouts signalled the outskirts of a settlement.

Shaded by flat-topped thorn trees, Sarmento was a scattered cluster of mud buildings overlooking the river. The figure of a slightly-built, middle-aged white man emerged from the lengthening shadows as they climbed the bank. Wearing faded, sweat-stained khakis and broad-brimmed hat, he had the yellowing, parchment-like skin Clarissa was beginning to recognise as the mark of a European too long in the tropics. Although his astonishment was apparent, he greeted them with continental courtesy and an almost pathetic eagerness, introducing himself as Antonio Andrade, representative of the Mozambique Company.

Clapping his hands for servants, he directed Mukwasi and the porters to a nearby compound where ragged hens pecked in the dust, children with runny noses gaped, and skinny dogs sprawled, scratching languidly. He escorted Clarissa and Emma to a small hut furnished with two camp beds and a large piece of sacking laid on the mud floor. Clarissa examined the interior warily, alert for the rats that had plagued them at Mpandas. They had barely time to tidy their hair and dust off their clothes before their host was back with an offer of refreshments.

He showed them into a large thatched building in the centre of the settlement. In a vast, sparsely furnished room adorned with animals skins and horns he offered them strong hot coffee, and bombarded them with questions in his broken English.

"When I see you, I cannot believe my eyes. Two ladies, with no gentlemens, only porters..." He rolled his eyes in amazement.

He listened sympathetically to their story, invited them to join him for dinner, and then rose. "And now, you wish to refresh?" he asked as they set down their cups. "Please," and they followed him curiously to a small reed enclosure behind the house.

Inside, a vast black woman was filling an enormous iron tub with steaming buckets of water.

"A bath," whispered Emma reverently. "You could not have offered us anything better."

Beaming with pleasure, he bowed and withdrew.

They savoured its pleasures with slow deliberation. The relief of peeling off dusty, crumpled garments and handing them to the waiting woman to take away and wash. The sensual delight of sinking into the hot water, feeling its warmth seep into their tired, aching limbs, and soaping away the grime of three days. They washed each other's hair and talked idly, lingering long after the water had lost its heat, their pleasure heightened by the novelty of bathing in an enclosure roofed by sky and canopied by branches in which tiny birds twittered busily.

"Even my feet feel better," sighed Clarissa, as she drew on fresh clothes and Emma wound her damp hair into a knot. Afterwards, they strolled down to the water's edge where men were fishing, some from the bank, others in dugouts. The air was cool, the sun had almost set, and monkeys chattered like children as they capered through branches overhanging the water.

But the mosquitoes were so insistent that they returned to their hut. Mukwasi and the porters squatted around a fire cooking their meal, and Andrade, in clean khakis and slicked-down hair, waited to escort them in to dinner.

In the orange glow of paraffin lamps suspended from the rafters, the large room was more welcoming than by day. "Please," said their host, seating them on either side of a heavy table set with silver and china, and taking his position at the head. A manservant carried in bowls of vegetable soup, and a woman set down a flagon of wine.

"Very special occasion for me, to have two English ladies for dinner," he said as he filled their glasses.

"It's like a dream for us too," acknowledged Clarissa.

After enamel mugs, it seemed very wonderful to hold the stem of a wine glass and sip ruby liquid that gleamed in the lamplight. The soup was followed by chicken cooked in a hot spicy sauce, accompanied by rice, roast sweet potatoes and pumpkin. While they ate, they answered Andrade's questions, and Clarissa told him about their lives in England, feeling a sense of unreality as she spoke of the London hospital.

He had come to Africa from Lisbon some twenty years ago, he told them. "First I work in Lourenco Marques for five years, then in Beira. Now," and he shrugged, "I am here." ("Must have lost favour with someone to end up in Sarmento," Emma remarked later).

"Do you have a family?" Clarissa asked.

"Yes," he nodded. "I have wife – she is from here. I have five children."

She wanted to ask where his wife was, but felt it would be rude.

"Do you ever want to go back to Portugal?" asked Emma.

His eyes darkened. "It is too late. This is now my home."

Wondering why his wife was not at the table, Clarissa studied the woman who had brought in the bottle of wine when she returned later to murmur in his ear. Middle-aged, she had a round, placid face and striking eyes, but Andrade addressed her in a peremptory way, as though she was a servant.

The wine had made them both sleepy, and after a dessert of mangoes and coffee they thanked him and rose to leave. But he insisted on escorting them to their hut and bowing low over their hands before saying goodnight.

As they rolled themselves up in blankets on the straw-covered beds, familiar, scuttling sounds were already issuing from the rafters. The gibbering of a hyena shattered the silence, but no longer did the cackles arouse the terror of their first night. "Not that I'll ever like it, but it makes a difference just knowing what it is," reasoned Emma.

In the morning, while the river was still splashed with topaz, they ate a rapid breakfast of mealie-meal porridge sent over by Andrade, and suppressed pangs of remorse as they resisted his pleas to stay another night.

"I'm afraid we really can't," said Clarissa gently, casting a wistful glance towards the reed-enclosed bathroom. She felt at home in the small settlement – it was a lively, dirty place, rather like Mpandas. Scores of children capered in the dust around Andrade, and he shooed them away as though they were a flock of irritating chickens. Several had pale skins and light-coloured hair, and it was the middle-aged woman of the previous evening who now came forward and presented them with a basket of fresh eggplant, carrots, sweet potatoes and mealies. She carried herself with authority, and the other women stood back to let her pass.

"We have nothing to give in return," protested Clarissa.

"You have give your company," Andrade countered with a gallant bow.

Although their feet were no less painful, their bodies were beginning to adjust to the routine of walking, and they had by now recognised that early morning was the time in which they made the most progress. The bush was coming to life, and Clarissa felt a sense of delighted discovery, of entering a landscape newly created. It was as though she too was being discovered, that the humans were the new players on this stage. To her surprise, the curiosity of the animals seemed largely untainted by fear – immense gatherings of impala, zebra and wildebeest, a jackal with a coat glittering with dew, and a vast herd of buffalo rolling like a slow dark river over the plain. She had read about the treachery of buffalo, but these animals moved as peaceably as cattle, and she felt no apprehension, only immense pleasure.

As the porters had consumed the meat provided by Philips, Mukwasi suggested she shoot one of the hundreds of antelope scattered across the plain. "Good *nyama* for eating," he pointed to a handsome impala bull with spiralling horns.

Recalling Philips' advice: "If you keep them supplied with meat, they'll stick with you," Clarissa agreed. But Mukwasi had told her that several porters came from the *kraal* which lay directly ahead. They had been recruited on their way home, and Copeland had warned her not to risk losing them by lingering there.

"I think," she decided, "I will shoot this evening. Tell them we will not stop more than half an hour at the *kraal*, but tonight they will have *nyama*."

She was glad of her decision when they reached the small cluster of dwellings surrounded by long-legged, waving palms and rustling bamboo. The four homecomers were greeted by shrieks of welcome from their women, and hordes of naked children swarmed around them, laughing, shouting, and climbing their fathers' legs.

Clarissa and Emma were offered golden-fleshed pawpaw, and they presented calico and blankets in return. One of the porters brought forward a small child with a festering wound on its chest, and when Emma opened the medicine box, its contents drew hisses of amazement from the circle of wondering onlookers.

But audible murmurs of rebellion from the four porters greeted the signal to move on. A rotund man with a sullen face became loud and aggressive, shouting at Mukwasi and glaring arrogantly at the two women. Mukwasi's eyes flashed, he lashed him with his tongue, then softened his tone winningly. Clarissa guessed he was reminding him of the promised *nyama*, and the payment awaiting at the end of the journey.

Finally, in sullen silence, the four men picked up their loads. I only hope my marksmanship is still good enough to let me keep my promise, she thought nervously.

It was not difficult to find the next campsite marked on the map, as it bore signs of previous occupation in a scattering of rusty cans and the ashes of old fires. Despite the debris, it was an attractive spot, shaded by large trees and bamboo clumps bordering a small stream of clear water.

"I make big fire tonight," Mukwasi informed them, "too many *shumba*."

"Lion?" queried Emma quickly – she had been studying the list of words and phrases supplied by the young Irish engineer in Mpandas. Mukwasi nodded.

Clarissa sat down with a mug of tea and took out the diary she had started keeping, in desultory fashion, since Cape Town. Now it was assuming greater importance: she realised their expedition was something out of the ordinary, and wanted to record their progress along this track that would one day be widened to carry a road or railway.

Afterwards, she took the Holland and, with Emma, Mukwasi, and one of the porters, went in search of *nyama*.

They did not have to go far. A few hundred yards from the camp, strung across the horizon, the tawny silhouettes of impala glowed in the soft evening light. Mukwasi's eyes gleamed, and Clarissa's pulse quickened instinctively. At home, she had been an enthusiastic participant in duck and pheasant shoots, and had joined her father and brothers hunting red deer in Scotland; now, she felt the familiar surge of adrenalin as she selected her quarry. A lithe young buck was surrounded by a harem of soft-eyed females; close by, a group of young males frisked and jousted, waiting their opportunity to challenge his supremacy. All were perfect specimens with gleaming coats; Clarissa selected an animal on the outskirts of the group, and laid the stock of the Holland against her cheek.

At the crack of the rifle, the herd erupted, and her quarry bounded gracefully through the tasselled grass as though unhurt. It had covered several yards, and she was about to fire the second round, when the creature faltered, stumbled and sank on its forelegs, and Mukwasi and the porter whooped their delight.

She had not lost her eye, she saw, as they stood over the animal, whose liquid, sightless eyes stared blankly at the sun-bleached grass in which it had fallen.

The herd had already regrouped; some stood poised and alert, ears pricked, sniffing the air, but most had resumed grazing, as though nothing had disturbed their routine.

At Emma's stricken expression, Clarissa spoke briskly: "It's food, Emma, don't start getting sentimental. Just wait until you smell roast venison."

Emma frowned, grinned uncertainly and straightened her shoulders. "First time I've seen an animal shot. Good shooting," she added diffidently.

The light was fading fast, and they had almost reached camp when a series of deep low grunts echoed across the plain, a chilling sound that died away on a descending scale, almost seeming to shudder through the ground at their feet. Mukwasi and the porter, carrying the carcass strung from a bamboo pole, muttered inaudibly.

"Lion?" asked Clarissa, glancing at Emma, and he nodded. "Will the smell of *nyama* bring them here?"

"Can be," he agreed, "better we eat tonight."

Later, as they feasted on the roasted meat, accompanied by Andrade's mealies and sweet potatoes, the distant roars reverberated through the darkness, and Mukwasi gathered a large pile of wood to keep the fire going.

"I'll get my violin," Emma announced.

Clarissa had heard her play often, sometimes in London, sometimes during visits to Elderbrook. Now the music revived vivid memories of evenings at home: her father doing his best not to nod off; her mother, whose hands were seldom at rest, busy with a needle; Denis lounging against the mantelpiece with his pipe, Nicholas sprawled on the rug beside the dogs.

Mukwasi listened intently, still as an ebony sculpture, watching the sparks from the fire fly up to join the cascade of stars overhead. Emma was no virtuoso, but she played with feeling, and when she laid down her instrument Clarissa's eyes were brimming.

Emma looked at her with a wry grin. "Didn't do me much good either. I hoped it might make me feel less homesick."

They made their beds close to the fire, but even with its warmth Clarissa shivered as the deep-throated roars echoed through the moonless night.

In the morning, when Mukwasi went to the stream to fetch water, he called to her and pointed to the ground. A chain of massive, doglike pugmarks were imprinted like dusty flowers in the powdery earth. "So close," she gasped, "and we never knew." She said nothing to Emma.

The porters chanted in impromptu praise of the fine meat as they set off down the track. "They too happy," explained Mukwasi. "They not know if a madam can get *nyama*. Now they say you good – like man."

"Like man," Clarissa grinned. "Praise indeed." If it was that easy to keep them contented, she determined to provide more meat as soon as possible.

As she got into her stride, she grimaced with pain. To add to blisters on both feet, she was suffering from a festering insect bite on her leg. Despite cleaning and dressing it each night, the angry red swelling around the bite was spreading. Emma was nursing an infected toe, and they both limped as they walked towards the distant haze of blue hills.

Bamboo forest loomed ahead. Once inside, it was so dense and dark they could barely see the sky overhead, the fronds rustled and whispered secretively, and scuffling sounds suggested the scurrying of small animals. The track wound tortuously through tangled undergrowth, and it was nerve-racking to be able to see no more than a few paces ahead. They advanced slowly, fearful of the strange sighs and crackles that accompanied their passing, and breathless in the heavy, moist atmosphere. The smell of rotting vegetation hung in the dim, green, filtered light, and small, irritating flies swarmed about their heads. Perspiration ran in rivulets into Clarissa's eyes, seeped down her neck and into her shirt.

It was midday before they emerged on to an expansive landscape scattered with feathery palms, and it was good to walk in open, undulating country again. Their days were developing a natural routine: an early start in the cool morning air; a pause for a biscuit and a drink of water around mid-morning. In the early afternoon, when the sun was at its fiercest, they rested again, and then, as their shadows lengthened behind them, the search for a campsite began.

Then followed the most treasured moments of the day. Setting up camp, lighting a fire, easing aching feet out of dusty boots, brewing a pot of tea or coffee, relaxing for half an hour before washing, and preparing dinner. Mukwasi would squat by the fire, rolling a cigarette or taking snuff from the duiker horn dangling from a thong around his neck.

Each campsite had a character and personality all its own, suggested by a hill or stream, an animal or bird seen during their stay, Clarissa decided. On this occasion, the site presented no unique features – a level glade surrounded by trees, near a stream with just enough water to allow them to restock their supplies, and paddle blistered feet. Emma scrubbed away the irritating spines of some velvety pods her bare arm had brushed against during the afternoon. Clarissa changed the dressing on her throbbing leg. The swelling was worse.

"You'll have to lance it," she said reluctantly.

Emma examined the infected area and her face contracted with sympathy. "'Fraid so."

"Do it now, quickly, please."

Sending Mukwasi for boiling water, Emma cleaned the area, selected a small scalpel and, as Clarissa closed her eyes and set her teeth and Mukwasi hissed sympathetically, she cut swiftly into the distended flesh. The stabbing pain was intense, and Clarissa gasped and bit her lip as yellow fluid oozed from the wound.

Emma worked fast and neatly, but once she had put a fresh dressing on the leg, she raised a pale face beaded with sweat. "I don't know why it is affecting me like this," she admitted, "must be because I know you so well. Where's the brandy?"

It was midnight when Clarissa woke with a start from a confused dream, and lay rigid and trembling, staring into the darkness.

What was it? Every nerve was alive and receptive, alert to danger. But what? At first she could hear nothing, just the thudding of her heart. Then something else – padding feet, a rustle, a coughing grunt. Heavy blowing sounds, cut off by a terrible, muffled shriek, someone shouting, someone screaming.

With the feeling of waking to a chaotic nightmare, she lifted her net. In the firelight, the naked limbs of porters tumbled away in all directions. The muffled shriek came again, standing her hair on end. And a smell, a strong, earthy, animal smell.

Emma was clutching her arm. "Lion! A lion has taken someone," she whispered feverishly.

"Where? I can't see," she reached out for a flaming log, held it high. Shadows leapt and danced in the flickering light.

"Over there!" Emma voice rose hysterically.

On the far side of the fire, a huge, dark-maned form loped towards the edge of the clearing. It dragged what looked like a long slack bundle, from which emerged gurgling, whimpering sounds.

As she raised the brand, the lion turned and stared straight at her. Screaming, she flung the burning brand with all her strength towards it. "Let him go! Let him go!" she yelled. It fell short, but propelled the creature forward, still clutching his burden.

"The gun, where's the gun!" She scrabbled feverishly in the dark. "Get light! I have to see!" But Mukwasi was behind her, whispering urgently, passing her the weapon. As her fingers closed around the steel barrel, she thanked God she had kept it loaded.

A flaming branch trembled violently in Emma's shaking hands. The lion continued to drag the whimpering man towards the trees. Clarissa's fingers fumbled sweatily. "I can't shoot! I might hit the man!"

"Ya, madam, ya! You shoot!" urged Mukwasi, and she raised the Holland to her shoulder, forced her shaking hands to be still.

The explosion of sound merged with a scream. The lion dropped his burden, staggered drunkenly, then veered towards her, stumbled and slumped to the ground.

Silence, broken only by the crackling of the fire, and the pounding of her own heart. As she stood, frozen, the shapeless bundle beside the body of the lion came to life, crawled a few yards, rose unsteadily and stumbled, whimpering, into the darkness of the trees.

Clarissa's stare was riveted to the motionless shape on the ground, about fifteen yards from where she stood. Shakily, she reloaded. There was no movement from the tawny body beneath the massive dark mane.

"Wait!" Mukwasi hissed. Seconds dragged past. Very slowly, without taking her eyes off the recumbent form that flickered orange in the light flaring from the log in Emma's wavering hand, Clarissa reached down and felt for a stone.

She threw it. In the same instant, the dark form heaved up in a convulsive movement, and surged forward with a low panting snarl, yellow eyes glittering. He came fast and low. Emma screamed and flung the flaming brand, Clarissa fired. The bullet struck home, and Mukwasi's spear sank into its flank, but still the lion came. The foul hot stench of his breath swamped her as he struck her a glancing blow on the shoulder, throwing her to the ground, and crashing past her to roll over, shudder, and lie still.

Again, a deafening silence. The burning brand flickered in the dust beside the heavy form. Clarissa sprawled where she had been flung, beside Mukwasi. Every nerve shrieked at her to flee, but she dared not move a muscle. The fallen brand flared with new strength, its ruddy glow rippling over the inert animal.

"He's dead," Emma whispered at last, "I can see his eyes. It's all right. He's dead."

Mukwasi nodded slowly, and Emma moved very cautiously to Clarissa and knelt down beside her. They clung together, breathing hard. Clarissa reached slowly for the gun, and together they edged back and away, toward the light and warmth of the fire.

Mukwasi tossed a stone at the body, striking its rump. There was no movement. He threw another – again nothing. She laughed shakily, with a sound that was almost a sob.

In death the lion was almost as terrifying as in life. His mane was heavy and black as night, his shoulders powerfully-muscled, eyes like cold yellow topaz. Looking closer, she saw that he was past his prime: his hide was mangy and scarred with ancient wounds, and one massive paw was swollen and festering.

She swallowed and turned away. Emma put an arm around her, and slowly they sank together to the ground. Clarissa began to laugh, releasing the awful tension in helpless giggles.

As they clutched one another, out of the darkness, in ones and twos, emerged the figures of the porters, whispering, laughing nervously, hugging themselves in silent fear. Gathered in a half-circle around the lifeless form on the ground, they stared from the dead lion to the giggling women.

Clarissa made a supreme effort to pull herself together. She remembered the porter. "The man who was attacked – where is he?"

Mukwasi picked up the still-burning branch and carried it towards the trees, calling as he went. Slowly the two women followed. Mukwasi shouted again, and pointed. Fifteen feet above the ground, in the branches of a tall tree, a figure was slowly and clumsily climbing down. Sliding the last few feet, he tumbled into the circle of light, eyes vacant, mumbling incoherently.

It was Kandenga, a stocky, amiable man who had come to Clarissa the previous day asking for a dressing for a gash on his leg. Blood trickled from the side of his head, and his left shoulder was a bleeding mass of torn flesh. The shoulder was hunched too, and he clutched his upper arm.

Mukwasi brought blankets, and they laid him down and covered him. While the two women examined his injuries he lay quite silent, trembling violently. After a while the tremors ceased and he only whimpered intermittently. Mukwasi brewed hot water, while Clarissa rummaged for the brandy bottle. The porters stood around the lion, chattering loudly now, and laughing, as though to dispel their sense of outrage.

Kandenga swallowed a little brandy and stopped whimpering. A couple of gashes were deep, and Clarissa staunched the bleeding with strips of calico from the trade box. While Emma doused the wounds with antiseptic, she threaded a needle with twine, and fed him more brandy before stitching up the larger gashes; he endured the pain in stoic silence, grey-faced, barely wincing as she drew the bloody lips of the wound together.

After they had made a bed for him near the fire so that they could watch him, Mukwasi brewed tea which Clarissa laced with brandy. Tending to the porter had helped calm her nerves, but she was far too tense to sleep.

"Get some men and move that animal away, please, Mukwasi," she instructed, "we can't sleep with it there – the smell."

"Tomorrow we get skin for you," he told her once the porters had dragged the carcass to the edge of the clearing and covered it with branches.

She shuddered, seeing again the giant form surging across the ground towards her, the heavy pungent smell, the implacable eyes.

Emma took the first watch and Clarissa lay down and tried to sleep, but the images of the night continued to replay in her mind. She dozed intermittently, and when dawn broke, both were bleary-eyed with strain. Kandenga stirred restlessly, groaning from time to time.

"What now?" asked Emma.

"He came from the *kraal* we passed through. We could make a stretcher, and take him back."

"Let's wait till tomorrow. If he seems better, we can send him back with two others from the *kraal*."

The day dragged by. Vultures gathered in the trees, and hyenas slouched around the edge of the clearing as Mukwasi and two porters skinned the lion. The injured man ate nothing, but drank copiously. By nightfall Clarissa was satisfied that he could travel the following morning, and a rough stretcher was fashioned from lengths of bamboo and a blanket. Two of the man's comrades were appointed to carry him home, and their loads split between the remaining porters.

"When you think of what lions feed on, I don't see how his wounds can fail to become infected," said Emma gloomily. "Do you think he has any chance of surviving?"

"We must make them understand that the wound has to be kept clean." Clarissa had seen villagers deal with various infections in less than sanitary ways. "I expect he'll consult a witchdoctor and have dung or some such substance plastered all over it. On the other hand, they might well have some local herb that will serve as an antiseptic."

Sleep did not come easily that night. Although the men collected bundles of thorn bush and built a *boma* around the campsite, nerves were taut, and even familiar sounds caused her heart to thump, her stomach to contract. The fires were fed constantly with wood, and Clarissa's dreams were haunted by terrifying visions. She woke often, and lay tense and alert, staring into the darkness, where every creaking branch or flitting shadow carried a threat. Again, she was assailed by a longing for the security of her bed at Elderbrook and her old blue eiderdown.

But, in the light of dawn, the phantoms dissolved, and her heart lifted when she saw that their patient was livelier, and the dazed, unseeing expression had disappeared from his eyes. After a breakfast of mealie-meal porridge, he was lifted on to the improvised stretcher, and the small party set off along the road back to the *kraal*.

"Our numbers are steadily dwindling," sighed Emma.

"And the others aren't looking too happy about having to carry extra," Clarissa muttered. To appease them, she promised more *nyama*, and there was a slight but perceptible lightening of the atmosphere. She could not help noticing that several men who had been inclined to regard her with indifference now looked at her with a glimmer of respect. Well, that's something good that has come out of that awful night, she reflected. She felt different too – a little more confident of their ability to reach their destination. She had been blooded.

An hour beyond the camp they were enveloped in a cloud of light rain which stayed with them all day. Although it was not unpleasant weather for walking, the ground became water-logged, their boots squelched through the mud, and by the afternoon their blistered feet throbbed with pain, and their spirits became as damp as the swampy earth through which they paddled. Only the animals seemed unconcerned. Ebony and white zebra coats gleamed and wildebeest lumbered through the mist like bedraggled clowns.

It was impossible to find a dry spot for a camp, and they settled on a small hillock where three tall trees formed a canopy, and the earth beneath was marginally less sodden than the surrounding terrain. Mukwasi struggled to get a fire going with damp wood, and the meagre glow continually threatened to go out. The sun came out briefly, just in time to stain the clouds crimson before the the mist closed in, the drizzle started again, and visibility was reduced to a few yards. Clarissa was unable to keep her promise to provide more meat, but Mukwasi roasted mealies and sweet potatoes.

Sonorous roars from the south reminded them they were still in lion country and, with no fire to discourage interlopers, they built a thornbush *boma*, and huddled inside, the men sullen and untalkative. Despite the cold, mosquitoes whined incessantly. Mukwasi rolled a cigarette and stared impassively into the feeble flames of the fire, unlike his talkative, expansive self.

Emma yawned as she struggled to find a comfortable position. "By the time our two years are up and we go home, if this trip is anything to go by, I will have had enough excitement to last a lifetime."

"What will you do?" Clarissa asked.

"Get married and have four children. I shall live in the country, grow sweetpeas and Brussel sprouts, and breed Labradors." She paused. "I suppose you would disdain such a conventional existence? You'll be off canoeing up the Amazon."

"Not quite." Clarissa stared into the fire, remembering the burnt child. "But perhaps I'll come back one day, when I'm rich, and build a children's hospital."

Although the rain stopped during the night, their restless sleep was interrupted by a pair of hyena patrolling the perimeter of the camp, their falsetto howls punctuated by the drip of raindrops from the branches overhead.

A light drift of rain accompanied them for most of the following morning, doing little to improve their spirits. In the grass alongside the track, a slope-backed hyena lifted a blood-stained muzzle from the carcass of a newly-slain young wildebeest. Emma shuddered. "It's the only animal that isn't beautiful – it has the most sinister look."

"You could hardly call a wildebeest beautiful. Or a warthog."

"No, but there is something endearing about wildebeest, and warthogs always look as though they are hurrying to an important appointment. But there isn't a single appealing thing about hyena, especially that unspeakable noise."

"Remember that dirty little pawnbroker with the shop in the alley near the hospital?" asked Clarissa.

"Mmm – always slunk around and never looked you straight in the eye. You're right – he was rather like a hyena."

"Whereas those warthog we saw yesterday," she smiled at the memory, "the big one looked a bit like my uncle – stout and quite aggressive, but with his heart in the right place."

It was a new game, one they would turn to for diversion when aching feet, fierce heat or a sense of isolation threatened to drag their spirits down. If the creature in question did not resemble an acquaintance, they awarded it a profession. The secretary bird, fussing officiously through the grass on spindly legs, needed no title; lilac-breasted rollers, looping and darting, became trapeze artists showing off, and a group of ostriches tripping rhythmically across the plain, rustling their exotic plumes, were aging dancers.

The sun came out, and their spirits lifted. As they followed the track through valleys shimmering with heat, and over granite kopjes shaded by spreading acacias, Clarissa had the feeling of walking in a dream – a sensation that came often these days. Sometimes she would shake her head and say in wonderment to Emma, "What do we think we are doing here?" And they would look at each other in mutual astonishment as they struggled with yearnings for the familiar surroundings of home, and the people they had left behind.

Equally often, they reacted by dissolving into laughter so helpless they had difficulty walking. "Hysteria, I assume," said Clarissa.

At other times, she felt a strange sense of *déjà vu,* as though this had all happened before – or, that it was meant to happen. In the past, she had scoffed at people who talked of fate and destiny, but now it sometimes seemed to her that they had sailed to the Cape of Good Hope specifically to receive a message diverting them to the country north of the Limpopo. This is what her whole life had been leading up to – Robbie's death, nursing in London, her illness, Chas and his stories of Africa – all directing her to this wilderness of grass, so dense and tall that she regularly lost sight of the porters.

In the immensity of their surroundings, their small party seemed frighteningly small and vulnerable. And all they had to guide them was a track that sometimes disappeared, a scribbled map, a compass, and a black man who had walked it before. At such thoughts, she was overcome by a swamping rush of fear. Fear that they might get lost, and walk on and on through the bush, never reaching their destination, pacing forever towards smoke-blue mountain mirages that receded ever further away.

She remembered one of Chas' stories – about a white man who became separated from his companions during a northbound trek from the Cape: how he had become completely disoriented, panicked, lost all sense of direction, and walked round and round in circles, slowly growing mad with thirst and terror. How, when a party of men finally found him several months later, he was like some wild creature, with long unkempt hair, matted beard and staring eyes. She shuddered and thrust the image from her mind.

They made camp beneath a large spreading tree on a promontory with a view of the blue mountains towards which they had been walking for the last two days.

"I have to find water – I'm dirty all over," announced Emma, running her fingers through her hair.

Armed with soap, towels, and the rifle, they walked to where a line of dense papyrus and palms indicated water. It was only a shallow stream, but it was running fast and they stripped off their clothes and stood ankle-deep, shielded by tall reeds, washing away their tiredness, and examining each other for ticks, a daily routine that generally netted at least half a dozen.

"A bit like Moses, isn't it," Clarissa plucked a plump grey specimen off Emma's back. "You expect a baby in a basket to come drifting past at any moment."

The reeds rustled noisily, and they both leapt from the water and scrambled unceremoniously up the bank, Clarissa seizing the Holland, Emma a towel to hug about her dripping form. Two Egyptian geese erupted into the sky with outraged honks.

Emma looked at Clarissa and began to laugh. Naked, dripping with water, she crouched with the gun against her shoulder, aimed at the clump of reeds. Clarissa grinned back and lowered the weapon, but her mouth was dry, her hands shaking, and the spell of the secluded stream was broken. Alert and watchful as a pair of antelope, they dressed hurriedly, and walked to the end of the promontory to look for dry firewood in the shadow of a granite outcrop.

"Look," Emma pointed upwards. The rock face above her head was covered in a tracery of faint brown markings. Moving closer, Clarissa saw that they were paintings of small, stick-like ochre figures pursuing animals across the weathered, lichen-clad face of the rock.

"Impala, kudu, buffalo," Emma traced the figures with her finger, "and a giraffe."

"And elephant." Clarissa stared in awe at the ancient mural. The animal likenesses were marvellously accurate and alive. Who were the artists, she wondered, who had taken such pains to record their hunts in such infinite detail? How long ago had they passed through this land?

She asked Mukwasi later, as they sat around the fire, and he squatted comfortably on his haunches, spindly legs splayed like a giant frog, his horn of snuff swinging in the firelight. And in a curious sing-song voice, quite unlike his normal tones, he told them there were many such paintings scattered across the landscape, the legacy of a race of small brown men who passed through from the north. Carried away by his own eloquence, he related tales of chameleons and hares, wily baboons and wise tortoises, stories that reminded Clarissa of Aesop's fables. As a bushbaby screeched from the dark, he told of ancestral spirits who lived on in the form of trees, plants and animals; and of witches and demons who rode through the night astride hyenas and antbears.

It was dawn when Clarissa woke to find Mukwasi shaking her shoulder urgently. She shook her head to dislodge a vivid dream in which she had been walking with Nicholas on the hill behind his farmhouse in Hampshire.

"Madam, you come quick."

Heart thudding, she reached for the Holland, crawled out of her blankets and stumbled after him down the track through the trees. He pointed, and she relaxed.

A flock of guinea fowl were foraging systemically through the grass, in immaculate, polka-dotted plumage and brilliant aquamarine helmets. "I thought it was another lion," she protested.

Mukwasi's eyes gleamed, "Can make good scoff tonight."

"But I haven't even woken up properly." She rubbed the sleep from her eyes before taking aim. To her surprise and gratification, she dropped two birds before the remainder took to the air, and another as they flapped heavily away to the north.

The sight of the birds generated a murmur of appreciation from the porters.

"A regular Annie Oakley you're becoming," Emma yawned, as she fed twigs into the ashes of last night's fire.

"Your hair is full of grass."

Emma put an exploratory hand to her head. "It feels as though it has other things besides grass in it."

"I could cut it," Clarissa said thoughtfully, "and you could cut mine. Think how much easier it would be. All right, I was joking," and she grinned at the expression of outrage on Emma's face.

Dewdrops glistened on spider webs, and the sun gilded the rocks where the long-forgotten artists had left their timeless records. "I love this," murmured Clarissa as they left the camp. "Don't you love the early morning?"

She was discovering how much she loved to walk. At first, her muscles had stiffened so that every morning she had to crawl out of her blankets, and hobble to the bucket of water in which she dipped her handkerchief to wash her face. Sometimes she walked for an hour before her limbs regained their flexibility, but now that they had been on the track for a week, she was beginning to feel she could walk forever.

Every day, as they climbed further from the coast, she could feel herself grow in strength and vitality. It was as if she was drawing up through the worn soles of her boots the strength of the vast, antique land. The further they walked, the stronger was the feeling. With the humidity of the swamps behind them, the air was sharper, keener, and she breathed it with relish. The heat was still intense, but it did not drain the energy from her; she was surprised at how well she adjusted to it after the damp chill of London.

Tall red anthills reared like an encampment of Indian wigwams, and by the time they halted at midday the air quivered with rolling waves of heat. By late afternoon Emma was lagging, and complaining of a headache when, on a hillside sloping down to a river, they came upon a deserted village with a forlorn and desolate air. Some of the buildings were quite sizable, but most of the thatching had collapsed inwards and the mud walls had crumbled. A few huts were still intact, however.

Clarissa consulted the map. "It could be an old Portuguese settlement," she decided, "maybe we can have a roof over our heads tonight."

But she quickly abandoned any thoughts of staying when she peered into the nearest intact hut, and a rat the size of a rabbit hurtled past her. There was something else too – something more tangible than just the desolate atmosphere of empty dwellings in which families had once eaten and talked and slept. Something else – a feeling that crawled along her spine as she walked through the silent *kraal*.

Emma stooped to enter the low doorway of a small hut. Almost immediately, she withdrew again, a handkerchief clutched to her ashen face.

"What is it?" Clarissa started towards her, but she turned and stumbled around to the back of the hut, and Clarissa heard the sound of violent retching. When she re-appeared, she was wiping her face with hands that trembled.

"What is it?" Clarissa repeated, but already she had guessed. Because by then she had caught a whiff of a heavy, cloying, sickening smell from the darkness of the hut.

"Is it ... someone.....?"

Emma swallowed and nodded. "A man...," she gulped, "what's left...a white man. Must have died some days ago. Don't go in, it's horrible."

Behind them, the porters drew back, shuffling uneasily and muttering amongst themselves.

"But we can't just leave him," said Clarissa weakly, "we should bury him at least."

Emma looked at her strangely. "There's not..." She began, then paused. "Perhaps you'd better go and look."

Mukwasi stepped forward. "I will come," he said gruffly.

Steeling herself, Clarissa took a handkerchief from her pocket and, holding it up to her face, stooped and went into the hut, Mukwasi at her shoulder. She heard the hiss of his sharply indrawn breath.

As Emma had said, the man had been dead for some days. He lay on a filthy, stained blanket, a rifle beside him, a knapsack beneath what was left of his blackened face. For the rats – or maybe hyenas – had visited the hut, and half his face was no longer there. All that was left were the straggling remains of a once-blonde beard, clinging to a cheekbone, above which two gaping eye sockets stared at the roof. On the gaunt arm that rested on the grey blanket, the few tattered shreds of rotting flesh were a crawling mass of flies and maggots.

The stench was so overpowering she thought she would faint; pushing past Mukwasi she stumbled outside to draw in huge gulps of fresh untainted air.

"We must bury him," she said at last, "we can't leave him there ...."

But why must we? she wondered, half hysterically, as she told Mukwasi to take some porters and dig a grave. He will be eaten by maggots in the end, anyway.

When the grave was ready, Emma cut a length of calico which they laid on the ground next to the body. Only Mukwasi and Manwera were willing to help, the others shook their heads and kept their distance from the hut.

They did not try to raise the body itself (Clarissa was afraid it might disintegrate); instead they lifted the blanket on which the dead man rested, and laid it on the fabric which they wrapped around the remains.

When the task had been completed, and the soil replaced in the grave, Clarissa searched gingerly through the knapsack and found a leather wallet. Inside was some money, and a faded, dog-eared photograph of a buxom, dark-haired woman in a big hat, and two young children. There were also two letters, addressed to 'Dearest Thomas' and written in a cultivated hand by someone who signed herself 'Connie'. The letter bore no address, and the only other items in the hut were a few dirty articles of clothing, the gun, an ammunition belt, and some cooking utensils.

Clarissa wrapped the wallet in a length of fabric and packed it away. "Maybe we'll meet someone who knows him," she said without conviction. "Mukwasi, take the gun and the belt."

Emma hugged her elbows and shuddered. "Where was he going? How long did he lie there," she said slowly, "all alone, before he died?"

And did the hyena wait until he was dead, wondered Clarissa. "Let's go," was all she said, but Mukwasi intervened.

"We burn," he gestured towards the hut. "Kill bad spirits."

"Good idea," agreed Emma quickly.

He set the brittle thatching alight, and within minutes the hut had crumbled into a heap of smoking debris. The porters watched in silence, but their faces cleared, they picked up their loads silently, and led the way swiftly out of the *kraal*.

By tacit agreement they did not make camp at the usual time, but kept walking for another hour, to get as far as possible from the stench of death, halting at last in a small valley, in a glade surrounded by slender trees and backed by a wall of granite.

The tinkle of trickling water prompted Clarissa and Emma to push through the long grass and around enormous boulders towards the sound. Two small duiker bounded away in alarm as they scrambled over tumbled rocks, and almost tripped into a small clear pool of water fed by diminutive waterfalls. Fringed in soft fern and shaded by young trees with pale yellow flowers, it was screened from view behind a curtain of rock and undergrowth.

Fetching towels, soap and clean clothes, they returned to the secret pool. Although the air was still heavy with heat, the water was cool and silky. Filtered sunlight gleamed on tiny bronze lizards and glittered on flecks of quartz in the granite rocks, and small brown frogs with delicate emerald markings plopped into the water and swam away as they plunged in.

Clarissa felt as though she was scrubbing away not just the smell, but the images of death that had followed them from the deserted *kraal*. Emma lay on her back, taking pins from her hair and allowing it to float free. "I can feel acres of Africa floating off me," she announced blissfully.

They shampooed each other's hair, and washed their clothes the way they had seen the African women do it, slapping the garments vigorously against the rocks. They splashed and frolicked, laughing at the contrast between their sun-tanned forearms and necks and the milky purity of the rest of their bodies. Suddenly, it was inexpressibly important to affirm their own youth and vitality, the fact that they were alive and strong and invulnerable.

5

Emma woke hot and feverish, with a throbbing head. Her face was flushed, her eyes too bright.

"You don't think it could be anything to do with yesterday – that dreadful place?" she faltered.

"Don't be ridiculous," Clarissa, who had immediately wondered the same thing, spoke more sharply than she intended. "It's probably just the sun. But we had better not move today, just in case it is malaria." Damn, she thought, damn, damn, damn. We were going so well, now we could lose days. Instantly, she felt guilty.

"No." Emma shook her head. "It's not that bad. I'm well enough to walk."

Clarissa was undecided, concern vying with pragmatism in her mind. "It would be better if we could move on," she conceded. "If the map is right, we should get to Chimoio today. There's another Portuguese base there, and we have a letter of introduction from Philips. If it is malaria, at least you can have it in relative comfort. But suppose you get worse on the way?"

"I'll be fine," Emma repeated.

"All right. Poor Emma, I'll get the quinine."

For the first few hours they made good progress despite the hilly terrain. Emma's fever seemed to drop, but by midday it was rising again and her headache was worse. When they stopped to rest in the dappled shade of a dense clump of bamboo, she sank to the ground, beads of sweat trickling into her hair from her pale face.

"Just a short rest, then I'll be fine," she muttered, gulping water from her bottle with closed eyes.

"How about if we made a stretcher?" But Emma shook her head irritably. "If the porters carry me, they'll have to leave behind their loads." She closed her eyes again, and flies buzzed about her face. Please, God, don't let her have a bad attack, Clarissa prayed, remembering the chilling figures quoted in Beira about deaths from malaria – one in every three, wasn't it? Hastily, she thrust the thought from her mind.

After a while, Emma struggled to her feet, and they walked on. The track was uphill now, and Clarissa deliberately slowed the pace and called for frequent stops, despite the half-hearted protests from Emma, torn between her increasing weakness and a determination not to hold up progress.

Towards mid-afternoon, Clarissa sent Mukwasi and one of the porters ahead to the village to announce their impending arrival. She was worried that, at their present pace, they would not get to Chimoio before nightfall, and she wanted the Portuguese resident to be aware of their whereabouts.

Pale and silent, Emma walked steadily, her eyes fixed on the track ahead. The landscape was more like parkland than bush, the trees were large and spreading, although still interspersed by clumps of feathery palms. Zebra, wildebeest and impala cropped the short grasses, barely lifting their heads as the column passed.

By late afternoon, Emma was shivering and beginning to stumble. She stared at Clarissa with frightened eyes. "My legs are like jelly..."

"Lean on me," Clarissa slipped an arm around her waist. "Chimoio is probably just over the top of that rise." Fighting a wave of panic, she kept her voice quiet and steady.

Emma's white face was streaked with dirt where she had wiped away perspiration. "Don't think I can go much further."

The sun had disappeared behind the trees, the way ahead was in deep shadow, and as they crested the hill Clarissa's heart dropped. The track fell away down a steep slope into a wooded valley through which a small, clear stream splashed over a tumble of rocks. A ribbon of track climbing the opposite bank disappeared into trees.

"Just one more hill, and it's not as high as this one," she said with determined cheerfulness. "And a stream to cool off in." Emma's weight was sapping her strength, her own legs were starting to feel weak, and the water, when they reached it, flowed deliciously cool on her blistered feet.

It was getting dark when the unmistakable deep low grunts of a lion rumbled from the head of the valley, some way away, but close enough to set her heart thumping against her ribs. Ahead, the porters spurted up the track, and Emma tried valiantly to walk faster.

"Nothing like a lion to put a spring in your step," joked Clarissa, but her stomach contracted.

On the crest of the hill, she breathed a prayer of thanks. Small fires glowed along the river bank below, and tendrils of blue woodsmoke spiralled above the trees.

"Are we there?" Emma's words were cloudy and slurred.

"Very nearly. See the fires?"

Slowly, they began the descent, Emma leaning more heavily against her at every moment. Then a movement caught Clarissa's eye. In the gathering darkness a short way down the slope, two white men stood watching a small, brown-skinned man who crouched over something in the grass.

The taller one glanced up as the two women stumbled down the track. "Well, I'm damned," he said slowly, removing a wide-brimmed slouch hat.

"Hullo," Clarissa gasped, staring in surprise. This was no Portuguese resident.

Emma sagged against her, and he frowned as he took in her appearance. "Are you all right?" he asked.

His companion, an expression of almost comical astonishment on his face, murmured, "Jerry Shawcross, at your service."

"You look as though you could use some help," the tall man was saying. "Simon Grant. Allow me," and he helped Clarissa lower Emma, barely conscious now, to the ground.

"Are we there?" she muttered through dry lips.

"Your friend is sick?" he inquired, somewhat needlessly.

"Yes," gasped Clarissa. "Is that Chimoio?"

"Yes. Give me a hand, Jerry. We can carry her between us."

"With pleasure. Allow me, ma'am." They helped her to her feet, and supported her between them.

"All right?" asked Grant gently, and Emma mumbled inaudibly, her head slumping forward. "Relax, we'll have you tucked up in no time." He spoke rapidly to the brown-skinned man who was skinning the carcass of an eland with quick slashes of his curved knife.

Clarissa followed them down the hill. Relieved of the extra weight, she felt suddenly weak and shaky.

"We'll take her to our hut until Ramores – he's the man in charge – can make arrangements for you," said Grant over his shoulder.

"Thank you," she said breathlessly.

It was almost dark, and fires glowed as they entered the compound. A small boy, herding goats into an enclosure, stared at the women with large frightened eyes, and a plump, swarthy man hurried towards them.

"Good evening, my ladies, yes, I expect you – your carriers arrived one hour ago. I have bed ready for the lady. Come, please."

He led them to a small hut on the edge of the compound, and stood back to allow them to enter.

Inside, the two men lowered Emma on to one of two rough wooden stretchers covered in shabby grey blankets. Clarissa noticed that Simon Grant's brown hands were gentle as he spread a blanket over her. She lay quite still, terrifyingly pale, breathing in short, shallow gasps, and shivering intermittently.

Clarissa uncorked her water bottle. "All right, Em. Drink this. We made it, you can rest now."

The sick woman gulped thirstily, licked hot, dry lips, and lay back with a deep sigh, staring past Clarissa at the men behind her. She frowned. "Timmy," she whispered in a barely audible voice, "what are you doing here?"

Timmy was her brother's name. Delirious, thought Clarissa. "Sleep now," she said softly, and turned to the hovering Ramores. "I'm sorry to arrive like this. My friend has malaria......," her voice tailed off. She was suddenly overwhelmingly tired.

He nodded, clasping and unclasping his hands, staring down at Emma. The two Englishmen murmured politely and ducked their heads to leave the hut, and Clarissa summoned the energy to follow them outside.

"Thank you both so much," she said fervently. "You appeared just in time. I would have collapsed back there if you hadn't come along."

For the first time since their meeting, she was able to look at them properly. Both were travel-stained, burnt nut-brown by the sun, and clad in worn khaki shirts and trousers tucked into boots. They carried weapons slung behind their shoulders and ammunition belts hung about their waists.

It was too dark to see their features clearly, but Simon Grant had thick dark hair and a kind of restless energy. Jerry Shawcross looked a little older, thirty-five to forty; he was lanky, and had a thin face and a drooping moustache.

Suddenly conscious of her stained and dusty apparel, the mosquito bites on her face, and scratches and welts on her forearms from the long grass, she brushed a damp strand of hair from her face, and held out her hand. "I haven't even introduced myself," she said a little shyly. "Clarissa Hamilton – lately of Buckinghamshire, though it seems a lifetime ago."

They both grinned. "Hertfordshire," said Grant, and "Sussex," said Shawcross with an elaborate pantomime bow.

"Do you have quinine?" asked Grant.

"Yes, thank you."

"Then we'll leave you to rest. We're billeted here for a couple of days, so let us know if you need anything."

Ramores hovered in the background. "I bring more blankets, water for the lady. Everything is to your pleasure?"

"Perfectly. Thank you very much." Mukwasi arrived with their belongings and she asked Ramores where he and the porters should camp.

"I fix," he assured her. "English ladies like tea, yes?"

"Oh yes," she said fervently, "English ladies like tea very much."

He nodded. "I fix," he said again. She was longing to subside on the bed in the hut. Ramores patted her arm. "You rest. I bring."

Mukwasi returned with tea for Clarissa and a large pot of water for Emma, who had sunk into an exhausted sleep. Clarissa sponged her face and hands, before lying down on the stretcher with the steaming mug of hot sweet tea.

When she woke later, in darkness, she lay for several moments trying to remember where she was. From outside, she could hear the muted rise and fall of voices; beside her, Emma breathed lightly and evenly.

She felt her way to the door. Ramores and the two Englishmen were seated around a fire beneath a giant fig tree. From its spreading branches oil lamps cast long flickering shadows, and the scene looked comfortingly domestic. Nearby loomed the dark bulk of a large building. She shivered involuntarily in the cool night air, and Ramores saw her, and immediately rose. Sweat gleamed on his face and neck. "Miss Hamilton, you will join us?" and he gestured towards the table.

He was unshaven, and she found his manner unctuous, but perhaps he was as unaccustomed to the presence of white women as Andrade had been. "Thank you." She hesitated. "Can you lend me a lamp until I can find our own?"

A paraffin lamp was produced and she returned to the hut. Emma still slept, drenched in perspiration, but her pulse had steadied a little. Clarissa sponged her face and straightened the blanket; pulling a woollen wrap around her shoulders, she left the lamp burning and went back across the clearing. A nightjar whistled, and the sound of splashes rose from the river.

The three men stood as she approached, their shadows long in the lamplight. Ramores bowed low and scurried into the darkness, returning with a rough wooden chair which he set down near the fire.

"Please," he gestured politely.

"How is your friend?" asked Grant, tossing a log on to the flames and stirring them up with a suede-booted foot.

"She has a high temperature. But she's sleeping now, which is what she needs most."

She heard laughter and the murmur of voices. Mukwasi and the porters sat around a second fire on the edge of the clearing.

"Your porters have joined up with ours," said Grant, "We shot a couple of buck this afternoon, so they have plenty to share. Have some chicken." With a knife, he speared one of the slices of roasted meat sizzling on a flat sheet of iron in the ashes, and put it on a tin plate for her.

"Excuse the lack of Wedgewood," he grinned.

"Is good," Ramores assured her. "Peri peri, Portuguese recipe."

The chicken was spicy and delicious, and he poured her a glass of wine. "From my homeland," he murmured with a half bow.

The wine glowed deep crimson in the firelight, and its warmth filtered through her. Easing her shoulders, she leaned back and felt some of the strain of the day evaporating. *Thank God we made it. Now I can look after Emma and she will get better soon*, she told herself. Ramores seemed as eager to help as Andrade had been, and the presence of the first Englishmen they had seen since Mpandas was comforting. Hearing her own language spoken – not in halting, broken accents, but in real English voices – somehow made her feel secure.

"This is the second time in a few days that your Portuguese wine has worked miracles," she said, smiling at Ramores.

"You stop at Sarmento?"

"Yes. Mr Andrade was very kind."

"You are travelling on your own with porters?" Jerry Shawcross leaned towards her. "That's a little unusual."

Clarissa told them about Copeland's departure.

"Umtali? That's quite a trek." Grant's voice sounded so incredulous that she was immediately on the defensive.

"We've done well up to now. Emma is strong and healthy, and I hope she will not be too ill. Is it all right if we stay here until she is better?" she asked Ramores.

"But, yes, of course you stay." He nodded vigorously.

"Good for you," said Shawcross, "I salute your courage, both of you." He raised his glass, and she laughed ruefully.

"Courage has very little to do with it," she said frankly. "Boredom and frustration were our main motivations. We were so tired of waiting around in awful places like Beira and Mpandas that we barged off into darkest Africa without much thought. There were many who tried to dissuade us."

"Well, here's to a successful journey," he raised his glass again.

"Thank you." She munched on the morsels of chicken Ramores laid on her plate, licking her fingers and feeling better by the minute. The crackling glow of the flames and the spreading warmth of the wine enclosed her in a comforting cocoon. As the men talked, she began to feel as though she was hearing them from a distance.

Ramores was reminiscing about Portugal and his yearning to return to the country he had not seen for five years. Simon Grant explained that he had met his companion on the Kimberley diamond fields, soon after pegging a claim which was being worked by a business partner. Together he and Shawcross were travelling to Beira on the first stage of an expedition that would take them up the coast to the mouth of the Zambezi River. From there they planned to follow the river, by boat and on foot, to the interior.

"For what purpose?" asked Ramores.

"For my part, mainly curiosity. Ever since I first heard of the Zambezi and Livingstone, I've wanted to explore it. Shawcross here is collecting specimens for the British Museum in London, so I'll help, and do a bit of prospecting."

"Plants or animals?" asked Clarissa.

"Plants, I'm a botanist," explained Shawcross. "But we've also bagged some ivory on the way, which we're taking to Beira."

As she listened from the safety of her wine-induced cocoon, Grant spoke about their wanderings through Bechuanaland, along the waterways of the Okavango swamps, across the hippo-infested Limpopo, and up to Fort Salisbury shortly after the raising of the flag in the new colony.

From his voice, she sensed that, unlike Ramores, who had little good to say of the continent, he was revelling in the freedom of wandering footloose through Africa with a companion who shared his enthusiasm.

As he listened, Ramores drank his way stolidly through another bottle of wine, becoming progressively more morose, until he lapsed into a brooding silence. Finally, he stood up, bowed unsteadily and steered erratically towards the large brick building.

Clarissa began to excuse herself too, but Shawcross protested. "Don't go yet. We're starved of civilised feminine company. Tell us about your trek," he prompted her.

"All right, but I must go and check on Emma."

The sick woman looked as though she had not stirred, but when Clarissa touched her shoulder gently, she opened her eyes. "If you don't stop interrupting, I'll never get finished and we'll miss the train," she mumbled accusingly.

"What train?" Clarissa lifted a mug of water to her lips.

"The train to Victoria. It leaves at five-ten." She sipped and stared up at Clarissa. "My head hurts," she said conversationally, and sank back, closing her eyes.

Clarissa dampened her face with a wet cloth. "I know. It'll be better tomorrow."

"Take off the blanket, please," she muttered without opening her eyes.

When Clarissa returned to the fire, the two men had lit up cheroots. Leaning back in their chairs, they listened intently as she began, tentatively at first, to weave a picture of their days on the trail, culminating with the encounter with the lion. Although she made light of the incident, she could not repress an involuntary shiver, and Simon Grant was quick to notice.

Changing the subject adroitly, he launched into a humorous account of some of his own misadventures, and Clarissa listened gratefully, sensing once again the depth of his feeling.

"You really love this continent, don't you?" she asked impulsively.

"Yes," he said slowly. "I suppose I do."

"Why?"

He was silent for a few moments, staring into the glowing embers as he drew on his cheroot. From the darkness, a zebra barked.

"Lots of reasons. Freedom, lack of bureaucracy, because it makes its own rules," he said at last. "In England and Europe, man is in control, most of the time anyway. He has sliced up the land, made towns and cities, roads and bridges, governments and rules. He's put up fences and borders and cultivated almost every inch of the soil.

"Here, you can go places where no white man has ever been before, sometimes where no black man has been either. It's all new, untouched. You get the feeling that anything could happen, and does, and you have to go along with the inevitable. There's only one rule – survival."

"That sounds merciless – frightening."

"Sometimes it can be." He paused. "How can I explain? In England, let's say, you arrange to meet someone in London in two weeks' time, and you do. Here, you arrange to meet someone at a certain place at a certain time – and a river comes up in flood, and there is not a damn thing you can do about it except wait for it to go down in its own good time.

"We don't set the rules here, not yet. Nature does – and we have to fit into the pattern, not change it to suit our convenience. In the bush you get up with the sun and go to sleep when the sun is gone. I like that – the thought that a force greater than man is still in control – call it what you will."

Shawcross glanced at him in surprise. "He doesn't usually go on like this. Must be the unexpected company." He grinned at Clarissa.

"You don't have much faith in humanity, then?" she persisted.

"In certain circumstances, I have a lot of faith in humanity – particularly the British – and particularly when their backs are against the wall. It's their bureaucracies, their need to meddle, and their greed that I came here to escape from. I'm not so naive as to think they won't change all this. It's already happening. We're here at the perfect time, the beginning. And I want to make the most of it because it won't last."

"How about you, Miss Hamilton? What are your impressions?" Jerry Shawcross asked her curiously.

"Me?" Her mind ranged back over the past weeks. "Exciting, cruel, mysterious, terrifying. As though, deep down, it has all the answers to all the questions you could ever ask, about ourselves and the planet and the universe. But it's not telling. It's sort of – indifferent." She paused. "But so beautiful." She thought of the plains surging with vast herds of game. "All the animals seem perfect. Hardly ever do you see one that is diseased or deformed."

"As I said, a matter of survival. Only the strong survive; the weak die or are killed," Grant interposed. "That's why they look perfect."

"I suppose so. But it's as though God had just made them and set them down on earth at the beginning of creation."

"If you look closely, you'll see that many of them suffer from parasites," said Shawcross matter-of-factly.

"The voice of science," murmured Grant, turning to Clarissa. "Go on."

"Sometimes it's like the Garden of Eden, sometimes so frightening you want to crawl into a hole and hide." She suppressed a gigantic yawn and stood up, "and now you'll have to excuse me while I crawl off to bed."

Emma was tossing restlessly, murmuring in her sleep. She awoke at Clarissa's touch, and stared at her with glittering, almost hostile eyes, but accepted a drink of water before sinking back into sleep again. Clarissa curled up in her blankets, but sleep would not come. She was assailed by remorse and guilt. What if she dies? I persuaded her to come, I persuaded her not to go to Johannesburg, she's here because of me, sick because of me.

The night passed in a haze of waking and sleeping, piling blankets on the feverish woman when she shivered violently, taking them off as her temperature soared and she became delirious. Towards dawn, Clarissa drifted into an uneasy slumber, disturbed by nightmare visions of lions prowling through the compound and pounding with raking claws on the wall of the hut.

She awoke with a start to see Mukwasi in the doorway, silhouetted against the light. Emma was still asleep, her face beaded with sweat.

I'll make a soup for her, she decided. A good strong broth with meat and vegetables. She went in search of Ramores, who emerged from the central building with red-rimmed eyes and khaki shirt hanging loose over a bulging midriff. At her request, he snapped an order, and a woman appeared a few minutes later with a squawking fowl, a basket of green cabbage-like leaves, sweet potatoes and marrows.

Clarissa regarded the bird with alarm, but Mukwasi took out his knife, slit its throat with one practised gesture, and began plucking it.

She went back to the hut to fetch a bucket, and when she emerged, Simon Grant was standing in the shade of the fig tree talking to the brown-skinned man who had been skinning the carcass the previous night.

The Englishman raised his hat and strolled over. "Good morning. How is Miss Clarke?"

"Good morning." She noticed for the first time his eyes, brown with gold flecks. "Much the same, but no worse thankfully."

"Do you want water? Rukore," he spoke to his companion who took her bucket. Lithe and bright-eyed, he had a ageless face and a wispy growth on his chin. He wore a loin cloth of indeterminate colour, and moved fast and lightly as he clambered down the bank towards the river. The soles of his bare feet were like grey leather.

"He'll get it for you. I have a job to do today – something you might be interested in."

Ramores had approached him about a report from a nearby village – a bull elephant was destroying crops and terrorising the occupants, and he had asked Grant to shoot it.

"I hear it has a good set of tusks. Do you feel like coming along?" he asked. "It is not without risk, but you seem quite capable of looking after yourself."

"Thank you," she was flattered, and a little flustered. "If I can leave Emma for a while, I'd like to. Where's Mr Shawcross?"

"Jerry went out hunting early this morning. He'll be back this evening."

Walking behind Simon Grant in the noon silence of the forest, clutching her skirt close so that it did not rustle against the grass and undergrowth, she could see in the dappled shade his shirt damp with sweat, the gun held lightly in his hand. A fly buzzed close to her eyes, and the air about her face was oppressively hot.

They had been following the tracks of the elephant for over an hour. Ahead, the tracker Rukore lifted his hand warningly, and Grant motioned to her to stop. The trees had thinned out now and the grass grew thick and high, but she could see nothing and could hear only the chirr of crickets and doves warbling from the river.

Rukore glided forward again, spear glinting. She was two paces behind Grant, who moved almost as lightly, with a smooth animal grace. A small black beetle crawled up the back of his faded khaki shirt, his dark, springing hair grew to a point on the nape of his neck, and she caught the scent of tobacco and male sweat. Every sound, sight and smell seemed magnified a hundredfold, and the crackle of leaves and twigs snapping beneath her feet sounded deafeningly loud. The fly buzzed irritatingly and perspiration dripped down her face, and as she lifted her hand to wipe it away, Grant stopped again.

She halted at his shoulder and opened her mouth to speak, but he raised a warning finger and leaned down to place his lips close to her ear, his breath brushing her cheek. There was a small tear above the pocket of his shirt, beads of moisture in the hollow of his throat, tension in the bulk of his shoulders.

"We're close," he said quietly. "Stay a few paces behind me, and do as I tell you. There should be only one, but you can never be sure."

She nodded, adrenalin singing in her ears, and he suddenly grinned. "Fun, isn't it?" he whispered, brown-gold eyes glinting. She nodded doubtfully, swallowing, trying to smile, and felt a little of her fear evaporate.

They moved out of the deep green shade into the blinding white glare of the sun. At first, there was nothing but a grassy glade about a hundred yards across, a few scattered shrubs encircled by spreading thorn trees. Rukore halted beside a large thorn bush overgrown with a tangle of white-flowered creepers, motioning them behind him. Then Grant raised his arm slowly and pointed and, with a shock of surprise, she saw the grey bulk of the elephant.

He stood at the far side of the glade, sideways on, feeding from an overhanging branch, his trunk grasping clumps of leaves, tugging them free and curling underneath to his mouth. She could see the dusty, wrinkled, leathery folds of skin, the small twitching tail, the creamy crescents of ivory gleaming in the sunlight, great fanlike ears flapping to and fro.

As though suddenly aware of their presence, the creature swung towards them with a swaying motion, seeming to look directly at the bush behind which they stood. Clarissa's throat closed, and she clasped her hands tightly against her ribs. Slowly the elephant extended his trunk, testing the air for endless moments, then he turned and went back to browsing.

Signalling her to stay still, Grant stepped soundlessly out of the shelter of the bush, and crept forward a few paces, Rukore at his shoulder. She heard the click of the safety catch as he raised the gun to his shoulder. Slowly, as though he had all the time in the world, he sighted along the barrel.

The explosion filled the air, echoing and reverberating with a shocking loudness, sending a hundred birds shrieking into the air from the surrounding trees, and a young duiker springing in panic through the grass into the cover of the forest.

The elephant flung his trunk skywards, swung around sharply and lumbered towards Grant, ears fanned wide like massive sails, screaming with anger and fear. Grant fired again, and still the creature came on, filling her vision. And then, almost in slow motion, the heavy legs buckled, the vast grey body swayed like a giant vessel in a high wind on an ocean of grass, and crashed to the ground. The earth shuddered beneath her feet, and the birds shrieked again in the ringing silence of the African noon.

An echoing pause followed the crescendo of sound. The trio stood motionless for perhaps half a minute, then Grant gestured, without turning around, that she should not move – she would have been incapable, anyway. The sound of the shot still resounded in her ears, and it was as though the scene was replaying itself in her mind: her vision was filled again by the massive grey bulk, the extended trunk, the vast, widespread ears.

"Don't move," he said quietly, breathing lightly and rapidly as he reloaded and moved forward, Rukore at his shoulder, murmuring softly under his breath.

They stepped quietly through the grass, the figures of the tall white man and the small brown man dwarfed by the mountainous bulk of the fallen animal. Grant held his gun with both hands and Rukore clasped his spear easily at his side. Together they halted before the carcass, bent over to examine it, and walked slowly around it. Grant beckoned to her and she approached hesitantly, her legs still weak, arms clasped defensively about her waist.

The elephant had fallen on his side, and she was conscious first of the swelling belly, the pale arc of ivory spearing the air, the underside of his massive feet, caked with mud, scored and hardened by long years of tramping the brown earth of Africa.

A small trickle of blood ran in rivulets from the side of his head across the fissured hide. His trunk lay outstretched on the grass, as though finally abandoned, and somehow defenceless. A large unwinking brown eye, fringed with thick lashes, stared past her, heedless of the flies that crawled across it, and tentatively she stretched out her hand to touch the folds of wrinkled skin where the trunk merged with the head. The unseeing eye still stared and, almost unthinkingly, as she had done in the past with patients who had died, she touched the skin above the eye and found she was able to close the eyelid.

Grant had not noticed the gesture. He was stroking the protruding tusk – the other had speared the earth – with an acquisitive gleam in his eye.

"A fair set," he said in satisfaction. "At least seventy-five pounds each. See where the tip has broken off, probably a long time ago."

She touched the cool ivory: close to, it was dark and stained, scored with scars, the legacy of ancient clashes. "It's so powerful... awesome..."

His eyes gleamed with understanding. "The first time you get close to an elephant can be a bit overwhelming."

"Did you hit it twice?"

"Yes. First a head shot, the second in the chest. Just down here," and he showed her the second hole, partly obscured by folds of skin.

"What now?" she asked, noticing for the first time the thousands of tiny hairs that sprouted on the outstretched trunk.

"We get the tusks cut off, and then let the natives deal with the carcass."

"Can you eat the meat?" she wondered.

"Certainly, I've had it myself. Here they come, along with the vultures."

On the edge of the clearing stood half a dozen young men in loin cloths, carrying spears, chattering loudly and gesturing towards the corpse. Others were approaching, and the sound of singing and shouting rang from the forest. In the blue overhead, black specks wheeled.

"How do you know they're vultures?" she asked. "They're so far away."

He shrugged. "You just know – they sense when something dies."

He spoke to Rukore, who had been joined by two men, and all three began sawing at the leathery grey-brown hide above the tusk. It took ten minutes for them to remove the upper tusk from its socket, leaving a raw, bloodied hole.

She tasted bile in her mouth, and turned away, walking to a fallen log under a tree on the edge of the glade. The heat was oppressive. More people were arriving, shouting, laughing, chanting a joyous, exultant song. The men carried spears and axes, the women and children a motley array of containers – closely-woven mats, baskets and clay pots.

Accustomed to the frank stares of curiosity her appearance generally evoked, she stared back. Two children halted close by, regarding her with large eyes. Both were naked but for strings of beads around protruding bellies. The older boy held one arm to his chest: the skin, from elbow to wrist, was a mass of swollen, suppurating flesh. She made an involuntary gesture towards him, and immediately both children retreated behind a large woman.

Searching for inspiration, Clarissa drew from her breast pocket a small gold fob watch on a chain, which her father had given to her when she started nursing. Casually, she swung it gently and the gold winked in the sunlight. The children stared in wonder and edged nearer. When they were close enough, she smiled and nodded and held it out.

Slowly and cautiously, they inched closer. She let the injured boy play with the watch as she looked at the wound without making any attempt to touch it. It could have been a burn that had become infected; flies hung over the raw, ruptured flesh, and the child made no attempt to wave them away.

When she made a move to examine it more closely, he pulled roughly away, his huge eyes never leaving the watch. She went to Grant, who was supervising the removal of the second tusk.

"There's a small boy there with an infected arm. I have a medicine box in our hut. Would his mother mind if I treated him?"

"You're wasting your time. If you start looking closely at these people, ninety percent of them need some kind of medical attention. You'd be here all week."

"I could go back if you lent me Rukore to show me the way," she persisted. "If I don't treat it, it will get worse."

He looked at her with a pained expression, then called his tracker and spoke to him rapidly. "Rukore will go faster on his own. Would your man be able to find the box for him?"

She nodded, and Rukore saluted and set off at a trot towards the camp.

"On the other hand," Grant looked at her consideringly, "perhaps you should have gone too. You might not be too keen on what happens next."

"Why? What happens?"

"My boys will peel back the skin, and this lot here will dive in and get as much meat and fat as they can. They also puncture the stomach, and the smell is – well, let's say – a little rich. It tends to become a free-for-all. You are a nurse, of course, so it may be all in a day's work," he added teasingly.

She was still feeling queasy, but once again he had put her on the defensive. "No need for you to worry about me," she told him.

But it was hot, and she settled on the ground beneath a spreading thorn tree, beckoning to the two children, whose mother had joined the men around the carcass. She showed them her watch again, then played a game in which she pretended to remove the end of her thumb. Every time she pretended to grimace with pain the children rolled on the ground laughing. Several times, the wind wafted in their direction, carrying an obscene, sickly sweet stench that only she seemed to notice.

A shout erupted, and the assembled people surged towards the carcass. Clarissa's curiosity overcame her repugnance and she left the children and went to investigate.

"It was like a scene from hell," she told Emma that evening. "The elephant lay on its side, a gaping wound where once the upper tusk had been, and the entire carcass was swarming with men and blood and guts. The hide had been peeled back, and they were hacking at the flesh with all kinds of implements, mainly short spears and axes. They stood on its legs and shoulders and head, and inside the stomach cavity."

Behind the men, women and children passed chunks of fat and bloody meat from hand to hand, to be packed into pots and sacks, bags and baskets. Some of the children already had full loads on their heads and were leaving the clearing. Men crawled over one another to reach the farthest caverns of the carcass. Up to their elbows in blood, they flung chunks of glistening fat and meat and intestines over their shoulders as they hacked at the great walls of muscle and sinew, flesh and bone. It was difficult to know which blood oozed from the dead elephant and which from the people, because in their urgency to seize all they could, they sometimes slashed at one another with their spears.

From the uppermost ribs of the animal, festoons and loops of flesh and entrails and gore dangled like macabre streamers, until one of the men reached upwards and slashed at them, pulling them down and tossing them to a waiting woman.

Near the carcass, a fire had already been built by some of the women, who began roasting slices of meat. Overhead, the sun was briefly obscured by dark shadows, and the branches of the thorn tree were heavy with the hunched silhouettes of vultures. A marabou alighted on a dead tree stump, its naked neck blue-white in the glare. Grant approached, his eyes following her gaze. "If you come back tomorrow, there will be nothing left but bones. Africa has a most efficient rubbish disposal system."

Her eyes turned back to the frenzied activity inside the carcass, where the near-naked, bloodstained figures worked feverishly, screaming, laughing, swearing. An old crone hobbled past, a loaded basket balanced on her head, a large pot of entrails clutched in her arms. She grinned fiendishly at Clarissa as she passed.

Grant pointed. "You could have another patient."

Out of the mêlée hurtled a young man, panting, bloodstained and sweating, clutching one arm and shouting over his shoulder. Brilliant red blood oozed through his fingers, and a woman handed him a dirty piece of rag which he hurriedly wrapped around the wound and, without more ado, leapt back into the bloody cavern, wielding his spear.

"More important things to worry about than a mere arterial bleed," Grant murmured.

"It's like a swarm of ants – or maggots," she said, mesmerised. At that moment, Rukore approached with the medicine box. "Mr Grant, that little boy. Please ask his mother to bring him here."

"The name is Simon." He said a few words to Rukore. The woman was summoned, and she approached hesitantly, staring at Clarissa suspiciously. The boy hung behind her, large eyes staring fearfully. Flies still buzzed about his arm and his nose was running.

When the woman pulled the child forward, he clung to her leg, and she spoke impatiently. Clarissa held her watch close to her own ear, and then extended it invitingly. When he had taken it, she swiftly opened the medicine box, and Rukore explained to the mother what she wanted to do.

The woman stood silent and fearful, hypnotised by the array of bottles and instruments. Clarissa worked rapidly, cleaning and disinfecting the wound, and covering it with a dressing and large white bandage that contrasted sharply with the ebony skin. By now, the child was watching the process with mild interest as he played with the watch.

"Please tell her she must keep the dressing on," she said to Simon. The boy was persuaded to hand the watch back, and his mother looked at Clarissa with an unfathomable expression, aiming a question at Rukore.

Simon grinned artlessly. "She wants to know if she can have one too." He spoke rapidly to Rukore who grinned. The woman laughed, took a chunk of meat from her basket and held it out to Clarissa.

She was about to decline politely, when Simon said, "Go on, take it. She has no other way of thanking you, and she would be offended."

"But it would feed her family for days," protested Clarissa. "Ask her to cut off a slice for me. Tell her I have a small stomach and no children."

The woman grinned a little pityingly. She cut a slice, and Rukore wrapped it in a handful of broad leaves. Mother and child moved away, the boy holding his arm out stiffly, as though it was a separate entity.

"I suppose they'll have to eat all the meat quickly, before it goes bad?" she queried, closing the medical box.

"They'll gorge themselves for a couple of days, and the rest they will make into biltong – that's what the Boers call dried salted meat. It lasts indefinitely."

Engrossed in her work, she had not noticed the activity around the carcass. Now she stared in astonishment. All that remained of the creature which had, only hours ago, been browsing on the shiny green leaves now tipped with late afternoon sunlight, was a skeleton, hung with a few tattered ribbons of tissue, lying in a patch of blood and bile-stained grass trampled flat by urgent feet. The villagers were leaving, and the waiting congregation of vultures flapped heavily to the ground, the smaller ones making way for a large black bird with flesh-coloured folds of skin on its face and neck.

Emma was awake when they returned. Although still weak, her skin was cooler than the previous night, and she was able to swallow a little soup. She listened alertly to the saga of the elephant hunt, but by the time Clarissa had finished, her eyelids were drooping. "I'm sorry to be such a nuisance, Lissa, I know you want to move on," she murmured tiredly.

"Don't be silly." Remorse surged over her again. "We're in no hurry, and it's been very pleasant to have a rest." She realised it was true, that it was a relief to have this period of respite.

After sponging Emma's face and hands, she went to the fire, helped herself to soup from the pot, and wandered with her mug down to the river. From the opposite bank drifted the throb of drums and the sound of chanting voices. She sat on the bank, and sipped the soup. The evening was clear and cool and the sounds of celebration mingled with other nocturnal sounds – grunts, splashes, rustles in the grass. Bats flitted soundlessly, brief smudges against the cool sky.

"How is Miss Clarke?" She had not been aware of Simon Grant's silent approach. He sat down beside her, in clean shirt and trousers. He was smoking a cheroot, and she sniffed the familiar scent appreciatively.

"Reminds me of my favourite uncle," she said – it was easy to imagine Chas at this moment. "She seems a little better, but she won't be able to travel for a few days at least."

"When she is strong enough, you want to start slowly. Don't try to do a full day immediately. There's a good campsite near a *kraal* about six miles from here. It's beside a stream and there are shady trees."

"Thank you. I'll remember."

"If you feel like a walk, we've been invited to the celebrations across the river. They're roasting the meat."

She looked at him doubtfully. "We won't stay long," he assured her, "it should be quite a spectacle. You'll have a chance to taste elephant meat – unless you've already sampled some?"

"No," she laughed. "I gave it to Mukwasi, and he's going to dry it for us and make – what did you call it?"

"Biltong."

"Yes, biltong. All right, I'd like that. I'll make sure Emma's asleep. Where's your friend?"

"He's coming with us."

"Did he have a successful day?"

"Yes, got a kudu, and some more specimens."

"Would you both like some chicken broth?"

"Sounds good."

In the lamp-lit hut, Emma breathed easily, a fine sheen of moisture on her forehead. She woke and Clarissa gave her water, and told her where she was going. Emma raised one eyebrow ever so slightly. "Mr Grant seems to be amazingly attentive," she whispered weakly, the hint of a smile at the corners of her mouth. "It's all very hazy, but I remember one of them was quite good-looking."

Clarissa laughed, immeasurably relieved Emma was able to joke again. "They're both madly handsome. Go to sleep. I won't be too long. The village is just across the river."

The two men were waiting by the fire, finishing mugs of soup with evident appreciation. Rukore walked ahead of them down a narrow track to the river. The moon was rising, casting deep shadows on the track, and the sounds of the night intensified: the hoot of an owl, the chirr of crickets, hippos communing in comfortable grunts.

A dugout was waiting on the bank, and Rukore poled it across the still dark water. On the far bank, the throb of drums and the sound of singing were much louder and the glow of fires winked through the trees. The track was narrow and they walked in single file behind Rukore.

At the village they followed him past a group of huts, the smaller ones raised on stilts, to a central clearing where fires were burning. The fragrance of roasting meat mingled with woodsmoke, the smell of dung and human sweat. The drums were very loud and the firelight leapt and danced, burnishing the limbs of the assembled people.

Celebrations were well advanced. The drummers pounded their instruments – hollowed logs covered in stretched animal hide; totally absorbed, with half-closed eyes, they swayed to the beat, mesmerised by the rhythm. The men danced in an outer circle, the women in the centre, facing them, stamping the dust, their bodies moving rhythmically and unselfconsciously. The men wore loin cloths, the women brief skirts of animal skin, and beaded belts. Beyond the dancers, small children pranced, pounding the earth and leaping into the air, giggling and shouting as they imitated their elders. Firelight gleamed on ebony skin, and Clarissa's eyes smarted from the swirling smoke. At a word from Simon, Rukore melted into the throng of undulating bodies.

They stood together watching, and she felt the pulse of the drums and the thudding of feet through the soles of her own feet. Firelight danced on breasts, gleaming arms and thighs, and gilded the swirling dust.

Simon touched her arm and pointed to one of the dancers – a young man with broad powerful shoulders, and she saw that a white bandage was wrapped around his head, the end floating free. She had seen him with the injured child earlier in the day.

"I did warn you," he remarked. "Obviously a fine white bandage has other uses."

She simmered with annoyance. "How could he take it off that child? D'you think if I put another one on tomorrow.....?"

"Probably end up the same way."

The man was lost in the throng of dancers. Someone brought a calabash of beer, and Simon proffered it to her. She sipped experimentally, it was strong, pungent and sweet, and she gasped as it took her breath away and sang through her body. Simon and Jerry drank thirstily, and then a man came and led them around the circle of dancers to a small group of elderly men. They were introduced to the *kraal* head, a stout man with a cherubic face, who smiled and nodded his thanks to Simon, called for stools to be set out, and offered them chunks of roasted elephant impaled on sticks.

The meat tasted good. "I thought it would be a tough as a boot," Clarissa said in surprise.

She was offered more beer, and sipped slowly, unaccustomed to its potency but enjoying the sense of lightness that flowed through her body. With the knowledge that Emma was on the mend, she felt carefree and irresponsible.

"They have so little," she said, as she stared at the animated, pulsing scene, "yet they seem so happy."

"The beer helps," said Simon dryly.

The tempo was building up, dust rose from the pounding feet. Rukore, standing nearby, poured beer down his throat in a single stream.

"Does Rukore come from this area?" she asked.

"No, but he seems to be able to communicate with these people. He's from the south – the Cape."

Now the dance was coming to an end, the dancers breathed long and deeply, their bodies glistening, and they began to clear the central area, moving back to gather in a semi-circle around its perimeter.

From the darkness beyond the firelight emerged an extraordinary figure, wearing a full skirt of animal tails and feathers, anklets of animal teeth, a painted wooden mask and a lavishly feathered headdress.

The drums throbbed to a different beat, the man stamped his feet, leaped and gyrated with immense agility. After a few minutes he took from an onlooker two warthog tusks which he fitted to holes in the mask while he began a series of slow ponderous movements which seemed vaguely familiar. It was a couple of minutes before she realised what he was doing.

"He's your elephant," she whispered, and Simon nodded, watching intently. The dancer mimicked the movements of the creature, using one hand as a trunk to browse on imaginary leaves. He danced the moment of danger, the attack, the charge and the sudden death, and finally, leapt into energetic life once more, while the men encircled him in a dance of celebration that involved much shouting, and stamping, accompanied by ululations from the women.

The headman reappeared with some meat skewered to a stick. With a formal flourish and a few words, he presented it to Simon, who accepted it gravely, and bit into it. He nodded appreciatively and the headman grinned, showing large gaps in his yellowed teeth.

"This is the heart," Simon told Clarissa. "It is a great delicacy. Try some." Tentatively, she took a small piece, and was again pleasantly surprised by the taste. The drums surged and pounded like surf on a beach, and the firelight leapt and painted the sweating faces of the dancers. They seemed to move in a kind of trance, and Clarissa had the strange feeling she too was being drawn into the hypnotic pulse of the dance. A sense of exhilaration, almost overwhelming in its intensity, surged through her. After the miles of walking through the bush, her body felt stronger and more electrically alive than at any moment she could remember, but the feeling was more intense than merely a sense of well-being or the urge to dance.

She was suddenly conscious of the bare breasts of the women, the burnished torsos of the men, the overtly sexual movements of the dance, and of the tall silent Englishman beside her, smoking his cheroot.

She had the same feeling that she had experienced earlier in the day while walking behind him – an intense awareness of her surroundings, as though her senses had become acutely sensitive antennae. She felt the warmth from his body and was suddenly aware that he was young and strong and immensely attractive, and she had to suppress an overpowering urge to put out her hand and touch the sun-browned skin, feel the sun-bleached hairs on his arm as he raised the calabash to his lips.

The wind veered and smoke from a nearby fire stung her eyes and made her cough. He extended the calabash, grinning. "Here, have a drink."

She had intended taking just a sip, but the liquid flowed out in a sudden jet, running down her chin and making her splutter. He took the calabash and handed it Jerry, who had rejoined them. "Steady. This is vicious stuff."

"I didn't meant to…" Her eyes watered and she was gasping and laughing. As she lifted her hand to wipe her mouth, he took a handkerchief from his pocket, tilted her chin and carefully dabbed it dry. The firelight flickered on his face, and there was laughter in his brown-gold eyes.

"You'll be on the dance floor in a minute," he said lightly, handing her the handkerchief.

She dabbed the front of her shirt where the beer had spilt. As she gave the handkerchief back to him with a murmur of thanks, his fingers brushed hers, and it was suddenly as though the people and throbbing drums faded and there was only the two of them.

She blinked. "Why not?" she countered, trying to match his lightness of tone.

"Go on, then," he dared her.

She stared at him, their eyes locked, and she laughed and turned away.

"Jerry has no such inhibitions," he remarked, and she caught a glimpse of his friend gyrating in the crush of bodies. She would like to have danced, but something held her back. Inhibitions, the thought of her mother's disapproval. The beer sang in her head and through her veins, she was acutely aware of his gaze, and when she looked up, his eyes were staring at her with candid curiosity, and a kind of watchfulness.

"I think perhaps I should get back," she said, "…. in case Emma needs me."

"Of course. You must be tired." His hand on her elbow was warm and dry and strong. "You coming, Jerry?"

His friend tilted the calabash to his lips. "Later," He waved them on. "Goodnight, Miss Hamilton," and he smiled with deep contentment.

"Feeling no pain," said Simon resignedly.

Away from the fire and the crush of people, the night was cool and the moon silvered the leaves overhead. He took the lead, and she followed him down the narrow track, the throb of drums an insistent echo within her. She knew she had drunk too much beer, and although she saw that Simon had unslung his rifle and held it at his side, she felt no sense of threat from the surrounding night. It was too beautiful for danger to be lurking in the shadowy trees bordering the track. Once she saw the gleam of green eyes in the undergrowth, close to the ground, but when she looked again they were gone.

Back at the settlement, the fire was out under the tree where they had sat the previous evening, and there was no sign of Ramores. Outside her hut, she turned to Simon, still buoyed by the inexplicable sense of well-being, the moment of tension at the village now dissipated.

"That was special," her eyes were bright. "Every day seems to bring a new experience."

"A little different from the balls you would have attended in Bucks?"

She grinned. "Perhaps. But not so very different from some of the celebrations I've seen up in Scotland. They have been known to get quite boisterous." She looked wistful. "Do you think there will be balls in Mr Rhodes' new colony?"

"Certainly. Wherever the British go, they take their traditions with them – and cling to them with much more determination than they ever do at home."

"Good. Well, thank you again, I'll see you in the morning," but as she turned to go, he put his hand on her arm.

"Don't go in just yet." His voice was almost tentative. "Come and sit for a few minutes."

"All right."

She walked with him to the tree, where the stools were still standing from the previous evening. They sat down, and the night was so still and quiet that the throb of drums sounded clearly from across the river. She could even hear, very faintly, the sound of voices.

She asked him about himself, and he told her his father, William Grant, was a zoologist and explorer, who had written a number of scientific and popular books on India.

"I think I remember seeing that name on some of my father's books," she recalled. "He's keen on that kind of thing."

A cloud passed in front of the moon, casting a shadow on the night, and Simon looked up at its silvered edges. "When I was a small boy, looking at the moon through my window, my mother used to tell me that when a cloud went in front of it, the moon was washing its face. She used to say, 'Watch and you'll see that when the moon comes out again, it will be much cleaner and brighter than before.'"

"And was it?"

"It seemed so at the age of six." As he spoke, the African moon emerged slowly into a gap in the cloud – a silver melon – and they grinned at each other. "She used to say that the moon could see the whole world as it sailed across the sky – continents and oceans, mountains and rivers, Europe, Asia, Africa, America. My father used to be away a lot, and I asked whether the moon could see him too, and she always said, 'Yes, of course'. Once I asked her, 'What does the moon see my father doing?' And she said, 'Riding through the jungle on an elephant draped in red tapestries with golden tassels'."

The cloud had passed across the moon again, and she could no longer see his expression. "It was around about that time that I decided I wanted to be like the moon, to be able to see the whole world, including elephants with gold tassels."

"And did you go to India too?" she asked.

"No, India belonged to my father. By the time I grew up, I wanted to go somewhere different. A place that would be mine – but it had to have elephants."

She smiled in the dark. "And here you are."

"And here I am."

"Shooting them instead of riding them."

"Yes, well, ivory pays, and one has to eat. Besides, African elephants are too proud to let you ride them."

"And here is your moon, still watching," she looked up as the cloud drifted away and the clearing was bathed once more in radiance.

He looked at her quizzically. "I don't know what made me tell you that. I haven't thought about it for years. Tell me about your family."

She told him about her parents, and Chas, and her brothers, and Nicholas' country farmhouse with its crooked walls and winding stairs. The yard bordered by stables, where Nicholas's dogs lay panting on the cobblestones and the air was heavy with the smell of warm hay and horse manure. The garden sloping down to a stream where dappled trout gleamed in the shadow of moss-clad rocks, the old ruined castle on top of the hill behind the house.

"We have picnics up there sometimes. Do you miss England?" she asked suddenly, besieged by images of the past.

"Not at all. Do you?"

"Mostly I haven't had time to think about it. But sometimes, yes, especially at night."

"Is that you, Lissa?" Emma's voice was clear and frightened, and she stood up quickly.

"Yes," she called. "Coming, Emma." She turned to him as he rose. "I'm sorry, I must go. But thank you for this evening."

"It was my pleasure."

"I'll see you in the morning."

"Yes, we're moving on tomorrow."

"Oh." She was startled at the wave of disappointment that surged through her. "Of course, I'd forgotten. Will I see you before you go?"

"You will." He walked to the hut with her, and picked up the rifle leaning against the mud wall. He stared down at her with a half-smile. "Thank you for coming, Clarissa. Sleep well." He reached out a hand and touched the tip of her nose gently with his forefinger. It was the first time he had said her name.

"Goodnight." She turned and went into the darkness of the hut, and when she emerged a few minutes later to fetch hot water from the pot resting on the still-glowing embers of the fire, she saw the silhouette of his figure walking back in the direction of the village.

By morning, Emma's eyes had lost their feverish glitter, and her skin was cool and moist. Although still weak, she immediately began talking about moving on.

"No," said Clarissa firmly.

"Look, I'm fine, and we've lost so much time."

"You're not fine, and I'm not having you walk after a fever like that. You can get up if you insist, and walk around a bit here. If you still feel well tomorrow, we might move on then, but only a little way."

"What were you up to last night?" asked her friend innocently. "Did I not hear you having a tête-a-tête with Simon Grant while I was lying at death's door?"

"We were just talking." Clarissa felt herself flushing.

"Talking – about what?"

"About the moon and elephants."

"The moon," Emma's inflection was heavy with meaning.

"And before you get any ideas, he's leaving this morning and I'll probably never see him again. He's going up the Zambezi."

"Not a moment too soon, by the sound of it," Emma said with mock severity, and Clarissa was glad to hear the familiar lilt in her voice.

Mukwasi had cooked the now-familiar mealie-meal porridge for breakfast, and today even Emma took a few spoonfuls, sitting up in bed, her dark hair hanging in lank coils about her face.

There was a flurry of activity outside, and Clarissa went to the door to see Simon's porters assembling, ivory tusks prominent in their luggage.

"They're leaving now," she said.

Emma threw back her blanket. "I need some fresh air," she declared, standing up slowly in her shift, "and I am determined to have a look at your Mr Grant before he disappears."

"He's not my Mr Grant." Clarissa helped her to dress, carried a stool outside into the sun, and wrapped a shawl about her shoulders.

"I wish my ears would stop ringing," she sighed, holding her hands up to the sides of her head.

"That's the quinine. It'll wear off in a few days." Clarissa went into the hut to tidy the beds, and when she emerged, Simon was talking to Emma.

"I'm much better, thank you. Ready to start walking again," she was telling him blithely.

He raised his eyebrows, and turned at Clarissa's approach, smiling at her. "Good morning."

A rifle was slung over his shoulder, and morning sunlight glinted on his sun-bleached forelock. He exuded pent-up energy.

"Good morning," she replied. "And don't listen to her. I have no intention of letting her walk today, perhaps not even tomorrow, but when we do, I'd like us to stop at the place you recommended."

"Do you have a map?"

When she returned with van Heerden's map, Jerry Shawcross was there too, eyes red-rimmed and bloodshot.

Simon glanced at him. "Here's someone who would rather not be walking today," he jeered heartlessly. His friend smiled sourly, bowed carefully to Clarissa, and went across to speak to Emma.

Simon studied the map, and showed her the campsite. "Be careful along this next section," he warned. "Don't ever think of walking after the sun has set. The place is thick with lion. You have a gun? Yes, of course, I forgot, you've already bagged yourself a lion."

"That's right," she said.

"I don't need to worry about you then." The tawny eyes laughed at her.

"No, you don't. We'll be fine."

"I believe you will." He gazed at her silently for a moment, and then withdrew an oilskin bag from his pocket. "Would you do something for me? Look after this?"

The request was so unexpected that she stared at him blankly. "What is it?"

He opened the bag and drew out a small ornament. Curiously, she took it in her hand: it was a stone carving of a bird of prey poised for flight from a tree stump.

"I've been carrying it for weeks, and I'm afraid I'll lose it. I got it from an old man down on the Limpopo and I'm rather attached to it. With all the travelling I'm going to be doing, especially by river, anything could happen to it."

"What is it?"

"A fish eagle, they're found all along the rivers around here. They have white heads and darkish bodies, and the most magnificent call. To me they're the essence of this part of Africa."

She was puzzled. "But, Simon, why me? How will I return it to you? We'll be in Umtali for two years and then we're going back to England."

"I expect to be passing through Umtali next year. In a place like that, where white women are few and far between, I think I'll manage to track you down."

"How?"

"All I need to do is ask for the English nurse who has shot a lion and has a taste for the local brew. How is your head this morning?"

"There's nothing whatsoever the matter with my head," she retorted. "And you can talk. I saw you going straight back there after we said goodnight."

He grinned. "Couldn't leave Shawcross, he would have stayed all night and been in even worse shape than he is at the moment. Rukore was just as bad, had his eye on one of the local beauties, so I hauled them both back. Will you keep it for me?"

"All right," she said slowly, "but I'm not exactly in the most sedentary situation myself."

"I know, but women look after these things better than men. Anyway, it means that I'll have to find you." He was smiling, but his eyes were serious.

"So I will see you again?" She spoke lightly, felt unaccountably breathless, and looked quickly down at the stone carving, turning it over in her hand.

"You will see me again. But give me your address in England, just in case. With ships like us, passing in the night, you never know. I should be going back home myself after this trip is over – for a short time."

She wrote her address in a small, dog-eared notebook which he put in his pocket.

"Now," he said briskly, "you have a compass?"

"Yes. One thing I do worry about is water – I'm so afraid of running out," she confessed.

"Tell you a tip I got from an old prospector. As the sun goes down, look for birds, doves especially, they fly to water in the evening. And look for fresh tracks. Most animals tend to drink in the evening."

"I'll remember."

"And take good care of my eagle," he reminded her.

"I will. I hope you get a good price for the ivory." She extended her hand, and he held it for a moment, his eyes on her face.

As he donned a broad-brimmed hat decorated with a speckled guinea-fowl feather, Jerry Shawcross approached to say goodbye, and Ramores hovered nearby, his skin more than ever like sallow parchment, his slack, heavy physique in sharp contrast with the tall, hard bodies of the Englishmen.

Simon lifted his hand to her, and set off along the track by which they had arrived two days ago. She watched them climb the hill. His khaki-clad figure was already merging with his surroundings, becoming part of the rustling grass and copper earth. The nimble Rukore took the lead, spear in hand, feet scarcely seeming to touch the ground. A francolin called harshly from the undergrowth. One by one, the line of figures disappeared over the ridge, and then there was only the heat shimmering in blue waves, and the day was a little emptier.

She looked down at the small bag, and withdrew the stone eagle. The unknown artist had captured the bird in the moment before flight – neck arched in anticipation, wings outspread.

"What's that?" Emma rose from her stool. In the sunlight, her face was still luminously pale and thin, eyes encircled by dark rings. "I had to go and get sick just when we meet the first two presentable men we've seen in weeks," she grumbled. "Mr Shawcross looked rather nice. What *is* that?"

"A fish eagle. Simon asked me to look after it for him. He's afraid of losing it on the Zambezi – or in it."

"Hmmm," Emma's voice was heavy with significance. "Simon now, is it? And how and when is he going to reclaim his fish eagle, pray?"

"When he comes back through Umtali. You see – he thinks we're going to make it." She put the ornament back in the bag. Suddenly, there was nothing to keep them in Chimoio except Emma's recovery, and she felt a restless urge to move on. Maybe she will be up to it tomorrow, she thought.

"Come," she said briskly, "I'll wash your hair. Perhaps that will make you look a little less like the Lady of the Camellias."

6

A troop of baboons loped across the track and a line of giraffe formed a symmetrical frieze on the horizon. The sun was still hot, but a breeze, for which Emma was silently grateful, fanned the dry grass. The landscape was breaking up, the plains giving way to kopjes and wooded valleys, the grassy slopes were pierced by jagged granite outcrops. Gone were the feathery palms and dank rustling bamboo forests; they walked beneath massive umbrella-shaped acacias that spread pools of shade for animals retreating from the heat of the day.

They had not made an auspicious start. The porters had been drinking beer at the village since the previous morning, and those that had returned were in varying stages of semi-consciousness when the time came to leave. Although Mukwasi had been in the compound the previous day, he too moved with a dull-eyed lethargy, and admitted to having visited the village himself overnight.

"We are leaving in two hours," Clarissa told him curtly. "Anyone who is not ready to go will get no pay. I will ask Mr Ramores to find other porters."

With an impassive look, he disappeared. When Ramores heard about the porters, he offered a more immediate solution: "Give me two of your boys and I will beat them. They will give you no more trouble."

She recoiled. "No, thank you, that will not be necessary. I can handle it."

"As you like. But I live here a long time, sometimes is necessary," and he shrugged.

Two hours later, a silent, listless company had assembled on the outskirts of the encampment. Only one man was missing. Too drunk, she fumed, but when she tracked him down in a small dark hut smelling of wood-smoke, she realised he was genuinely ill. Feeling contrite, she dosed him with quinine, and paid him off in blankets, beads and copper wire.

Irritated by the sullen expressions and leaden feet of the men, and because she wanted Emma to walk at a comfortable pace, she sent Mukwasi ahead with them, instructing him to make camp at the site recommended by Simon Grant. The track was easy to follow, and so the two women walked alone for the first time.

Clarissa had persuaded a bemused Ramores to part with two pairs of khaki drill trousers and, after spending several hours the previous day adjusting them to fit, she stepped out with an exhilarating sense of freedom, under the amused – and slightly scandalised – gaze of her companion.

"You should try it," she told her, "It's so comfortable. And don't try to walk faster, because I won't let you. Just think of today as a pleasant stroll through an

African park. We only have a short way to go." She was buoyed by a sense of well-being that had not been diminished by Simon's departure, despite the small void it had left.

As he had predicted, they walked no more than two and a half hours before she spotted tendrils of smoke rising through the trees. Mukwasi had set up camp on a level grass clearing on the western face of a hill overlooking a stream. Two fires were crackling, a kettle was on the boil, and the porters, cheered by the brevity of the trek, were a good deal livelier than they had been at the outset.

"God bless you, Mukwasi," said Clarissa, as Emma sank down against a fallen tree trunk, pale and perspiring but weakly triumphant. "My legs turned out to be a bit more wobbly than I expected," she confessed.

"Lie back and rest. I'll get you something to eat, and then you can have a siesta. Later, Mukwasi and I will see if we can bag ourselves some nice plump guinea fowl or impala."

While Emma slept, she studied the map. The route that should have taken three days to travel was now likely to take twice as long, and she hoped their provisions would last. Thank goodness for the potatoes supplied by Ramores before they left she thought.

Lying back on her blanket she closed her eyes, but her mind was too active for sleep. She wondered how far Simon had travelled, how long it would take his party to reach Beira, and whether he would stop at any of their campsites. She suspected she was a little in love with him; she felt different but, curiously, she was not downcast by the knowledge that they were now moving in opposite directions, that – logically speaking – there was no knowing if and when they would meet again. In her present buoyant mood, anything was possible, and she smiled to herself.

Male voices – English – intruded on her drowsy sense of peace, and she sat up quickly. Two bearded white men approached along the track beneath the trees. They wore battered felt hats, carried rifles, and were festooned with ammunition belts, knives and water bottles. Behind them were two heavily-laden porters.

They halted, gaping at the small encampment. Clarissa rose hurriedly, straightening her trousers, but Emma slept on.

"Good afternoon," she said cautiously.

"Bloody 'ell," said the taller, removing his hat to reveal thinning red hair and pale blue eyes. He grinned through tobacco-stained teeth. "Good day to you, ma'am. 'Strewth, for a moment there, thought we was back in 'yde Park."

Clarissa grinned at the familiar accent. "But the sun is out, so you knew you were wrong?"

"Too right," said his companion, a gaunt, undersized man with a sallow complexion and straggly beard.

With a warning gesture towards the sleeping Emma, she beckoned them to the fire and offered them coffee, which they accepted with alacrity. That two

Englishwomen were travelling unaccompanied by a white man seemed to them inconceivable, and when she told them of Emma's illness, they glanced at each other dubiously.

"Never make it," insisted Bert Lumsden, the taller man. His companion, Josh Topping, nodded sagely.

"But we're almost there," she protested.

"You don't know what it's like back there," he waved vaguely towards the western hills. "All the way from here to Umtali is bloody great mountains, grass way over your head. And lion – the place is crawling with them. We could tell you a story or two, eh Josh?"

Josh nodded lugubriously. "With a sick woman, not a chance."

Clarissa was instantly irritated by their dire predictions. "Of course we'll make it," she retorted, refilling their mugs. "Anyway, she's not sick any more – just recuperating. We only have another three days or so to go."

With ghoulish relish, between gulps of coffee, Lumsden itemised the various ailments suffered by his partner over the past two years, moving on to a graphic summary of his own encounters with fever and dysentery until Clarissa, exasperated beyond measure, changed the subject by asking where they were heading.

They had brought a load of trade goods up from the Cape, Lumsden explained, but had met with a series of misfortunes and much of their cargo had been lost or stolen before reaching Fort Salisbury. Now they were making for the Pungwe delta in search of ivory to finance their return to England.

"We've had Africa," Topping assured her.

Lumsden looked curiously at the pile of boxes in the shade. "You're carrying a lot of gear there."

"Yes. Mostly medicines and equipment for the new hospital in Umtali," Clarissa explained. "And some food and trade goods."

"Medicines and equipment," repeated Lumsden, his eyes sliding over the boxes. "Well," he turned back to her, "I 'ope you get 'em there."

"We will." She shrugged away a sudden prickle of unease.

He grinned at her. "How about if we doss down with you tonight? Be good to have company for a change – female company."

"We're not staying here," she found herself saying quickly. "We just stopped to give my friend a rest. We're moving on in a little while. We want to get a lot further tonight."

"Ah." He looked not quite convinced.

"Sorry." She smiled guilelessly, praying Emma would not wake up and say the wrong thing. "Would you like more coffee before I pack up the pots?"

Her offer was declined, and she stood up. "I won't keep you then. It was nice to meet you."

"Well, best of luck," Lumsden said reluctantly, picking up his rifle.

She stared after them, disconsolate, as they called to their porters and ambled down the track.

"What those men want?" Mukwasi had come silently to her side.

She shrugged. "Nothing, Mukwasi – just passing through." He grunted, watching until they were out of sight.

The conversation with Lumsden had reawakened her doubts about the wisdom of allowing Emma to walk in her weakened condition. Should they have stayed longer in Chimoio – given her more time to recover? When Emma woke up, she confided her qualms.

"Nonsense," was the sharp response. "Some men have the idea that women can do nothing more strenuous than lift a saucepan. Not black men, I notice. Have you noticed it's the women who do all the work – hoe the land, plant the crops, fetch water and firewood, walk miles with enormous loads on their heads. I haven't seen the men do much except sit around and drink beer – apart from the occasional bit of portering," she added.

"Mukwasi says they do the fighting."

"And when there are no wars?"

"I expect they are planning the next one."

Later, as the sun subsided behind the tree-line, she heard the chittering of guinea fowl nearby. "Just what we need," she exulted.

Emma got to her feet. "I'll come with you. I'm feeling much better," she added in response to Clarissa's frown.

They followed the chirring sounds and rustling grass, but the flock was on the move and they walked for several minutes before catching up with the birds. Clarissa shot two before the blue-helmeted flock dispersed with flaps and outraged squawks, and as she picked them up she noticed, on the crest of a ridge ahead, the silhouette of an eland bull moving unhurriedly through the trees.

"You go back, Emma, or you'll get tired. I'm going to see if I can get close enough to shoot. The meat would see us through to Umtali. Take the birds and send Mukwasi and a couple of porters."

She followed the eland, stepping silently through the lengthening shadows. Mukwasi would be pleased – he had told her its meat was greatly prized. The sun had gone and soft evening light cloaked the woodland. But the trees grew more thickly here, and she lost sight of the animal. Unwilling to give up the chance of a windfall of *nyama* she walked on, but the eland had melted into the landscape, and reluctantly she had to turn back, conscious that she had strayed some distance from the camp.

The light faded rapidly and she walked fast, nervous at the thought of losing her way. When she found the clearing where she had shot the guinea fowl she relaxed, but almost immediately a prickling sensation at the nape of her neck warned her she was not alone.

A figure stepped out from the shadow of the trees into her path. Bert Lumsden, grinning in a way that made her tighten her grip on the Holland.

"Mr Lumsden." She spoke as calmly as she could.

"Thought you were moving on." He stood with his hands in his pockets, casually, still grinning, and blocking her way. She smelt whisky fumes.

"We changed our plans. My friend was not feeling well when she woke up. The fever came back. I was after an eland, but I lost it. I must get back to her." She tried to speak easily as she made to move past him, but he thrust out a hand and caught her arm.

"What's the hurry?" He grinned again.

"Let me pass!" She wrenched her arm but he held it fast.

She raised the other hand to strike at him with the rifle, but he was too quick, wrenching it out of her hand, tossing it aside and clamping a hand over her mouth as he pulled her against him.

More outraged than frightened, she tried to call out, and struggled furiously, kicking out at his legs. He stumbled and lost his balance, swearing, dragging her down with him. She fell on top of him, still struggling, but he shoved her violently against the ground and rolled over on top of her, pinioning her legs.

"Changed your mind, eh," he panted, his eyes close to hers, breath heavy with whisky on her face, "Good. Plenty of time then."

She screamed before his hand clamped down on her mouth again, stifling her. Intensifying her struggles, she pushed against his chest, pummelling him with her fists, but he was too strong for her. His hand over her mouth was blocking her breath, her ears were singing. She was suffocating. With a desperate effort she twisted her head sharply, his hand slipped and she bit into it, hard.

"Bitch!" he yelped, and clamped both hands around her neck, forcing her head back. She wrenched at his arms, trying to release his fingers, trying to scream. His breath was putrid. "Bitch!" he grunted again, and the branches wheeled and spun overhead. Her consciousness was fading, her vision blurring, she could not breathe.

From far away, she heard a shout, a thud, and another. Lumsden's grip loosened, he was gasping, cursing. Above him was a figure – Emma, yelling furiously, "Get off! Get off, you bloody bastard!"

She was hitting him with something heavy, striking him again and again. And he was rolling off her. "Leave her alone, you bastard!" screamed Emma, as he struggled to his feet.

Clarissa rolled over and gulped mouthfuls of air. Emma was still shouting, and now she heard Mukwasi's voice, approaching fast. Lumsden swayed drunkenly, there was blood on his face, then he was stumbling away, lurching into the darkness, and Emma was on her knees beside Clarissa, seizing her by the shoulders. "Are you all right? Did he hurt you?"

"Yes! No! I'm fine," Clarissa gasped, swallowing to ease her constricted throat.

"Was he the one who came earlier?" Emma asked feverishly.

"Yes, it was him – Lumsden," she was gasping for breath. "He was drunk...." She lifted a hand to her bruised face. "He was too strong. I couldn't..."

"He didn't....."

Clarissa shook her head. "No," she laughed weakly, "thank God I was wearing trousers."

Her voice trailed off as Mukwasi's tall figure was etched against the sky. He leaned over her. "The *mukiwa*?" he demanded harshly.

"He went that way." Emma pointed, and Clarissa saw the glint of a panga in his hand.

"No! Mukwasi! Leave him. He's gone."

"Better I fix," he spoke urgently, and his teeth gleamed as he strode towards the trees.

"Go, Mukwasi!" urged Emma.

"No," Clarissa shrieked again. "You mustn't! He was drunk, he's gone, he won't come back... Mukwasi!" But he had gone.

"Oh, God, what is he going to do?" She sat up, shivering, staring into the darkness.

"I shouldn't worry your head about that," Emma's voice was hard. "Can you walk? I'll help you."

"I think so." She stood up slowly, shakily, and remembered something. "Emma, what on earth did you hit him with? You practically knocked him cold."

"I almost forgot them," Emma looked around her in the gloom. "Here," she held aloft a limp guinea fowl carcass.

Hysterical laughter welled in Clarissa's throat. "Felled by a guinea fowl!"

"It makes a fine weapon," retorted Emma. "Where's your rifle? It didn't do you much good."

Back in camp, she uncorked the brandy bottle, and by the time Mukwasi returned an hour later, they were both wondrously revived.

"Did you find him?" Clarissa asked quickly. He grinned – a wolfish grin she had not seen before.

"Ya, I find."

"Mukwasi, what did you do?"

"He is not coming back," he said, without looking at her.

"You didn't – kill him?"

"I did not." He moved away, but she was uneasy.

"Did you hurt him?"

His teeth flashed. "The madam should not worry about this. These men, they will not come back." He spat on the ground, picked up the guinea fowl and walked away.

"Good," said Emma vehemently.

The track climbed through a range of rugged hills, densely forested. The sun burned down, and as they struggled up the steep incline, a pair of eagles circled lazily in the rising thermals. It was mid afternoon, and Emma was perspiring heavily. Her face was flushed, and Clarissa called a halt in the shade of an acacia.

"I can go with the porters and find a place," suggested Mukwasi, and she agreed. "We will rest here a little."

When Emma felt better they moved on, and when the track crossed a shallow stream they stripped off their clothes, revelling in the knowledge that they were quite alone. The water eased the new set of blisters Clarissa had developed since Chimoio. When they resumed the track, she handed Emma a mealie cob roasted by Mukwasi the previous night, and they munched as they walked, flinging the cobs into the long grass.

Reaching a fork in the track, they paused, looking for a clue to guide them. Footprints travelled in both directions. "I think this one," Emma pointed to the right.

"No, I think the left – the tracks look newer." They took the left, and the sun slid behind the trees.

"We've come the wrong way," admitted Clarissa at last, when they reached the forlorn remains of a deserted *kraal*. Tired and sweaty, they retraced their steps. I shouldn't have let Mukwasi go ahead, I'm getting over-confident, she thought guiltily.

By the time they reached the fork the sun had set, and they walked rapidly in the gathering gloom. Clarissa remembered Simon's warning about walking after dark, and when a francolin erupted from the grass, clucking stridently, her heart thudded against her ribs. She grasped the rifle with sweating fingers, and as her eyes strained to follow the track, she caught a faint but detectable whiff of a pungent, overpowering odour that brought an instant image of the night of the lion. Driven by the chilling vision of cold eyes and raking claws, she quickened her pace. The skin of her neck was prickling and, behind her, Emma was breathing fast. It was very quiet as they emerged from the cover of trees into the open. There was not the faintest breath of a breeze, but the long grass beside the track trembled imperceptibly as though something was passing through it, soundlessly. A baboon alarm call rang out loudly, and from the track ahead came the soft padding of footsteps. Her mouth was dry, and her terror so strong she felt her bladder almost give way as she raised the rifle.

Emma gasped, a shadow moved – and Mukwasi emerged from the darkness, panga glinting. She gulped, and a great surge of relief left her weak and trembling. Shakily, she grinned at him. But he was not smiling.

"The madams must not be walking late." He took the rifle from her.

They camped in a clearing Clarissa was to remember best for a pair of small owls that perched primly on a branch overhead, flapping silently away in search of prey, and hooting softly as she lay wrapped in her blankets by the fire. With luck, they would reach Massekesse the next day. The Portuguese outpost was, she recalled, the last before the border, and the site of the skirmish between British and Portuguese troops Captain Edgar had told them about. *I just hope no new trouble has been stirred up since then*, she thought.

In the grey dawn, she was woken by Mukwasi's hand on her shoulder.

"What is it?" She sat up, her hand automatically seeking the cool comfort of the Holland.

"The porters – they have gone."

"Gone!"

"All of them?' Emma sat up beside her.

"We have three."

Three, out of the original twelve who left Mpandas with them. She stared at him, wanting to cry with frustration. "Why?" she asked stupidly.

He shrugged. "They like to go home. Many time they say these madams walk too far. They take some boxes," he added.

Three boxes were missing. They took a rapid inventory. "Mainly the trade stuff, but food too, mealie-meal and the tinned stuff," she said wearily. "We could be short of rations. I suppose it could have been worse. At least they left all the hospital supplies."

"But how are we going to carry them?"

The hospital supplies were the most important items, along with their personal belongings, and the remaining food stores. At Massekesse, they would probably be able to rely on Portuguese hospitality. From there, if Emma continued to recover, it was probably no more than a day or two to Umtali.

"We'll take what we can, and find somewhere to hide the rest. The bishop can send for them later," Clarissa said distractedly.

Fifty yards from the track, behind a tall termite mound, a clump of trees was shrouded in tangled vines. In the centre, two trees had fallen, leaving a concealed space. It was hot work carting the boxes through the long grass, but they would be reasonably well hidden, and easy to locate. "It will have to do," said Clarissa once they had covered them with branches.

As they rejoined the track, she cursed herself for not having noticed anything amiss with the porters, and wondered how she could have avoided the defection. Was it because they were tired of taking orders from women? Damn them.

Emma broke the silence. "It's not anyone's fault, you know – that they ran away."

"I should have taken more notice."

"Don't you remember what Mr Philips said – and the doctor? That porters have a habit of running away. We're probably lucky to have kept them as long as we did."

"That's true." She felt a little better. "I'm worried about those boxes. Perhaps we should have buried them."

"We just have to get to Umtali as soon as we can."

The morning was breathlessly hot and close, and progress slow as they climbed one steep incline after another. For the porters it was heavy going and they were relieved, around mid-morning, to walk, for a while at least, on relatively level ground. Having left the delta far behind, Clarissa had hoped they were done with swamps until they reached a broad waterlogged *vlei* in which Mukwasi, who was in the lead, rapidly sank almost to his knees. Mosquitoes swarmed about her face and arms as she rolled up her trouser legs and waded in, Emma behind her with her skirt wrapped around her thighs and the hem trailing in the water.

"You see," Clarissa told her with a grin. "When are you going to abandon that ridiculous garment and wear something sensible?"

"I hope you don't intend wearing those in Umtali."

"Haven't decided yet."

When they stopped to rest, Clarissa took out her diary.

"Have you mentioned Simon Grant?" Emma asked slyly, and she found herself flushing because, unaccountably, she had not. Her feelings about him were not easy to express, and she wanted more time to unravel them. That in itself was strange, because the diary was proving a therapeutic outlet. Whenever the strangeness of their surroundings aroused feelings of loneliness or fear, recording them in her impulsive, sloping handwriting lent an order and meaning that was somehow comforting. It was a way of capturing an unsettling experience and fixing it to the page in a controllable form. It had helped even to record the lion incident, which still returned almost nightly to menace her dreams.

"It brings things into perspective and helps me sort them out in my mind," she had explained to Emma. But she was not ready to write down her feelings about Simon; she preferred to think about him as she lay in her blankets, staring into the fire.

Now she riffled back through the pages. "My writing is changing. In Cape Town it was small and sort of feathery. It's bigger now. D'you think that means something?"

"It means you have survived two weeks walking through Africa," Emma said. "That's something."

In mid-afternoon the fort at Massekesse loomed in the distance, and they approached it warily, uncertain of their reception. The outer walls showed grim evidence of the battering from the English, but the Portuguese *commandante* and his small platoon of troops greeted them with the same elaborate courtesy they had received from Ramores and Andrade. They accepted his refreshments, but when he offered them accommodation in a dark, stuffy hut, Emma shook her head from behind his back, and Clarissa declined.

"I thought you would want a roof over your head?" she commented as they walked back to the porters.

"No, it was hot and smelly. Suddenly I couldn't bear the thought of sleeping there. I've got used to being out in the open. You go in the hut if you want."

"No. We'll be sleeping like normal people again soon enough. I can't believe how well I've adapted to the ground. Besides, I like to look at the sky and hear the night birds."

The campsite was bordered by a citrus grove planted by some earlier visitor to the region. "All neat in regimental rows," Clarissa said. "I wonder who planted them." It was somehow cheering to know that this evidence of man's passing had not been obliterated by the enveloping tide of African bush.

Emma retired early, but Clarissa dined with the *commandante*, who told her it was possible to walk to the new British South Africa Company camp at Umtali in one day. But she had already made up her mind to split the distance into two days to make it easier for Emma, and reluctantly she decided not to change her plan.

In the morning, the encampment was shrouded in a mist so dense visibility was reduced to a few yards. While they waited for it to lift, they unpacked the medicine box and held an impromptu clinic: lancing boils, dosing stomach ailments, treating burns and malaria.

The track ran directly uphill, and after an hour it became difficult to decide which was more strenuous – scrambling up a steep ascent while grappling for footholds, or skidding and sliding on loose scree down the other side. Downhill is worse, Clarissa decided, as she dislodged rubble in a headlong slither down a steep incline.

"Do you think we are in British territory yet?" Emma removed her hat and wiped perspiration from her face, still pale under its light tan.

"We must be close. I must say," she brushed grass, leaves and earth from her clothes, "that if our own people are half as helpful as the Portuguese, we won't have anything to complain about."

"Yes, but have you seen how they treat the natives?"

"Yes." She recalled a disturbing scene the previous evening when the *commandante* had struck one of his servants on the side of the head and, when he fell to the ground, kicked him with his booted foot. And she remembered Ramores' offer to beat her porters. If he ever learned about their defection, no doubt he would attribute it to lax discipline. "Do you think it is Africa?"

"What do you mean?"

"Well – lions, hyena, jackals, vultures – nature is pretty brutal here. Perhaps it is infectious."

"Nonsense. There's no reason for men to behave like animals," Emma retorted.

The sun was directly overhead when they crested the shoulder of a high ridge. The summit extended away on either side in rugged granite peaks, and distant ranges faded into a blue haze; immediately below, the hillside was scattered with lichen-encrusted rocks sprinkled with crimson aloes and carpeted in bracken and heath. In the south, from a jutting spur of rock, a waterfall cascaded down an almost sheer granite face to meet a river coiling through a valley. Impala grazed in a glade beside the river, and a herd of elephants with calves at heel stood in the shallow water close to where it flowed into a steep ravine. It was very quiet.

"Yes," breathed Clarissa softly.

"What?" inquired Emma.

"I don't know," she shook her head. "It feels sort of familiar, as though I've seen it before or..... I can't explain. It's a strange feeling."

"All those hills," groaned Emma. "No wonder those men doubted our capacity."

"But it's so beautiful."

"Mmm."

Clarissa quelled her impatience with difficulty. Couldn't Emma feel the grandeur? No, she reminded herself, Emma was still recovering. "Sit down and rest," she urged, feeling remorseful. "I think we have crossed the border."

She felt the tiredness draining out of her body, replaced by exhilaration. The feeling was partly due to lightheadedness – they had been climbing steadily. But what a country we have reached, she exulted. No wonder Mr Rhodes wanted it.

It was about half an hour later, in the hot, still afternoon, that she skidded on a patch of loose stones. Flinging out her arms, she tried desperately to seize the branch of a nearby shrub, but missed and fell heavily, her ankle twisting beneath her.

The pain was sharp and sickening, and she sat up slowly, nausea rising in her throat. Mukwasi climbed back up the hill, while Emma scrambled down beside her and helped ease off her boot.

"Does it hurt badly?"

"Yes," she gasped, "but I don't think it's broken."

After a gentle examination, Emma agreed. "Not broken, but probably a bad sprain." She fetched the medicine box and bound the ankle with a wide bandage.

Clarissa gritted her teeth. "I'll put the boot back on. It will give support. We can't stop now."

"Why not? We can camp down there. You can't walk on that."

But Clarissa was adamant. "We must get further today. We have to reach Umtali tomorrow or we'll run out of food." Tears of pain and frustration stung her eyes. "Mukwasi, come and help me."

Emma turned away and walked down the hill. Mukwasi helped Clarissa to her feet. Leaning on him, she put her injured foot down, and winced. Slowly, she limped forward.

The next two hours passed in a haze of pain. Several times Emma urged her to stop, but Clarissa just stared at her, all her reserves of strength focused on putting one foot in front of the other. On level ground it was not so bad, but mostly the track climbed upwards or descended steeply. Her shirt was soaked with perspiration as she hung on to the silent Mukwasi, and forced herself forward.

To take her mind off the pain, she would look at each slope and estimate the number of steps to the top, then count them, keeping her eyes fixed on the rocky surface of the track. Only fifty to go, keep going, only another twenty-five. When she underestimated and saw that there were many more steps to go, her heart would sink.

When she reached the summit, she saw that Emma and the porters had stopped in a small valley below, intersected by a stream. The men were already lighting their fire as she limped slowly down on Mukwasi's arm. Her ankle throbbed with each step, the pain knifing upwards into her leg.

Emma stared at her defiantly. "We're stopping right here. We can stretch the food we have, so your heroics are quite unnecessary."

All the fight ebbed out of her, and she sank to the ground. Emma took control. Easing Clarissa's boot off, she bathed her swelling foot in stream water so cold it almost numbed the pain.

"Sorry. I was being pig-headed," said Clarissa, watching her.

"Yes, you were," Emma said placidly. "Just remember, although you've been leader all the way, and I've been sick and useless for a while, I'm fine now, and Mukwasi and I are quite capable of taking over."

"I know," she said humbly. "Sometimes I get carried away."

Later, as she sat with her foot propped up, watching a dung beetle resolutely roll a ball three times its size over a hump in the ground, Mukwasi approached with a handful of broad fleshy leaves. "This tree good for making your foot to be better."

"What do you mean?"

"I show you." He squatted, and took her foot gently in his hands.

"Do they stop the swelling?" guessed Emma.

"Ya," his teeth gleamed in a smile, "tomorrow it will be not so big."

He wrapped the leaves carefully around her ankle and Emma secured them in position with a broad bandage.

"Do you realise," Clarissa mused later, as they lay wrapped in their blankets by the fire, "that this is probably our last night on the trail?"

"I wonder how far we've walked altogether," murmured Emma. "It was not what I had in mind when I agreed to come to Africa with you."

"Wasn't what I had in mind either – and it certainly wasn't what my parents or

Uncle Chas had in mind. But," she added thoughtfully, "I wouldn't have missed it. Would you? Think what a story for our grandchildren."

"Mmm. I'm thinking of donating my boots to the museum – if they hold together just one more day. The soles are in shreds."

The pain in her ankle had eased slightly by morning and the swelling was no worse. Emma was impressed by Mukwasi's treatment. "Theoretically, your foot should be much bigger." But Clarissa had another problem – she had woken with a headache, nausea, and a slight fever. Please not malaria now, she pleaded silently as she rolled up her bedding, not when we're so close.

"How long to Umtali?" she asked Mukwasi, but he would not commit himself. "Can be tonight," he said, "but too many hills."

He had made her a stout walking stick, and with its help she managed to limp along slowly without his support, except on the steeper slopes. They made a bad start, taking a wrong turning and walking for half an hour before Mukwasi realised his mistake. Retracing their steps, they picked up the right track, and paused at a village where they were immediately surrounded by its occupants. Emma stared at the children playing naked in the dust. "Just think of all those poor London children crowded into slums, what lives they could have out here. So much space, and the air so clean and fresh."

Buoyed by the knowledge that the end of the trail was approaching, the porters had stopped complaining about their loads, and although Clarissa felt sick and lightheaded, the same incentive spurred her forward. But her ankle was slowing them all down.

"We could send Mukwasi to the bishop to send a stretcher for you. Wouldn't you like to be carried in comfort the last few miles?" Emma suggested.

"Certainly not," Clarissa was surprised at her own vehemence; it had become a matter of pride to complete the march on foot. We've been on the road two weeks, we've survived a lion, malaria, attempted rape, she reflected; and I am going to walk into Umtali.

But, as the heat grew in intensity, she had to ask for more rest stops, oblivious now to the grandeur of the scenery. When they stopped at midday, Mukwasi made coffee, which restored her flagging energy, but she was now feverish and her head pounded with each step.

"We don't need to go any further," urged Emma. "What are you trying to prove? Whatever it is, it isn't necessary."

"I know. My feelings are purely selfish. I want to arrive on my own two feet and I want to get there today."

"That's just silly. What difference will a day make?"

"The porters will be getting fed up. I don't want any more running out on us. I'm fine now. Come on, let's go."

They trudged on through an endless afternoon of blinding glare, up rock-strewn kopjes, through dappled forests and swampy *vleis*. They were all moving slowly now, the sweating porters struggling beneath their burdens, and even Mukwasi's steps had lost their spring.

The shadows lengthened, and there was another hill, and another, and another, and the day assumed the quality of a dream – the boxes on the heads of the porters bobbing up and down, Mukwasi's figure floating ahead of her, Emma's voice coming and going, the need to concentrate on putting one foot down in front of the other. Before her the ground sloped steeply upwards, hard and unyielding.

"Maybe, we should......" she was beginning to shape the words unwillingly when an exultant shout from Mukwasi stopped her. Blinking the sweat from her eyes, she leaned on her stick, too short of breath to speak, and stared up at his silhouetted figure on the shoulder of the hill.

"What, Mukwasi?" panted Emma.

He grinned widely, white teeth flashing. "British campi!"

Emma turned, reached for Clarissa's hand and dragged her up the last few steps.

The valley below was shrouded in deep shadow, but on the topmost ridge of the hill beyond, on a flagpole rising from a clutter of tin and thatched roofs, a familiar flag fluttered lazily in the slanting rays of the sun.

7

Seventy years before Clarissa and Emma trekked to Umtali, and hundreds of miles to the south, in the fertile hills of Natal, Shaka – the brutal, autocratic chief of the Zulu nation – hounded a once-favourite general from his kingdom for refusing to hand over cattle looted in raids on neighbouring tribes.

The *induna* who fell from grace was Mzilikazi, of the House of Kumalo who, with several hundred followers, fled north across the rugged Drakensberg mountains. They had learned well from their ruthless former commander and, to discourage pursuit, plundered and killed the inhabitants of villages in their path, slashing a trail of desolation along their passage into the Transvaal highveld.

For two decades Mzilikazi rampaged through the countryside, swelling his army with young warriors routed in battle with local tribes, and wielding such power that even white traders and missionaries acknowledged his supremacy and sought his permission before venturing through the region under his control.

Until the arrival of the Boers, trekking north from the Cape, with their ox-wagons, families, cattle and horses, to escape the frustrations of British rule. Searching for new land on which to settle, the hardy, independent Boers had no intention of negotiating with a ruler they considered no more than a murderous black savage.

The two groups clashed head-on in the Transvaal bush. The Matabele ('people of the long shield,' as Mzilikazi's followers were now called) attacked Boer wagon-trains and massacred men, women, children and babies, but not for long. The Boers fought back, on horseback and from their circular laagers of wagons, and it did not take long for Mzilikazi to realise he had seriously underestimated the determination, weapons and outstanding marksmanship of the resilient newcomers. After a number of bloody skirmishes and the loss of thousands of head of cattle, he reluctantly withdrew his warriors and turned his face to the north once more, crossing the Limpopo River into the country that would one day be called Rhodesia.

Renegade Zulu leaders had passed this way before him. Now the same trail of destruction scarred Mzilikazi's route through the rugged landscape north of the broad, brown river, as his warriors torched crops, looted sheep and cattle, and killed, captured and terrorised the inhabitants of small *kraals* sheltering in the shadow of granite kopjes. This time his victims were the gentle, peaceable Mashona, and once he had fired a few *kraals*, slit numerous throats, and dragged off a number of terrified captives as slaves, they were swiftly cowed into acquiescence.

The old warrior finally settled with his followers in the awe-inspiring, monumental landscape of granite outcrops known as the Matopos. Mzilikazi lived well. In fact, he became so obese he had to be carried around his court in an armchair borne by his numerous wives; and when he died, his son Lobengula continued his father's iron hold over both his people and neighbouring tribes from the Royal *Kraal* at Bulawayo, the Place of Killing.

By this time white men – explorers, traders and missionaries – were crossing the Limpopo in increasing numbers, and Lobengula realised they were a different breed from the submissive and demoralised Mashona.

Like his father, he was tolerant towards the intruders. As a child, he had been looked after by a young girl captured by the Matabele in a skirmish with the Boers, a relationship that may have heightened his genuine liking for white people. He enjoyed the company of legendary hunters like the club-footed Henry Hartley, and the artist Thomas Baines; as long as they sought his permission before embarking on hunting expeditions during the dry winter months, he smiled on them and sometimes even accompanied them on safari.

But now the newcomers wanted more than ivory and skins. They wanted to prospect for gold and diamonds. And the day came when the powerful but pragmatic king, worn down by weeks of haggling, put his cross on a piece of paper presented to him by three white representatives of mining magnate Cecil Rhodes, soon to become prime minister of the Cape Colony.

Lobengula did not fully understand the document, and Rhodes' henchmen were not about to enlighten him as to its subtle, and not-so-subtle implications. But he was no fool, and may well have guessed he was signing away more than just permission to dig for gold and diamonds in his '*kingdoms, principalities and dominions*'.

The concession also gave Rhodes and his subordinates a wide-ranging right '*to do all things that they may deem necessary to win and procure the same*'. Did the old king suspect he was being out-manoeuvred by these men with their guns, smooth tongues and glib promises? Perhaps so, because he described Cecil Rhodes as the 'big man who eats countries for breakfast'.

As for the big man himself, once he had the precious concession he wasted no time in sailing north to ask Whitehall for permission to occupy the area north-east of Lobengula's kingdom, known as Mashonaland, which was so crucial to his dreams of extending British power and influence north through the African continent.

But the 'Imperial factor' (Rhodes' nickname for the British Government) was not interested in extending its financial commitments to yet another irksome colony, and he was obliged to drum up support from other sources.

Nor was he alone in his eagerness to grasp the riches of the mysterious north. The Matabele king was besieged by rival concession-hunters streaming into

Bulawayo. Incensed at being outflanked by the master manipulator, they persuaded the king he had been duped and was in danger of losing not only the mineral rights to his kingdom, but the kingdom itself.

Already uneasy, and conscious of the simmering discontent of his warriors, Lobengula repudiated the concession and sent two *indunas* to London to ask Queen Victoria for protection against the white invaders. The sovereign's response was an obscure letter that included the phrase: *A King gives a stranger an ox, not his whole herd of cattle...*

To pacify Lobengula, who was already slaughtering those among his people who he believed had betrayed him by giving the wrong advice, Rhodes dispatched his second-in-command, the wily, charismatic Dr Leander Starr Jameson, who quickly insinuated himself into the king's confidence by relieving his painful attacks of gout with morphine. Lobengula was finally persuaded that the queen approved the agreement.

Back in England, through shrewd and persistent lobbying, Rhodes had won over not only the influential Tories but the Liberals as well. The support of the Irish Party he won with a donation to the Home Rule fund. To remove any remaining obstacles, he adopted a device that seldom failed: he bought off his rivals. Whitehall granted him a royal charter to finance the acquisition of land north of the Limpopo, and the British South Africa Company was established with himself as managing director in Africa.

His plan was to send a column of men to take occupation of Mashonaland (over which Lobengula in fact had no legal control as it was under the command of various chieftains). Returning to South Africa, Rhodes looked around for the man to entrust with the task, and at breakfast in the luxurious Kimberley Club, met the energetic, aggressive Frank Johnson, the same entrepreneur who would later win the contract to build the road from Portuguese East Africa to Mashonaland. Johnson contracted to train and outfit a corps of men, cut a road through to the new territory, and raise the flag in Mashonaland for 87,500 pounds.

The corps was made up of around two hundred men, hand-picked from thousands of applicants fired by the prospect of being part of an expedition infused with all the romance of a Rider Haggard novel. In occupations ranging from artisans to professionals, they would form the nucleus of a society. Only the legal profession was vetoed: "I want no lawyers in my country," Rhodes was reputed to have declared, although he was eventually talked into including just one.

The expedition was to be protected by a police force of four hundred; provisions would be carried by wagons manned by Africans, and Jameson would travel with the column as Rhodes' representative.

Most recruits were given military rank for the duration of the expedition, the remaining civilians were mainly prospectors. Bearded, blue-eyed Frederick Courtney Selous, the celebrated hunter-explorer, was appointed guide and intelligence officer, and charged with the task of finding an alternative to the traditional route through Lobengula's capital Bulawayo, where the Matabele warriors were respected by the white people as much for their courage as for their legendary brutality.

The Matabele king was deeply worried about the wisdom of allowing the expedition to cross the Limpopo at all, although he had, for the moment, curbed the aggression of his militant young *indunas*, who were itching for a fight. It was customary for all newcomers to seek Lobengula's permission to travel through his country: only the king had the right to 'give them the road', and the prospect of the column taking a different route, to avoid contact with the Matabele, troubled his peace of mind.

The first groups of would-be pioneers set out from the railhead at Kimberley in April of 1890, and gathered at Macloutsie, a dusty outpost in the flat, sun-baked thorn scrub of Northern Bechuanaland, where they were drilled into a disciplined force.

It was mid-winter, a time of clear sparkling skies, when the column left Macloutsie. Jumpy and trigger-happy, the men were acutely conscious their progress would be followed, that the invisible eyes of Matabele *impis* would be shadowing every move for the next four hundred miles.

With Selous and his scouts riding ahead to cut the road, the first leg of the march passed without incident. The corps crossed the broad Limpopo, and it was not until the men had painstakingly dragged their wagons, oxen and supplies across the fast-flowing, hippo-infested Lundi River that their commander, Lieutenant-Colonel Edward Pennefather, received a message from Lobengula warning them not to go any further.

Pennefather replied briskly that his orders came from Rhodes, not Lobengula, and the wagons rumbled forward once more, but when the oxen were outspanned at nightfall and the wagons formed into a circular *laager*, he doubled the guard and set up a powerful searchlight to scan the surrounding bush. Through the long night, as jackals yelped and hyenas gibbered from the darkness, tense sentries strained their eyes for the lithe shadows of warriors gliding soundlessly through the scrub beyond the ring of wagons.

Still they were not attacked, although the route wound through dense bush and rugged kopjes that offered countless opportunities for ambush. The corps marched in a double column fifty yards apart, with a train of wagons stretching one and a half miles, presenting an almost-too-easy target. Slowly, the cavalcade crawled on, through a landscape denuded of people by the plundering of Lobengula's *impis*. At the few occupied villages, usually perched high on granite kopjes for safety, the terrified occupants begged them to move on for fear of attack. When the column finally reached the comparative safety of open savannah on the highveld, they gave the name Providential Pass to the gap through which their wagons rolled.

Tension eased, and the column reached its destination on September 12. The British flag was raised in the rich red earth of Mashonaland from the gnarled trunk of a msasa tree, and the site named Fort Salisbury in honour of the British prime minister. Rhodes was exultant, and Frank Johnson reaped a profit of two thousand pounds from the expedition. The corps was disbanded, and each man awarded fifteen mining claims and the right to three thousand acres of land. Shouldering picks and shovels, they headed into the bush to dig for El Dorado.

The first year was plagued with difficulties. A drenching rainy season flooded rivers, destroying the primitive communications with the south and cutting vital supply routes. Company officials worked ineffectually to re-establish contact, while the new settlers cursed them vengefully as they struggled to survive in damp and hungry wretchedness until the onset of dry weather brought an erratic flow of supplies once more.

Now, a year later, conditions had only marginally improved. The constant setbacks had dampened the enthusiasm of some and killed more than a few, but the majority of men still scoured the landscape with picks and pans, convinced that untold wealth lay just over the next kopje in the next glittering reef of quartz. And gradually their numbers swelled.

Some left the Fort Salisbury region and made their way three hundred miles to the south-east, to set up camp on a cluster of ridges forming part of a mountain chain along the ruggedly beautiful country bordering Portuguese territory. A mixed bag of prospectors and traders, they lived on a diet of whisky, maize meal and hope, alongside two hundred police sent from Fort Salisbury to keep some semblance of order in the remote settlement known as Umtali.

The Bishop of Mashonaland was a tall, handsome, clean-shaven man, wearing a cleric's collar that looked strangely out of place above his khaki shirt and trousers, thought Clarissa through a haze of exhaustion as he led them to a hut shaded by a giant fig. Beneath its spreading branches, Mukwasi and the porters made camp for the last time.

In the morning, clear-eyed – her fever having miraculously evaporated with their arrival – she paid each porter the agreed fee of blankets, copper wire and beads, and spoke to them through Mukwasi. "Tell them we thank them from our hearts for helping us to come such a long way, for staying with us when the other men left. Now we will be able to open a hospital which we hope will help many people. We could not have come here without their assistance, and we wish them a safe journey back to their homes."

She turned to her translator. "And you, Mukwasi? What are you going to do now?"

"I myself will stay with the madams," he declared decisively, his tone suggesting he was conferring a priceless favour. "The madams need help."

She fervently agreed. The sight of the departing porters, chanting as they had done so often during the trek, left her desolate, and it cheered her to think she would have his familiar presence at her side and his unfailing confidence to lean on in her new surroundings. She was beginning to realise how much she had come to rely on him.

The bishop dispensed coffee, informing them of a change of plan. Although he was building his mission nearby, it had been agreed after discussion with Fort Salisbury that the hospital would be built and operated by Rhodes' British South Africa Company.

"The police are at this moment putting up huts for you," he told them. "I think it is a much better arrangement. They have lines of communication and access to regular supplies – or as regular as things get around here."

They walked with him to the police camp, where rows of huts were lined up with military precision in an area cleared of bush, and Clarissa and Emma were mobbed by a throng of bronzed and bearded young men, all volunteering to show them around.

"I don't know what I expected," Clarissa said later, "a brick building maybe, but a mud hut in the process of being thatched was something of a shock."

"Quite a well-built hut," Emma had pointed out charitably.

"I know. They do say mud and thatch are the coolest materials, but even so...." Although her fever had gone, her ankle ached, and she felt tired and disoriented by the sudden end to what had almost become a way of life.

Over the next few days, news of their arrival spread. There were few women in the settlement, and they were besieged by miners and prospectors, eager to conduct them around the mines already in operation. The countryside swarmed with ragged, bearded, sun-burnt prospectors scrambling along the beds of streams and rivers, panning quartz samples for the elusive streak of gold. Every other day brought yet another jubilant report of a strike, and every new discovery was the excuse for another round of riotous celebration and the sinking of quantities of whisky and Cape brandy.

As Emma commented tartly, "Whisky seems to be about the only thing that is not in short supply here."

While the prospectors still grumbled about the hardships of survival, most of the talk now was about how fast the country would be settled once the railway line reached Umtali from Beira. As their own experience had revealed not even the semblance of a road, let alone a railway track, Clarissa listened to their speculation with scepticism.

In less than two weeks, the police had erected three huts for them – high on a hill overlooking sweeping views of the surrounding kopjes – and produced an assortment of furniture: chairs, a table, and a fine pair of brass candlesticks to replace the bottles generally used to hold precious candles. It wasn't until after the furniture had been arranged that they were told the items were part of the loot taken during the attack on the Portuguese fort at Massekesse a few months earlier.

Emma was aghast. "The Portuguese were so kind – and here we are using their stolen property."

"Spoils of war," one of the officers told her matter-of-factly. "Don't you worry about it. They would have done the same if it had been the other way round."

"Do you think so?" she said uncertainly, looking longingly at the chairs. "They are very comfortable."

Emma was revealing an unsuspected talent for carpentry. While waiting for their accommodation to be built, she had amused herself by knocking together a few rough cupboards and chests, using old packing cases and nails provided by the police. Punching holes in the bottom of an old paraffin drum, she also rigged up a shower in a tree near their hut, around which a grass fence was erected.

To brighten the drab brown walls of their new home, Clarissa hung lengths of colourful cotton fabric bought from a local trader; on the floors – a mixture of earth and cow dung pounded cement-hard – they spread reed mats. And around the huts the police erected a low stone wall to discourage wild animals.

The police recovered the cache of supplies concealed on the track, and while they were unpacking, Clarissa drew from the depths of a dusty bag Simon Grant's carving. She set it down on a crate draped in blue and white trade fabric, and memories flooded back. Where was he now?

Two weeks later Dr Copeland appeared, thinner but otherwise little the worse for his illness. The hospital opened, beds filled rapidly with sick and injured men, and the two women began the work they had come to Africa to do.

To provide their patients with a nutritious diet, they bought a cow from a nearby *kraal*, and some poultry, which were closed up at night in a grass shelter on stilts. Police officers kept them regularly supplied with venison, some of which Mukwasi cut into strips and hung from the rafters of the kitchen hut to make biltong. When weevil-infested flour was available, he taught his assistant, a young African boy from the mission, to bake bread on a heap of ashes buried in the ground.

Beyond the mud walls of the hospital hut, spring transformed the parched landscape and msasa trees sprouted new young leaves in a palette of wine-red, russet-gold, rose and soft green. Emma bought seed from a passing trader and planted cabbages, carrots and tomatoes in a small patch of cleared land behind the hospital.

With the first rains, her vegetables burst into exuberant growth and she was soon adding variety to the hospital diet. The sea of bleached grass sweeping away from their doorstep flushed with new green growth, and rich, damp aromas rose from the steaming earth.

The rain brought more than new growth. The newly-thatched roofs sprang leaks, rivulets of red mud seeped into their huts, and supplies were held up by flooded rivers and impassable roads. Spiders and beetles, scorpions and shiny black millipedes, called *chongololos*, invaded the huts. And when columns of ants marched across the earthen floor, Mukwasi placed the legs of their makeshift furniture in old tin cans half-filled with paraffin. Each day brought a new challenge, a new test of their ingenuity.

March 1892
Dearest Mother and Papa,
You will be pleased to hear that we are at last settled in the new hospital. As I told you in my last letter, the powers-that-be decided our original site would never do for a town, so we had to be moved to another spot five miles away, which is supposed to be higher and healthier. Now that we have got over the shock, the move has been worth it: the new hospital is much bigger and even has an operating room, with wards on either side that can take up to thirty patients. The new township even boasts a High Street, wide enough for cricket matches, and a baker, although his bread is of a rather inconsistent quality.

The last few months have not been easy, but we are at last getting organised. We work hard and our hours are long. Most of our white patients are police, prospectors or traders suffering from malaria or dysentery, and we can now nurse them on canvas stretchers, a welcome change from planks of wood covered in grass (a haven for fleas and heaven knows what else).

The men are grateful for whatever we can do for them – which, because of our limited medical supplies – is sometimes very little. When they leave, they often return with small presents: a bunch of bananas, sometimes a real luxury like a tin of foie gras. Poor souls, they miss their homes and families so much, although they claim to enjoy their vagabond lives and the thrill of searching for gold.

Most of our black patients are from the nearby mine, and usually present us with broken bones or fingers crushed in mining accidents. They are still wary of us, and suspicious of our medicines, but they are coming round slowly. I think they realise that, while mere white women may not be as powerful as their witchdoctors or spirit mediums – certainly we are a lot less decorative – we have not killed off too many as yet, and have even helped a few.

Very slowly, I'm learning to speak the local dialect, but I am still thankful to have Mukwasi to translate when I get stuck. We have several other native assistants, but our ways are totally alien to them, and from time to time they tire of working for crazy white people obsessed with hygiene, and disappear into the bush.

We have made some good friends amongst the officers. Captain Maurice Heany, an American, who was in charge of a unit of the Pioneer Corps, brought us a small monkey a few weeks ago. He found it in the bush while hunting – it's mother was probably killed by a leopard – and it was only a few days old. Although it nearly died, we nursed it through, and now it is as fit as can be and growing fast. We call it Pepe and it is a guaranteed tonic for our patients.

And there are many men who come close to despair at times. Despite the high hopes they arrived with, there have been few gold strikes substantial enough to celebrate. To crown their disappointment, they get malaria or dysentery, which is enough to discourage the most optimistic soul.

The news from Fort Salisbury is similar. Although some gold has been found, it seems Mashonaland may not be the El Dorado expected when Mr Rhodes made his treaty with Lobengula.

Personally, I cannot understand why the men fail to see the enormous potential in areas other than mining. The countryside is very lovely, and the soil rich and bursting with life now that the rains have come. I wish you could see how quickly and easily the native crops grow – the mealies are way over my head. If the prospectors put away their idle dreams of overnight wealth, staked out some land and started growing crops instead of sitting around drinking and complaining about their bad luck, we might see some progress.

We have started a vegetable garden ourselves, but the buck and other small animals are a constant menace, despite the grass fence Mukwasi has built. Sometimes I get frustrated. Supplies are so hard to get, things we took for granted in England, like candles and flour. You can't imagine what it is like, as you wallow in the luxury of the new electric light. And here I can see you pursing your lips and saying, "Well, who was so eager to run off to Africa?"

So let me say immediately that I don't regret it for a moment. Despite our grumbles, we love our work, and the people, black and white, and manage to turn the most frustrating situations into cause for laughter. I miss you all, but we have made new friends here, and because this is such a small community, have a host of social events to enliven our days – when we have the time to join in. As there are so few women here, a dance means we are never short of partners.

We have started a fund to build a proper brick hospital. We will probably be back in England before there is enough money, but hope our successors will continue fund-raising. On my optimistic days, I dream that someone *will strike gold and make us such a handsome donation that we can start building immediately.*

A few weeks ago a leopard started sneaking into the compound at night to take chickens. We had no doors on our bedroom, just a reed mat, and one night, when we had left it up because of the heat, I woke up to see a dark shape in the doorway. I screamed, and it disappeared. We made a barrier of furniture and boxes in front of the door, and next morning, when we found the spoor, you can imagine how quickly we asked the police to make us a stable door.

I have had a dozen proposals of marriage since I arrived – but before you start planning a wedding, read on. Six were from men too overcome by whisky to appreciate what they were saying (or to remember anything the next day), and four from fever patients whose gratitude got the better of them. Only two could be taken halfway seriously, and I would not dream of accepting either.

I have met one man you would approve of, however. His name is Robert Hammond, and he arrived here on a hunting trip. He has a business in London, and returns to England soon, but will be back again next year, when I hope to see him again. I like him very much and he is very persistent. But marriage – I don't think so. Emma has a serious suitor, although she refuses to consider marriage until we have completed our term here (thank goodness). His name is Frank Harrison, and curiously enough, we met him at Mpandas just before we started our trek. He is an engineer, with abundant Irish charm, and totally smitten. I like him well enough, but I am not sure that he is a very strong character.

And if there is one thing I have learnt here it is that the survival-of-the-fittest principle applies not only to wild animals but to people, and not only to physical but to mental strength. Although conditions are slowly improving, life is very hard in many ways, and I have seen men overwhelmed by the enormous demands of day to day survival. On the other hand, we have learned to use our imagination and ingenuity in a thousand ways. Anyway, I doubt I would consider any man good enough for Emma, and she seems very happy. We have seen very little of Frank, as he is building bridges between here and Beira and will soon be surveying the new railway line.

Countless visitors pass through, either on their way back to England or en route to Fort Salisbury. The most recent was Mr Rhodes himself. He came up from Beira with a small party along the same route we travelled, so we had that at least in common. After meeting him, I can understand how he has achieved so much. He left the hospital with a long list of supplies we had been trying to get for some months, and they arrived by coach soon afterwards.

Despite his somewhat rumpled appearance, he is a compelling character – tall, with clear, almost transparent blue eyes and curly hair. He has a quality that turns heads and attracts people, and a strange voice that can rise to a high-pitched falsetto and does not fit in with the rest of him.

People adulate him – they are convinced that, whatever the problem, Mr Rhodes can solve it. And usually does. He is renowned for his generosity, but his sympathies are clearly with people who get out and do things. Despite his fame and power, he seemed ill at ease with us, and only relaxed when we talked about the hospital and its needs. Perhaps he prefers the company of men – he has never married.

We also had a visit from the hunter Fred Selous, a charming man who had some hair-raising stories and was even kind enough to pretend interest in our adventures. Scores of hunters pass through en route to the Pungwe flats in Portuguese East Africa. We never realised the area we walked through would become one of the most popular hunting grounds in the region. In many parts of South Africa much of the game has been shot out, so hunters have to travel further north to find the vast herds that used to roam the entire continent. You know I enjoy shooting, but their excesses enrage me. They call it 'buck fever' here, and it seems to infect almost every new arrival with an almost obsessive need to shoot every animal in sight, and to compete with each other for the highest scores. The bush abounds in wildlife, but the British have not been here long, and one has to wonder how long the game will last if they continue treating the place like their shooting estates back home.

Mother, thank you for the lovely dress which arrived on the coach last month – I am the envy of every woman here. Dearest Papa, I send you a special hug and hope the news about your health is much better next time I hear from you. My love to Nick and Denis.

Your affectionate daughter,
Clarissa.

Days merged into weeks, weeks into months, and when the anniversary of their arrival came round, they were too busy even to notice. By nightfall, Clarissa was so tired she fell on to her bed into instant sleep. Sometimes her moods swung sharply, from exhilaration to acute homesickness: with the trek over, it was as though her guard came down, and for months her dreams were regularly invaded by the spectre of the lion on the Pungwe delta. Nightly, she re-lived the terror of that evening, waking sweating, with Emma shaking her, murmuring: "It's all right, Lissa. You're dreaming again."

But she revelled in the wild rugged landscape, the hills teeming with birds and animals. She loved walking alone in the bush (to the despair of the police, who feared for her safety), waking to the mournful lament of the emerald-spotted wood dove, and falling asleep to the bubbling call of a nightjar. She liked the ramshackle settlement of Umtali, the friendly people who did not stand on ceremony, Sunday cricket matches in the street, and occasional hunting expeditions or picnics.

Sometimes, her thoughts turned to Simon Grant. The carving she had packed away in a box under her bed, but occasionally she took it out and set it on the packing case that served as a small storage cupboard. Lying on her bed, she would stare at it, wondering where he was. She asked passing travellers whether they had met or heard news of two Englishmen travelling up the Zambezi; and once she found a man who had met them at a place called Chinde at the mouth of the river. But that was before his expedition had set off inland.

By now she had tended so many young men dying from malaria or dysentery, and had heard so many horrifying reports of attacks by lion, leopard, buffalo, or crocodile, that she had no illusions about the chances of living to a ripe old age in this corner of Africa. And so she steeled herself to accept that Simon could have met his death in half a dozen unpleasant ways since their meeting. Even if he were alive, there seemed little likelihood of seeing him again.

Although her life gave her little time to brood or daydream, the memory of him persisted in intruding on her thoughts. It could be a chance remark reminding her of something he had said, a laugh with echoes of his own, or the mention of the great river in the course of conversation.

Most of the time, she thrust the thought of him from her mind and turned to more pressing matters: the ever-present problem of supplies – medical and household, the whereabouts of a snake glimpsed disappearing behind a cupboard, how to get more cats to keep the rat population down, ants eating into her stored clothes, her father's deteriorating health. Both she and Emma had lost weight, they suffered skin ulcers and brief bouts of fever, but there was never time to get sick.

A few months before the end of their term of service, the strain began to tell. A young policeman, James Forrester, was struck down with dysentery. Tall, carefree and goodlooking, renowned for his batting skills in cricket, he had been a regular visitor to the hospital and they counted him a special friend. When, despite all their efforts, he died, they were both devastated by the loss of yet another young life. "Why him of all people?" raged Clarissa.

She was overcome by a sudden longing to be away from it all – the frustrations, the tragedies, the shortage of supplies, the endless toil. As Mukwasi had taken leave, they had both been working long hours, and no sooner had he returned than Clarissa fell ill, her normal resilience weakened by her emotions.

It was her first serious attack of malaria, and it came just as she was beginning to believe she possessed some magical immunity. As her fever grew in intensity Emma coped with the work of two, spending as much time as she could spare at her friend's bedside. Between them, they had trained several black assistants to help look after the patients, and Emma was able to leave Mukwasi in charge of them for short periods. While Clarissa tossed restlessly on the low camp bed, eyes glittering with delirium, hair lank and dull on the rough pillow, Emma held water to the parched lips and spread damp cloths on her burning forehead.

When she was busy with patients, she would often send Mukwasi, who brought water, straightened blankets, sponged her face, and sat cross-legged on a mat beside Clarissa's bed for hours at a time. Copeland called daily, and late at night, when the patients slept, Emma pulled her own camp bed next to Clarissa's and sank into an exhausted sleep, to wake with a start at the slightest call. Her slumber was racked by nightmares in which Clarissa died and left her alone to tackle the work they had faced with such confidence together. Their shared experiences over the past two years had brought them as close as it was possible for human beings to be, and the thought of losing her was unbearable.

Officers and men from the camp called regularly for bulletins on Clarissa's progress, and to leave behind a can of soup or other tinned luxury, some fruit perhaps, or a posy of wildflowers. But Clarissa had retreated to a sphere beyond communication, her consciousness ebbed and flowed, carrying her in and out of a realm inhabited by nightmares. When she swam to the surface, she knew she was very ill, that Emma was not only taking care of her but doing the work of two. Sometimes, in her delirium, her conscience, in the form of her mother's voice, called to her: "Come on Clarissa, you shouldn't be doing this to Emma. You've got to pull your weight, that child will kill herself trying to nurse you and all those men."

Wearily, she tried to answer, "I'm trying, mother, but I just can't seem to get up. There is this fire in my head." And her mother said, "Nonsense, you're just being lazy, get up at once. Your father wants you to help him down at the stables...." and words and visions tumbled over one another in surreal images.

Sometimes, the lion came back, a monster vaster and more terrible than the reality, roaring, filling the universe with his body, his cold yellow eyes, his gigantic claws. Pounding towards her through the campfire, black mane quivering with light. She tried to run, but her skirt was heavy with dew from the long grass, and it dragged at her legs. She tried to scream, and then Mukwasi was by her side with a mug of water, and she was sweating as she lifted her head to drink.

Once she was in a dark gorge on the banks of a wide river, watching Simon Grant in a dugout with Rukore, rowing through turbulent water towards a waterfall that thundered and crashed from an immense height. She shouted at him to come back, but the roar of the water drowned her words, and the craft was enveloped in pounding foam, and then she heard his voice quite clearly, echoing through the gorge: "Britannia thinks it rules the waves, but Africa makes its own rules..."

One night, as Emma sponged the sweat from the face on the pillow, she knew that Clarissa was drifting away. She had seen the same look too often over the past two years: deep-sunk eyes, ashen pallor. Come back, she pleaded silently, please don't die. Don't leave me alone – please, Lissa.

She realised she was talking out loud, but she was suddenly desolate. "Clarissa, you've got to try, you can't give up. We've come too far, you've got to come back and finish it. Be strong, Clarissa, you're always telling me how strong you are, come on then, prove it. Prove it!"

Far down at the end of the gorge, on a dark tide carrying her into a nameless sea, Clarissa heard Emma's voice – but the tide was too strong and she was too tired. And then another voice said very clearly, "Only the strong survive, the weak die or are killed." And deep inside her, a tiny spark glowed as though fanned by a light breath, and although the surging tide still bore her away, she made an immense effort, and turned, and began to swim slowly, wearily, back up the dark gorge. Strong, she gasped with every stroke, you have to be strong... the weak die or are killed, but you are strong. Keep going, you are strong.

Leaning over her, Emma heard the faintest sound – a change in the rhythm of Clarissa's almost imperceptible breathing. A fine sheen of perspiration beaded the translucent skin. Clarissa's eyes half-opened, she stared up at Emma, and a small thread of sound emerged from the dry, cracked lips. "Told you..."

"What? What did you tell me?" whispered Emma, bending close.

"Told you I was ...." And her eyes closed again, and Emma did not wipe away the tears that welled in her own eyes and splashed on to the grey blanket. She stared down at the tired young face for a long time.

"Thank you, God," she whispered, "I can do the rest."

She straightened the covers, wiped the perspiration from the damp forehead, then picked up a blanket, wrapped it around her shoulders and went outside, unlatching the looped string that still held in place the stable door installed by the police after the leopard intrusion.

It was not quite dawn. Only a faint crimson flushed the horizon, and the morning star still glimmered in the immense, hushed sky. In the purple depths of the valley, mist wreathed tumbled kopjes, a cock crowed, and a single bird tried a few notes experimentally, as though not quite sure of the key. The air was cool, and she sat down on the earthen step, drinking in the new day.

For days Clarissa did little more than move from the camp bed to a chair and back again. She was so weak she was often brought to tears by the sight of a burly police officer arriving with a dead chicken dangling from his hand, or a former patient bearing a large golden pumpkin.

For the first time, she thought about the future, and her return to England. Then what? Another nursing post, in London or closer to Elderbrook? It worried her that she could not feel any enthusiasm at the prospect. This was what she most enjoyed doing. I'm just depressed because I've been ill, she told herself, it'll be all right in a week or two. She was thin and listless, and she knew Emma was worried about her slow recovery, but she was unable to bestir herself.

And then one day, an old African woman, who visited the hospital regularly with vegetables for sale, arrived at the door with a large clay pot balanced on her head. She laid it at Clarissa's feet with a broad, almost toothless grin, and began talking and gesticulating.

"What is it?" Clarissa asked.

"It is special beer," said Mukwasi. "She say is very good for make strong. You drink every day." The woman looked at her sternly. Obediently but dubiously Clarissa took the pot – and as she lifted it to her lips, the taste and smell of the brew transported her back to the night of the celebration after the elephant kill, the night she had drunk native beer with Simon Grant.

"It's good," she pronounced with a radiant smile, clapping her hands in the traditional gesture of thanks. Cackling in satisfaction, the woman departed.

Whether or not it was the beer, Emma was never sure, but Clarissa's strength began to return, and with it her spirit. Within a week, she was taking up some of her duties again.

When the doctor told her gravely that another attack could kill her, that it was lucky she was going back to England, she grinned ironically. "That's funny. I came out here because I was told I needed a healthier climate."

He shrugged. "If it wasn't for malaria, this would be a healthier place. Once we have better treatment, once the swamps are drained, the long grass cut, things will be different."

Then came the news that replacement nurses were on their way from England, that Clarissa and Emma could expect to be relieved within a few months. And suddenly, events moved rapidly. Frank Harrison appeared with a diamond engagement ring for Emma and the news that he had built a small house in Fort Salisbury. They were to be married there in July, and Clarissa was to accompany them and act as maid of honour before returning to England.

Emma bubbled with vitality. She was in love, her friend was on the road to recovery, and the only shadow on her life was the fact that her wedding would take place far from home. Her family would not be present, except possibly her younger brother who wrote to say he would try to make it. She was philosophical, making plans for a new life, cheered by the knowledge that many Umtali friends would travel up to Fort Salisbury for the occasion. What a long way she has come, reflected Clarissa, from the shy, scared young creature who sailed from Southampton with me more than two years ago. But then, I have changed too.

"Soon you'll be gone," Emma's voice was wistful, "and I don't know when I'll see you again. I'm going to miss you so much. Do you think you will ever come back?"

"One day, when I'm very rich, I'll come back and build a children's hospital. I'll miss you too, but let's not look too far ahead – just enjoy the next few months."

"If you marry Robert Hammond, he might be persuaded to bring you out to visit from time to time. Maybe he'll even finance your hospital."

Clarissa laughed. "I have no plans for marriage – to Robert or anyone else."

As Mukwasi was the only African staff member with the necessary experience, he agreed to stay on at the camp hospital to help the new nurses. But only for a few months. "My place is with the madams," he declared grandly.

Clarissa looked at him affectionately. Her respect for him had continued to grow over the past two years; she valued his optimism, his independence, his humour, and counted him as both friend and mentor. When, unwillingly, she told him she would be returning to England, the expression in his eyes made her feel like the worst kind of traitor.

Emma promised that if he stayed at the hospital for six months, she would find him work in Fort Salisbury, either in her household or elsewhere. He agreed, with one qualification. "When the madam comes back, I will go to her."

"But I told you – I'm not coming back, except maybe for a visit," Clarissa tried to explain.

His expression was calm but sceptical. "The madam will not stay in Inglandi," he declared, "she will come back to this place."

She was taken aback by his confidence. "What makes you so sure?"

"I know it here," he said, touching his heart.

8

On the outskirts of Fort Salisbury, a rutted track followed the course of a small river meandering through msasa woodland. The wagon skirted a scattering of mud huts, coming to a halt in the shadow of a kopje on a large cleared area of dusty red earth occupied by several other wagons and teams of oxen. A group of white and black men were unloading mailbags from a weathered, mud-spattered passenger-mail coach, and a team of mules drooped in the traces.

Emma's fiancé Frank was waiting for them, a broad smile on his genial sunburnt face. Calling for porters to carry the luggage, he guided the two women along a rough, potholed road bordered by low mud-plastered buildings with thatched or corrugated iron roofs. It was midday, and the street was thronged with people: white men on horseback or on foot, in worn corduroy breeches, flannel shirts and broad-brimmed slouch hats; black men, some in tattered western clothes, but most clad only in triangles of goatskin or cheap calico, their limbs decorated with bead and copper wire ornaments. Some carried blankets around their shoulders, others capes of soft tsessebe hide. Bare-breasted, straight-backed African women balanced baskets or clay pots on their heads. Bead and iron necklets encircled their necks, waists and ankles, and bracelets covered their arms from wrist to elbow. Their heads were shaved, except for a small crown threaded with beads, and their foreheads, shoulders and arms were marked with the scars of small decorative incisions. From the bundles on their backs emerged the fuzzy crowns of small black heads, and at their heels scurried children clad in brief beaded waistbands. Parasols shaded the faces of the few white women who picked their way carefully on the uneven surface of the dirt road, long skirts sweeping the dust.

Although aware of the hardships suffered during the birth pangs of the fledgling settlement, Clarissa sensed an air of youthful energy and optimism in the faces of passers-by, most of whom seemed to know Frank. Bearded men stared in candid curiosity at his companions. Although the initial ban on women during the early months of settlement had been lifted for more than a year, and the birth of the first baby had since been recorded, a fresh female face was still enough to attract attention from the overwhelmingly male population.

Long accustomed to their novelty value, Clarissa and Emma returned the curious glances with equanimity, examining their new surroundings with interest.

"Look at it," boasted Frank with proprietary pride, although not long a resident himself. "Two years ago there was nothing but grass, swamp, lion and hyena."

Already brick buildings were beginning to replace the original, hastily-erected mud huts, and he pointed out newly-opened government offices and law courts as well as several hotels. From the appearance and gait of the clientele emerging from their doors it seemed that, whatever other shortages were suffered by the town, liquor was flowing as lavishly as it had in Umtali. And now the settlers had science on their side, new evidence having confirmed that whisky was more effective against malaria than quinine. "And it has fewer side effects," Frank added triumphantly.

Clarissa was more interested in the small stores lining the street. Some were no more than ramshackle huts but others were built in brick, and they paused to gaze in wonder at the town's first shiny plate-glass window in the new Store Brothers building.

Frank led them to a long, low mud-and-thatch boarding house surrounded by a wide verandah. Marigolds and zinnias bloomed in flowerbeds bordering the entrance, and their rooms were adequately but sparsely furnished with beds and a few pieces of rough furniture. Through the window, Clarissa glimpsed a troop of monkeys capering through the slender branches of msasa trees.

Fort Salisbury sprawled at the foot of a kopje on which three forts, barely visible from below, overlooked a broad grassy plain intersected by low ridges and wooded hills. "The forts were built by the police who came up with the pioneer column," Frank explained.

From the kopje, the town – which was beginning to look less like a mining camp and more like a permanent settlement – spread north to the edge of a glutinous black swamp teeming with waterbirds and infested with mosquitoes. Most of the original settlers had erected their rough dwellings at the foot of the kopje in an area that rapidly mushroomed into a disorderly, ramshackle commercial district. When the subject of town planning was raised, they had flatly refused to have their homes demolished to suit the tidy rectangular layout prepared by Tom Ross, the ex-US Army captain delegated the job of town planning. In the end, he drew up a two-part plan that left the area untouched, and the 'rebels' free to run their businesses in a chaotic muddle of streets known henceforth as 'the Cow's Guts'.

It was a frontier town where vagrants rubbed shoulders with English nobility. The police force raised to accompany Rhodes' corps of settlers had been drawn from all walks of life, from the cream of London clubs down to the roughest of Cape farmers. Along with this diversity came a broad range of talents. Frank introduced Clarissa and Emma to Lord George Deerhurst who ran a butchery in Pioneer Street at the foot of the kopje; they sampled bread baked in an oven carved out of an ant heap; and met William Fairbridge, journalist son of a Cape Town doctor, who had started the first newspaper, The Mashonaland Herald. Launched as a handwritten sheet laboriously duplicated in homemade ink, it was now a professionally printed weekly, though he told them ruefully he was seldom paid cash, and more often than not with a pot of jam or packet of candles.

They visited the hospital run by a small party of Dominican nuns, and were shown around by the diminutive Irish Mother Patrick, already a legend for her tireless dedication. Frank showed them the first school, recently opened, and several churches, including a synagogue.

"The story goes that when Rhodes arrived two years ago, he was disappointed by the ramshackle buildings. He was expecting to see a city – he obviously hadn't heard that there wasn't enough food, let alone building materials, for the first year," said Frank. "Anyway, when he was told that a synagogue was being built, he relaxed and said: 'If the Jews come, my country's all right'."

He pointed out the unassuming circular thatched hut where Rhodes' representative Dr Jameson lived; and his four-roomed office, in a building shared with the town's first bank, where the accountant slept under the counter, using his Gladstone bag as both safe and pillow.

The British South Africa Company had opened a post office, a telegraph line from Kimberley had speeded up communications with the south, and a mail coach had supplanted the original teams of police dispatch riders who, in the early months of settlement, had carried the mail bags the three hundred and sixty miles to the border.

For cricket and other sporting activities, the settlers used any available area of level cleared ground – like the yard on Frank Johnson's property where rugby matches were held.

North of the kopje, a couple of paddocks had been cleared and roughly fenced, and a small grandstand and racetrack built. And here, on their first weekend, Clarissa and Emma were escorted by Frank and several male friends.

As horsesickness was a continuing plague, the horses were a mixed bunch, and the jockeys mainly police. Few had colours, most wore jodhpurs, khaki shirts and an assortment of headgear, but their mounts carried numbers, course officials scurried about busily, and there was a semblance of order to the program of events. A carnival atmosphere prevailed amid the pervasive dust, and the women wore frivolous wide-brimmed hats and carried parasols. Beneath a shady tree, a trestle table was set up with refreshments, and bookmakers were doing a brisk trade at makeshift stands.

Swept along in the good-humoured throng, Clarissa and Emma were astonished to encounter a number of old acquaintances ("Comforting to know how many of our patients have survived," remarked Emma after greeting yet another bearded veteran of the Umtali hospital). Tall, dark Henry Borrow, who had passed through the small settlement a year earlier, introduced them to his business partner, burly Frank Johnson, former leader of the Pioneer Corps. As the man contracted to build the road from Beira to Umtali, he was not at all discomfited when Clarissa ribbed him mercilessly about its failure to materialise. "All a misunderstanding," he declared blandly.

The race meeting was essentially a social gathering – the races were almost incidental, an excuse for people to come together from farms and mines, to mingle in the dust churned up by thudding hooves, which made it almost impossible to see who was riding which mount. For although grass had been planted on the track, it was mid-winter, there had been no rain for several months and most of the ground cover had withered.

The two women were quickly surrounded by a throng of bronzed, leather-booted men, drinking beer and placing bets with reckless abandon.

"So many people," commented Clarissa, sipping tea beneath the trees near the grandstand, and sampling scones dripping with fresh cream. "After little Umtali, it is all a bit overwhelming."

The final event was a cross-country race that began a mile or so beyond the course. The progress of the riders through the brown winter grass was marked by a cloud of red dust that swung in a wide arc before entering the far end of the track. Although Clarissa had no idea who was riding, she was caught up in the general excitement and cheered as urgently as the rest of the spectators as the cavalcade rounded the final bend in a scattered field led by three horses and followed by a riderless animal with stirrups waving.

Crouched low over the necks of their sweating mounts, the leading trio were enveloped in dust as they thundered past the winning post to whoops, cheers and whistles of delight.

Clarissa's party surged along with the boisterous crowd to the paddock where the prizes were to be presented. As the winners cantered in through the gate and lined up before the waiting officials, Emma gripped her arm.

"Look! Do you see who it is?" And she realised, with quickening pulse, that the rider in the centre was Simon Grant.

"Who?" asked Frank curiously, and Clarissa felt her herself flushing.

"Just a friend," she murmured.

Face streaked with red dust, shirt stained with sweat, he sat his chestnut mount easily, joking with the other two riders, and when he removed his battered felt hat and leaned down to shake the hand of the official presenting the prizes, she saw again the sun-bleached forelock she remembered from Chimoio.

The punters cheered and shouted ribald remarks, and as the riders doffed their hats and waved, Simon's eyes swept the onlookers leaning on the paddock rails, and lighted on Clarissa.

A slow smile of recognition spread across his face. He raised his hat and nodded, and with gladness welling up inside her, she smiled in return, both hands gripping the fence.

Then the riders dismounted, and there was Rukore grinning, taking the reins as Simon patted his horse's neck.

And now he was striding towards the fence, taking off the dusty, wide-brimmed hat with the guinea fowl feather in the brim – the same he had been wearing at their last meeting. And she was suddenly shy as she held out her hand, and introduced him to her companions.

After congratulating Emma and Frank on their engagement, he turned back to Clarissa.

"What are you doing here? You're not nursing in Salisbury, are you?" he asked.

"Oh, no. We have just arrived. Emma and Frank are to be married here next week."

"That's great news, and what about you? Are you still working in Umtali?"

"No. After the wedding I go to stay with friends in the country, and after that back to Beira to sail for home."

"So soon? Probably just as well – it seems the Matabele are getting restless. But," and he looked at her keenly, "this time, it's you, and not Miss Clarke I have to be concerned about. What has Africa been doing to you?"

"I'm fine," she flushed in embarrassment. "I had malaria, but I'm over it now. Congratulations, by the way – that was quite a race. You must have been the one who nearly came off at the finish. Do you always ride like a madman?"

"Clarissa!" Emma exclaimed with a shocked laugh, but he only grinned. "Only when Danny O'Keefe is behind me," he nodded towards the stocky, shock-headed rider who had been placed third. "Couldn't let an Irishman beat me. So, you're staying here for the moment?"

"Yes. For a few more days. And you? How did the expedition go?"

"Excellently well. We got further up the river than we expected."

"And your friend, Mr Shawcross?"

"He had to go back to England with the specimens we had collected."

As he was speaking, a tall, blonde young woman in a pale green dress and wide white straw hat trimmed with flowers, came to stand beside him. With smiling assurance, she slipped a gloved hand around his bare arm. "Simon, I've been looking for you. Father has someone he wants you to meet."

He drew her forward. "Allow me to introduce Miss Sally George-Brown, she is visiting from England with her parents. We are old friends."

"How are you enjoying Africa?" asked Emma politely.

"It's perfectly fascinating, thank you. Simon, I'm sorry to break this up, but father..."

"Of course." He said to Clarissa, "We must go. Where are you staying?"

She told him, and after saying goodbye to Frank and Emma, he turned back to her.

"It's good to see you again – even if you are skin and bone. Take care of yourself." The gold-flecked eyes looked at her quizzically.

As he turned to leave, his impatient blond companion again slid her hand inside his elbow. On a sudden impulse, Clarissa called after him, "I still have your fish eagle."

He turned back. "So you have." And Sally George-Brown looked at her with sudden sharp-eyed curiosity.

"Hold on to it a little longer, will you?" he said. "I'll be in touch."

Her eyes followed them as they walked away. She noticed the way he smiled down at the slim woman by his side, the intimate way her gloved hand clung to his arm. She had a shapely figure, and the soft fabric of her skirt swirled in smooth folds over her hips as she moved.

Emma was watching too, with narrowed eyes. "Hmm – possessive creature. But what a surprise, Lissa." She squeezed her arm. "Aren't you pleased? I never thought we would see him again. And more good-looking than ever."

Clarissa laughed ruefully. "And obviously otherwise engaged."

"You don't know that. *She* was clearly staking her claim, but he didn't look particularly interested."

"She's very attractive."

"Not his type." Emma's voice was decisive.

"What do you know about his type?"

"She's definitely the Mayfair set. And from what you told me about him, he's here to escape people like that."

"What's all this about?" Frank stared from one to the other, and Emma grinned. "Tell you about it later."

Clarissa laughed and linked arms with them both. "There's nothing to tell. Look, there's Maurice Heany – let's find out what he's been doing with himself."

The tall, red-headed Virginian, who had helped them on several occasions with hospital supplies, introduced them to his companion, Dr Leander Starr Jameson. Clarissa looked at him with keen interest. The name was so well known in southern Africa that she had shaped her own clear image of him as a tall, imposing figure, and was surprised to be presented with a dapper, balding man with gleaming black eyes and an irresistible smile.

As Rhodes' right hand man and administrator of the new settlement, Dr Jim was either worshipped or loathed, he seldom inspired neutral emotions. Although she had heard him described as devious and scheming, Clarissa found herself instantly disarmed by his keen and sympathetic interest in their work, and the knowledgeable questions he asked about the Umtali hospital. His visible disappointment at the news of her imminent departure was equally flattering. "I hope you will come back," he urged seriously. "We need people like you."

"I don't think that's very likely," she replied, "but I will miss it – for all its frustrations."

Emma put an arm around her shoulders. "Don't give up hope," she told Jameson with a grin. "I'm working on her."

9

Fort Salisbury seethed with rumours of unrest among the Matabele in the southwest. It was the first time since the British South Africa Company had taken control of Mashonaland that such rumblings of discontent had been heard, but veteran hunters and prospectors, familiar with the country and its inhabitants, had been warning for months that Lobengula's warriors had been remarkably passive and peaceable since the arrival of the white invaders. Despite the suspicion with which his subjects – and in particular his *indunas* – viewed the influx, the king had continued to provide the newcomers with protection, and to rein in the simmering hostility of his people.

The descendants of the warrior Zulu nation were still fiercely proud of their military heritage, and their bloody raids on neighbouring tribes were an annual event. Ranging as far north as the Zambezi River, they looted cattle to swell their vast herds, massacred men and made slaves of their women and children, returning in triumph to the Royal *Kraal*, trailing their wretched victims. Missionaries and hunters gave graphic accounts of the celebrations that followed the raids, with the old king presiding as each victorious *induna* presented a theatrical re-enactment of his triumph, crowing about his often wildly exaggerated conquests.

Once Rhodes' chartered company had established a base in Fort Salisbury, its officials wasted no time consolidating their position, and among the first laws introduced was a ban on attacks against neighbouring tribes. For the first time, the Matabele were forbidden from carrying out their annual raids. Idle now, with no outlet for their restless energy and aggression, their discontent fermented, and it was only their fear of the king that compelled them to bide their time, sharpening their assegais and honing their battle skills. As they waited, they watched in mounting suspicion as telegraph poles were erected to speed up communications with the south. "You white men bring wires to tie up our king," an incensed *induna* told a prospector.

For two years, Lobengula kept his warriors under a tight leash. Then an unforeseen incident changed everything. It happened in the south, near the tiny outpost of Fort Victoria, where the local tribespeople had become lax in yielding the customary tribute of cattle to the Matabele king.

Lobengula dispatched a regiment to the region to teach them a lesson. Although heedful of his strict instructions against harming a single hair on the head of a white man, his *impis* unleashed their pent-up aggression in an exultant and bloody rampage through the district, slaughtering tribesmen and seizing women, children and cattle.

The terrified survivors fled into Fort Victoria to plead for protection from the whites, but the warriors had tasted blood. They pursued their victims into the settlement and hacked them to death in the dusty streets beneath the appalled eyes of the settlers.

A frantic message was sent to Jameson, who immediately rode down from Fort Salisbury and ordered the *indunas* to leave. Some sulkily withdrew their forces, but several hundred warriors defied the order, and Jameson sent out a small force of white men against them. It was a rout: the Matabele spears and oxhide shields were no match for bullets and Maxim guns, and the surviving warriors fled.

In England, a public outcry erupted and the white settlers were condemned by Whitehall for marching on 'helpless natives'. But in Mashonaland the reaction was very different. Aghast at what they considered wanton slaughter by the Matabele, the settlers demanded Jameson take immediate action and pound home the message, once and for all, that the British, not the Matabele, were now in control.

Dr Jim faced a problem largely of his own and Rhodes' making. To save money he had reduced the company police force by half, with the result that the settlement was hopelessly under-protected. He set about tacking together a hodge-podge force, recruiting civilians to make up the shortfall. But that was not his only problem. The ever-present scourge of horsesickness had ensured that there were not enough horses for a mounted force: before he could contemplate marching into Matabeleland, he had to find more. A message was dispatched to the south, and the restless recruits were forced to wait.

It was in this atmosphere of mounting tension that guests gathered on a crisp late winter afternoon for the wedding of Emma and Frank. The ceremony was held in the new Anglican Church, a barn-like brick building erected after the original shack had threatened to collapse on the congregation whenever the singing became too enthusiastic.

Emma stood before the altar demure in a simple high-necked gown of ivory lace over silk, fashioned from material sent up by coach from Cape Town, and stitched by hand, with Clarissa's help, during long candlelit evenings at the bedsides of patients. Her soft brown hair was swept back and coiled beneath a finely-embroidered tulle veil sent by her mother from England, and she carried a small posy of white rosebuds, grown in one of the newest gardens north of the town. Her heart-shaped face glowed with happiness, the arrival of her high-spirited brother Timothy setting the final seal of joy on her wedding day.

As maid of honour, Clarissa stood behind her in one of the few elegant gowns she had brought out from England: creamy-white, with a low neckline and soft sleeves that clung to her shoulders. For the occasion, she had trimmed the neck and sleeves with lace left over from Emma's gown and now, as she stood in the dimly-lit church, she was proud of her handiwork. Only she knew how long it had taken to invisibly mend a series of tiny holes in the slim skirt where ants had chewed through the fabric while the dress was stored in a trunk in the hospital hut.

The ceremony was attended by what seemed to be the entire population of the town, swelled by a delegation from the Umtali police camp, not to mention most of the dogs in the settlement. Like the gregarious Umtali dogs, they were sociable animals with a taste for public events, and after the church service was over, a rowdy canine concourse escorted the two carriages, borrowed for the occasion, to a nearby hall.

Earlier in the day, with the help of a few friends, Clarissa and Emma had decorated the tables with greenery, wildflowers and candles, and the hall presented a festive air. In one corner, a pianist and violinist played a selection of music from one of the latest London shows, and on the bridal table sat the wedding cake, the very first to be produced by the town baker, who had only recently graduated from a hole in the ground to the sophistication of an indoor oven. As the bridal party entered amid cheers, the canine escort lunged through it and bounded en masse in the direction of the cake. The leader, an exuberant black Labrador, was intercepted by a flying rugby tackle from Emma's brother, an Oxford blue, and the rest of the pack were chased out by the guests, launching the celebrations off to a riotously informal start that set the tone for the evening.

The champagne, transported from the Cape in one of Doul Zeederburg's coaches, was a fine vintage, and once the bridal couple had been cheered around the dance floor, Clarissa found herself constantly in demand. Robert Hammond, who had resumed his wooing immediately on his return from a hunting expedition in the Pungwe delta, had to fight his way through a determined forward line of bronzed young bucks to dance with her.

Not that she was complaining. To be whirled round a dance floor again after her long convalescence was wonderful, and she intended not to sit out a single dance, even if some of her energetic partners were not as nimble-footed as she would have wished, and she was often hard-pressed to keep her toes out of reach of their hurriedly-polished boots. Although the guests wore formal clothes, some of the finery was not as splendid as others, and showed the wear and tear of two years in the bush.

"I don't think I can afford to let you go again this evening, or I won't get another chance," Robert told her when he finally claimed her for a waltz.

She laughed. "Well, I only hope my feet hold out. I'm not being rude about your dancing, Robert, it's just that I haven't worn these shoes for ages and I think my feet must have expanded since I've been in Africa. Isn't it a beautiful evening? Emma looks so happy, especially with Timmy here, and Frank so proud. I believe he is almost good enough for her."

"Almost?" Robert grinned. "Would any man pass your test?"

"Probably not," she conceded, "she's somewhat special. When I go back to England, I'm going to feel as though one of my arms is missing."

"We are going to be shipmates, you know. I'm travelling home on the same boat."

"Oh." She was surprised. "But I thought you were planning to go down south for a while."

"Change of plan. My business needs me," he replied, a little too casually, and she guessed that he had deliberately engineered the arrangement. What had begun as a casual friendship was fast developing, on Robert's side at least, into something more serious. Although he had not yet mentioned marriage, she knew he was in love with her, and sensed he was waiting until they were back in England and he had met her family, before proposing. Smitten though he was, Robert was not going to break with protocol.

He was an attractive, attentive escort, with impeccable manners and a dry sense of humour that appealed to her, but she was not in love. It was enough, for the moment, to be able to be carefree again after two years of demanding, often heart-wrenching work that had left little time for the more frivolous aspects of being young. She was having fun, enjoying the atmosphere of this youthful, high-spirited settlement, revelling in the almost forgotten sensation of wearing a lovely dress, and dancing and flirting with handsome young men. Instead of wearing serviceable uniforms, ministering to a succession of sick or injured young men and – too often – watching them die.

With bubbles of champagne sparkling through her veins, she smiled at her partner and he tightened his arm about her waist. And then, between the revolving couples, she glimpsed a tall, familiar figure standing with a group near the entrance, and her heart performed an unexpected skip.

As Robert waltzed her past the group, Simon Grant turned and saw her. He nodded and bowed, and she smiled. The evening suddenly scintillated with an extra glow, and when the music ended and Robert led her back to the table, she found it almost impossible to concentrate on what he was saying.

She was standing with him, chatting to Henry Borrow, when Simon appeared at her side and asked her to dance. A little flustered, she introduced him, explaining to Robert, "Simon and I are old friends," before he led her on to the floor.

They danced in silence for a minute. Clarissa was glad because she was suddenly breathless and at a loss for words, though not too bemused to notice that he danced with a natural easy grace.

"So," he looked down at her with a smile, "they do have dancing in Mashonaland."

Recalling her words on the night of the elephant hunt – and pleased he had remembered – she laughed, "Yes, indeed. Even in little Umtali we had the occasional ball. Well, almost a ball, sometimes the music left a lot to be desired. But I didn't expect to see you here tonight. Emma didn't know how to contact you."

"You obviously didn't know that a couple of nights ago, at the Mashonaland Arms, Frank invited everyone in the bar?"

She smiled. "That sounds like Frank."

He looked at her critically. "You're looking better than last weekend. You looked as though you hadn't had a square meal for weeks."

"Thank you," she retorted, "just the sort of thing a woman wants to hear when she has dressed up for the first time in years."

He grinned. "Sorry. I have got out of the habit of paying compliments." He looked at her consideringly. "You do, in fact, remind me of a ... a frangipani flower. That better?"

"Much. You look very elegant too."

"I feel as though I've forgotten how to wear formal clothes. This collar is strangling me – I can't wait to get it off."

"What are you doing here?" she asked. "Have you finished exploring Africa?"

"Never – I'll never get tired of it, but I'm taking a short break. I've bought some land north of town, got it for a song from a fellow who got fed up when he didn't strike gold overnight." He halted in the middle of the floor. "Can we sit down? I've lost the art of talking and dancing at the same time. Lack of practice." Without waiting for an answer, he took her arm and led her outside on to the stoep running along the side of the building.

The hall backed on to the shadowy bulk of the kopje, silent and dark in the still, moonless night. They found a bench, and as he lit a cigar and sat down beside her, a jackal barked from far away and a nightjar warbled.

"Tell me about your land," she invited him.

"I think it's got potential. My idea is to run it as a farm and a mine. I've put a manager on it for the moment. I'm going out there to build a cottage next week, then I'm off again."

"Off where?" She felt a quick stab of disappointment.

"The museum has asked Jerry for more specimens, which suits me fine. There's still a lot of the Zambezi we haven't seen yet. We'll pick up ivory on the way."

"How far did you get last time?"

"As far as a place called Kariwa, where the river runs through deep gorges, wild country, hot as hell, the natives are incredibly primitive. By then, we were running out of ammunition and most other supplies, so we called it a day. We followed the elephants trails back up the escarpment, came down here and have been hunting and prospecting."

"So you'll go back and start from there?"

"Yes." His plan was to continue upriver to the Victoria Falls, brought to the attention of the world by the now-legendary Scottish missionary David Livingstone.

"We want to follow the river to its source," he told her. "Having gone so far, I think we've both developed an obsession about it. But," he shrugged, "who knows? In Africa, there are so many imponderables. Anything can happen, and the best laid plans... When we've achieved that, I'll come back down here and settle for a while. Perhaps," he added with a candid grin.

"You've having a good time, aren't you?"

"The best." His eyes glowed as he drew on his cigar. "But, as I think I said to you once before, I'm not stupid enough to think it will stay the way it is now. For a little while, we can enjoy this wilderness the way it has been for centuries, but things are going to move fast now. The whole place is opening up. The road is coming through from Beira, next thing you know we'll have a railway line to the sea. Rhodes wants to take it right through to Cairo: if he succeeds, that will put an end to this paradise."

"But that will be good, won't it? To bring hospitals, education, give the people a chance to live healthier, less primitive lives. Get rid of malaria, and dysentery and sleeping sickness – all the terrible diseases I've seen in the last two years."

"They've survived for centuries without our help. They've survived wars and drought and floods and disease, and would go on surviving if we left them alone. But we won't. We won't be able to keep our greedy hands off the place. The churches are already putting out their tentacles, and Rhodes and the company are making quite sure they get their fifty percent.

"In case you haven't noticed, there's a race on. If we hadn't raised the flag here, the Germans would have done it, or the French. They're staking their claims up north, so are the Belgians. And from what I've seen of their colonising methods, I think the locals are lucky we got here first. The British Government was lucky too, of course, didn't have to fork out a penny. Rhodes financed the whole thing, and Victoria can sit back and gloat over a new pink bit on the map."

"You sound so cynical."

"Not cynical, just realistic. In twenty years, you won't recognise the place."

"But despite everything, you're going to stay, make it your home?"

"Of course." His voice held no doubts. "It still has a whole lot more to offer than England. I could never go back – knew that almost as soon as I arrived, but I want to get to know it first. So it's back to the valley."

"The valley?"

"Zambezi Valley."

"How difficult is it to travel up there?"

"It's tough – unbelievably hot and wild, there's malaria, tsetse fly, unpredictable tribes. But it has a fascination, it's a world of its own. And the Falls – did you know that you can hear the thunder of the foam from ten miles away, and the spray forms a permanent rainbow?"

"Tell me more."

He drew on his cigar and, with his eyes gazing unseeing into the moonless night, told her of the way the great river wound through the vast heat-hazed valley between two escarpments, of the huge concentrations of game that congregated on its shores when the water in the pans and streams of the hinterland dried up. Of herds of over a hundred elephants wading to islands in midstream; of thousands of tiny bee-eaters building nests in sand cliffs along the bank, and a tribe called the Vadoma, in which some of the men had only two toes.

"Did you see any slaves?"

"Some. The slavers stop at Tonga villages, capture people, take them down to the coast yoked together, like animals."

"How dreadful. Who are the slavers?"

"Portuguese half-castes run the business on the river, helped by blacks. Further north the blacks sell their own people to Arabs – not a pretty business. Enough about me. What has happened in your life since I last saw you? I heard on the bush telegraph that you and Emma have been doing good work."

She brought him up to date, and then remembered the carving. "I must give you your fish eagle before I go back to England."

"When do you leave?"

"In about three weeks."

"So soon?" He flicked the butt of his cigar into the darkness, and paused. "Will you be in town till then?"

"Not all the time." She explained she would be visiting friends she had met through Frank, staying on their farm north of Fort Salisbury for a couple of weeks. "They've promised me a short safari. I want to spend a few nights under canvas again before I leave. Peter and Nell Ashton. Do you know them?"

"Sure I know them, everyone knows everyone here, but my land is not all that far from their farm." He was silent again for a moment. "Look, if you're going to be staying out at Shangara, would you like to come and have a look at my place? It's beautiful country, only a few miles away from them."

"I'd like that." She smiled at him, and her heart soared.

The music had started again and Robert appeared in the doorway to claim his dance. As she rose, Simon said quickly, "I'll talk to Peter and Nell. When do you go out there?"

"On Monday. I'll bring the fish eagle." She took Robert's arm, smiled up at him. "We've been catching up on the last two years."

The two men nodded to each other, and Simon watched as they went back into the hall and onto the dance floor.

"What's this about a fish eagle?" Robert's expression was wary as she explained.

The dancing continued into the small hours, but although he danced with Emma and several other women, Simon did not ask her again, and Clarissa found her eyes continually seeking him out amongst the increasingly boisterous guests.

This is ridiculous, she chided herself. I'm about to sail for England, he's about to go off again into the wilds. It's just as it was the first time, we are destined to meet only to say goodbye. If only we had longer, if only.... She turned resolutely back to Robert and tried to concentrate on what he was saying.

In a shower of confetti and a rowdy chorus of farewells, Frank and Emma departed. They were to set off the following morning to spend a week in a cottage, loaned by a friend, a few miles from Salisbury. "It's not a real honeymoon," Emma had explained, "we'll have that when we go back to England in a year or two."

As the carriage rolled away, and the guests began to disperse, Clarissa looked around for Simon but he had already disappeared.

Peter and Nell Ashton were an exuberant, extrovert young couple who had come out from Dorset, with their five-year-old son Jamie, to join Nell's brother Harry on his farm in Shangara, a district of rolling hills and fertile valleys north of Fort Salisbury, where a number of farms had already been established and a multitude of mining claims pegged.

As the couple were in town for the wedding, Clarissa had arranged to travel out to Shangara by wagon with them. But on the morning of their departure, rumours were circulating that Jameson was about to call up his recruits to ride on the Matabele. Peter shrugged them off.

"Been saying that for two months now. We're not staying here waiting for the doctor to snap his fingers. I've got work to do."

Peter was big and blond, with a cheery, gregarious manner and bristling moustache. Beside him his petite wife, with her smooth dark hair, olive skin and black eyes, looked even smaller than her five feet. "There's no chance of trouble spreading here, is there?" She glanced apprehensively at Jamie, a blond miniature of his father, who was helping load supplies into the wagon.

"None whatsoever," he reassured her. "The blacks around here are nothing like the Matabele."

The road north from the settlement meandered through grassy plains and wooded valleys. Peter rode beside the wagon, and when they stopped for refreshment at midday, he offered Clarissa a turn. It was good to be on horseback again, she relished the familiar sense of freedom that rekindled memories of the English countryside and her brother Nicholas. Sunlight shafted through slender msasa trees and she was filled with a surge of well-being as the small party travelled across the plateau. She was going to see Simon again.

They rode past grazing cattle, sheep and goats, past acres of red earth cleared and ploughed by oxen, and stopped to exchange news with a friend of Peter's who – having noticed tribesmen smoking homegrown tobacco – was experimenting with different strains on land a few miles from town.

Mashonaland had been slow to reveal its potential to the gold-hungry newcomers from the south. Torrential rains driven by violent storms had swept across the highveld, seeping through cracks in their inadequate, hurriedly-erected shelters. Flooded rivers and an almost non-existent communications system prevented the arrival of desperately-needed supplies, and the men fought near starvation by trading for pumpkins and mealies from the locals. Swarms of mosquitoes from the swampy ground bordering the small outpost wrought their own maddening and debilitating evil. Some young hopefuls died before they had time even to peg a claim, others packed their bags and left.

But many stayed, by choice or necessity, and their numbers were gradually swelled by others to whom news of the current setbacks had not yet filtered along the bush telegraph. And, once the drenching rains had eased and the sparkling highveld air had dried the churned-up mud on the rough-hewn tracks, they rode out from their shanties across rolling expanses of sweet grass and verdant woodland, through valleys cleft by green rivers and over glittering granite kopjes, and discovered a land that offered riches other than gold.

The Ashton party stayed overnight in a makeshift mining camp, and resumed their journey next morning, arriving on the farm at midday. The rough track leading to the homestead was bordered on both sides by acres of ploughed red soil in which Peter would plant maize as soon as the rains came. Built in the shadow of a giant granite kopje, the house was the usual mud and thatch dwelling surrounded by outbuildings, but it had been given a coat of whitewash and the indefatigable Nell had already started a small garden. The wagon drew up outside the back door between the house and a small thatched kitchen hut.

They were greeted by the distraught faces of two black servants: Jess, the family spaniel had been taken by a leopard from the front stoep the previous night. They had found the spoor the following morning, and bloodstains on the cement stoep.

Jamie was inconsolable. The spaniel had been his constant companion and playmate, and when Nell put her arms around him and murmured words of comfort, he pulled free and ran into the house.

After the wagon had been unloaded, Clarissa found him curled up on his bed, hugging his pillow. To distract him, she asked him to show her around the farm, and he raised a face on which tears had dried in dust-smeared rivulets.

He said slowly. "Do you want to see where Jess slept?" She nodded, and he climbed off the rumpled bed and led her out to the stoep that ran the length of the house.

"There," he pointed to a basket holding a blanket and a half-chewed shoe. "That was her bed, but sometimes she used to sleep with me. If she had been on my bed, the leopard couldn't have taken her, could it?"

"No, I don't think a leopard would come into the house," she agreed.

Jamie looked as though he was about to cry again. "We can't even make a grave for her, because the leopard ate her all up. I'm going to get my gun that Dad gave me and shoot it."

"I would feel like that if it was my dog, but the leopard isn't really bad, you know. It lives on meat, and it can only get that by killing animals."

"Well, it's got enough animals in the bush without taking Jess," he replied fiercely.

She had an inspiration. "We could make a memorial for her."

"What's a memorial?"

"It's a bit like a grave. It can have a cross and some writing about who it's for, and stones around the edge, and flowers. They make them for soldiers who have died in foreign countries."

He rubbed his nose. "She was a bit like a soldier because she guarded us. Will you help?" He sniffed and kicked at the low stone wall surrounding the stoep.

"Of course. Can you think of a good place to put it?"

"I know," he brightened. "I'll show you." And he led her across a small patch of cleared ground where Nell had planted cannas, marigolds and roses, to a cluster of msasa trees.

"When I climb these trees, Jess sits – used to sit – and wait for me. Just here."

It took them a couple of hours to carry stones for a small cairn, make a rough cross from packing-case wood and inscribe Jess's name on it. Jamie was tired but quietly triumphant by the time it was finished. Peter and Nell joined them in a brief ceremony in which each placed a flower on the flat stone on top of the cairn.

Nell squeezed Clarissa's arm gratefully. "He's going to be your friend for life. Come in and have a cuppa."

As they sipped tea on the broad stoep, a clattering of horses hooves and the sound of voices announced the arrival of visitors. Dogs barked, and two figures strode through the house and out on to the stoep. Leading the way was the biggest man Clarissa had ever seen. Flame-haired, bearded, with a thick neck and massive sunburnt arms emerging from a tattered bush jacket, he bellowed greetings and seized Nell in an enthusiastic bearhug. His companion, only slightly less enormous, with bushy black eyebrows and beard, removed an ancient slouch hat from his head and grinned awkwardly.

Nell extricated herself and straightened her hair. "Clarissa, meet Koos Villiers and Willie Marais – Miss Clarissa Hamilton. These gentlemen are from the Transvaal. They're up here hunting, and they've been camping down on the river. They are already running my life."

The red-headed giant nodded and grinned, fixing his startlingly clear, light blue eyes on Clarissa as he thrust out a large brown hand. "Good day, ma'am."

He turned back to Nell. "Brought you some more *nyama*, left it in the kitchen with Jandu," he boomed. "We came by to make a plan for Friday."

"We're going on safari with Koos and Willie," Nell explained to Clarissa. "Clarissa is coming with us," she told the big man.

"More the merrier," he bellowed, "just so long as Peter brings the *dop*."

"I heard that," Peter Ashton approached across the grass, hands deep in this pockets. "I believe the only reason we've been invited is because you found out we still had some cases of Cape brandy."

Koos roared with laughter. "Why else would I want a bunch of bloody *rooineks* getting in my way?"

The men sat down on the stone wall, and Nell told them about the leopard while she poured more cups of tea.

"*Ag*, shame, man," Koos commiserated with quick sympathy, "Peter, what say we put out a goat, and sit up for it?"

"Yes, I was planning to do that. I'd appreciate your help."

Nell invited them to stay to dinner, but they declined. "We got some boys outside and the dogs, and *nyama* to get back to camp," Koos explained.

The men went off to find a suitable spot to set up a bait for the leopard, and Nell poured a second cup of tea for Clarissa.

"Haven't had time to tell you the arrangements yet. We've got people coming for dinner day after tomorrow, including your friend Simon Grant. I understand he wants to show you around his place, so I thought he could stay the night. After he's shown you around, he'll bring you to Koos' camp, down by the river. We'll meet you there, and be ready to set off on safari next morning. How does that suit you?"

"Fine, Nell." She spoke matter-of-factly, but she was singing inwardly.

"I understand you're old friends?" Nell's expression was openly curious, and Clarissa told her the story of their meeting.

"My dear, how romantic," sighed Nell, "he's very good-looking. I hear Sally George-Brown has been pursuing him relentlessly, without much success. But what about Robert?" she asked teasingly.

Clarissa flushed and laughed as she set down her cup. "Stop match-making, Nell. Robert and I – we're good friends. As for Simon, I've only seen him two or three times in my life."

"Once is often enough," murmured Nell.

"It is scandalous. Nowhere else in the world do you have to give away half of everything you earn," said Count Edouard de la Panouse in his excellent English. "Rhodes is exploiting us – the very people who are opening up this country for him."

"But the flag wouldn't have been raised here if it hadn't been for Rhodes. He financed the whole thing himself," argued Peter peaceably.

It was early evening, and an owl 'hu-hooed' from the trees. Although Simon had not yet arrived, Clarissa was being richly entertained by the other dinner guests.

She had heard a good deal about the colourful and mysterious count and his wife Billie. Reputed to be a French nobleman, he had met his wife in an English boardinghouse, and brought her to Africa with him. Billie – slim and vivacious – was already something of a legend in the settlement: her real name was Fanny, but she had changed it when she donned men's trousers, tucked her hair into a cap, and sneaked into the country with her husband at a time when women were still banned from entry.

Heavy, dark and striking, the count had pegged a claim not far from the Ashton farm and, like many other prospectors, was furious about the company's claim to fifty per cent of profits from mining activities.

"Rhodes does nothing he is not going to profit from. He expected us to find veins as rich as the Rand, so that he could just sit back in comfort, waiting for his cut. Well, this is not another Rand. There is gold, yes, but not so much that we are all going to get very rich."

Simon Grant approached on horseback through the long shadows on the road bordering Nell's garden. Handing the reins to a servant, he strode across the grass, a small box under one arm.

After making his greetings, he turned to Nell. "Where's Jamie? I have something for him."

Jamie was summoned, his eyes large with curiosity.

"Sorry to hear about Jess, Jamie, she was a good dog," Simon held out the box. "Here's someone who badly needs looking after."

Inside, on a bed of dried grass, was an extraordinarily ugly little fledgling, with an enormous beak but very little in the way of fluff or feathers. It crouched motionless, huge eyes darting from side to side.

Jamie stroked the frail scraggy head. "Is it an eagle?"

"Baby peregrine falcon. There is a pair on top of the kopje near my camp, and I found it when I was out riding yesterday. Must have fallen or got thrown out of the nest. I don't have time to look after it properly. D'you think you could take over?"

"A peregrine falcon," Jamie's voice was awed. "They're for hunting, aren't they?"

"That's right," agreed his father. "Kings and queens of England used to train them to hunt."

"What do they eat?"

"I've been soaking bread in milk or water, and cutting up bits of meat very small."

Jamie's eyes were shining. "I'll go and get some from Jandu." He disappeared, cradling the box tenderly in both hands.

"That was very kind, Simon," Nell said gratefully.

"It was lucky it turned up when it did. I'd heard about Jess from my boys."

Later, at the long oak table, illuminated by tall candles, the mood was celebratory and Cape wine flowed freely. Peter, Koos and Willie had built a hide the previous day and lured the leopard with a small, frightened goat tethered to a tree. The predator's velvety black-and-gold pelt was drying in an outbuilding, and would soon lie on the cement-hard mud floor. From the African compound drifted the throb of drums: the beer flowed there too, for the leopard had taken two goats the previous week.

Everyone seated around Nell's table had experienced adventure and hardship over the past two years and, as the wine bottles emptied, the stories became more extravagant. Peter made them laugh with anecdotes about mishaps that had befallen the Ashtons since their departure from England; and Simon, twirling the stem of his wineglass, told bloodcurdling tales of encounters with elephant and lion in the Zambezi Valley, while Billie flirted outrageously with them both.

I like these people, thought Clarissa, I like their direct approach to life, the way they take difficulties in their stride, the way they laugh at themselves.

Now the count was again thumping the table over Rhodes and the chartered company. "Why bring the telegraph line up to Salisbury before the railway line?" he asked rhetorically. "The railway should have been the first priority. Supplies could have come through during that first rainy season, and we would not have lost so many men. You know why they were in such a hurry with the telegraph? So that conniving physician and Rhodes could send messages to each other. A lot of people have put their souls into this country, but the company doesn't give a damn about them. Money, that's all they're interested in."

"Most of us wouldn't be here if we didn't think we were going to make money," Simon pointed out, but the count was not listening.

"Why cut our police force in half? To save money. Never mind that now we can't put together a force to attack that black savage in Bulawayo."

"I hear Jameson has got his horses. They've crossed the border and are on the way," said Billie.

"About time too. The sooner we go into Matabeleland the better."

The track to Simon's land twisted between tree-clad kopjes, through waist-high grass and across dry streambeds. They stopped at the site where he was building his house on the crest of a hill overlooking a valley. The mud-plastered walls were finished, and two Africans were perched astride the roof timbers laying fresh thatching grass. It was a simple rectangular structure with a stone chimney at one end. Pitched nearby were a couple of tents, and a familiar figure was crouched over an earthenware pot on a wood fire.

"You've brought Rukore with you." She waved, and the tracker saluted her, a wide grin creasing his lined brown face.

"Couldn't manage without him. Come and see the house."

"Very basic," he told her as they went inside. "One room for living and eating, and one for sleeping, but I can add on to it later. The kitchen will be out at the back."

"You mentioned a manager?"

"Yes, he will live here when I'm away, until he's put up his own place. He's away at the moment, getting supplies for the mine."

They went back to the horses and rode into a valley, where he showed her the area pegged out for mining.

"How did you know where to start?" she asked.

"The boys showed me where the old gold workings were."

"There were miners here before?" she asked in surprise.

"Sure. That's what attracted all the interest. Not just geologists' reports, but the fact that the ground had already been worked a long time ago. Watch your step. I keep finding new workings by falling into them."

As they walked the horses through the bush, he pointed out a series of overgrown mounds of earth alongside long narrow trenches, and small circular shafts sunk into the ground, their entrances almost invisible behind tangled undergrowth. Clarissa peered into one but could see nothing except a few rotting timbers.

"They used primitive methods, so they never got at the really deep stuff but they took a lot of surface gold out," he explained.

She followed him down a narrow track to a sandy riverbed in which only a few scattered, shallow pools of water still remained. The pools were flanked by a belt of trees and they dismounted beside an outcrop of rock and left the horses in the shade.

He showed her where the smooth rock face had been painstakingly chiselled away to form crude basins. Squatting comfortably, he picked up a stone. "See how smooth it is. They would light fires over the exposed rock – back there where we've just come from. The heat would crack it into pieces, then they would bring the pieces down here, and use these stones to crush them. Then they'd take the crushed rock down to the water and pan for gold."

"Who is they? The same people who live here now?"

"No one seems quite sure. There have been lots of waves of migration from the north. But yes, I suppose the ancestors of the present tribes. They're a pretty demoralised bunch now – the Matabele have seen to that. They certainly don't do any mining, although they can show you where all the old workings are."

He tilted his hat to the back of his head as he balanced on his haunches. "An archaeologist told me gold has been mined here for hundreds of years. The miners traded first with the Arabs who came inland from the coast, and later with the Portuguese.

"All the stories about fabulous gold mines and lost kingdoms and the Queen of Sheba – they all came out of travellers' tales. Why do you think the Portuguese wanted to control this part of the world? Not just for gold of course, slaves as well."

"What about the church – the missionaries?"

"They came too, and had some small successes in a few places. But it was gold, not souls, that motivated the Portuguese."

"You know a lot about it."

"Been reading it up on long evenings in the bush." He stood up. "See that line of palms?" and he pointed to the far side of the riverbed. "They were planted by a missionary who met a rather unpleasant end. He was travelling down to the river when the natives caught him. They took him and ....."

"Please spare me the details," she said hastily, rising to her feet.

They walked beneath the tall rustling palms planted by the unfortunate missionary before returning to the rocky outcrop where, in the shade of a mimosa tree, Simon unpacked a basket filled by Nell's cook with cold venison, bread, and a bottle of wine. Tiny bronze lizards glittered as they darted over the surface of the rock where he spread the picnic.

Clarissa asked him about his family in Hertfordshire, and he told her he had two brothers, both younger, and a country home where his father still lived.

"He was a scientist and explorer, wasn't he?"

"That's right. He has spent most of his life travelling, and published a number of books. He can't do much these days – gout has slowed him down, and the effects of various tropical diseases."

"Did that mean you didn't see much of him when you were growing up?"

"We hardly knew him." Although his tone was matter-of-fact, his eyes had darkened, and Clarissa sensed unspoken bitterness. "We were all packed off to boarding school while we were still very young. I think I saw him about four times during my schooldays."

She thought of her closeness with her own father and felt a quick stab of sympathy. "It must have been hard for your mother to bring up three boys?"

He grinned as he carved a slice of venison with his sheath knife. "Let's say she turned grey at an unusually early age. We ran rings around her, and once we got older she more or less gave up on us."

"Didn't your father ever take her with him?"

He shook his head. "Not a chance, although I know she would have loved to travel. No, her role was running the house and us, not gallivanting around the world." He extended a slice of meat to her on the tip of the knife. "She died about four years ago, just before I came out here." His eyes narrowed, and he stared across the riverbed. "She had a lonely life, because we grew up and left her as well. My father was in Asia when she died. I wasn't there either, I was up in Scotland when I received a message that she was ill. By the time I got back it was too late. Only Jack, he's the youngest, made it back in time. I still feel guilty about that."

He tossed the bone he had been gnawing into the undergrowth, and offered her more wine. "What is the news of your father?"

"Not so good. I'm glad I'm leaving soon. I only hope..." her voice tailed off. She found it difficult to express the fear that she might not arrive home in time.

"I hope the news is better when you get there."

Warmed by the sun and the wine, he lay back on the rock and talked idly of his plans for the property.

"What are you going to call it. Have you got a name yet?" she asked lazily.

"Yes. I was sitting by the tent having breakfast the other morning. The sun was shining through the msasas, and I asked one of the boys for a word that might describe it. He suggested 'Mushana'. It means something like 'sun in the morning'."

"Mushana – that's lovely." She leaned against a rock and stared up into the leaves overhead, enjoying the sense of drowsy well-being. Her eyes closed, and she was drifting away when she became aware of something crawling up her bare arm. Glancing down, she stiffened. A spider – monstrous, hairy, chocolate brown – stared back at her. Her flesh crawled and she froze.

"Simon!" she whispered urgently, not daring to move.

"What?" he mumbled, half asleep, his hat tilted over his eyes.

"Quick! Get it off me," she gasped, prickles of sweat breaking out on her face.

"What?" He sat up immediately.

"There! Get if off!" The creature advanced deliberately towards the opening of her sleeve. As he leaned over, grinning, to knock it away, it jumped lightly on to her neck. She screamed, scrambled to her feet, and danced up and down, brushing feverishly at the front of her shirt.

"Where's it gone?!" Hopping from one foot to the other, she twisted her head from side to side, peering down the front of her shirt, the back of her skirt. "Is it still on me? Simon! Where is it?!"

He had sat down again and was leaning back against the rock, his shoulders shaking with laughter. "Down there – by the basket. Scared out of its wits."

"Why are you laughing? It's not funny! Why didn't you help me?" she demanded crossly.

"I was trying to," he made a not-very-serious attempt to control his mirth. "Sorry. It just never occurred to me that the slayer of man-eating lions would need help with a spider."

She shuddered. "I hate them, I can't help it. Give me a lion any day." She gazed with deep hostility at the motionless creature.

"In that case, allow me," and he got to his feet and squashed it underfoot, kicking the remains into the dust. "And I promise not to tell Koos. He might think twice about taking you on safari."

They retrieved the horses and rode north through a golden afternoon, sometimes following the riverbed, sometimes leaving it to climb out of the valley and gallop along the ridge, racing each other through the tall silver grass. They surprised a herd of zebra, almost invisible in dappled shade, and an impala ram that bounded lightly away followed by a harem of tawny does, so delicate and beautiful Clarissa wished she was an artist.

It was early evening, and they were riding side by side in the white sand of the river bed, when Simon pointed to a blue spiral of wood-smoke above the trees ahead. "There's the camp."

She instinctively put her hand up to straighten her shirt and smooth the strands of hair that had escaped the combs and pins holding them in place. "I must look a fright," she murmured, brushing ineffectually at the grass and leaves that clung to her sleeves, a legacy of their last gallop. She looked up and saw him watching her. "What?"

He took a handkerchief from his pocket. "Keep still," he said, and brought his mount close to hers.

Leaning towards her, his knee against her thigh, he carefully rubbed a smear of dirt from her cheek. His face was so close that his warm breath fanned her face.

"There you are, a respectable Englishwoman again, except for the hair, but I can't help you with that." He pocketed the handkerchief.

The camp was set up beside a rocky pool that still held a few inches of water. The Ashtons were already there, and Nell emerged from a tent alongside two wagons to welcome them. Several horses were tethered nearby and three or four dogs stretched and came to meet them, tails wagging furiously. Strips of salted meat hung on lengths of wire beneath a tree, and an African in a tattered loincloth was cutting up a carcass on a small table, a sack of salt beside him. Koos sat in a canvas chair watching Jamie feed his falcon chick with small pieces of meat.

Simon refused an invitation to stay for dinner, but accepted a brandy. Nell joined them, and Peter and Willie arrived soon afterwards.

Koos reminded her of Chas, Clarissa decided, as they sat around the fire listening to him recount a recent hunting expedition in the north. When Koos' throat was lubricated by the mug of brandy that was generally at his elbow after sundown, his eloquence flowed. Although rough and illiterate, he shared Chas' boundless enthusiasm for the simple pleasures of life, and his eyes had the same snapping vitality.

"*Ag*, Simon, man," he said at last, as Simon got to his feet, "why don't you just stay and come shooting with us tomorrow."

"Can't," said Simon regretfully, "love to, but I've got to get the house finished."

Clarissa walked with him to where his horse was tethered beyond the orange circle of firelight. A hyena whooped from the direction of the river, and she smiled. No longer did the sound frighten her – it was part of the African night.

"Thank you for today," she said as he swung himself into the saddle. "It was lovely."

"Yes," he agreed, "it was. Thank you for coming." The brown-gold eyes looked down at her thoughtfully.

"Will I see you when we get back?" she asked impulsively.

"Yes. I'll ride over here in the evening." He leaned down and touched her cheek lightly. "Watch out for spiders."

10

The old buffalo bull was hiding up in a dense thicket of thorn bush surrounded by head-high grass. He stood quite motionless, heavy head hung low, tail and ears flicking irritably at the flies that swarmed about his glistening nostrils, red-rimmed eyes, and the festering wound on his swollen left foreleg. He had caught it in a wire snare made from pilfered telegraph wire, set by villagers to trap smaller animals. His struggles to free the leg had tightened the noose until it cut into his flesh and rubbed against muscle and bone. Although he had wrenched the injured limb free, the noose had remained in place, and now the poison in the suppurating, maggot-infested wound was spreading through his old body.

No longer able to keep up with the herd, he had been abandoned to wander alone through the hills until the creeping infection weakened him, and hyena and jackal, attracted by the putrid smell of rotting flesh, forced him to take cover. The previous day he had been harried by two inquisitive young lions, but he still had the strength to threaten them with his massive grooved horns, and they had eventually loped off in search of easier prey.

Now he stood in his pain, waiting for the cool of evening to filter through the thorn bush, when he would gather strength to hobble down to the river bed to drink. A white egret, perched on his back, pecked at the ticks that hung in the dark heavy folds of his mud-caked hide and dangled from his drooping eyelids.

It was late afternoon when Koos' hunting party walked in single file through tall grass down the narrow track.

It had been a fine safari. For four days they had travelled a circular route, hunting along the way, making camp in the early evening. The men had shot eland, kudu and impala, enough to provide quantities of meat and hides. Koos had even shot a hippo – "Makes *lekker* bacon," he informed a surprised Clarissa, who was satisfied with her own modest bag of several guinea fowl, a bushbuck and a wild duck. As Nell did not shoot, she had stayed in camp with Jamie and Koos' black servants.

The previous evening, they had returned to the main camp on the river. Tomorrow would be the last day of the safari.

In the lead, chewing on a grass stalk, Koos halted in his tracks so suddenly that the gun-bearer and Willie almost walked into him. Close behind them, Clarissa heard the sound of rifles being cocked. Koos held up his hand warningly, and she saw tension in his shoulders.

"Something in there," he said very quietly, squinting towards the thicket.

He got no further. As he jerked up his rifle, the long grass parted – and a squat black shape emerged at a rush, huge curving horns thrust forward, hooves pounding, dust boiling as the creature plunged towards Koos.

Rifle fire crashed, and the animal struck him in the thigh, lifting him bodily and hurling him against a tree trunk. Instantly, the creature whirled and pounded into Willie, flinging him against Clarissa, throwing them both to the ground before wheeling around in the dust towards Peter, who was on his knees, firing. Peter took the force of the charge in his left shoulder, somersaulted, and crashed into a thorn bush. The animal pulled up and turned.

Pinned for an instant underneath the weight of Willie, Clarissa was momentarily stunned and winded. Dust, rifle shots, shouts, and the powerful sweet-sour stench of rotting flesh and excrement filled her nostrils as she gulped painfully for air. Above the turmoil, Koos was bellowing, and as she lifted her head the black form pounded towards her. She could not move, her gun was gone, and her shocked brain registered crazily that the hunter who had told her buffaloes lowered their heads to charge was wrong. This one thrust his dark broad head forward so that the blood-rimmed eyes and coldly gleaming crescent horns were terrifyingly clear. She covered her head with her arms and flung herself desperately out of its path. Three shots crashed out almost simultaneously, and she felt rather than saw the animal halted in its charge. With a hoarse, terrible bellow, he swayed drunkenly; slowly his forelegs buckled and the ground trembled as the heavy body struck the earth.

In the silence, the smell of cordite mingled with dust and the odour of putrefying flesh. Above the thudding of her heart, she heard Koos' voice, swearing loudly and fluently in a mixture of Afrikaans and English.

Someone was groaning. She pulled herself onto her elbows, conscious of a sharp stabbing pain under her ribs. Willie staggered to his feet clutching his rifle, his black beard matted with dust, blood spreading on his sleeve. Peter was on his knees, shaking his head. A few paces away, the buffalo had fallen on his side. Dark blood oozed from his nostrils and flies buzzed around the wound on his leg.

Koos was propped on one elbow, clutching his thigh. Both hand and thigh were stained red with his blood, it trickled through his fingers, but he was still swearing furiously.

"Bugger got me too quick, hit him in the shoulder but he never stopped," he was gasping. "Bastard just kept coming. *Magtig*, but that was some bloody charge."

Willie helped Clarissa to her feet, and together they stumbled across to him. The horn had ripped through his trouser leg and gouged a ragged crimson hole in his thigh.

She forced her shocked brain to think clearly. "Give me something to stop the bleeding," she said quickly, pulling the scarf from around her neck and ramming it into the wound. Willie began peeling off his shirt, wincing as he eased his arm out of the sleeve.

Later, she could not remember who went for the horses which had been left tethered near the water earlier in the day. She could not remember working desperately to stem the bleeding on Koos' leg as he sprawled in the dust with his head propped against a rock, still trying to give directions in a voice that every now and then died to a whisper before surging back almost to full volume. Or how, between them – the gun-bearer, Peter with his dislocated shoulder, Willie reeling from the impact of the massive horns – they managed to lift Koos, who was rapidly losing strength, on to his horse. She vaguely recalled Willie remembering the brandy in his saddlebag. "Give him some *dop*, that'll keep him going till we get back."

They poured brandy down his throat, and somehow heaved him astride the massive chestnut, where he slumped, swaying and mumbling drunkenly, his face ashen beneath the shock of beard. During the nightmare ride back to the camp, on a track that wound through dense undergrowth over rocky ground, she lost count of the number of times the injured giant slumped over the horse's neck and began sliding out of the saddle, the number of times they had to stop and push him back upright, as he swore and cursed incoherently.

It was dark by the time they stumbled into camp, to be met by a white-faced Nell and the wide, terrified eyes of Jamie. Koos swayed in the saddle, and Willie and Nell caught him as he slumped to the ground. Peter, ashen-faced beneath his tan, dismounted and put his uninjured arm about his wife. "Right as rain," he assured her cheerfully, before collapsing on the camp bed in his tent.

Once Koos had been half-dragged, half-carried – still cursing intermittently – to his tent, and Nell had assured herself that Peter was not seriously hurt, she turned to Clarissa: "What about you? Are you all right?"

She nodded, rolling up her sleeves. "I'm fine, Nell, but we must work fast. Willie, bring boiling water, and whatever antiseptic or spirits you can find – the brandy will do. Bandages – sheets, whatever. Nell, you look after Peter."

Hours later – she had no idea what time it was – she woke up with a start. The flickering light of the paraffin lamp threw long dancing shadows on the roof of the tent, and Simon Grant was leaning over her, shaking her gently.

She stared up at him, confused, on the edge of a dream in which she was being pursued through a suffocating forest of bamboo.

"What...?" Then she remembered, looked past him to where Koos snored stertorously, and leapt guiltily to her feet. She should not have fallen asleep.

But his pulse was slightly steadier. As she straightened, dazed and barely awake, Simon took her by the shoulders.

"He's sleeping, he's all right. What about you? I heard you...."

"I'm fine," she blinked at him, happy that he had come. "How did you know?"

"Willie sent a message. I brought some stuff – antiseptic and bandages. He thought you might need help taking Koos into hospital."

"We can't move him tonight," she lifted a hand wearily to her forehead and rubbed it. "He's lost too much blood, he's been in deep shock."

"Tomorrow perhaps. Come," and he took her arm and led her out of the tent.

"What time is it?"

"Half past two."

"He should have someone with him..."

"Nell's coming to sit with him, then I'll take over. I've made you some tea, then you're going to bed."

"What about Peter?"

"Asleep." He grinned. "We fed him some whisky, and Willie and I put his shoulder back for him. I've done it once before – for one of my brothers. His arm is a bit mangled, but it'll be all right in a day or two."

"I should look at it – ."

"Tomorrow," he said, and she allowed herself to be guided into a chair by the campfire. The night was very silent, only the flames crackled as Nell walked past quietly, touching Clarissa's shoulder briefly, saying, "I'll watch Koos."

He poured her a steaming mug of tea, added a tot of brandy from a half empty bottle, and sat down beside her. "Here, drink this."

She took it obediently. The brandy flowed down her throat in fiery trails, and she smiled up at him faintly. "This is the second time you've fed me spirits." She started to laugh, and then winced and held her ribs.

"What is it? Are you hurt?"

"Willie fell on top of me – I think my ribs are just a bit bruised. How is Willie?"

"Fine. Tough as old boots – you've got a gash on your face. Stay there and drink your tea."

He returned with an enamel bowl of water and antiseptic. While she sipped her tea, he carefully washed the blood away and cleaned the wound. She leaned back in the chair and closed her eyes, tired to the depth of her being but at the same time, oddly content. The touch of his hands on her face was wonderfully soothing, the brandy flowed warmly through her veins, and she thought she could happily sit there forever, letting him take care of her.

"All done. Now, drink up, I'm going to take you to your tent." She emptied the mug, and set it down on the table.

"That was wonderful. Almost as good as that native beer you fed me."

He grinned briefly. "I don't remember you needing much persuasion then either. Which is your tent?"

"That one," she pointed.

He took her hands and pulled her gently to her feet, and led her across the clearing. "Promise you'll go straight to bed and not back to Koos."

"If you promise to call me if anything changes."

"Done."

"Thank you for the tea and brandy and medical treatment."

"You're welcome." He looked down at her and the smile went out of his eyes to be replaced by an expression that startled her, because it was close to fear. His hands tightened on her shoulders, and when he spoke, his voice was low and uncertain.

"Don't ever give me a fright like that again," he said softly. "When the message came, I thought you'd been badly hurt. It was so garbled – it didn't make sense. The boy said – I was afraid it was you." He stopped. "I was afraid," he whispered again.

She stared up at him. "But I'm fine." She tried to joke: "The only thing that hit me was Willie."

"Thank God," he whispered. "I didn't realise how much...." and he cupped her face in his hands. His lips were warm, he smelt of cigars and horses and brandy, and even in the depths of her exhaustion, she responded instinctively. Her arms reached up and around his neck and she moved her body against his. His arms tightened, and his lips were in her hair. They stood together for a long moment, then he lifted his head and let the tip of his nose rub gently against hers, before releasing her reluctantly.

"Go and sleep." He lifted the tent flap, held it as she ducked her head to go inside.

She turned back to him. "You won't go?"

"I'll be right here. Sleep tight," and he let the canvas flap fall behind her. She stood quite still, staring at it, in the sudden surging realisation that if he had followed her she would not have stopped him.

By late the following afternoon Koos' condition had stabilised slightly and she made the decision to take him to Fort Salisbury. "We have to get him to hospital," she told Willie. "The wagon ride will be bad but it will be worse if we don't. I can't give him the care he needs."

"He's not going to like it," Willie shook his head dubiously. "If I know Koos, he'll kick up one hell of a fight."

Which he did. Flatly refusing to be moved, he told them all to get the hell out and leave him with a bottle of brandy – he'd take care of himself. There was no way he was going to lie in a hospital bed in Salisbury and have a bunch of women flapping around him. At one point, he even reached for the rifle by his bed and threatened to shoot anyone who tried to move him.

It took an hour and the combined force of all their persuasive powers to wear down his resistance. Collapsing back on the camp bed, grey-faced and panting, he finally gave in, muttering dire consequences if they did not guarantee his return within a week.

"He's scared," Willie told Clarissa. "Only time he's ever been in a hospital was to see his brother die of enteric fever."

He went off to make up a bed in the back of the wagon. It was agreed Simon would accompany the Ashtons back to their farm. Peter's shoulder was still painful, his arm had stiffened up, and Nell was afraid he might not be able to manage his horse. Clarissa would travel into town with Koos and Willie, and see Koos settled in hospital.

"Are you sure you'll be all right? He's a hellish patient," Simon asked as he carried her bag out to the wagon.

"I'll be fine, Willie will back me up if I have any trouble – but I don't think we will. He's used up all his strength for the moment, and I think he's going to be in too much pain to give trouble."

The transfer to the wagon was accomplished with muted abuse from the patient, who was settled on a pile of blankets alongside Clarissa's medical box and the brandy bottle.

She said a hurried goodbye to the Ashtons, and Jamie followed her to the wagon, the falcon on his shoulder now sprouting fluffy feathers.

"You'll come back, won't you?" he urged, as Simon helped her to climb in beside Koos.

"Yes, of course, Jamie, Willie will bring me back after we've taken Koos to hospital. I want to see how your father is getting on."

"Good," said Jamie. "Come back soon."

Behind him, Simon's eyes caught hers. "You heard him. Come back soon."

Koos' voice croaked weakly in her ear. "So, what's the hold-up, hey, Marais? Let's get the bloody show on the road."

"*Ja, ja*, we going now." Willie hauled himself up into the driver's seat, cracked his whip and the wagon lurched forward.

Although she had planned to return to Shangara with Willie as soon as Koos was settled, his condition had deteriorated so much by the time they reached Fort Salisbury that neither wanted to leave until they were assured he was out of danger. The journey had been an agony for the injured man, and almost as agonising for Clarissa, who was able to do little more than sponge his face and utter soothing words. Before a scattering of buildings heralded the outskirts of the town, he had developed a fever, and by the time they reached the small hospital he was semi-conscious and babbling incoherently.

She went back to the boarding house, wishing Emma was still there to confide in. A message from Robert was waiting for her, and she stared at it blankly: she had not thought about him at all during the past week. She dropped the slip of paper on the table, and sank down on to her bed.

Time pressed in on her. She was leaving the country in a couple of weeks and now she was not sure she wanted to go. She ached to see her father, but Simon? I love him, she acknowledged. For the first time in my life I am sure of that. He is someone who will be more than a lover, he will be my friend. I think he feels the same, and will say it when I go back. If he doesn't, I will. I must get back quickly.

When she visited the hospital the following day, Koos was delirious and did not recognise her, but by the third morning he was lucid, and by the fourth agitating to be released, although as weak as a newborn impala fawn.

Willie suggested they slip out of town the following morning without telling him: he was afraid Koos would try to discharge himself if he sensed he was being abandoned.

"We'll leave a message, tell him you'll be back next week," suggested Clarissa, as eager as he to be gone.

But the following morning, when she went down to breakfast in the boarding-house dining-room, it was to hear that Jameson had called up all members of the Mashonaland Horse. The long-awaited horses had arrived, they were waiting at an outpost south of the town, and messages had already been sent to outlying areas, calling in the recruits. The troop would begin moving out the following day.

Unable to eat, she returned to her room to pace the floor, her mind in a ferment. She did not know whether Simon had enlisted, but she suspected he would have done so. Peter at least – she reasoned – would now be exempt from riding out.

Willie was coming to fetch her within the hour. If she went back with him, she might miss Simon, who could have left already. She might not even meet him on the road: as he was on horseback he would take the shortest route.

She decided to stay. He would have joined up, she was certain, and would be on his way to town. The thought of him riding into Matabeleland to confront a tribe whose military prowess and brutality were legendary was something she could not contemplate at the moment, so she thrust it to the back of her mind.

When Willie arrived, he told her his own plans were unchanged. He and Koos were due to return to the Transvaal before the onset of the rains, so he would go out to Shangara, hunt for the rest of the week, then pack up the camp and return to pick up his companion before starting the long trek back to the south.

Although not averse to the prospect of a scrap, he deeply feared the reaction of his wife if he allowed himself to be drawn into this conflict. "I would rather face the Matabele than that one, true's God," he told her frankly.

She waved him on his way, and for the rest of the day agonised over whether she had made the right decision. To take her mind off her inner turmoil, she visited Koos, and when she broke the news that Willie had gone, his outraged reaction assured her he was no longer at death's door.

She estimated that if Simon came in on horseback, he would reach town that night and she could expect to see him before the troop left at midday. If he did not come to the boarding house, she would go to Market Square, where the men were due to assemble.

But at breakfast the following morning, she was called out to attend a trooper who had been thrown from his horse near the government buildings. He had broken his leg, and she improvised a splint and stayed with him until the arrival of a wagon to transport him to the hospital. When she returned to the boarding house, the proprietor was waiting.

"You 'ad a visitor, dear – a Mr Grant," her black eyes were bright and inquisitive. "Called just after you left, but 'e was in a hurry – said 'e 'ad to leave with the advance party. Said to let you know 'e came to say goodbye and would be in touch." She smiled archly.

She bit her lip to hide her despair. "Did he say anything else?"

"Not that I recall. Nice-looking gent, looked ever so 'andsome on his 'orse. Oh yes," she added vaguely, "'e did say something, come to think of it. Something about a bird. An 'awk, was it?"

"An eagle?" Clarissa restrained herself from shaking the woman. "It's a carving."

"Eagle, that's what it was. Said you was to keep it for 'im. Funny sort of message."

"Which way did he go, Mrs Foley?" she asked hastily.

"Back to Market Square. But you'll be wasting your time," she called as Clarissa turned on her heel. "They'll be gone by now, shouldn't wonder – and 'e was going ahead of the others."

"Thank you," she called over her shoulder as she picked up her skirt and broke into a run. It wasn't far to Market Square. Please let him not have left, she prayed, let me see him once before he goes. Just once....

But even before she reached the dusty arena, it was clear she was too late. The crowd that had assembled to cheer the troop on its way was already dispersing, and although a few people lingered in groups, the men had gone.

She halted on the edge of the square, barely acknowledging the greetings of friends and acquaintances, desolation sweeping over her in a great grey wave.

Locked in her misery, she was faintly aware of someone calling her name. It was Nell. Clarissa stared at her in a mixture of confusion and despair.

"Nell, what are you doing here? Peter hasn't gone with them, surely?"

"He has," Nell said grimly.

"But – his shoulder, his arm?"

"It was on the mend, and he swore that by the time they reached Matabeleland, it would have healed. I tried to stop him, but it was useless. He could sit on his horse, he said. It's a salted horse too, and because they're in short supply, he wasn't going to hand it over to anyone else. Besides," she shrugged resignedly, "you know men. He had the light of battle in his eyes."

"Nell, that's awful." She hesitated. "Was Simon with him?"

"Yes, you only just missed them. They left five minutes ago. Most of the men were on foot, they were going to pick up their horses at Charter, but Simon and Peter were with the mounted group. They'll be well on their way by now. He went to find you," she added.

"I was called to an accident. I missed him."

"They both said to say goodbye. Simon was quite upset to miss you. He didn't say much but I could see – ," she grinned impishly, but her expression changed when she saw Clarissa's eyes. "Oh, I'm sorry, of course, you'll be leaving in a week or so."

"I wanted to see him...." Clarissa whispered, and Nell put an arm around her shoulders and hugged her.

" Oh, dear, I didn't realise things had gone so far, although the other night, when he arrived in the camp, and thought you'd been hurt, I did wonder. Don't you worry, he'll be all right."

Clarissa tried to smile. "How were they when they left?"

"In the best of spirits – in more ways than one. The whisky had been passed around. Looked as though they were off on a picnic, like a bunch of schoolboys."

"Aren't you worried about Peter?"

"'Course I am." She took Clarissa's arm, and as they began to walk back in the direction of the boarding house her eyes darkened briefly. "But everyone seems to think it will all be over in a couple of weeks. Just a question of letting old Loben know who's boss. Peter can take care of himself."

They parted outside the boarding house, Nell to visit Koos. Clarissa paused as she opened the door, then changed her mind, closed it again and walked around the back to follow one of the many small footpaths that meandered to the top of the kopje.

There were a few houses on the lower slopes, and she climbed past them slowly in the noonday heat. It was quiet, the monkeys that daily entertained her with their almost-human antics outside her window had retired into the dappled shade of msasa trees, and there was no sound save for the mournful descending plaint of a wood dove, and the harsh 'Go 'way, go 'way' of a lourie. She passed the remains of mud huts, and remembered someone telling her that tribespeople had once lived on the kopje a long time before the coming of the white settlers.

It was not very high – only a couple of hundred feet. She had never been to the top before, and saw for the first time the forts erected by the police, buildings she had only glimpsed from a distance. They were well placed, for the view of the town and surrounding countryside was panoramic. To the north, the reed-fringed swamp, a scattering of buildings, and beyond them a ridge of hills; to the south a line of trees bordering the river, and the road to Umtali.

And to the southwest – she shaded her eyes with her hands – yes, there it was.

A column of marching men, barely visible, and some distance beyond, a small cloud spiralling upwards – the dust churned by horses' hooves.

Hugging her arms tightly, she followed the dust cloud with her eyes, struggling to quell the chilling images that rose in her mind. Campfire tales of the ingenious ways in which the Matabele king dealt with those who lost his favour; and the hunter who had told her once that the name of Lobengula's stronghold, Bulawayo, meant 'the place of killing'. Stories of the way Matabele *impis* attacked in the traditional 'horns of the bull' formation inherited from their Zulu forebears. How the warriors advanced in crescent moon configuration, with seasoned fighters bunched together in the centre of the crescent – the head of the bull – while the fleet young warriors on the outer tips of the horns closed in to surround and crush the enemy.

Keep him safe, she prayed, her eyes straining as the dust cloud merged into the blue heat haze on the horizon. Peter too, all of them, but especially him. Bring them back. What is it Mukwasi says? *Hamba gashle.* Go well.

When she returned to her room, she sat down on the bed and stared out of the window for a long time. Then she stood up, pulled a cabin trunk away from the wall under the window and began packing, working fast and methodically, finding relief, as always, in action.

Until her fingers closed around the fish eagle, lying under some clothes at the back of the cupboard. I meant to take it to Shangara, she thought, but I forgot. How did I forget? Slowly, she sat down on the bed, allowing the tears to slide unchecked down her cheeks and over her lips, tasting their saltiness.

A forgotten image appeared in her mind. Simon, standing in the sunlight outside the hut at Chimoio, wearing the hat with the guinea fowl feather, asking her to look after the carving.

What was it he had said? "It means I'll have to find you if I want it back."

She stared down at it through a blur of tears, turning it round and round, so that the sunlight gleamed like copper on the arcs of its outspread wings.

11

London, 1895

Clarissa and Robert emerged from the building where the lecture had been held into the London twilight. The street was a bustle of hurrying grey forms hunched against a dreary drizzle from a darkening sky. Distant figures merged into a deepening yellow fog in which the gas street-lamps shed a blurred radiance.

"Wait here, my dear," Robert's protective arm halted her beneath the portico, "I'll find a cab." He walked into the drizzle, turning up his collar.

As she stepped back into the shelter of the doorway, the wheels of passing hansoms hissed on the wet cobblestones, steamy breath puffed from the nostrils of horses splashing through muddy puddles, and a young boy in a ragged overcoat and dirty, too-large cap brushed past her, clutching a bundle of newspapers.

Her breath misted in the cold air, and she pulled her heavy cape closer about her shoulders, glad of its warmth. The sudden transition from the sights, sounds and smells evoked by the lecture, back to the grey reality of winter in England, had momentarily disoriented her.

The lecturer – a zoologist from the Royal Society – had been a compelling speaker, and his words had transported her effortlessly back to the landscape of vast plains and limitless skies which she had left – it seemed – a lifetime ago. Standing at the podium in the draughty lecture hall, bearded and still lightly tanned from his sojourn in the African sun, the speaker had seemed strangely out of place as he looked down on the rows of pale, rapt faces. As he spoke of his travels and his work, Clarissa sensed in him a barely restrained impatience to be gone from the physically and emotionally claustrophobic restraints of his surroundings – away to the wild, free spaces in which he had spent a number of years studying the fauna of Southern Africa.

But instead of lifting her spirits as she had hoped it would, the talk had merely underlined the blandness of her present existence. How distant – in both time and space – it now seemed, that other life.

A cab arrived and Robert stepped out, skirting a puddle to take her arm and bundle her solicitously inside – with all the fussiness of her mother, she reflected as he settled in the seat beside her. Doesn't he remember that I ran a hospital in the bush, shot a lion, walked miles in every kind of weather?

He had enjoyed the lecture, and chatted comfortably while she half-listened, staring out at the sea of jostling umbrellas in the shiny, rain-swept street. If this was Africa, it would still be light and sunny at five o'clock. She felt as though she had just returned from a long absence, instead of having been back in England for more than a year. Seated on the hard wooden benches in the cavernous hall, she had been so completely transported to the African bush that, at one point in the lecture, she had tasted dust in her mouth, and run her tongue involuntarily around her lips to moisten them and remove the familiar grittiness. Just as she had done so many times crossing the hospital grounds in the hot, parched months before the start of the summer rains, or riding through the bush at Shangara.

"Why is it," she asked Robert a little later, as they sipped tea from porcelain cups in the subdued elegance of the Grosvenor lounge where her aunt was meeting them, "that when you look back on something that was – a lot of the time – exceedingly uncomfortable, and often quite horrible, you remember only the good bits? Perhaps it's the only way the human race has managed to survive for so long."

"If you're talking about Africa," Robert paused in his evident enjoyment of a large buttered scone dripping with raspberry jam, "I assure you I remember every painful detail, especially my trip from Kimberley. I still have dreams about it, unloading that wretched wagon piece by piece, in scorching heat, so that the oxen could haul it across a drift and up the bank. Carting every bit of luggage up the bank and loading up again only to repeat the process in another couple of hours.

"And that was when things were going well," he grinned, "which wasn't often. Mostly, the axle broke, the oxen died, or the wagon got stuck. As for the rats," he began buttering another scone, "the mozzies, the flies, the heat. My word, it's still as clear as daylight."

"Mmm." She gazed unseeingly across the sea of snowy linen, silverware and coiffed heads. "I do remember the rats – some as big as rabbits. But somehow, in retrospect, those bits don't seem so bad. While the good bits – they just get better and better. One night after a picnic in the hills, Emma and I and some men from the police camp – Frank was there, I remember – walked back in the dark." Her voice had a hushed, dreamy quality. "There was no moon, and I've never seen a sky so clear and stars so close as they were that night. So close and so many – millions and millions.

"And the smell of impala meat roasting on a wood fire, and the smell of the bush after a thunderstorm," she mused, "and the way the frogs came out and hopped all over the place, and we kept tripping over them when we walked to the wards at night, and squashing them...."

"I can see that the thought of squashed frogs must be particularly alluring," Robert's tone was dry. "But could you keep the details till after we have finished tea?" He lifted the silver teapot and refilled their cups. "Your aunt is late," he pointed out unnecessarily as he offered her another scone and took one himself. "I hope she won't mind that we have started." Robert took his food seriously, but she refused to be side-tracked.

"You know what I mean," she said impatiently. "Don't you ever miss it, Robert? You were there almost as long as we were."

"But I thought you liked being back in England." He looked at her in surprise.

"I do, I do. It's only...," and she looked around at the ornate surroundings, the only sounds the tinkle of crockery and the subdued hum of voices, "it's just that after a while, it starts to get so ...so..."

"Tame?" he interrupted, with a gentle understanding that made her look at him sharply.

"Yes, tame, predictable. Say what you like about Africa, it was never predictable."

"Agreed." He set down his cup and his brown eyes looking steadily into hers. "It was a tremendous experience, unforgettable, and I wouldn't have missed it. But it was an adventure, and it's over."

"I know, but I keep having this strange feeling that all the time I'm not there I'm missing something, missing ..."

"What you narrowly missed was a war, brief though it was. As I said, it was memorable, but no place to settle down and raise a family." His eyes became serious. "Which brings me back to a subject which, as you know, I have raised a dozen times since we have been back."

"But..."

"Don't 'but' me, Clarissa," his voice was gentle but determined, "you are about to change the subject again."

"Well, it's just that this isn't a good time, Robert – not now. I can't think about serious things when I'm eating cream scones. And here's Aunt Kitty."

She leaned back in relief as her aunt's imposing figure bustled towards them. "We'll talk about it when you come down to Elderbrook next weekend – I promise." She leaned across the table and squeezed his hand.

"I can wait, I suppose," Slightly mollified, he dabbed his mouth with a snowy napkin, and his eyes were smiling. "My patience, as you know, is endless. But I won't let you forget."

He stood up and pulled out a chair. "We haven't eaten all the scones, Mrs Harcourt."

But later that evening, in Kitty Harcourt's box at the Haymarket, watching a performance of 'A Woman of No Importance', Robert found it difficult to concentrate on the dialogue he normally found so entertaining. He was restless, and unable to prevent himself from glancing covertly at Clarissa by his side, wholly absorbed in the witticisms floating up from behind the footlights. Although the ballet was her greatest love, she enjoyed the theatre, and Oscar Wilde's sophisticated comedies were among her favourites.

Robert stared at her in the darkness, savouring the opportunity to love her with his eyes without intrusion, willing her to feel about him the way he had felt since their first meeting in Umtali, when he had called at the hospital in the early evening to deliver a message from a former patient. He had caught her at a bad time: she was busy, tired and harassed, but she had come out of the ward, drying her hands on a towel, and talked to him out on the small stoep. There were stains on her apron, her hair was dishevelled, but her eyes glowed when she laughed, and it had taken him no more than twenty minutes to fall irretrievably in love.

She looked very different tonight, in this sophisticated setting. Different too from the thin, fragile waif with lifeless hair he had met up with again in Salisbury after her bout of fever. The hollows in her neck and throat had been smoothed away, the wheat-gold hair was combed back from her face in a classic chignon that accentuated her slender neck and the white shoulders emerging from the décolletage of the slim wine-red gown.

But despite her return to health and vitality, despite her obvious pleasure in his company, despite the fact that her family had made him welcome – and he knew that her mother wanted nothing more than to see her only daughter happily settled – he was instinctively uneasy, unsure of his ground.

God knows he had already called upon all his considerable powers of persuasion in this lengthy courtship, and he intended to persist. But, sometimes, she just wasn't there. Sometimes, she seemed to be somewhere else – and after the tea-time conversation, he realised she still dreamed of Africa and, perhaps, of that brief encounter which Emma, in a moment of indiscretion, had once hinted at.

It was difficult to believe that after all she had gone through: all the discomfort, drudgery, ill-health, the unbelievably primitive conditions in which she had worked (and come close to killing herself), she still hankered for the place. He recalled someone saying to him once that Africa was like a dose of malaria. "Once you've had it you never get over it, it's in your bloodstream."

Well, he had got over it, and he would see that she did too. He knew he had her family behind him. With his thriving business, comfortable London home and country house in Kent, he was confident that, in the eyes of the old lady, he was a supremely eligible candidate for her daughter's hand. Even the old man, who had died before Robert had been able to get to know him well, had made his approval abundantly clear.

Clarissa must have become conscious of his insistent gaze because now she turned and caught his eyes, and smiled absently before turning her attention back to the stage.

She's stubborn, he reflected, but then, so am I. It was just a matter of perseverance, a quality he had in abundance.

Sometimes, as she lay – wide-eyed and far from sleep – in her childhood bedroom, she found herself re-living the trek to Umtali, recalling their camping sites with a clarity that amazed her. Each one had its own unique spirit, and she remembered that when they broke camp each morning it was as though the small patch of ground, where they left behind only the ashes of their fires, had become woven into the fabric of her life. Especially that first night on the bank of the river: the wind rustling in the bamboos, the splashes and grunts of hippos heaving themselves out of the water, the high squeaking of bats skimming overhead, the smell of wood smoke, hot sweet tea the way Mukwasi made it. And the morning after the doctor had left them, when they had walked through billowing waves of grass into the unknown.

Sometimes, despite all the time that had elapsed, she could not prevent her thoughts turning to Simon Grant and their last meeting in Koos' camp on the river.

A few days after his departure with the Mashonaland Horse, she had left for the coast with Robert, and sailed for England with conflicting emotions, torn between a longing to stay until his return from Matabeleland, and a yearning to see her ailing father before it was too late. She had written him a letter before she left, wishing him a safe return and asking him to write. She had wanted to say more, to open her heart and reveal her feelings, but something held her back. Was it that she was suddenly unsure, afraid he might not feel the same?

During her first weeks in England, she had followed the reports of the war through *The Times*. With quickening pulse, she had read of the doomed, defiant stand on the banks of the Shangani River, where Major Allan Wilson and some thirty troopers, massively outnumbered, had been surrounded and slaughtered by Matabele warriors. Scanning the list of casualties with hammering heart, she had breathed a prayer of thanks when Simon's name was not among them. But she had remembered the major, and recognised other names, men she had laughed and danced with, including the tall, charming Henry Borrow, friend of Maurice Heany, who had waltzed with her at Emma's wedding. So young they had been, coming to Africa in the carefree certainty of finding adventure and making their fortunes. And their corpses had been left for hyenas and vultures to squabble over. At least they had not been mutilated: the victorious Matabele had refrained from their customary tradition, praising their courage and saluting them as 'men of men'.

In terms of British lives, the incident had marked the only major loss of the entire four-month campaign. Overall, casualties among Company forces were light, though hundreds of Matabele had been slain. The members of the Shangani Patrol, as the doomed unit came to be called, had been sent in pursuit of the old king Lobengula, who had burned down the Royal *Kraal* in Bulawayo and fled into the bush with his followers. He had made one last bid for peace, sending a message and a bag of gold with two British troopers. But he had chosen the wrong messengers: the pair absconded with the gold, and the old king of a once-proud nation, alone with a few faithful *indunas*, had taken poison.

With the conflict over, Clarissa had expected a letter or message of some kind. When neither materialised, she made excuses for Simon, consoling herself with the fantasy that he was not writing because he was on the way home by ship, and would walk in one day and surprise her.

Her spirits were buoyed by this comforting image, and the realisation that her arrival seemed to have given back to her father some of his old strength and vitality. Her older brother Denis had long since taken over the management of the estate, but Richard Hamilton still retained his interest, hobbling about with the help of a stick, or driving out in the pony trap.

And so, during those early months, she had been content to wallow in the comforts that had been missing from her life for the past two years: her own enormous four-poster bed overlooking the orchard at beloved Elderbrook, the new electric lights in her aunt's house in Kensington, outings to the theatre and Kew Gardens. Despite the yearning for the letter that never arrived, she spent happy interludes riding and fishing on Nicholas' farm, where she met the current object of his affections – cheerful, horse-loving Felicity Stewart, daughter of a neighbouring landowner.

With her mother, she had sorted through the clothes left behind on her departure to Africa. Most of them were out of fashion, they decided, and would have to be made up into bundles for charity. That meant a new wardrobe, and together they took themselves off to London to stay with Kitty, and indulge in day-long explorations of the newest shops in Oxford Street, where Clarissa exclaimed in delight over the latest styles: the frivolous puffed sleeves, small chic hats, the new skirts that fitted sleekly over the hips and swirled outwards to the hemline.

Aware that both her mother and aunt were doing all they could to help her settle back to life in England, she indulged them by immersing herself in Kitty's social round. For a short time she found it entertaining, but taking tea in stuffy drawing-rooms and listening to conversations about servants, the weather and the latest scandal very soon lost its novelty. She took a temporary post at a London hospital while looking for a permanent position, but although it was good to be nursing again, she felt flat and restless, and impatient when those around her complained about their working conditions, poor equipment or long hours. When she tried to explain what it was like waiting months for vital equipment and medicines, or assisting at operations performed by the light of flickering candles, her colleagues raised disbelieving eyebrows, or did not care.

There was Robert, of course. Already he had proposed marriage several times, and while she had not exactly refused him, she had so far managed to stall by postponing a decision until she had become accustomed to being back. When she was at Elderbrook, her parents watched anxiously, afraid her restless eyes would turn southward again. Chas, older now and in failing health, listened to the stories of her adventures with deep, nostalgic pleasure, and then proceeded to echo her parents' words.

"You were lucky," he warned. "You might not be lucky twice, and you've seen enough of the place to know that yourself. I'm glad you went, and I'm delighted to see you back in one piece. Don't tempt fate, my girl."

"I'm not even thinking about it, Uncle Chas."

"Good. Thank God you met Robert. I was afraid some bronzed frontier type would throw you across his saddle and ride off with you. Your mother would have killed me."

While she looked into various options for a permanent position, her father's health suddenly deteriorated. He retired to his bed, and suffered a stroke soon afterwards.

"It's almost as though he was just hanging on to have some time with you," sighed her mother, "and now he's giving up the struggle."

Clarissa left the hospital, cancelled her social engagements, and moved back to Elderbrook to help nurse her father and support her mother.

As his condition worsened, she spent long hours by his side, reading his favourite books or talking about her time in Africa. During those last weeks, it was his greatest pleasure to lie with his eyes fixed on her animated face, chuckling wheezily as he listened to her tales.

Then one evening he sank into a coma, and two days later, quietly and without fuss, the spark went out and he drifted peacefully away, to be laid to rest in the small family plot by the old Norman church.

After his death, her mother clung to Clarissa for comfort and support, another reason she gave Robert for postponing a decision about their future. "I can't think about marriage just yet," she told him, "she's strong, and she'll get over this, but she needs me now."

As always, he had been the soul of understanding and sympathy, visiting regularly and bringing small, thoughtful gifts down from London for them both – gestures which made her feel all the more guilty and remorseful. Because, in her heart, she knew she was not being fair to him.

And then, while she was struggling to come to terms with the loss of her father, a letter arrived from Africa. But it was in Emma's familiar hand, an Emma bubbling with *joie de vivre* and local news:

You'll be glad to hear that Mukwasi is now with us, she wrote. *He arrived on the doorstep one day and announced that he had had enough of Umtali, and was going to hold me to my promise. He asked for news of you, and wants to know when you are coming back. I told him you were happily settled in England, but he just gave me that look that I'm sure you remember – as though I was feeble-minded – and said you would be back. As you know, it's a waste of time arguing with him.*

I have not seen anything of Simon Grant since the rising, she continued, *but Danny O'Keefe (who nearly died of enteric fever a few months ago)* told me that as soon as the fighting was over Simon went back to the Zambezi with Jerry.

I know how you felt, Lissa, and I cannot blame you, as the man is undeniably attractive. But he is not the marrying kind. Frank and I agree he is too much the free spirit, and I hope you will have put him out of your mind by now.

What about Robert? she breezed on. *Every week, I hope to hear that you have accepted him. When that happens, I will truly rejoice because he would make you the very best and most loving of husbands.*

Clarissa reread the words, but there was no mistaking their message. She was not really surprised. She knew her capacity for self-deception, that in her heart she had guessed the truth a long time ago. She thought of her letter to him, and burned with pain and humiliation at the knowledge that she had even hoped for a response.

Resolutely, she put the brief interlude at Shangara out of her mind, and set about encouraging her mother to pick up the strands of her life again. But it was not that easy. Several weeks later, she fell ill, and the doctor diagnosed a recurrence of malaria. The parasite had entered her bloodstream, he informed her, which meant the disease could recur for years to come. Once the fever had ebbed, he warned that her health had suffered profoundly from her African sojourn and she should not, under any circumstances, think about returning.

Turning her face to the wall to blink away the tears that came too easily in her weakened condition, she murmured that she had no reason to.

During her recuperation, Robert came down regularly from London, and they spent long hours sitting in the garden, or walking together in the spring countryside. Slowly, to his intense relief – for he had been frightened by the severity of her illness – her strength returned, her natural high spirits reasserted themselves, as she began to accept the fact that Simon Grant had never had any intention of making her a proposal of marriage.

Now her conscience reminded her once again that she could not keep Robert waiting for an answer. Her mother was almost back to her vital and enthusiastic self, and had thrown herself into the activities of the local parish with a new vigour and sense of purpose. She was also making it quite clear that she considered her daughter's treatment of her suitor less than admirable. There was no longer any excuse to prevaricate.

The weekend after the lecture, when Robert came down from London on the train, Clarissa was at the station to meet him with the pony trap, startling and delighting him with the warmth of her welcoming kiss. She handed him the reins, and as they rode back to the farm, examined his profile surreptitiously from beneath lowered lashes.

She tried to pretend she was seeing him for the first time – the erect, almost military bearing, the sandy hair, receding just enough to give his face a touch of distinction. The brown eyes were clear and honest, there was no guile in Robert, she thought. He's like one of those clear brooks that run through the estate: it never comes down in torrents, never promises anything wildly exciting, but is always reliable. And not unattractive.

Logic and reason tell me this is right, she reflected, as he flicked the whip gently to urge the aged pony into a more energetic pace. I feel no great passion for him, but I like it when he kisses me. He fits in with the family, and I would like to have children with him. Mother will be pleased, Denis and Nicholas like him. What else is there?

It was a mild summer evening, and after dinner they walked to the old whitewashed windmill on top of the hill, to watch dusk sift across the tranquil countryside. In the field below, rabbits frisked in the grass, sheep grazed peacefully and swallows twittered in the fading light. Yes, she thought, it will be all right, and when he took her hands and asked her again, as she knew he would, she gave him the answer he had been waiting for.

He tilted her face up to his, and was startled for the second time that day by the warm pressure in the lips that met his own; his arms tightened, and he pulled her against him, and kissed her deeply. Again she responded, winding her arms about his neck, moving her lips against his.

For Clarissa, it was the first time her body had been stirred since the night Simon had come to her after the buffalo attack, and she was glad it was happening, glad that she could feel this way with someone else. See, she thought fiercely, he isn't the only person who can do this to me.

They announced their engagement the following week, and set a date for an autumn wedding. Her mother beamed with delight, Kitty was in raptures, her brothers approved and, gazing at the diamond and sapphire ring Robert had slipped on to her finger, Clarissa felt as though a great weight had been lifted from her shoulders. With a new sense of purpose, she threw herself into wedding plans and, soon after the announcement, travelled down to Kent to meet his parents.

Dorinda Hammond was a small, querulous, self-indulgent woman with a quavering voice, who doted on her son and was, Clarissa quickly decided, unlikely to be satisfied with any bride she had not personally selected for her only son. She was hospitable enough, but despite Clarissa's valiant efforts she failed to strike up a rapport with the older woman, and it was with Robert's father that she formed an immediate, conspiratorial bond. Gordon Hammond had Robert's tall, erect bearing, the same eyes, and an air of patient, humorous resignation developed, no doubt, through years of enduring the vague, complaining mannerisms of his wife.

Robert suggested a variety of activities and outings designed to include his mother, but she seldom accompanied them – it was too cold, too far, too exhausting. And so they so were left, to Clarissa's relief, to form a comfortable, convivial trio, fishing in the nearby river, visiting Canterbury Cathedral, and exploring Dover and the surrounding villages.

Although Robert kept a country house close to his parent's home, it was agreed they would live mainly in London where he was a partner in a trading company with a range of interests in Asia and India. Clarissa spent much of her time planning the redecoration of the London house.

"Do whatever you like, sweetheart," he told her indulgently, "I have every faith in your taste."

She was enjoying herself. The prospect of a home of her own was exciting, and Kitty, who had a natural flair for decorating, was on hand with advice in picking out the right curtaining, upholstery fabrics and furniture.

On a hot, airless afternoon in late August, two months before the wedding, she returned to Kitty's house, armed with fabric samples from a shop in Oxford Street, her mind preoccupied with colours, designs and textures.

Singing out a greeting to her aunt, she poked her head around the sittingroom door. A tall figure was silhouetted against the window. Before he had even turned around she knew it was Simon Grant.

12

As he came towards her, she was swept by a rush of emotion so strong it was as though the breath had been sucked from her body; the colour ebbed from her face, and she gripped the door frame for support. He had been smiling, but when he saw her expression his smile faded and he put his hand out instinctively.

"Clarissa, I'm sorry. I didn't mean to startle you." He looked at her uncertainly.

"No, it's all right. It's just ... a surprise. I hardly recognised you – in your London clothes." She moved unsteadily into the room, her heart thudding, and held out a gloved hand as she fought to regain control. "How long have you been waiting?" she asked weakly.

"Not long. Your aunt said she was expecting you back any minute." As he spoke, Kitty fluttered into the room, chins wobbling, draperies flying, eyes alight with curiosity.

"There you are, darling. I see you've already found your surprise visitor. I understand Mr Grant is an old friend from Rhodesia," and she looked keenly at her niece.

"That's right, Aunt Kitty." Her cheeks were hot and flushed as she tugged at her gloves. She was having trouble with her fingers, they were suddenly stiff and clumsy. "We met when Emma and I were walking to Umtali – and then... and then later, in Fort Salisbury."

"In that case you'll have a lot to talk about. I've asked Alice to make tea – ah, here she is." The maid entered with a tray which she set down on a table beside Kitty's chair.

"Do sit down, Mr Grant. You will have some tea, won't you? Cream and sugar?"

"Thank you."

How she endured the next half hour Clarissa would never know. But she was grateful for Kitty, chattering animatedly, dispensing tea in her best *grande dame* manner, and bombarding Simon with a barrage of questions that gave her a chance to fight for composure.

From his replies, she gathered he had been in England only a few days and planned to stay for two months to attend to business and visit relatives. The expedition up the Zambezi had been successful, and Jerry Shawcross had delivered the specimens collected for the museum. The mine was yielding a modest profit, and he was planning to put in maize and tobacco, and experiment with fruit trees, on his return.

Although he wore his dark tailored suit with casual grace, he brought into the room a sense of belonging elsewhere. His skin was deeply tanned, and he still carried the familiar aura of suppressed energy. When he rose to hand Clarissa her teacup, he moved with a lightness more suited to sun-bleached plains than the cluttered, upholstered elegance of Kensington.

"You would have been through the Matabele War, Mr Grant?" Kitty asked.

"Yes. I saw some action, though I was mainly on reconnaissance patrols. We were lucky to get away with so few casualties, but I lost some good friends at Shangani." He turned to Clarissa. "You would have known some of them?"

"Yes. Yes, I did. I was so sorry to hear of their deaths."

"It was a bad show all round, should never have happened. Wouldn't have if Jameson hadn't been in charge. He overplayed his hand as usual." There was a pause. "Your aunt tells me you are engaged to be married," he said abruptly.

"That's right," she replied brightly, flushing, "I believe you have met Robert."

"Yes," he said steadily. "Unfortunately, I didn't have the chance to get to know him." He paused. "My congratulations to you both."

"Thank you."

In the silence that followed, Kitty looked quizzically from Simon to Clarissa. He cleared his throat. "When is the wedding?"

"In October. Robert has a house in Kent, but we will be living in London most of the time."

"So nice for me," interposed Kitty chattily. "It will be marvellous having Clarissa close by. I did so miss her when she was away in Africa. More tea, Mr Grant?"

"No, thank you, Mrs Harcourt." He set his cup down and looked about him restlessly.

"Well, in that case," Kitty rose tactfully, "I'll leave you two to catch up with the latest news, and go and get dinner organised. Delighted to have met you, Mr Grant. I do hope we see you again before you leave," and Simon rose and took her hand, murmuring his thanks before she bustled from the room.

There was a long silence. Clarissa rushed headlong to fill it. "Are you sure you wouldn't like some more tea?" She lifted the teapot. "There's plenty in the pot."

"No. No, thank you." He sat down opposite her, loosened his jacket and gazed at her, as though it was his first opportunity to look at her properly. "You're looking well, Clarissa. No more malaria?"

"I had a recurrence a while ago. But since then, I've been fine." To her ears, her voice sounded strained, almost shrill. "You look very well too. How are things in Fort Salisbury?"

"Better than when you left. The Matabele have laid down their assegais for the moment, though for how long I wouldn't like to say – as the company has treated them shabbily since the war. Taken their land, their cattle, put badly-trained black police in control."

He stood up restlessly and walked to the fireplace. "There are plenty of new buildings, new roads, new arrivals. Bulawayo – Lobengula's old stronghold – is flourishing, a lot of the action moved there after the war. The railway line to Beira is being built, and there's a line coming up to Bulawayo from the south. You probably wouldn't recognise the place."

"You won't be pleased about that – civilisation encroaching on your wilderness." She stirred her tea with a hand she struggled to keep from shaking.

"No," he grinned briefly, "I'm not. But it's not too serious yet. Still plenty of wilderness. What about your father? He was ill, I remember."

"He died some months ago."

"I'm very sorry."

"Thank you."

"Look...," he hesitated. The silence spread between them.

"Look at what, Simon?" Her voice was tense, and a small tight core of anger was forming below her ribs.

He shook his head in an oddly helpless gesture. "I rehearsed what I was going to say to you a hundred times, but now I've forgotten the words. It seems they aren't appropriate any more, anyway."

"I can't think what you could possibly want to say to me," she stood up quickly and walked around to the back of the sofa, so that it formed a barrier between them, "that you couldn't have written any time in the last year."

He followed her with quick strides. "You have every right to say that, Clarissa. But if you'd let me explain..."

She rounded on him, her voice shaking. "Explain what, exactly? Why you didn't write, why I never had a single word from you in all that time. After Shangara – that night – I thought....I thought we had," her voice dropped to a whisper, "a future. You let me think so. Or did I just imagine it?"

"No. You didn't. Just listen..."

"You could have written," she said fiercely, "I waited over a year, but you didn't even answer my letter," and she turned away so that he would not see her eyes, and walked to the window.

"Your letter? I didn't get any letter from you. When did you write?"

"Before I left." She shook her head, staring out of the window, her voice shaking. "It doesn't matter now. You could have written anyway, but you didn't care enough."

"No, that's not how it was." He was behind her, his hands on her shoulders, turning her around and leading her, stiff but unresisting, to the sofa, sitting down beside her on the edge of the seat. "Listen. Just hear me out. Please."

She stared fixedly down at the diamond and sapphires sparkling on her finger.

He spoke in a low, rapid voice. "When we came back after the fighting was over, you had gone back to England – with Hammond. I knew I had to make a decision – whether to follow you or to stay. What happened at Shangara was important to me, but despite the way I felt about you, despite what happened, I knew – in the cold light of day – that I wasn't ready for marriage then, the kind of marriage I thought you deserved, anyway. I admit that."

She started to say something, but he rushed on. "Hear me out. Remember me telling you about my parents – that day in Shangara? What I didn't say was that all those years, when I watched my mother becoming bitter and angry about my father's long absences, the way she was left to bring us up on her own, I realised the same thing could happen to me. Because I was like him in that way. I wanted to live the same kind of life – free, unfettered. I had no ambitions about settling down, I wanted to explore the world.

"But I was not going to make any woman suffer the way my mother suffered. So, I made the conscious decision not to marry. That way I could do what I liked with a clear conscience, without hurting anyone. The thought that I wouldn't have children didn't particularly trouble me at the time.

"So I enjoyed the company of women, but I was always careful to disentangle myself if things started to get serious. And then you came along, and for the first time, I was confused. Maybe I had been wrong, maybe it could work – that's how I was thinking in Shangara that evening.

"But once I was away, riding down to Matabeleland, I knew I still wanted to go back to the Zambezi and finish what I had started.

"Don't interrupt," he said as she opened her mouth to speak, her face flushing with anger, "you are going to say I was being selfish, and you're right. But it was part of my plan, and I still wasn't ready to throw it out. There were things I wanted to do where a woman would have been a hindrance. Even," and he smiled faintly, "one who had killed a lion and walked from Beira to Umtali. Besides, you had to get back to your father.

"I couldn't write and say 'Wait a couple of years until I've done what I want to do'. Why should you? I knew Hammond was on the scene, knew he would make you a better husband – that you would be better off without me.

"So I decided to put you out of my mind and carry on exploring Africa and getting as much pleasure from it as I always had before. And I headed off to the Zambezi with Jerry."

He was on his feet again, pacing. Now he stopped before her, rubbed his chin and gazed ruefully down at her as she sat motionless, staring fixedly at her fingers pleating the fabric of her skirt. He went down on his haunches so that his eyes were level with hers.

"I tried for more than a year, but couldn't forget you. I've been carrying you around with me all this time, wishing you would go away and leave me in peace. Whenever I saw something that excited me – and there were so many things, Clarissa," his eyes glowed, "the Victoria Falls with a double lunar rainbow, elephants squirting each other with water in the river, a million fireflies one night – my first thought was: Clarissa would love this. I wanted to show them to you, and you weren't there.

"In the end, I realised it wasn't working. Without you, nothing was as much fun any more." His voice was low now. "So I came back to find out whether, by some miracle, you were still free, and whether I had a chance."

"And you found it was too late," she said flatly.

He rose and walked to the fireplace. "Not until half an hour ago. When I saw Emma in Salisbury, she hadn't heard about your engagement. I told her how I felt, she gave me hell, and then told me to get back here as fast as I could before you accepted Hammond.

"She also told me I didn't deserve you, but she thought that, for some obscure reason, you might still have some feeling for me. I came on the next boat," he paused and his voice deepened, "but not quickly enough, apparently."

She drew a deep breath, looked at him squarely. "So. You are now ready to take on the hindrance of a wife," she said levelly.

He rubbed a hand across his face. "Say it, say it all. I deserve it. I behaved appallingly."

"Yes," she agreed tightly. "You did."

"But it wasn't pure self-interest, Clarissa. Believe me, I know what I am, and I knew when I was being honest with myself that Hammond would make you a better husband."

"Well, I am sure you are right," she replied, staring past him. "Things have obviously turned out the way they were meant to, and now you can go back to Africa and continue to live your free, unfettered life."

He stared at her for a long moment. "Yes," he said quietly. "It would seem so. Is there nothing I can say to change your mind?"

"Nothing."

She saw pain in his eyes, and looked away quickly. She wanted to stay angry with him.

"Very well," he said heavily. "But please, Clarissa," and he crossed swiftly to her side and sat down, "at least, let's not part like this. I've said I'm sorry – what else can I say? Can we at least be friends?"

"Friends? Yes, of course," she said stiffly, for her face felt brittle. "Which reminds me," and she rose, "I must get your fish eagle for you. I've been wondering what to do with it. Excuse me." She whirled about and left the room before he could stop her.

Concentrating furiously on keeping her mind a careful blank, she mounted the stairs, went into the spare room and rummaged in the cupboard where she had left some of her luggage on her arrival in England. There it was, still wrapped in newspaper – a sheet from the Mashonaland Herald. As she picked it up, memories surged back and she felt her resolve weaken. I want to go with him, her heart cried, why can't I? Why can't I just forget Robert, and go? He wants me... and I've waited so long. She held the smooth stone against her cheek for a long moment, and then straightened and went back downstairs. Outside the door she drew a deep, steadying breath.

He was staring out of the window and turned at her approach. A nerve twitched in his cheek.

"Here you are – all in one piece." She ran her fingers over the cool curving lines of the carving. "Come to think of it, it's a bit like you, isn't it, Simon? Forever spreading its wings and preparing to fly away." With an abrupt movement, she held it out, spitting out the harsh words, unable to help herself. She wanted to hit out at him for the pain of the past, and for the new ache growing inside her.

"That's not fair. I want you to fly away with me," he said softly.

"Yes, well, that's impossible. Why did you give it to me in the first place? From what you've just said, it was strictly out of character."

"I don't know why," he said slowly. "I didn't know at the time. It wasn't planned. I just suddenly wanted to keep some link with you. It was just a crazy impulse." He hesitated. "Here's another. If you won't come with me, I'd rather you kept it – as a memento..."

"I don't think a memento would be a good idea." She felt a warning prickle of tears behind her eyes and fought them back, holding the carving out again, blindly. He took it, put it on the arm of the chair without looking at it, and she extended her hand. "Goodbye."

He took her hand and held it, tightening his grasp when she tried to pull away. She drew a long shuddering breath and looked directly into the gold-flecked eyes, and he lifted her hand slowly and deliberately, turned it palm upwards and brought it to his lips. They were dry and warm, and she did not move, and when he raised his eyes again, they held the same expression as they had done the night after the buffalo attack.

"Come with me," he said softly and urgently. "I love you so much. You don't have to go through with this, my darling. Marry me and come back to Africa. I'll take you down to the Zambezi. We can follow the elephant roads across the flood plain....."

"I can't," she whispered, but she did not try to pull her hand away. "You know I can't. You left it too late."

"Do you love him?" He kept her hand in his.

"You've no right to ask that."

"Do you?"

"I think I could be happy with him."

"Do you love him?"

"Yes," she said despairingly, "yes, I do!"

"Don't lie," his eyes were searching her face. Very slowly he took her other hand and drew her towards him, took her face in his hands and kissed her. His arms were around her, his hands on her hair, and all the strength and fury she had summoned began to ebb, and her will to dissolve in a flood of feeling.

"No!" With a desperate effort, she wrenched herself free. "I can't do this," she gasped, backing away. "I can't do it to Robert, don't ask me to. Go now. Please, Simon."

"Say you'll come with me. Then I'll go."

"No, no, I won't. I can't. It would break his heart. He's waited so long, he's been so good to me, he loves me."

"But you don't love him," he spoke swiftly. "He'll find that out, he's not stupid. Come with me," he repeated.

"Go, please, go," she begged him, her voice rising almost hysterically.

"All right." All at once his voice was quiet and pacifying, almost humble. "I'm going, I promise. Don't cry, please don't cry. I'm sorry." He picked up the carving. "I'll be in London for the next two weeks, then away in Hertfordshire for a few days, then back here at my club in the Strand." He took a folded slip of paper from his pocket, scribbled an address on it, and held it out to her. When she didn't move, he put it on the mantelpiece.

"If you change your mind, send me a message. I won't be leaving until the fifteenth of September."

She stood with her arms hugged defensively about her body. He walked across the room and picked up his hat. At the door, he turned. "Clarissa, change your mind. Think of what we could do together."

"Goodbye," she was trembling, "please go."

He turned and went out, and she heard the front door close quietly behind him.

She did not move, made no attempt to wipe away the tears that slid down her cheeks. Minutes passed – she did not know how many – before Kitty's quick footsteps on the stairs brought her to her senses, and she dabbed feverishly at her cheeks with a handkerchief, and smoothed her hair hurriedly.

"Has Mr Grant gone already?" her aunt asked in puzzlement. "I expected you two to be chattering away for hours. You're always looking for someone to talk about Africa with."

"He had an appointment," she said abruptly.

"What an exceedingly good-looking man, Clarissa, I hope we will see him again." She paused and looked closely at her niece, "Are you all right, darling? You look flushed. You don't feel feverish, do you?"

"No, no. It's just a little hot in here," Clarissa said hastily. "I believe I'll go for a walk in the park to cool down. I won't be long," and before her aunt could reply, she had left the room, seized a wrap from the hall table and opened the front door.

"Don't be late, dear," Kitty called, following her to the door. "Don't forget you're dining out with Robert tonight," her voice trailed away and she stared at the receding figure of her niece in perplexity.

In the small gardens two blocks from Kitty's house, Clarissa paced the paved walks beneath chestnut trees, their leaves already tipped with autumn gold. Pigeons and sparrows pecked about in the grass, and a nurse in a grey uniform trundled a pram, talking crossly to a little boy she was pulling along by the hand. Two elderly men in dark suits sat on a bench deep in conversation, and a woman in a shabby blue dress read a book nearby. Her brain registered these details detachedly as she walked around and around the perimeter of the park, her mind in a turmoil.

Don't think, she told herself, just walk, walk and calm down. Nothing has changed, nothing. You are still engaged to Robert, you've done the right thing. Yes, the right thing. The only thing. Don't think, and above all don't remember his eyes.

After an hour or so, her tightly-stretched nerves began to relax, her breathing to become regular again, her thoughts to cease darting about like swarming, panic-stricken bees whose hive has been overturned. And still she walked, until the shadows grew long, the sultry air cooled and the park was filled with hurrying figures bound for home.

When she re-entered the house she saw, through the diningroom door, that her aunt – already dressed for dinner – was arranging yellow roses in a cut-glass vase. "There you are at last. I was beginning to get worried."

She forced a smile. "Sorry, Aunt Kitty. It was such a lovely afternoon I walked further than I meant to. I didn't realise it was so late."

"You really don't look well," her aunt's sharp eyes were searching her face. "This afternoon you were so flushed, now you're quite pale. Do you think you ought to be going out this evening?"

"I'm fine, truly," interposed Clarissa, "but exceedingly late. Robert will be here in a minute."

Kitty went back to her flowers. She was perfectly fine until that young man this afternoon, she mused, a frown creasing her forehead. So good-looking, handsomer than Robert. I wonder whether he knows Mr Grant is here. She clipped the stem of a yellow rose and sniffed its fragrance thoughtfully. There was something about the way he had looked at her niece that reminded her of..... She shook her head and put the rose into the vase. The sooner Clarissa and Robert were married, the happier she would be.

As Clarissa dressed, and combed her hair into a coil behind her head – a style Robert particularly liked – she studied her face in the mirror. Kitty was right, she was much paler than usual, and she concealed the deficit with a little rouge. When Robert rang the bell half an hour later, to be admitted by the maid, he was in unusually good spirits. His business was thriving and he was looking forward to the evening. His spirits lifted even further, a few minutes later, when his fiancée tripped down the stairs in a pale green confection that accentuated the gold glints in her hair. A gauzy wrap lay around her shoulders and she smiled brilliantly into his eyes.

Taking her hands, he kissed them one after the other. "I love your hair like that. You look beautiful."

"Do I?" she said quickly. "I was hopelessly late – went walking in the park and forgot the time."

Outside, a hansom cab was waiting, and she was seized by an overwhelming urge to avoid sitting close to him in the intimacy of its interior. "Robert, let's walk – it's not far, and such a beautiful evening."

He agreed good-humouredly, dismissed the cab, and she took his arm, chattering about whatever came to mind: her plans for decorating the sittingroom, gossip about Kitty's expected dinner guests. He listened absently, content to be walking through the twilit streets of London on this warm and mellow evening, with a full moon rising and his love beside him. But as he looked down at her animated, uplifted face, he felt a small, inexplicable flicker of unease.

"Kitty was right – she said you were looking pale, my love. Have you been overdoing things?"

"Probably," she responded quickly. What else had Kitty said? Surely Robert wouldn't be looking so happy if she had mentioned Simon's visit. From scraps of information he had let slip in the past, she suspected he knew something had happened between them in Africa. "I'm perfectly fine – just a little tired."

"Then why on earth did you suggest walking to the Temletts? It's the last thing you should be doing, sweetheart."

"I thought the fresh air would do me good," she said hastily, "and it is. Tell me about your week."

The evening passed in a dreamlike blur. James Temlett and his plump, vivacious wife Francesca were Robert's closest friends. He and James had been to school together, and Clarissa knew he dearly wanted them to form a good impression of his fiancée. She hoped she was behaving well, but she was not sure because she felt as though only a part of her was present at the diningroom table. She knew she was talking too much, as she had been doing during the walk, and she caught Robert looking at her oddly from time to time, but she prattled on, drawing on the most amusing anecdotes in her repertoire of stories about her life in Africa and her meeting with him.

She tried so hard to be charming that by the time Francesca led her through to the sittingroom after dinner, leaving the two men to their port, she had a throbbing headache. "That was a beautiful dinner, Francesca," she said as she sank thankfully into an armchair, easing the taut muscles in her neck.

"Call me Fanny, everyone does." She had a wide, engaging smile, and Clarissa had been instantly drawn to both her and her amiable, bespectacled husband. "James and I have been so looking forward to meeting you," Francesca confided as she poured coffee. "When Robert told us he was engaged, we couldn't believe it. I can tell you now that we were both quite anxious. You know how it is, people you are fond of don't always marry the person you would have chosen for them. But," she handed her a cup, "we needn't have worried. I know we're going to be good friends."

Clarissa smiled gratefully. "I hope so. Robert has talked so much about you that I was a little nervous myself. That's probably why I talked too much at dinner," she added apologetically.

"But I loved your stories. All those adventures, and to think you met him there. Just to know he has found someone like you – well, it's set my heart at rest." Her face became serious. "You may not know it but he was badly hurt a few years ago, which makes me even happier now that we have met you."

But you shouldn't be happy, Clarissa was crying inwardly. You should be warning him that he is making an awful mistake, that he's engaged to someone who is not at all confident she can be a good wife to him. Outwardly composed, she answered, "No, I didn't know," and changed the subject, asking Fanny about her family. When the men joined them, they were discussing plans for the wedding, and before they left, a date for dinner and the theatre had been arranged.

In the cab, Robert took her hand and kissed it, and she kept her face in the shadows so that he could not see her eyes.

"Do you like them? They loved you," he murmured, leaning towards her in the dark.

"Yes, Robert, I do. Fanny is fun and James has a lovely sense of humour. I can see why you're so fond of them," She tried to smile.

"What is it?" He put his hand against her cheek, and she struggled to hold back the tears that threatened to flow at his gesture of tenderness.

"Nothing, a headache. Must have been the sun – I probably walked for too long."

"You're overdoing things. You've been tearing around with wedding arrangements and decorating the house. Never mind, when you go down to Nicholas next week, you can lie around all day and do nothing. Here we are."

He escorted her up the steps, and she was glad of the darkness as he drew her to him, and kissed her. She touched his cheek with a gloved hand: "You're so good, Robert. I don't deserve you."

"Stop talking rubbish," he said with a pleased grin. "Goodnight, sweetheart."

The following Monday, as she travelled down to Hampshire with her mother and Kitty, she felt a grateful sense of escape. Simply to leave London and the muddle of her life was a relief – away from associations with Simon, away from Robert, away from the whole disastrous mess, to the cosy security of Nicholas's seventeenth century farmhouse with its crooked staircase and sloping ceilings, and the calm, easygoing presence of her favourite brother.

She tried to thrust Simon to the back of her mind and focus on the present: riding with Felicity, walking the dogs, feeding the ducks that waddled expectantly to the kitchen door every afternoon. Her tangled emotions were soothed by the gentle contours of the smiling green countryside, where the warm autumn sunlight faded into soft lingering twilights, so much kinder than that other landscape, where a brazen sun flamed into swift, dramatic splendour at the end of the day.

She had not seen her brother since the announcement of her engagement, and when they went walking together on her second afternoon, he made a point of expressing his satisfaction. "Rob's a damn fine chap, Lissa, you couldn't have made a better choice."

"Do you think so?" she asked wistfully – she felt she needed all the reinforcement she could get to bolster her decision.

"Absolutely. I was afraid there for a while that you'd do something feather-brained like turning him down and going back to Africa."

"What made you think that?"

"Well, it took you long enough to make up your mind. There had to be a reason and I did wonder if there was someone else. I can tell you now that Rob consulted me about you once. Asked for advice from one who knew you well," he added with a grin.

"Oh. And what did you tell him, pray?" she asked as she gathered up her skirt to climb over a stile.

"Told him to stick to it, wear you down," he grinned. "Said you were the stubborn one in the family."

At the bottom of the meadow, a line of ancient willows fringed a stream. The dogs bounded into the water, and Clarissa and Nicholas sat down on the bank and tossed sticks for them. She had always been close to her brother, and was accustomed to confiding in him. Now she told him candidly: "One of the reasons I waited so long was because my feelings were not as strong as his. I wondered, and I still wonder, even now, whether that's fair on Robert."

"Not having second thoughts, are you?" He glanced at her sharply.

"No, of course not. It just seems a little one-sided, that's all. Lovely for me, not so lovely for him."

"Robert seems quite content with the arrangement. And who's to say your feelings won't grow stronger with time? It happens."

"Yes," she tossed another stick into the bubbling stream and four dogs pounced, showering them with droplets of water, "perhaps you're right."

By midweek, she was regaining her equilibrium, and when Robert came down on Friday evening, she was able to give a creditable impression of a woman in love. They spent a convivial two days playing cards when it rained, walking and fishing when it was clear, and only one incident marred the tranquil tenor of the weekend. During dinner on Saturday night, Kitty casually mentioned Simon Grant's visit.

"Who's Simon Grant?" asked her mother, and Clarissa glanced instinctively at Robert. His eyes were immediately alert, but he looked her way only once as he listened to her aunt's prattle. He asked no questions, and the moment passed, but later, when they were alone together, putting away the cards, he said quite casually, "You didn't tell me Simon Grant was in London?"

"It must have slipped my mind," she answered equally casually, "it was such a short visit – he only stayed half an hour. Besides, you didn't really know him, did you?"

"Well enough to be interested in his news."

She told him briefly about the expedition and the farm, and he said no more, but his eyes, when he kissed her goodnight, were sombre, and the old pangs of guilt and remorse surfaced again.

When she returned to London with Kitty the following week, a small parcel was waiting for her on the hall table. Kitty was agog with curiosity, but Clarissa, with some instinctive premonition, slipped away upstairs to open it. Inside was the fish eagle, and a note in a strong, slanting hand:

Please accept my apologies for the other day, she read. *I'm sorry I upset you, but I hope you will understand that I was not prepared for the news your aunt gave me, and not thinking rationally.*

I want you to know that, although my feelings will never change, I wish you and Robert all the happiness in the world.

Please accept the eagle back. It's yours now, and besides, it would always remind me of you. Yours ever, Simon.

"Damn you," she whispered. "Why won't you get out of my life and leave me in peace?"

Some days were better than others. On the night of the theatre date with James and Francesca, she relaxed in their congenial company and it was a good evening. James was at his entertaining best, the play was a sparkling comedy, and they were still laughing over it when they returned to the Temlett's for coffee. As they sat around the dying fire in the sittingroom, Clarissa watched Robert smiling and joking with James, and wished it could always be like this. We are so well suited in so many ways, she thought. Please, God, make me love him as much as he deserves.

She ordered new curtains for the house, and Kitty accompanied her for a fitting of her wedding dress – a simple, slim, high-necked gown in ivory silk. As Clarissa stood motionless on a little stool, waiting patiently while the dressmaker made last minute adjustments to the hemline, Kitty gazed fondly and somewhat sentimentally at the romantic image presented by her niece. She was admiring the way the skirt swept back into a graceful train when she looked up, caught an unguarded expression on Clarissa's face, and was struck by a sudden shocking revelation. Why, she doesn't look like a bride trying on her wedding gown, she looks as if she's being fitted for a shroud.

She pursed her lips on the shattering thought, and said nothing until after dinner. "Is everything all right with you and Robert, dear?" she asked. "Forgive me for prying, but I can't help noticing that you are not the same high-spirited person you were a month ago."

Clarissa was caught completely off guard. "Yes, of course everything's all right," she said quickly, but her aunt shook her head.

"I don't think so. I know you too well. What I want to know is: is it just the normal doubts that brides and grooms get before the big day or," and she looked keenly at her niece, "has it got anything to do with that Mr Grant who visited last month?"

"Simon? Of course not. Why should he...?" She stopped, for her aunt's gentle tones had pierced her armour, and the emotions she had fought to suppress so fiercely overflowed in a torrent of tears and words. Kitty let her cry, stroking her hair, murmuring soothing platitudes.

As the truth tumbled out, Clarissa realised that her aunt was the first person to hear the whole story. The relief at unburdening her soul was immediate and profound. "Tell me I'm doing the right thing," she pleaded. "Tell me it's right to marry Robert, even though I love Simon much, much more."

"What a tangled web," sighed Kitty. "Dear girl, I know your mother would say 'Yes'. I know he would make a fine husband – a fine husband," she repeated. "But I understand how hard this is for you."

"You see, I think he suspects something is not right."

"He'd be pretty obtuse if he didn't. I imagine he's gambling that if he sees this through, and you get married, everything will be all right. Robert's not a fool. He's sitting it out until you get this man out of your system."

"But isn't it unfair to marry him when I can't love him as much as Simon?"

"Not necessarily. There are few marriages in which both people love equally. Remember the old French saying: there is always one who loves, and one who turns the cheek?"

"And I am the one who turns the cheek." She blew her nose. "How was it for you, Aunt Kitty?"

Kitty sighed. "At the beginning, not so very different from you – perhaps that's why I was suspicious when I saw you together. There was someone. Quite unsuitable, so my parents took me off to Europe for a few months to forget him, and then married me off to Harold on my return. And I grew to love him in time, and we had a good marriage for twenty-nine years before he died. "But," she smiled crookedly, and for the first time Clarissa saw, behind the faded hair, the double chins and sagging contours, a hint of the young girl Kitty had once been, "in my secret heart, I always wondered what it would have been like with Max." She came back from a distance and said briskly, "Appalling, most probably. He had no money, few prospects, but abundant charm."

"So – I should go ahead with it?"

"Certainly not if it is going to make you unhappy. No one would want that, least of all Robert. Tell me, Clarissa, Simon Grant – I saw so little of him – would he make you a good husband?"

"I don't know. Why does everyone talk about 'a good husband'? I only know I love him, I love to be with him, I would go to the end of the earth with him."

"Including back to Africa, which you know would be bad for your health?"

"Especially back to Africa. That's something else I've been fighting all these months. I love it almost as much as I love him, they're mixed up together. They're both exciting and... and exhilarating..."

"And Robert is supposed to compete with that," murmured Kitty, shaking her head. "Look, dear, perhaps you should postpone the wedding. Give yourself a bit more time."

Clarissa stared at her. "I couldn't do that to Robert. I've kept him waiting so long. I must either go ahead or break it off now."

"Well then, Clarissa, my considered advice is to forget Simon Grant. That way disaster lies, I feel it in my bones."

Clarissa laid her head on her aunt's shoulder, too tired to think any more. "Maybe I should forget them both and go off and be a missionary somewhere."

"Not in Africa, you won't," said Kitty sharply, and they both laughed.

But opening her heart had brought relief, and she woke in the morning with a renewed determination. Once Simon's departure date had come and gone, she would be all right. Then there would be no turning back.

The fifteenth of September, the day of his departure, was bleak and blustery, and she passed through it in a daze, filling every moment with frenzied activity. She went shopping, met friends for lunch, cleared years of accumulated rubbish out of Kitty's attic and, in the evening, dragged her aunt to the theatre where she sat for two hours staring at the stage, never absorbing a moment of the plot unfolding behind the footlights. And next morning, she woke feeling an almost comforting sense of fatalism. He was gone.

A few days later, she was attracted by an advertisement for an exhibition of the works of the late, well-known traveller and artist, Thomas Baines, who had journeyed through Africa recording his impressions. She was not sure why she wanted to go – perhaps it was not a good idea, like rubbing salt in a wound, but she wanted to keep one last link with Africa. Robert agreed to take her, somewhat reluctantly. Not because he was not interested (he had himself begun collecting art in a modest way), but because he knew that anything that smacked of the African continent tended to unsettle her, and she was tense enough already. But she sounded enthusiastic, a quality that had been lacking in her voice recently.

The Bond Street gallery was crowded – Africa was very much in vogue, and although Baines had died some years ago, his name and exploits were still remembered with respect. She was glad she had come, and captivated by the skill with which the artist had captured not only the colour and atmosphere of the bush, but the minute details of safari life.

Robert was drawn back time and again to a small watercolour of a wagon stuck in a drift, surrounded by goods unpacked to lighten the load. A group of white and black men were urging the straining oxen up the muddy bank, and for Robert the picture revived vivid memories of his own experiences travelling from the Cape. After looking at the rest of the collection, he drew Clarissa back to it. "What do you think?"

"I love it. You can almost hear the wheels creaking and feel the oxen straining. But it's awfully expensive."

"I know, but it would be an investment. Baines is very well known."

"It would go beautifully in the diningroom." Clarissa was trying to look at the work objectively, thinking of the old gold and autumnal colours she had chosen.

"You're right. Let's go and get it before someone else does."

They threaded their way through the throng to the desk in the far corner, and as they did so, a knot of people parted to reveal Simon Grant, deep in conversation with a man who looked like a gallery official.

Clarissa stopped abruptly, suppressing a gasp, and Robert followed the direction of her eyes.

"I'll just wait here and have another look, Robert. You go ...." As she stammered the words, Simon glanced up and saw them. He stiffened, and she looked desperately around for a means of escape, but they were hemmed in by the crowd, and Robert's hand on her arm was suddenly like steel as he drew her forward.

Simon recovered first. "Clar – Miss Hamilton – Hammond," he advanced slowly. Hardly knowing what she was doing, Clarissa opened her mouth, words came out. Simon turned to Robert, whose face was strained but composed, and now they were saying polite nothings to one another, talking about the paintings, how well the animals had been captured – buffalo, sable, elephant. Robert asked Simon about the mine, Simon inquired about Robert's business, and she stood mute and frozen beside them.

But, when eventually there was an awkward pause, she was unable to prevent herself from blurting out, "I thought you had gone."

He looked at her directly then, his eyes hard as stones. "I should have, but family business delayed me – some papers that weren't ready for signing. It's done now and I'm off tonight." Silence spread, and he turned quickly to Robert, "Are you thinking of buying anything?"

"Yes – a small watercolour. What about you?"

"I was just arranging for a painting to be sent on after me. That's the fellow to talk to. Come, I'll introduce you." He led them to an official and tapped him on the shoulder. Introductions completed, he said abruptly, without looking at Clarissa, "Well, I'll leave you to it. Good to see you both again."

He turned and walked swiftly through the crowd towards the door. Robert was talking to the official and she stood stiffly at his side, barely hearing what they were saying. She had to get out, it was hot and airless, she had to get away from the throng that seemed to be pressing in on her from every direction. She walked to the nearest painting and stared at it, but it made her feel worse – for it featured a hunting scene: a hunter with a rifle at his shoulder, an enraged elephant with trunk held aloft and ears fanned wide.

Then Robert was at her side, his face set in unfamiliar, hard lines.

"Did you buy it?" she asked in a voice she hardly recognised.

"I told him we would think about it and come back next week," he said tightly, "come, let's get out of here."

Taking her elbow, he steered her to the door and hailed a passing cab. All the way back to Kitty's, he sat in silence, staring out of the window, but as they mounted the steps together he said abruptly – in the same tight voice, "I'd like to come in and talk."

"Of course," she answered miserably.

They went into the sittingroom and he closed the door. Clarissa took off her hat, jacket and gloves, dropped them on the nearest chair. Her heart was thudding and she felt sick and dizzy. Robert ran his fingers through his hair, and strode to the window where he stared into the street for what seemed like an age. Then he turned and his face was very pale.

"Clarissa, we can't go on like this. I've known there was something wrong for several weeks, and today has confirmed it. There was once something between you and Grant, wasn't there?"

She hesitated. "Yes," she whispered, "but it was..."

Robert interrupted her. "Did he come back to ask you to marry him?"

"Yes," she repeated in the same whisper.

"Do you love him?"

Her hands flew to her mouth as though to stop the words from escaping.

"Do you?" he insisted.

She looked at him pleadingly. "Yes, but...."

His shoulders slumped. "But you were prepared to marry me in spite of it. In the name of God – why?"

"Because I thought it was all over between Simon and me. Because I had learned to love you too – I do, Robert, and then, when he came back, I couldn't bear the thought of hurting you. You had waited so long, been so good. Everything," she spread her hands helplessly, "everything seemed right for us."

"Even after he came back?" His voice had a harshness she had never heard before.

"Even then. Nothing happened between us. I told him to go away, that I didn't want to marry him. That I loved you."

"But you were lying."

"No – I wasn't. I do love you – in a different way." She realised it was true. "I sent him away. I didn't see him again, I never intended to see him again and he didn't try to see me. I thought that once he had gone things would be all right again, like they were before. He was supposed to have gone. He should have been gone..." Her voice tailed off into a scraping whisper.

He looked at her with anguish in his eyes, and she felt a wave of remorse, of anger at herself for hurting him, at Simon for not having gone, for spoiling everything all over again. She went to him and put her hand on his arm and said imploringly: "Robert, I'm so sorry. But he is going tonight. Maybe if we postponed the wedding, so that I could have more time...."

"No," he put her hand away. "I don't want us to get married on those terms – because you've made a promise and feel sorry for me. I love you, Clarissa, but I don't want you marrying me as a consolation prize. That's not good enough."

"If only we hadn't gone to that gallery today," she said in despair.

"It was going to happen anyway," his voice was flat. "It just would have taken longer. It's better this way."

She dashed a tear away, and he immediately came and took her hands. "Don't cry. It's not your fault. I can see you did what you thought was right. I don't want you to be unhappy, you know that all I ever wanted was your happiness. I just thought you could find it with me."

"I know. I thought so too." They stood in silence, and then he released her hands, walked back to the window and stared unseeingly into the street again. When he turned, his face was set.

"Clarissa, whatever you do, think carefully, don't rush into anything. If you and Simon.... You would go back to Africa with him?"

"Yes," she wiped her wet cheek with the back of her hand, and he took out a handkerchief and handed it to her.

"You shouldn't go back – you know what the doctor said."

"I have to," she said softly, "I want to, if he still wants me."

"Believe me, he still wants you," he said grimly. "Then promise me one thing."

"Yes?"

"Promise me that if ever things go wrong, if ever you need help, you'll send for me. Promise me that."

"I promise. Oh, Robert," her voice scraped exhaustedly, "I wish so much this didn't have to happen."

He smiled grimly and watched as she slipped the diamond and sapphire ring off her finger and handed it to him. He dropped it into his pocket without glancing at it, walked to the window again, came back and stood before her, touching her cheek gently with his hand. "Friends?"

She nodded. "How can you be so nice?"

"I'm good at being nice," his voice was bitter. "You won't forget?"

"No. Robert, you'll meet someone else – someone who will make you a much better wife than I would."

He smiled briefly, painfully. "No doubt I will." His eyes glittered, and he took her hand and kissed it very lightly. He looked around blindly for his hat, picked it up quickly and went to the door. With his hand on the knob, he turned, as though he wanted to say something else. He shook his head and went out of the room.

Moments later she heard his steps outside and she stood by the window, holding on to the russet velvet curtains, watching him walk slowly down the street and around the corner.

After a while, the door opened and Kitty's apprehensive face appeared. She took one look at Clarissa's expression and came into the room. "What is it? What's happened? Was that Robert just leaving?" She looked intently into her niece's face. "Oh, my saints, what have you done? You haven't broken off..." her voice tailed away.

Clarissa nodded wordlessly.

"Oh, heavens." Kitty fluttered across the room and sat down on the window seat, taking Clarissa's shoulders in her hands. "You've broken it off?" Her eyes flew to the ringless finger. "Oh God, I was afraid of this. Why now? Simon Grant has gone."

There was a note of hysteria in Clarissa's laughter. "No, he hasn't." And she related the events of the morning, her words tumbling over one another in agitation. Remorse and guilt were still her dominant emotions, but now there was something else as well: deep in the core of her, beneath all the turbulence, a small singing spark was stirring.

"Oh, my saints," repeated Kitty, "that poor man." But her initial horror was rapidly subsiding, to be replaced by a mixture of apprehension and excitement. "What are you going to do? Does Simon know? When does he leave?"

"Tonight, he leaves tonight. Aunt Kitty, what shall I do?" She stared at her aunt. "A message – I must get a message to his club."

She flew to the writing desk, seized some paper and a pen and began to write, then stopped, crumpled the sheet and flung it into the wastepaper basket. "No, I must go myself."

"Do you know where he's staying?"

"Yes, he gave me the address," and she picked up her jacket and gloves and whirled to the door.

"Clarissa, wait!" Kitty wrung her hands. "When will you back?"

"As soon as I speak to him. I must hurry. What if he's left?"

"What will your mother say?"

"Mother!" Clarissa stopped in the doorway, aghast. "When does she arrive?"

"I think – about three this afternoon."

"About three," Clarissa muttered distractedly. "I'll be back as soon as I can."

But when she entered the dimly-lit, panelled lobby of the club in the Strand, the elderly, grey-haired man at the desk informed her, quite sniffily, that Mr Grant had already left.

"Do you know what his plans were? Where he was going?"

"I believe the gentleman was returning to Africa, madam." His voice was faintly supercilious.

"Yes, I know that. I mean, where he was going this morning?"

"I'm afraid I couldn't say, madam."

"It's just that....," she could feel his eyes taking in her hatless, dishevelled appearance. "You see, I'm his cousin, and I was supposed to meet him this morning to say goodbye, but I was late and I missed him, and I must get hold of him before he leaves. I must."

He unbent ever so slightly, said, "One moment, madam," and retired into an office. Looking past him, she caught sight of a cabin trunk and suitcases.

He returned with a sheet of paper. "All I can tell you, madam, is that Mr Grant asked us to deliver his luggage to Waterloo Station by five-thirty this evening."

She repeated the information breathlessly, then leaned impulsively across the counter and squeezed his wrinkled hand. "Thank you."

"Now I must pack," she told Kitty on her return, "oh, and write a letter to Nicholas," and she flew up the stairs, Kitty behind her. Opening drawers and cupboards, she threw clothes on to the bed. "Please let him not leave without me," she repeated over and over again, like a mantra. "Aunt Kitty, what if he's changed his mind? What if he doesn't want me?"

"Changed his mind, girl? He came halfway around the world to find you. Why should he change his mind?"

"I don't know. Because of the way I treated him." Kitty took her firmly by the arms and sat her down on the bed.

"Clarissa, if you don't calm down, you'll be in no fit state to go anywhere, never mind meet your sweetheart. I'll help you pack. There can't be too much, most of your clothes are still at Elderbrook. We can send them on to you. When we have finished up here, you're going to sit down and have something to eat." She dabbed her eyes. "Oh, I don't know if I should be helping you to do this – this will probably be the last time we'll have together till I don't know when."

Clarissa hugged her. "Don't. I can't bear to think about it. My mind is so mixed up. And I still have mother to face."

But Anne Hamilton, who was travelling down from Elderbrook with the wedding invitations, did not arrive at the expected time of three o'clock, or at four. Dressed in travelling clothes, Clarissa paced the floor, and Kitty flitted restlessly about the house, wringing her hands. She was rapidly losing her nerve.

"Perhaps you shouldn't try to meet him today," she pleaded. "Wait till he gets there and send him a letter, then everything can be arranged properly. We can all be at the wedding. Maybe you're right and he's changed his mind."

"If he has, I'll know as soon as I see him," said Clarissa, staring out of the window and up the street. "How could you even think I could wait? Oh, Mother, where are you?"

Another half hour dragged before they heard the sound of horses' hooves. Clarissa flew to the window. "Thank God," she gasped.

Although Anne Hamilton had always prided herself on rising to the demands of any occasion, she was caught hopelessly off balance. She knew, as she listened to her daughter's words and watched her face, that this was no time for tears and hysterics. But to see her hopes for Clarissa to be settled in England with a fine, steady husband – to see those so-nearly-realised dreams shattered in a moment, was almost too much for her iron self-control.

But even as she pleaded with her daughter to delay her departure, she knew instinctively that she might as well have saved her breath. And so she gathered herself together. "I always had the uneasy feeling that your heart was not in it," she confessed, "but that isn't so unusual, and I had every hope you would grow to love him. And I was always terrified you had not got Africa out of your system. And oh," she clung to Clarissa, "I'll miss you so much. Will you promise to be careful, and not let yourself get sick again? Will I ever see you again?"

"Mother, of course you will." Clarissa hugged her.

"The cab's outside," sobbed Kitty.

And then she was out on the steps, kissing and hugging them both again, feeling the softness of her mother's cheek, and Kitty's vast, scented embrace.

"Waterloo Station – hurry, please," she directed the cabman as she waved through the window to the two women standing with their arms about one another on the pavement. And then the cab turned the corner and they were out of sight. It was getting dark and beginning to rain, and she slumped back in the seat, trying to breathe deeply and slowly. But it was impossible to relax, the cab was moving so slowly, they would never get there in time, and she sat forward on the edge of the seat, and called, "Could you possibly go faster, please. I have a train to catch."

"This is as fast as the old girl goes, missus."

She twisted her gloves, stared out of the window at the wet streets, her thoughts racing in a tangle of hope, dread, fear, anticipation. She pressed her hands to her temples and forced herself to sit back against the upholstery. Suppose she had the wrong time, suppose he was already gone – how would she find him? Don't think about that. Take one step at a time. You'll make a plan.

At the station, a chaotic mêlée of cabs, carriages and passengers milled around in the sheeting rain. The cabman had trouble finding a place to stop, and there was another delay when he went in search of a porter. After an eternity, he was back followed by an old man with a trolley. Clarissa stepped down from the cab and stood in the rain while the driver, with painful slowness, took down her bags.

"Hurry, please hurry," she pleaded as she pulled out a valise and dumped it on the trolley. Swiftly she paid him, and whirled towards the entrance, calling to the bemused porter, "The boat train – which platform?"

"Platform four," he replied, but she was already pushing her way through the crowds.

He was an old man. He suffered from painful twinges of rheumatism in his back, and he had seen a thousand trains come and go, and an even greater number of passengers who arrived too late. He wasn't going to get fussed about one more, even if she was young and good-looking.

Trundling the trolley slowly in her wake, he muttered irritably, but kept an eye on her as she bought a ticket and wove through the throng of people. She was wearing a long dark green cloak, the hood of which had fallen back, revealing a bright halo of hair that made her easy to distinguish in the drab crowd.

By this time most of the passengers were saying their farewells and dragging suitcases on board. The massive engine was hissing quietly, and there was a good deal of laughter and tearful embracing. It was always like that with the boat train.

As the young woman pushed her way swiftly through the throng, she was scanning the crowd, looking for someone. She stopped several times to peer into compartment windows, and now she was clasping her gloved hands in agitation, talking to a conductor, who slowly and painstakingly consulted his list. Finally, he pointed to the far end of the platform.

The porter had almost caught up with her, but now she was off again and he lost sight of her completely as he patiently negotiated the moving mass of people and luggage. Only another half hour, he thought, and the old girl has fish and chips for supper. Wicked night it was set to be – maybe stop in at the pub.

Now where had she got to? He paused and looked around, grumbling under his breath. And then he spotted the bright halo of hair. She had stopped dead in her tracks and was staring at someone further down the line. She started forward again, calling in a shaky sort of voice, and then he noticed, standing beside an open carriage door, a tall figure in a dark coat – with two bags on the ground beside him – in the act of tipping a porter.

The man – he looked like one of them tea planters he had seen arriving from India on leave – glanced up, saw the lady, and sort of froze. He stared at her, she stood looking at him, and the old man paused again, glad of the respite, and leaned on his trolley.

Her heart was thudding so hard she could hardly breathe, and Simon was saying stupidly, "What is it? What's wrong? Why are you here?"

And she was saying, halfway between a laugh and a sob, "Nothing's wrong, Simon. Why do you think I'm here? I'm here because... if you want me..." she hesitated.

"If I want ..." A light was growing in his eyes, but he seemed rooted to the ground.

"If you still want me to fly away to Africa with you," she said softly.

And then he moved and she moved and he caught her up in his arms, and the bubbling well of happiness within her surged into glorious, exultant life, filled her body and mind, and overflowed. He was holding her tight, so tight, lifting her, twirling her round and round in his arms, and they were laughing, and kissing each other.

A whistle blew sharply and he released her, picked up his bags and flung them on to the carriage steps. He lifted her into the carriage doorway and started to climb in behind her.

The old porter called, "Hey, guv, what about these, then?" And the young lady leaned out, still laughing but with tears on her cheeks, and shouted, "My bags!" And the man seized them and lifted them on board, thrust a handful of coins at the porter and leapt on to the step as steam filled the vast vault of the station, and the train jerked and began to move slowly forward.

The lady leaned out again and waved at the porter and shouted, "We're going to Africa." And her face was as bright and glowing as the halo of hair that was fast unravelling from the neat coil in which it had been enclosed.

As the carriage passed him, moving very slowly, they were still standing in the doorway, holding hands, quite still, very close together, laughing.

The crowd waved and shouted, and the train gathered speed and chugged out of the lighted station away from the waving figures and into the rain and the dark.

The porter scratched his head and glanced at his mate, who grimaced in the direction of the departing train. "Love's young dream, eh? Cutting it fine, as per."

He nodded, counting out the coins the man had given him. "You off then? Fancy a pint?"

"Why not? Bloody awful night."

Side by side they trundled the trolleys slowly back up the platform. A long whistle echoed from the distance, and the sound of the engine faded into the night.

PART TWO

1957

13

Liz Pendennis opened her eyes to sunlight shafting through the curtains, and lay for a moment staring at the ceiling, confused and disoriented. Then her fingers touched the diary, which still lay face down on the blanket where she had dropped it shortly before dawn. And she remembered.

The room was warm, and she leaned over to look at her travelling clock. It was almost midday.

She found her uncle in the sittingroom on the phone, ordering spare parts for a tractor. It was an ancient wall telephone with a handle on the side.

"You had a good sleep," he said when he had finished, "I looked in a couple of times but you were dead to the world."

"It was the diary," she came over and kissed his cheek. "I couldn't put it down – read till half past four. Have I messed up your morning?"

"Not a bit. I'd offer you breakfast, but it's almost lunchtime. How about a cup of tea? We'll have it outside." He called to Samuel, the cook.

From the sittingroom, French windows opened on to a wide stoep running the length of the house and bordered by a low stone wall. Crimson bougainvillea tumbled from the thatched roof, and steps led down to a lawn surrounded by a border of shrubs and flowers. A sprinkler played on the grass, blue waxbills fluttered about a stone bird bath, and a gardener in navy overalls tinkered with an old lawn mower. Beyond the garden, the land sloped down to the dam they had passed the previous evening.

"So you read the whole diary?" he asked, pulling up a chair.

"Yes. It's a pity there are so many gaps, but as you said, research could fill in some of them."

"I might be able to help. I still have a few old letters of hers."

"She didn't write much after she went back to England," said Liz, her eyes following the fluttering of tiny bronze mannikins cooling off under the sprinkler. "Didn't she keep any more diaries when she came back here?"

"Not that I know of."

"It brought her so alive. Mum has told me the story, of course – many times – but it always seemed sort of remote, romantic make-believe. They never seemed real until now."

"They were real all right," Nicholas said dryly.

"I wish I could have met her," she said wistfully. "Were you and she close?"

"Yes, we were," his expression was reflective. "Before I went away to school we did everything together. And after we grew up, she would come for visits and we'd go shooting and fishing."

"Did you meet Simon?"

"Only once, when he came back to England on business." Samuel arrived with a tea tray and set it down on the table beside her. She poured, and handed Nicholas a cup.

"What did you think of him?" She was hungry to know everything he could tell her about Clarissa's life. She was like me, she thought, she came to Africa to get away from England and find a new direction. She loved adventure and travel.

"Simon? The type women fall for – good-looking, articulate, bit of an adventurer, bit of a visionary. Restless, selfish, everything Hammond wasn't."

"You knew Robert too?"

"Yes, liked him. Solid, thoroughly decent chap. Strong-minded, reliable – boring, Clarissa would say."

"Do you think she should have married him?"

He looked at her quizzically. "What a question. I expect so, she would have had an ordinary life and probably lived to be eighty. But then, Clarissa was never destined for an ordinary life."

"Look, it's a damn nuisance but I'm going to have to go back to town tomorrow – something's come up. Do you want to stay here, or come with me and have a look around?"

She thought for a moment. "I'd better come and put out a few feelers for a job. Could you point me in the direction of whatever newspapers and magazines are published here?"

"I can do better than that – I'll give you a few contacts. We'll stay over for the night, go to the races on Saturday and come back in the evening. I've just bought shares in a horse," he explained with a grin, "so we must have a bit of a flutter."

Salisbury was not a big city. Armed with a list of names and addresses from Nicholas, and using Meikles Hotel as her reference point, she found it easy to get around on foot. She visited the editor of the national daily paper, a couple of magazine publishers and several personnel agencies. By five o'clock, buoyed by the generally encouraging reception, she walked back to the hotel past the flower-sellers on Cecil Square, and found Nicholas having a beer in the high-ceilinged lounge with two couples from neighbouring farms.

After they had left he suggested going out for dinner, and as they left the hotel someone called her name. It was Mario Pallivera, the young Italian engineer she had met on the plane from England. He broke away from the group he was with, and came over. Seizing her hands, he kissed her on both cheeks and greeted Nicholas.

"Mario! I thought you'd be up at Kariba by now, starting work," she said.

"I come to town for a meeting, fly back again tomorrow morning. I have been trying to telephone you," he added reproachfully.

"How is it at Kariba?"

"It is fantastic, Lizi, you must come and see. Already I have seen elephants – and buffalo, and hippo...."

His companions were moving on, and he said quickly, "Next time I come, I ring you...... Take care, Lizi."

Nicholas took her to a small restaurant near the hotel, in Manica Road – one of the oldest streets in the city, he told her. The upper end was flanked by offices, department stores and banks, the older section by small shops, owned by Indians and Greeks, dispensing everything from bicycles and haberdashery to spices. It was a shabby, cosmopolitan area, livelier than the sedate pavements around First Street which she had walked during the day, and where most whites shopped and ran their businesses.

"If you don't mind a recommendation," said Nicholas as she scanned the menu, "the peri-peri chicken is excellent. It's Portuguese, but almost a national dish here. I'll have the same. What about avocado prawns to start with?"

While they ate, Nicholas talked about the farm and his life in Africa. Although arthritis had stiffened his joints, and his angular form was regularly racked by a cough that seemed to do nothing to discourage his chain smoking, he had not lost the irrepressible zest for life she remembered from his visits to England.

He must be over eighty. What must it be like to be that old, she wondered. He had lived in the reign of Victoria, been a young man during the Boer War, and his life had encompassed two world wars. What riches must be locked in his memories.

"I've met so many grouchy old men who seem to have stopped living – it's just their creaking bodies that go on," she wrote later to a friend. "Uncle Nicky is still young inside, and when you're with him, the thought of getting old seems less frightening."

Her mind went off at a tangent: "It was strange, wasn't it, that my mother never really liked Africa?"

"Yes. She came out twice, and enjoyed herself well enough, went dancing with some of the young bucks, but was always glad to go back home. I suppose you can hardly blame her. This country took her own mother and her father. Although she never knew them – we were her parents to all intents and purposes – it must have had some effect. She was always very level-headed about it."

"She said Clarissa's grave was never found."

"That's right. I had a look for it myself...." He stopped. Raised voices near the restaurant door had brought a sudden lull in the hum of conversation.

Two Africans were arguing with the manager, a swarthy, thick-set man. Although Liz was too far away to hear what was being said, it was obvious he was ordering them to leave – none too politely. They were standing their ground.

Both wore suits, and the younger one – tall, broad-shouldered and clean-shaven – raised his voice deliberately. "What about that table over there in the corner?"

"I told you, it's reserved," the voice of the manager was brusque and rude. The clatter of cutlery had almost ceased now; a number of diners had stopped eating, others bent their heads over their plates, embarrassed, pretending not to hear.

"We'll come back in a few minutes. I'm sure one of the tables will be free by then. Or perhaps we can wait," the second man – who sported a neat goatee, and was older and less aggressive – was saying politely.

"There would be no point. There will be no tables available."

"What you mean is you refuse to serve us," challenged his companion. As he spoke, Liz was aware of someone else – a white man in a dark blazer and light trousers – striding past her table towards the trio.

"You can see the notice," the manager was saying tersely. "The management reserves the right of admission."

"What's the problem, Johnny?" The white man clapped him on his shoulder and he stiffened. Complete silence had fallen in the restaurant.

"No problem, Chris," he said curtly.

"Good. This gentleman, Paul Masimba, is a mate of mine," and he indicated the tall African, who was now grinning broadly in recognition.

"If you've got a problem with space, Johnny," the man called Chris continued smoothly, "they can join our table." Paul Masimba looked challengingly at the manager.

"OK with you, Johnny?" pursued the white man, "just stick a couple more places at our table."

"Perfectly all right, Mr Rainier." The manager inclined his head stiffly and snapped his fingers at a black waiter who had been watching the exchange with an unfathomable expression.

"Thanks, Johnny." The speaker led the two men through the tables of silent, watching diners. As he passed their table, he noticed Nicholas and paused briefly. "Old Nick, how goes it?"

Nicholas grinned and inclined his head, his eyes following the trio to a table in the corner, occupied by a girl with long black hair, wearing a red dress.

The flow of conversation and clatter of cutlery resumed and Nicholas leaned towards Liz. "That's Chris Rainier – nephew of my neighbours. Bit of a stirrer, not usually renowned for pouring oil on troubled waters – in fact, it's generally the other way round. He's from the Cape, seems to be spending more and more time up here. We go fishing together."

"What was that about?" she asked in amazement. "Did the manager not want to let them in?"

"That's about the size of it," Nicholas returned to his chicken. "Most restaurants still serve only whites. There are a couple that are integrated – the ones businessmen patronise, but most stick to the old ways."

"So if you're black, you don't get served. Where do they go?"

"There are places in the townships. Until recently, dining out was not really a black man's thing – it's a western idea and this is a pretty conservative country. We're in Salisbury, my girl, not Soho. You have to understand that."

She shook her head in wonder. "I can't believe it. So why were they trying to get in if they knew they wouldn't be allowed?"

"Making a point. They don't accept the status quo the way they used to. They're getting organised, formed a couple of political parties, and there's a bit of a campaign under way. I recognise the other chap," he said thoughtfully, "not Chris' friend – the shorter one. He is the editor of a new magazine – what's it called now? Zimbabwe Sun...no, Zimbabwe Dawn. That's it."

The spicy chicken, served on a bed of white rice, lived up to its reputation, the sauce bringing tears to her eyes. Liz ate in silence, absorbing her uncle's words. Although politics held little interest for her, she was not unaware of the situation in Britain's African colonies. Apart from a certain objective revulsion for a system that denied franchise to a majority of citizens, she had never thought deeply about the issue. Now, she was aware of a growing sense of outrage, coupled with a quickening of interest, and she began to question Nicholas.

"This country is only sixty odd years old," he explained. "When the whites arrived, including your grandmother, there was nothing here – just miles and miles of bloody Africa. We've built it up – with black help, of course – into a pretty wonderful place. But it's not paradise, and while we don't have the injustices the Nats are perpetrating in South Africa, there's a lot of inequality."

"The Nats?"

"Nationalist Party, run by right wing Afrikaaners, which is now in power down there. As I was saying, not all whites here agree with the inequities, I'm not enamoured of them myself, and I think they're going to cause trouble in a few years. But it's hard to make the hardheads realise they can't go on living in the Dark Ages indefinitely. And frankly, I'm too old to get involved. Just want to see out my days in the country that has given me the best years of my life. Now," he topped up her wine glass, "tell me about your work."

Some time later, she saw the two Africans leave, under the sour gaze of the manager, who was deep in low-voiced conversation with a couple seated near the door. The waiter was serving coffee when Chris Rainier approached Nicholas' table, and her uncle introduced him. He looked about thirty or so, and as she took his hand, she was aware of direct hazel eyes and an expression of calm assurance tinged with humour.

"Liz is over from the UK for a visit. Just in time for the floor show," Nicholas grinned. "Take a pew, Chris."

"Mustn't be long." He pulled up a chair. "Annabel is just having a word with friends. So – this your first visit?" he asked her politely.

"Yes, I arrived two days ago. I've heard a lot about the country from Uncle Nicky."

"Well, you saw one side of it this evening," he said dryly.

"What did you think you were doing, *shamwari*?" interrupted Nicholas. "Did you really know that chap?"

"Paul Masimba? Sure – he's a protégé of Dad's. Dad's company started a scholarship scheme down in the Cape for young blacks. Paul was down at Fort Hare University when I was at varsity in Cape Town, I debated against him a couple of times, and told him to apply. He won it and went to the UK to study law. He's just come back, and it looks like he's on a mission to liberate the masses single-handed."

Nicholas grunted noncommittally, and the younger man continued, "To change the subject, I was going to ask you to come fishing in a couple of weeks – a mate in Sinoia has stocked his dam with bream, but perhaps you're too busy," and he glanced at Liz.

"Drop in for a beer, and we'll make a plan. Liz might want to come too. We could take the plane." Nicholas turned to her. "Had to give up flying, but I can't bring myself to sell it. So Chris sometimes flies me around. You could come and give Liz a flip around sometime, show her the country."

"Glad to," he said affably as he stood up. "Good to meet you, Liz. *Totsiens*, Old Nick."

Nicholas's grey stallion finished second at the races the following afternoon, and he was in high spirits by the time they reached the farm. "Samuel's left dinner in the oven. I think this calls for a celebration – I'll get a bottle of wine. Light the fire, dear."

To Liz the evening seemed wonderfully balmy, but firewood had already been laid, and she had a blaze going by the time he returned with a dusty bottle.

"That fireplace," he told her, "is the only part of the original house."

"Original house? You mean it was built by Simon?"

"That's right. When he bought the land, he built a mud and thatch cottage – pole and dagga, we call it. When they got married, they extended it. After they died, the manager and his wife lived in it for years.

"When I moved in permanently, it was in such a shocking state I decided to start all over again. Told the boys to knock the whole place down. Then I had second thoughts about the fireplace: it worked like a charm and it was the only link with the past, so I kept it and built this place around it."

"I'm glad. Does Simon's mine still operate?"

"No, it's all worked out. The shafts are still there – take you around sometime."

"Clarissa died a long way from here, didn't she?"

"In the Zambezi Valley, on one of Simon's expeditions. He was always restless, he worked the mine, had a manager who grew crops, but he was always off hunting or exploring, and she usually went with him. She loved the life here, despite the troubles."

"What troubles?"

"Well, there was the rebellion in '96, when a lot of whites were murdered. She never wrote about it, but I got the feeling something bad had happened and she didn't want to talk about it. That was when she started a clinic for the blacks – children especially – and threw all her energy into that.

"Then, a year or two later, we had a frantic letter from Emma – out of the blue – to say Clarissa had died in the Zambezi Valley, giving birth to Kathy – your mother, and that Simon had died shortly afterwards, from fever, on his way back to Salisbury with the baby."

"So sad," murmured Liz.

"Yes. Apparently they had been camping in the Valley, and were about to start back to town when it happened. The baby wasn't due for another couple of months, but something went wrong – I think she had a fall – and it came early. Of course, she should never have been down there in her condition. Not that the medical facilities in Salisbury were exactly five star," he added.

Liz took up the story as she remembered hearing it from her mother: "And after she died, Simon's tracker's wife nursed my mother and saved her life."

"That's right. Simon made it back up the escarpment with the baby, to a small mining camp on the Salisbury road. He collapsed there and sent Rukore for Emma, who got there just before he died. She brought the baby back to Salisbury and got in touch with us."

"What a terrible shock for you."

"Yes, though in some ways not entirely unexpected. Her health had been suspect for a long time, and my mother had often begged her to persuade Simon to bring her back to England. Anyway, Felicity and I hopped on the next boat and came out to fetch Kathy. Emma would happily have kept her, but Simon had wanted us to take her. I stayed on to sort out his affairs, and Felicity took the baby back to England. You know the rest."

"And Clarissa's grave?"

"Never found it. It's something I always regret. Didn't have much to go on. Rukore had vanished off the face of the earth, and he was the only person who could have shown me where it was. All Emma knew was that it was on a tributary that ran into the Zambezi, not all that far from the gorge where your young Italian friend is working right now.

"They were camped on the bank overlooking a kind of sheltered channel. The grave was marked with a cairn of stones and a wooden cross, under a mahogany tree." Nicholas paused, staring into the fire, feeling for his cigarettes. "I went down with a hunter and a couple of blacks, stayed several months, looking for it, talking to the locals. There had been a huge flood in the meantime, and some of the topography had been changed, parts of the bank washed away. For all I knew, the campsite had been washed away too.

"Never found a thing. Well, except for some tribesmen upstream who remembered them passing through several months before she died, so I knew I was looking in the right area."

"So you went back to England?"

"Yes. I couldn't afford to stay away longer."

He took a cigarette from his pack. "I've been down again, you know, since I settled here."

"And?"

"Still no luck. Got a dose of malaria, which left me so weak I had to come back."

"What about Simon's grave? Do you know where that is?"

He nodded. "Yes, he's buried in the cemetery at Sinoia, a small farming town about sixty miles from town."

"Did you ever meet any of his relatives?"

"Felicity contacted his father – told him Simon had asked us to look after the child. He visited us several times from Devon until he got too frail. Felicity didn't like him, she was afraid he would try to take Kathy, but he wasn't really interested. Disappointed she wasn't a boy. Crabby, unfeeling old bastard. Died when your mother was about eight. I believe there were a couple of other brothers, but I never met them. One went to Canada, I seem to remember."

Her attention was distracted by a new sound drifting through the window over the crackling of the fire. "Is that drums?"

"It is. Saturday night – there's a beer drink in the compound. Bloody nuisance sometimes, because they tend to get tanked up and start brawling. Still," he stretched his legs towards the blaze. "I enjoy the sound, if not the problems that sometimes go with it. It beats traffic any day."

She lay in bed in the dark later, thinking over what she had learned from her uncle. The rest of the story she knew: after settling Simon's affairs, Nicholas had left the farm and mine in the care of a manager. It would belong to Katherine one day, in the meantime its income would help support her.

He returned to Rhodesia once a year to check on the property, and gradually, as his sister before him, was infected by what he called 'the Africa disease'. His increasingly frequent visits were tolerated by his wife Felicity, an energetic, independent woman totally engrossed in Katherine, her own children and her beloved horses.

Felicity ran the farm in Nicholas' absence. Any passion that may once have sparked between them had long since died, and while they remained mildly attached to one another, both lived their own separate lives. The children grew up, and Nicholas's son took over the farm after Felicity's accidental death in a riding accident. It was then Nicholas decided to settle permanently in Rhodesia, his daughter having married and emigrated to America.

Liz's mother, Katherine, immune to the spell that had ensnared both her parents and her adoptive father, married a young lawyer, Harry Pendennis, who joined the air force when war broke out and was shot down over Germany in 1943.

Katherine never remarried. She raised Liz and her brother Andrew alone, assisted by the income from the African farm. Of her dead father, Liz had only the haziest memories. Nicholas replaced him as the father figure in her life, although she saw him only intermittently once he had settled in Africa.

Reading the diary had awakened her curiosity. She now wanted to know much more about her grandparents' life before their sudden deaths.

She drifted into sleep, and woke around midnight, disturbed by cries that seemed woven into a confused dream in which she was looking for Clarissa's grave in a dense, tangled forest. Mario, her companion on the flight from England, was standing on a high wall above a river, shouting words she could not hear above the roar of water.

Her heart thumped as she sat up in bed. The cries came again, they were not part of the dream, they were coming from somewhere in the house: a high-pitched wailing interspersed with a man's angry voice and, in the background, her uncle's gruff tones.

She could not find matches to light the lamp, but shafts of moonlight through the gap in the curtains gave sufficient light for her to pull on her dressing-gown. Feeling her way down the passage, she edged towards the kitchen door which was ajar, and as she stepped blinking into the glow of a paraffin lamp, the dogs leapt upon her joyously.

There were four people in the room. Her uncle, in a dark blue and red paisley dressing-gown, muttered under his breath as he rummaged in a wooden box. A black woman, who was wailing loudly, clutched her face with both hands. Blood oozed through her fingers, trickled down her faded cotton dress and dripped on to the cement floor. A young black man in a green shirt, wearing a sullen expression, was nursing his jaw, and another man stood in the doorway, arguing with someone outside.

"*Tula, bichana*! Can't hear myself think," Nicholas was saying in an irritated voice. He saw his niece and motioned her in. "Give me a hand, dear, I'm getting too old for this kind of thing. Grab those dishcloths and stop that bleeding while I find a dressing."

He gestured to the wailing woman, who slumped into a chair and rocked back and forth, still wailing but in a less piercing key.

Seizing two dishcloths, Liz folded one into a pad and approached the woman, who stared at her with apprehensive eyes. Murmuring in what she hoped was a reassuring tone, Liz gently prized the woman's fingers away from her head, and winced at the ugly gaping slash across her left temple, close to where her hair was parted into geometric lines and tightly plaited in a decorative pattern.

The woman stopped wailing, took the pad and held it in place over the wound. Gently removing her other hand from her cheek, Liz's stomach lurched. Although the facial wound was smaller, it had laid bare a glimpse of bone glistening white through blood and tissue. She used the second cloth to staunch the blood, swallowing to suppress the nausea rising in her throat. At her feet, one of the dogs began licking at the splashes of crimson on the floor, and Nicholas shouted at it.

He came across with a roll of bandage and peered beneath the padding, replacing it hurriedly. "She'll need stitches. We'll bandage her up, then Moses can drive her to the clinic. Head wound first, I think. Hold the pad where it is, I'll bandage over it."

"What happened?" she asked, as he wound the first bandage neatly around the woman's head, securing the pad in place, and a second bandage from the top of her head, down over the cheek wound and beneath her jaw.

"The old story, eternal triangle. Pass me a safety pin, there's a good girl," he muttered. "Luke over there – her husband – caught her with another man, gave him a broken nose and a thick ear. Then laid into her. Casanova's outside, licking his wounds. We'd better take a look at him as well.

"Casanova wants to charge Luke with assault, and her with using witchcraft on him. Novel excuse – we'll let the police sort that out. All right, let's look at the other fellow."

Moses went outside and returned with a tall, square-jawed man with a swollen nose, who glanced furtively at Luke, the wronged husband, and was met with a menacing growl. The woman started whimpering again.

"Get both of them out of here, Moses. *Kurumidza*," ordered Nicholas. "Luke can go to the clinic with her. Wait in the Land Rover until I have a look at this one."

Liz wiped the blood from the floor while Nicholas made a cursory examination of the man's face. "Broken nose. You'll live, Dendera. Can't very well send you in the Land Rover – that would be asking for mayhem." He spoke in Shona to the man, who mumbled and went outside. "He can go to the clinic in the morning."

Almost immediately, shouts and screams erupted and Nicholas slammed the first aid box on the table. "God dammit," he roared, limping to the back door. He disappeared into the darkness, shutting the door behind him.

Liz clutched the bloodstained dishcloth, uncertain whether or not to follow. She heard a sharp crack, a thud, then silence, followed by a groan and low voices.

A man laughed. Footsteps approached, and her heart pumped faster. The door opened to admit her uncle.

"Are you all right?" she gasped.

He shuffled inside, shaking his head. "I'm fine, fine," he soothed. "That was Moses, my foreman. He had to intervene again. Good chap." He grinned crookedly. The redoubtable Moses re-appeared, rubbing his knuckles, and Nicholas took a bunch of keys from a hook and handed them to him. "OK, Moses?"

"Ya, 'nkos." He saluted and disappeared.

Nicholas looked sharply at his niece. "You all right?"

She relaxed her hold on the dishcloth. "I'm not used to this sort of thing, especially in the middle of the night. Not much good with blood either," she confessed, aware that her legs were suddenly shaky.

"Sit down. I'll make a cup of tea, could use one myself." He shuffled over to the stove, put the kettle on and set cups and saucers on the table.

"What will happen tomorrow?" she asked.

"The police will come and sort it out. I keep out of these domestic squabbles." He lit another lamp, made the tea, brought her a cup and sat down beside her, lighting a cigarette.

"What was that about witchcraft?" she asked, as the shaky feeling began to ebb from her body.

"Dendera was just trying it on. Luke's wife Reta is a hot number, gives Luke a lot of trouble, but no one has suggested she has supernatural powers before. They're a superstitious bunch, but Luke's no fool, he won't fall for it."

Breakfasting on the stoep with Nicholas next morning, it was difficult to believe the incident in the night had not been a dream. The dogs sat in a semi-circle around her uncle, following the progress of each morsel of food from his plate to his mouth. In between writing a list on the back of his cigarette packet, he tossed them scraps of toast and bacon rind. Ducks flew towards the dam, whistling, and a hoopoe pecked for insects on the lawn.

"What news of the casualties?" she asked.

"All patched up. Luke's wife had to have stitches. I just spoke to the police, they're sending a constable over."

Later that afternoon, when she returned from a walk to the dam with the dogs, the injured woman was chatting with Samuel behind the kitchen, near the boiler where the water for the house was heated by a wood fire.

Despite the dressings on her face she appeared to be in high spirits, laughing loudly, in sharp contrast with the cowed, whimpering creature of the previous evening.

Liz nodded and smiled, and the woman clapped her hands and said something in Shona. For the first time, Liz noticed her lustrous eyes and shapely figure. The pert young breasts beneath her cotton dress had not yet begun to droop in the manner of so many of her older sisters.

"She say thank you for helping her," translated Samuel.

"Tell her I'm glad she is better," said Liz.

There was a car in the driveway, and she found her uncle on the stoep drinking beer with Chris Rainier, who rose to his feet. "Hi. How are you?"

"Pour Liz a beer," Nicholas told him, "she's getting a taste for Lion."

"Thank you. It seems like the thing to drink on a stoep in Africa," she agreed, curling up on one of the chairs. Grey herons winged overhead into the flaming sunset reflected in the pewter surface of the dam.

"We were talking about how to entertain you," Nicholas told her.

"You don't have to entertain me," she protested, "I'm very happy pottering around here, going for walks. I've been using your bird book, trying to identify the birds down at the dam." She remembered something she had read in the diary. "But there is one place I'd like to see. Clarissa mentioned a spot where she picnicked with Simon before she left Africa. A valley with a small river and some palm trees."

"We call it 'The Palms'," said Nicholas. "Tricky to get to by road, but easy on horseback."

"If you like, I'll bring a couple of horses over tomorrow and we can go there," Chris offered. "D'you ride, Liz?"

"She was a proper little pony club fanatic at school. Pigtails, braces, the works," teased Nicholas.

She grinned, "Don't remind me. Yes, thanks, I'd like that."

"It probably won't have changed much since Clarissa was there," said her uncle. "Not many of us know about the place."

The phone rang and he got to his feet, grumbling, and went inside to answer it.

"So, tell me," Chris turned to her, "is it just a holiday that brings you here?"

She sipped her beer and put the glass down on the low table between them. "Yes, well, a working holiday – I hope to get a job soon. I came to see my uncle and have a look at Africa. But," and she paused and then said slowly, "but now I'm here, I think I'd like to find my grandmother's grave."

She stopped, surprised that she had put into words the idea that had come to her during the day.

"Your grandmothers' grave?" He tilted an eyebrow questioningly.

"Reading her diary gave me the idea. And why not? No one else has had any luck, maybe I will."

"Slow down, I'm not with you. You'd better start at the beginning."

While she related Clarissa's story, Nicholas returned, handing Chris another beer. The younger man listened intently, his grey-green eyes never leaving her face, and when she had finished, he shook his head slowly.

"Quite a story. So how are you going to go about finding this grave?"

"What's this?" Nicholas interposed.

She turned to him. "Let's have another try, Uncle Nicky."

He laughed in disbelief. "Are you crazy, Elizabeth? I told you I looked for it twice. If I couldn't find it then, how could you possibly have a chance after all these years?"

"We could try," she said stubbornly. "Can you get to the Zambezi River by road?"

"Yes, there's a new road. But you'll have to move fast. From what you say," said Chris slowly, "it sounds as though your grave will be flooded by the new dam at Kariba. It'll be under water in a couple of years."

"Damn right, Chris," said Nicholas. "It's been on my mind, but there's nothing more I can do." He told Chris about his attempts to find the grave. "Quite apart from anything else, as I told Elizabeth, it could have been washed away by now – in one of those huge Zambezi floods. Not a pleasant thought, but true."

"But if it's still there, we should try one last time." she said, and Chris looked at her and shook his head slowly.

"I wouldn't give you a chance in a million," he said flatly.

"You're both so negative. What was it Clarissa wrote in her diary? *'Our doubts are traitors and make us lose.....'*"

"*... the good we oft might win by fearing to attempt.*" Nicholas finished it for her. "Shakespeare – one of her favourite quotations."

"So, at least let me try."

"Where would you start?" he asked dubiously.

"In the area you went to." She had a thought. "Did you ever check the newspaper archives, or talk to local historians?"

"No. I talked to people who'd been down there, and to the locals, of course." He looked at her ruefully. "You're just like your grandmother. When she got an idea...."

Chris looked at her sceptically. "So that's your mission, is it?"

"Yes." She felt elated, and a little defiant.

"And then back to England?"

"I suppose so" Her thoughts flew to Alex. Perhaps things would have changed by the time she went back. Perhaps there would be a chance.... "Yes. It's my home."

"It was your grandmother's home too, and from what you said, it didn't take her long to be infected by this place. It's called the curse of Africa. You'd know about that, Nick." He glanced at her uncle, who grinned.

"I think Simon had something to do with Clarissa's decision to come back," Liz pointed out.

Chris turned to Nicholas. "When you went down the Valley, did you have a boat, Old Nick?"

"No. Wagon the first time, the second time I drove part of the way and walked the rest."

"Well, why not try a different angle, go upriver from Kariba?"

"Upriver?" Liz leaned forward eagerly.

"Worth a try," her uncle said reluctantly. "Do you know anyone who has a boat at Kariba?"

"Yes," said the younger man, "it shouldn't be too difficult to organise." He stood up. "I must get back. My aunt will be having palpitations about her soufflé."

As soon as he had gone, she turned to her uncle. "Don't you know anything more about the grave than what you've told me?" she asked.

"No. By the time Emma got to Simon, he was dying and his mind was wandering. He wasn't very lucid."

"What happened to Emma?" she asked.

Nicholas stared out across the garden. "Emma – there's someone I haven't thought about for a while. I don't know. I lost touch with her."

"And before that – was she living here?"

"Yes. In the early days when Felicity was still alive – before I came out here for good – I used to see a lot of her. She stayed in Salisbury for years after Frank died."

"Her husband died?"

"Way back, alcohol poisoning mainly. Their marriage was all right for a few years, then things started to turn sour, though she never left him."

"What went wrong? Just drink?"

"A lot of things, exacerbated by drink. He was an engineer, so he was away a good deal – there were railways to build, and bridges, and when he was away he drank a lot. They all did," he grinned, "we all did – still do. In the end, it started to affect his work. Basically, Frank didn't have enough backbone, and so the vicious circle went on.

"When I came out to check on the farm, I used to do what I could to help her. She was bringing up two kids virtually single-handed. She had another – a little boy – who died as a baby. She didn't have an easy time.

"After Frank died, I was spending more time out here and we became quite close. She used to come out for weekends with the kids, when she wasn't nursing. In fact," he looked at Liz almost sheepishly, "if it hadn't been for Felicity," he paused, "we might have made a go of it."

"You and Emma?" Liz was open-mouthed with astonishment.

He grinned, looking almost embarrassed. "Me and Emma. But it was out of the question, of course, and after a few years, I think she got fed up waiting. When a chap she had nursed in the past showed up as a widower, she married him.

"They went down south to live, but we kept in touch for years. Then they must have moved, or maybe she died – I don't know, but my letters were returned."

"How long since you last heard from her?"

Nicholas coughed heavily, cleared his throat and promptly lit a cigarette. "Must be ten years at least. Little Emma," he said pensively. "A few years ago I heard her daughter was in Salisbury, but I've never been able to track her down – didn't know her married name. The son went to Kenya years ago."

"I wonder if she could still be alive," mused Liz. "I'd give anything to talk to her."

"Well," her uncle said briskly, as though coming back to the present from a long way away, "I think your chances of that are slim."

"What was her surname after she remarried?"

"Something like Somerset...Somerton...Somerville. That's it. Bob Somerville. He would have given her the security she didn't get from Frank Harrison."

"And what about Robert Hammond? Did he find someone else after Clarissa married Simon?"

"Yes. Married a pretty young thing from Kent who had been after him for years. I used to see him from time to time, we went shooting together up in Scotland. Never really got over Clarissa, devastated by her death. Had a couple of kids, and the last I heard he was still alive, but that was a few years back." He stood up and stretched. "Come inside. It's getting cold."

He turned on the radio to catch the evening news. In Kenya, an elderly white couple had been hacked to death by a Mau Mau gang, believed to have been let into their farmhouse by a Kikuyu servant. Liz had listened to such reports before, in her London flat. Now, curled up in an armchair with the dogs sprawled at her feet, surrounded by the sounds of the African night, she shivered as she stared into the blackness beyond the French windows. An owl hooted softly, and as the newsreader's noncommittal voice concluded the grisly details, Samuel padded into the dining alcove on silent feet and placed dishes on the sideboard. "Dinner ready, 'nkos."

"Thanks, Samuel," grunted Nicholas, putting his glass down.

Her eyes followed the cook's white-uniformed figure. But it couldn't happen here – in peaceful Rhodesia. Could it? Could affable, smiling Samuel one day let killers into the house to attack Nicholas?

"What's the matter?" asked her uncle. "Not cold, are you?"

"Goose walking over my grave," she rubbed her arms. "Uncle Nicky," she hesitated, "Mau Mau – could it happen here?"

He raised his eyebrows. "It could happen anywhere in Africa. Mau Mau is aimed at getting rid of the whites and establishing black government, and it's all tied up with tribal ritual and superstition. You remember Dendera last night, using witchcraft as a excuse?" She nodded. "Most of these people still think the witchdoctor's magic is a hell of a lot more powerful than the white man's. Don't forget that ninety percent of them are still rural people, easy to manipulate. And I have no doubt the Shona and Matabele are just as keen as the Kikuyu to get their own government."

"But would Samuel help people who wanted to kill you?" she persisted.

"Damn right – if he was scared enough. And when you see what those Kikuyu are doing to each other, who wouldn't be?" He grinned reassuringly, "Look, dear, it's not about to happen here, not in the near future, anyway. But," his face darkened, "I wouldn't put anyone's loyalty to that kind of test. It's not just the Mau Mau who indulge in obscene rituals. D'you know what Lobengula's father used to do to people he didn't like? He'd have them skinned alive, or fed to the crocs."

He got to his feet slowly, easing his back, "Speaking of which, it's roast chicken. I'll carve, you do the vegies."

14

"Will we see any wildlife?" she asked Chris Rainier.

"Doubt it. You have to get a long way from civilisation to see anything these days, except in parks and game reserves. Maybe the odd buck, a jackal or two sometimes, nothing bigger."

She remembered Clarissa's rapturous descriptions of plains swarming with animals. "Was it hunting or farming that killed them off?"

"Both. A lot were shot – and are still being shot – to get rid of tsetse fly. But there's still game in parts of the Zambezi Valley."

They were on the road past the dam. Chris, in khaki trousers and open-necked shirt, rode a muscular grey; she ambled along on a placid black mare with a benign expression. He turned off the farm road on to a track through the bush and they rode in silence, side by side. To make conversation, she asked "What do you do, Chris?"

His grin was sardonic. "That's what my old man keeps asking me. At the moment, I do flights to Kariba for the government and Impresit, the Italian consortium building the dam."

"So you're a pilot?"

"For the moment. I took law at university. Dad's a lawyer and it was always assumed I would follow in his footsteps. It seemed the logical thing to do. When I got my degree, I worked in his office for a while, then took off around the world. I had to get out, away from the politics and Afrikaaner paranoia. I ended up in the States, working on ranches, and got to thinking maybe I wasn't cut out for the law. After a few years I headed back slowly via the UK and Europe.

"Took a cargo boat to Algeria and worked my way down. I got this far and came to work on my uncle's farm. I had spent time here during school holidays, and I decided to stay while I made up my mind what to do next. The more I thought, the more the idea of putting on a suit and tie every day was not on.

"My folks kept phoning from Cape Town – when was I coming back to get a job and settle down? Then I heard pilots were in demand. I had learnt to fly in the States, so I applied and got a job. It's regular work, I get to see the country, and the more I see, the more I like."

"But you're not planning to fly as a career?"

"No." He paused, "but for the first time, I'm getting a sense of what I do want to do. For a start, I'm not going back to South Africa. It's going one way under the Nats – separate development and all that, so I'm applying for residence here. There's more happening, more of a frontier feel. It's still young. I'm saving to buy land and go farming."

"And your parents?"

"They'll spit tacks. Waste of a law degree, all those years' study, etcetera. Dad still wants me to go into the business and take over eventually. That's why I can't go back yet. Too much pressure."

"Would your mother support you?"

"Mum? She's an out and out snob," he said frankly. "There's nothing she would love more than for her son to become an eminent lawyer. Farmers are not on her social register, unless they're old families with vineyards dating back to Simon van der Stel."

They were following a track through the dappled shade of msasa trees. "What do you know about farming here?" she asked.

"Not much," he conceded. "But I'm learning. I've picked up a lot helping David, my uncle."

"Do you have any other family here?" asked Liz.

"A sister – Barbara. She met Derick, her husband, at university in Cape Town. They got engaged after they graduated, and Barbara came up here to work while they saved up to get married. Derick's a lawyer, so the old folk approved."

He reined in his horse. "We'll stop here. You can see the old mine, but watch where you walk."

It was a strange sensation to wander through the overgrown workings developed by her grandfather. There was not much to see: a few tunnels running diagonally down into the earth, some mounds covered in straggly grass. "Don't go too near," he warned as she bent to peer into a shaft. "It's started to cave in. Nick and I are planning to shore this one up and preserve it, but we haven't got around to it yet." He offered her water from a bottle on his belt.

"You get on well with my uncle?" she remarked as she took it from him.

"He's a good old guy, and we are both fishermen. He gets lonely, enjoys having a bit of youth around. It's good you're here for a while."

"I liked what you did the other night at the restaurant," she remarked once they had remounted and returned to the track.

"Did you now?" he raised an eyebrow sardonically. "The guys were none too pleased, but I didn't want to see Paul stuffing up a bright future by taking a punch at Johnny. We're going to need intelligent black lawyers."

"It's good to meet someone who wants to give them a chance to prove themselves. Some of the people I've met – the way they talk – they seem to tolerate blacks only as servants or farm workers."

"Farmers. Notoriously conservative. That's not to say the city folk are much better, but they're a lot more open-minded than down south."

"You mean in South Africa?"

"Yes. Strydom is a rabid fundamentalist, believes the Afrikaaners are the chosen *volk* – destined to lead *Suid Afrika* to great things, provided their blood isn't tainted by black blood. Which is a laugh – Afrikaaner and black blood have been mixed for centuries."

"So you don't believe in separate development?" she queried eagerly.

"Apartheid is unrealistic, unjust and plain stupid. But I don't believe in one man one vote either, not right now, not here."

"But in the restaurant...."

"Look," he interrupted, "just because I don't like to see people pushed around because of their colour doesn't mean I want them running the country."

"It's their country," she reasoned.

"Not any more it ain't. The Matabele didn't think so when they came in and clobbered the Shona. Then the Brits came in and fought two wars to stake their claim. People have been fighting over land since time began – Americans and Indians, New Zealanders and Maoris, Australians and Aborigines."

She stared at him. " But you can't think it's fair to deny people the right to vote?"

He sighed. "Ninety percent of them live in the bush, they don't understand what an election is. Fifty years ago, they were chopping each other up. They'd be doing it still if we hadn't come along and stopped them. They're not ready yet."

"But you can't suppress the voice of the majority," she tried to keep her voice level and reasonable. "You are – how many whites? Against how many blacks?"

"Roughly 150,000 to five million I think, and increasing rapidly – the blacks, I mean."

"Five million people. They won't stand for it indefinitely."

He grinned without humour. "Now, there you may have put your finger on it. Things are already hotting up. Kariba Dam and Federation are just the start."

"Stop a minute," Liz interrupted him. "Federation. Southern Rhodesia, Northern Rhodesia and Nyasaland have formed a federation – right?" He nodded. "When did that happen?"

"A couple of years ago. There was a referendum, and the majority voted 'Yes'. Kariba is the first big federal project, and already there's trouble brewing."

"What do you mean?"

"A lot of blacks in Northern Rhodesia and Nyasaland are against Federation. They think it's been engineered for our benefit – the whites in Southern Rhodesia – to give us access to the copper mines up north, and cheap labour in Nyasaland. It's a sore point in another way too. Northern Rhodesia wanted the dam on their Kafue River, but we won it. They see it as a political decision. One problem is that Federation has joined three very different countries."

"How's that?"

"Well we're different from the other two, because we've had responsible government for more than thirty years, they haven't. Things are slowly getting stirred up," he seemed to be almost talking to himself. "I get the feeling we are not going to be able to keep the peace much longer."

He was saying almost exactly what Nicholas had said in the restaurant. "Well," she said irritably, "if it's peaceful only because the majority are oppressed, it doesn't deserve to remain the way it is."

"Do I detect a revolutionary tone under that proper Brit exterior?" He glanced at her sideways as the horses plodded down a rough path into a valley. Doves warbled lazily.

"I'm not talking revolution. Just people standing up for their rights."

"And if we decide they are not ready to have a vote yet?"

He was taunting her and she rose instantly to the bait. "What makes you so sure every white uses it intelligently?" She could feel the heat rising in her face.

"Maybe they don't. But at least the majority understand what is involved in making a country work in the twentieth century. And I'll tell you something else. Even the brightest and most liberal don't particularly appreciate *rooineks* coming out and telling them how to run the country – after a week in the place."

She flushed, seething inwardly. Arrogant South African! They rode in silence. He did not appear in the least discomfited; the sun glinted on his light brown hair as he sat relaxed in the saddle, holding the reins loosely, whistling softly through his teeth as he led the way down the narrow track.

But after a few minutes, he turned and looked at her over his shoulder. "Truce, OK?" he grinned disarmingly. "Shouldn't talk politics with Old Nick's guest. I apologise."

She regarded him with deep suspicion. "I don't take back anything I said."

"That's all right – neither do I."

The sun was warm on her back and she was enjoying the ride too much to stay angry for long; besides, he had taken the trouble to bring her down here. "You're right about one thing only," she conceded, "I shouldn't shoot my mouth off until I've been here a bit longer."

"Most people wait at least two weeks before claiming to be experts on Africa," he agreed solemnly.

She ignored that. "What's a *rooinek*? It sounds rude."

"It's the South African equivalent of 'pommie'. Be careful, loose stones."

The path sloped steeply downwards, and the emerald fronds of the palms mentioned in Clarissa's diary rustled above the canopy of natural vegetation. Chris reined in on the banks of a sandy streambed where a trickle of water seeped into shallow rock pools. They dismounted and led the horses down to drink before tethering them in the shade.

"Strange," said Liz, taking off her shoes and rolling up her jeans, "to read about something in the diary and then actually see it."

They walked upstream, and she paddled in pools of clear water bordered by the line of palms. It was more than strange, it gave her a sense of making contact across time with someone she wished, more and more, that she had known.

It was hot, and they went back to the rock where Chris had left his rucksack. He opened two beers and unwrapped Samuel's sandwiches. "Take your pick: ham, cheese, avocado."

She had noticed he spoke with barely an accent. "I know South Africa was settled by the English and Dutch. Which lot are your family?" she asked curiously.

"Neither. We're Huguenot stock. My ancestors left France to escape religious persecution. If you look at South African names, you'll see that some of them sound French – de Villiers, du Plessis, du Toit. Did you learn about a thing called the Edict of Nantes at school?"

"Sounds remotely familiar."

"Well, the Huguenots were Protestants and they were left in peace under the edict. When it was revoked around the late seventeenth century, they were put on the Catholic hit list, had to get out. Some went to South Africa, and started vineyards in the Cape, some went into professions. One of my uncles is in the wine business. David – the other – served in Asia during the war, and stayed on afterwards until the troubles in Malaya. Now he farms here."

After they had eaten, he lit a cigarette and lay back in the shade while she pottered around the pools, watching small lizards darting across the rocks, and large black ants scurrying off with breadcrumbs twice their size. She wandered downstream past the line of tropical greenery; in the warm, still afternoon, the silence was broken only by the distant descending call of a wood dove.

When she returned, he was sitting with a finger to his lips, beckoning. She approached slowly and he put a hand on her arm, pointing to a shallow pool. The sun had moved and the water was in shadow. At first she saw nothing, then a flicker of movement caught her eye. About ten feet long, patterned in light gold and dark coppery-brown, the snake lay coiled half in and half out of the water, powerful neck muscles convulsing in regular spasms. It seemed to be swallowing something.

"You should have been here." His eyes never left the rhythmic undulations of the sleek, powerful coils. "I watched the whole thing. Hell, if only I'd had my camera."

"What is it?" she whispered. The dappled sunlight on the gleaming scales lent the snake the mythical quality of a dragon-like creature of fantasy.

"Python. Came out on the rock just after you left. I was willing you to come, but I didn't dare move in case it took fright."

The muscles convulsed once more. "What has it caught?" she whispered.

"Looked like a big cane rat." They sat in silence as the creature continued to contract its muscles, easing the bulge of its victim further along the length of its body.

She swallowed. "You mean that thing was there all the time I was paddling?" The skin crawled all the way up her spine and into her hairline.

His eyes glinted with laughter. "Probably."

"Shouldn't you kill it?"

"What do you suggest I use? Anyway, they're protected – royal game. It's bad luck too, the rains won't come if you kill a python. It's all right," he regarded her in amusement, "they don't go for *rooineks*. They're quite harmless to humans."

"I don't believe you."

They watched until the coils stopped convulsing and the creature lay supine, sunlight glancing on copper scales. Then they rose quietly and backed slowly away.

The sun had almost set, and the veld was carpeted in purple shadow by the time they reached Rugare, Chris' uncle's farm, where they were to meet Nicholas for dinner. They followed a dirt track past a compound of mud huts, where wood smoke spiralled from small fires, to the sprawling farmhouse.

Chris' aunt was in the kitchen with the cook, a gin and tonic at her elbow. Lilian Rainier was a stately woman with an ample bosom and a face that had once been beautiful and was now sagging into comfortable folds. Immaculate in pale green linen, she wore jade eardrops and her silver hair was coiled on top of her head in an elaborate, old-fashioned style. Liz was instantly conscious of her crumpled jeans and tangled hair, but the older woman did not seem to notice.

"I'm teaching Joshua to make mulligatawny soup," she said, while Chris nibbled chopped vegetables. "It's David's favourite. Chris darling, take Liz and give her a drink. The men will be back in a minute. We won't be late tonight – David has to go down to Gwelo tomorrow to look at a Charolais bull. No, no, Joshua, chop them much smaller, like this," she chided in a maternal tone.

The large sittingroom, overlooking an immense expanse of lawn, was crammed with intricately-carved ivory ornaments, jade figurines, lamps, carved chests, glass cabinets loaded with porcelain tea services so delicate they were almost transparent.

"Like I said – they lived out East," said Chris, following her eyes, "Lilian makes the best sweet and sour pork I've ever tasted. What'll you have – gin, whisky, sherry, brandy or beer?"

Nicholas arrived with David Rainier, a thickset, genial man with a bald pate the same nutbrown as his muscular arms. When Chris told him about the python, he fetched a large book from his study and riffled through the pages.

"There you are, m'dear," he handed it to Liz, *"'normally harmless to man but can inflict a painful bite if annoyed'."*

"I don't call that harmless," she said to Chris. He regarded her with amused tolerance, and she was irritated again.

David lit a cigarette, using an ebony holder which would have seemed an affectation on anyone less down-to-earth. His wife bustled in, bracelets tinkling, and led the way through to the diningroom where a table was laid with gleaming silverware; crimson hibiscus flowers floated in a crystal bowl. Nicholas grinned at his niece. "When you get tired of my scruffy bachelor establishment, you can come here for a bit for culture."

The Rainiers were entertaining hosts, well-travelled and amusing. Their affection for their nephew was as apparent as their devotion to one another, and she was touched by the old-fashioned gallantry with which David treated his wife. She asked Nicholas about them on the way back home.

"They have a son but they never mention him. I gather he married an Asian girl against their wishes."

"So they don't know where he is?"

"They don't even know whether they have any grandchildren. They're good neighbours – hearts of gold, very gregarious. They love having Chris – treat him like a son, and Lilian treats Joshua like her own child. Got him as a teenager, took him under her wing and taught him to cook."

Eyes gleamed in the headlights. He braked, and the slender form of a small antelope bounded across the road. "Bushbuck," he sounded pleased. "Haven't seen that little fellow for a while."

After two job interviews in the city, Liz was offered a part-time position on a small wildlife and tourism magazine, and a more promising but temporary post with the Rhodesia Herald, standing in for a journalist going on leave. In a couple of months there would be a chance of a more permanent position. Crossing her fingers, she accepted the Herald job, which was due to start in three weeks, giving her time to find somewhere to live.

"Am I going to lose you so quickly?" Nicholas grumbled as he poured his evening whisky.

"I'll still come out over weekends," she consoled him. "I love it here, so don't you dare give my room to anyone else."

Finding accommodation was less simple. Although she had a little money put by, she did not want to commit herself to a flat until the job was secure, so she scanned the classified pages for rooms to let. A week before she was due to start work, she still had not found anything appealing, and was beginning to feel mildly panicky, although Nicholas reassured her that he could find her temporary accommodation with friends.

Chris Rainier telephoned. She had not seen him since the evening at Rugare, but he had heard of her predicament. "I've persuaded my sister and her husband they need a lodger," he told her laconically. "They have a huge house – can't afford it, but fell for it heavily. Now they're stuck with a massive mortgage. Derick is a struggling junior partner and Barb is expecting a baby. They could use the money."

Liz was doubtful. "Are you sure you haven't pushed them into it?"

"My sister doesn't get pushed around. Anyway, they want to look you over, so I'll take you to meet them tomorrow afternoon. I've got the day off."

He drove her to one of the older suburbs, an area of shady flowering trees and quiet avenues. The house was set well back from the road, at the end of a driveway lined with blue and white agapanthus. On either side of the gateposts tall jacarandas spread feathery fronds; a third leaned over the faded green tin roof, casting dappled shade on white stucco walls.

As Chris' car halted near the front door a Great Dane, sprawled on the wide polished stoep, raised a huge head, unfolded a tawny form and bounded down the steps.

"Hey, boy. No – stay down!" Chris shouted as his shoulders were pinned against the car door by gigantic paws.

"Shumba, down, bad dog!" The door had opened, and a woman came down the steps. Except for her grey-green eyes, Barbara Coles did not look much like her brother. Small boned, she had fine blonde hair bobbed to frame a heart-shaped face sprinkled with freckles.

"My long-lost brother," she grinned placidly as he wrestled with the dog. "Put him down, Shumba." The dog retreated, and Chris grumbled and dusted himself off.

"You must be Liz," she extended a hand, "I'm so glad you've come to look at the room. Derick and I are rattling around here at the moment. Come inside, no, Shumba, stay. The floor's just been polished. How are you, brother? We never see you," she said over her shoulder as she led the way inside. The dog flopped down against the wall with a grunt.

"Overworked and underpaid, but the flying's good. How's the morning sickness?"

"Much better. We're expecting our first baby," she explained to Liz, "at the end of the year."

"And Derick wasn't too charmed," said Chris. "Is he coming around yet?"

"Slowly. He didn't want us to start a family until we were more established," she confided. "This was an accident. Well," she grinned, "sort of. We'll look at the room first and then have tea."

The old house was cool and airy, with high ornamental plaster ceilings, polished wooden floors and large windows opening on to the garden. It was furnished simply but comfortably, the kind of home in which you could put your feet up without worrying about the furniture, thought Liz as she sidestepped a large dog basket in the hallway.

Barbara showed her into a room at the back. It had the same high ceiling, and was furnished with a bed covered in a floral spread; matching curtains hung at the window, a set of bird prints on the walls. There was a rough coir mat on the wooden floor, cream-painted furniture and a cane chair.

"Nothing palatial, as you can see. The thing I hope will really take your fancy is out here," she said, crossing to a door in the opposite wall. "A sleeping porch, and you have your own entrance for when you want to sneak in at four am after a night on the town."

Warmed by her friendliness, Liz made up her mind as soon as she stepped into the mosquito-gauzed porch. The floor was the ubiquitous red polished cement she had seen in other homes built in the early years of the colony, the only furniture an aged but comfortable-looking settee, a couple of cane chairs and a bed. Jacaranda branches rustled against the mosquito netting, the garden surrounded the porch on three sides, and a green door led down steps to the back lawn where sunbirds hovered amongst the flowers.

"What do you think?" asked Barbara. "I love to sit out here when it's pouring and the thunder is crashing. Derick put up canvas blinds that you can let down if things get too wild, but the rain doesn't often come in."

"I think it would suit me very well," Liz looked around with appreciative eyes. "I like the feeling of being almost in the garden."

"So you'd like to take it?"

"If you'll have me."

She beamed. "Isn't that great, CJ?" Chris, leaning against the bedroom doorway, inclined his head tolerantly towards his sister.

"Hope you know what you're doing," he remarked, "she's a stubborn, argumentative Brit."

"Don't tell me you've met your match?" asked Barbara. "Someone who doesn't let you win every argument – especially about politics?" She winked at Liz. "Let's have tea. You will stay for dinner won't you? Don't look like that, Christopher, we haven't seen you for weeks and I want you to have a look at my car. Derick is hopeless with it."

After tea, while Chris tinkered beneath the bonnet of Barbara's aged diesel Mercedes, his sister conducted Liz around the garden until he reappeared, wiping his hands and loudly demanding a beer.

They were sitting out on a small patio at the side of the house, when Derick Coles joined them, planting a kiss on his wife's cheek and bestowing on Liz his slow, serious smile. The financial arrangements were quickly disposed of, and Liz agreed to move in the following week.

"There is a bus into town, but I can take you to work until you get a car," he told her. Tall and bespectacled, he looked several years older than this wife.

During dinner, served by a large, middle-aged maidservant with a good-humoured face, the subject turned to the new hydro-electric project at Kariba. Liz was instantly alert and began asking questions.

"It'll be the biggest man-made structure in the world," Derick told her. "When it's full, the water will cover an area the size of Wales. There'll be new jobs, new industries."

"I met one of the engineers on the plane coming out," she told him. "How far is it from Salisbury?"

"Between two and three hundred miles. The river is the border between us and Northern Rhodesia."

"Does anyone live there?"

"Fifty thousand tribesmen. Yes," he said, anticipating her next question, "they have to be moved – some have already been moved. They're a primitive tribe, grow a few crops and fish in the river, and they've lived there for thousands of years, so it's tough on them. My brother is involved in the exercise."

"How do they feel?" she asked.

"How would you feel?" he countered." They've had it rough, the Batonga. The Matabele used to cull them on a regular basis, the Barotse raided from the north before the whites moved in and put a stop to it. Now this."

"Where will they go?"

"New land has been set aside. The government is sinking boreholes, putting in schools, clinics, irrigation schemes, so I believe."

"They'll still have the right to fish in the new lake when it's full, won't they?" asked Chris.

"Yes. But of course there's been trouble. A bunch of hot-bloods are stirring them up, telling them it's all a white man's plot to get their land, that there's not going to be a flood and they must stay where they are. Ian – my brother – is a DO, district officer," he explained to her. "He's been travelling through the area, explaining what's happening. He says they don't really understand. They say, 'OK, so the river rises, but it's often done that'. In the past they have simply moved to higher ground and waited for the water to go down. No problem. Some of them can't grasp that this is not a temporary thing, the water level won't go down again. That their land will be gone – kaput."

"Don't think they're living in paradise," interjected Chris. "They're riddled with disease – bilharzia, malaria, sleeping sickness, you name it."

"True," Derick nodded. "But it doesn't make it easier for them."

Chris was looking thoughtfully at her. "Remember I said I could probably organise a boat trip up the Zambezi? Forget that – Ian Coles is the guy to talk to. He knows the Valley like the back of his hand."

Through one of her uncle's contacts Liz bought a secondhand Morris, loaded her suitcases into the back, and moved in with the Coles a few days before starting work.

It was strange to be back in harness in such a vastly different environment, one in which she had no network of contacts, but her colleagues were a relaxed, friendly group, who immediately absorbed her into their circle.

And a week after she started, the editor sent her to cover a press conference at Meikles Hotel on the progress at Kariba Dam.

With the aid of a ciné projector, Impresit's chief engineer outlined the principles of dam building: that, before you start, you have to push the water out of your way so that it does not interfere with construction work. The tall blond Tuscan explained that the designers had opted to divert a large volume of water through a tunnel built into the south bank. During the dry season a coffer dam was built on the north bank and the first stage of the wall had begun inside it.

As the projector hummed in the background, Liz was awed by the scale of the project unfolding on the flickering screen. The river was low at present, and dark forest mantled the steep flanks of the gorge, contrasting sharply with the startling blue of the sky. On the north bank, the circular coffer dam was dwarfed by its surroundings; vehicles crawled like beetles up the white roads cut into the hillside, and the figures of men working on the dam wall scurried about like a colony of ants. An aerial view showed a town mushrooming on the crest of seven hills overlooking the gorge, and a settlement for African labourers nearby.

In the presence of overseas journalists hungry for any sign of inter-racial tension, a government official took pains to stress the spirit of camaraderie prevailing between Italian and African labourers. He spoke of how a bank had been erected in nine days, a house in three. In a lighter vein, he reeled off figures for the quantities of beer imported from the city every week to quench the thirst of men working in temperatures of 120 degrees and more.

An African journalist asked a question, and Liz recognised the bearded man involved in the disturbance in the restaurant. Identifying himself as Joe Guve of Zimbabwe Dawn magazine, he queried rumours of malaria decimating the African work force. As though anticipating the question, a rotund, bespectacled Health Department official rose ponderously to present a string of statistics negating the rumour. "The medical officer at Kariba regularly distributes supplies of anti-malarial pills to all workers," he concluded.

Guve persisted, asking questions about working conditions, hours, wages, and the relocation of the Batonga. He was told that despite the efforts of the ANC to destabilise the situation and manipulate it to their own ends, peaceful relocation was well underway. Several overseas journalists picked up the issue but their questions were neatly fielded.

Afterwards, on her way out, Liz found herself walking down the stairs beside Guve. On an impulse, she introduced herself, mentioning the incident in the restaurant.

"Oh," he grimaced, "well, as you might have guessed, it didn't turn out quite the way we had planned. Masimba's white friend sabotaged it for us – with the best intentions, no doubt. We had to do it all over again the next day to get the photos we were after."

"And did you?"

"Yes, we chose a restaurant in Baker Avenue this time."

"What happened?"

"Worked like a charm. We were told in no uncertain terms that kaffirs were not served and we should go back to the townships where we belonged."

She winced, and he grinned cynically. "I ran the piece and it caused a few hackles to rise, which was the general idea. As you see, this is not London."

"You have been to London?"

"I worked on Fleet Street for a couple of years, until I missed the sun. It's a good time to be back, things are beginning to hum." They were outside the hotel now. "Are you going back to the Herald?" he asked. "I'll walk a little way with you."

As he loped along beside her, she noticed the oblique glances of people in the street. The sight of a white woman walking with a black man was not a commonplace occurrence in Salisbury.

He told her he published his magazine with a staff of three: "Myself, one other journalist – we take the photos ourselves – and a secretary. It's hard graft, but I love it."

"What did you mean when you said things were beginning to hum?"

"Well, start of Federation, this Kariba project. The decision to built it at Kariba, not in Northern Rhodesia on the Kafue River. The ANC being resuscitated. Interesting times."

Since her argument with Chris Rainier, she had determined to familiarise herself with the complex workings of state and federal politics in the young colony, and so far had only gauged the opinions of white Rhodesians.

Now she asked Guve, "What do you think of Garfield Todd?" referring to the country's handsome, charismatic prime minister, a combination of missionary, farmer and politician.

"Todd? Bit of an enigma, mixture of progressiveness and rigidity. He clearly wants to move towards electoral reform, wants to do more for us in the way of education and agriculture, and get rid of discriminatory laws. But he was tough on the miners who came out on strike. On the whole, I prefer his approach to Huggins'."

"Huggins? He's the federal prime minister?"

"That's the boy. Been around for years, part of the establishment, and has the paternalistic approach. Africa is changing fast now, people like him are becoming obsolete. I don't think he'll be around much longer, he's overdue for retirement."

"Who represents the black people?"

"That's the problem. At the moment, we have no real leadership. For half a century we've sat back and let it happen to us. Now there is Joshua Nkomo. He's been lying low the past few years, but my contacts tell me the ANC are going to resurrect him as leader. He's got the credentials but he lost credibility, because when he went to London with Huggins, he appeared to support Federation, then came back and said the opposite.

"Still, he's experienced, and the whites think he is more moderate than radicals like Chikerema or Edson Sithole."

"Do you count yourself a moderate?" she asked as they walked up Second Street towards the cathedral.

"I guess so, in comparison with them, and my friend Paul Masimba – the man I was with the other night. He wants 'one man one vote' today."

"Surely you want that too?"

"Of course, but I would be prepared to compromise on a few years of partnership before we take over." He grinned.

She sighed. "It's all very confusing."

"It's nowhere as simple as the media try to paint it. You'll soon get the picture, but watch closely, it's going to change fast."

"Why?"

"Well, in the north, there's a move towards independence and black majority rule. Down south, with the Nats in power, there's a hardening of white attitudes. And the meat in the sandwich is us, experimenting with the concept of so-called black-white partnership. But there are few among my people who believe in this notion of partnership."

She remembered Chris' words: "They think it's been engineered for the benefit of white Southern Rhodesians". "A bit one-sided, you mean?"

"Extremely one-sided." They had reached her office building and he held out his hand, "Good to have met you. Good luck."

At dinner, Barbara mentioned that Derick's brother was due in town for a few days. "Chris's right, Liz. You should meet him. He could tell you a lot about the river, perhaps give you advice about how to start."

"Good, because I'm cooking up a plan." She explained that the journalist she was standing in for was due back in a week, but there was now a definite possibility of permanent work. If she could persuade the editor to send her to Kariba to write a story about the relocation of the Batonga people, she might be able to begin her search.

"Ian would be pleased to see something balanced written about the Batonga instead of the emotional claptrap some of the overseas press have been churning out," Derick commented. "He could take you upriver into some of the villages. He loves those people, and the Valley. I believe he's happier there than any place else on this earth."

"Is he married?"

"No. Barbara says he's a confirmed bachelor. I think he's just too pre-occupied with his work, always off in the bush somewhere."

As soon as she realised that Ian Coles' reserved demeanour concealed a dry sense of humour, Liz relaxed and felt at ease with him. On the stoep after dinner, she asked hesitantly about the possibility of accompanying him into the Valley.

"That shouldn't be a problem," he said immediately. "I have to go upriver in a few weeks and you could come with me."

"I wouldn't be in the way?"

"Not at all. I usually drive, but the department has bought a boat because of all the to-ing and fro-ing recently, so we can do it in style. It can be hellishly hot, though it's not so bad at the moment. D'you think she could handle it, Barb?" he quirked an eyebrow at his sister-in-law. "A greenhorn from the UK?"

"'Course she can. She's not the helpless type."

"Are you sure?" He looked across to Liz, who was still in the tailored suit she wore to work. "She has that citified look about her," he teased, with a grin that suddenly made him look like his brother. "But the Brits are often tougher than they look."

"I'll be fine," she assured him. "Would I be able to talk to people who are being moved?"

"Sure. Some have gone already, but you can talk to anyone you like. Use one of my lads to interpret. A few of the men have a little English. They are a bloody good bunch, very friendly. Idle as hell, spend their lives lying around consuming the local brew. The women do most of the work. Their story needs to be told, without sentimentality."

"Will we see animals?"

"I think we can guarantee that." He leaned forward, fixing his intense gaze on her, ash building up on his cigarette. "I'll tell you the secret of the Zambezi Valley, why the animals are still there when they've vanished just about everywhere else. It's because of a little midgie called a tsetse fly, which has a bite that is death to cattle. That's why there has never been much human settlement. Just about the only blacks who live there are the ones along the river, they live mainly on fish and maize, and barely make a dent in the wildlife. Because of that, the place is an almost pristine paradise. Elephant, rhino, buffalo, lion, leopard, kudu, eland. And birds – just wait," and he grinned boyishly.

"She'll be expecting the Garden of Eden," Derick interrupted. "Don't give the wrong impression, Ian. Liz, the place is dry and dusty, hot as a furnace. A lot of it is dead flat and covered in jesse bush – almost impenetrable, and you'll get bitten by everything under the sun."

"He's right," Ian agreed, "to me, it *is* the Garden of Eden, but it can be somewhat inhospitable – and, as far as I'm concerned, long may it remain so. I can't imagine anything more God-awful than hordes of American tourists in pith helmets and safari outfits rubbernecking along my river."

"My river. See what I mean, Liz," Derick jeered. "Thinks he owns the place."

"When you live and work down there for any length of time, you get to feel protective about it," Ian said peaceably, stubbing out his cigarette.

"You must be upset about the dam?" Liz asked him.

"It's going to destroy something very special. I hate the idea."

When Liz approached her editor with her proposal, he agreed with barely a hesitation. "OK. It's time we did a follow-up. Don't go and get heat stroke, that's all I ask," he growled. "Do a piece that presents both sides, for and agin'. And you might as well have a look at the wall while you're at it."

She wrote to Mario, giving him her dates, and set about buying the kind of clothes likely to be needed in the Zambezi Valley. Although not so naive as to think a visit to the river would lead her miraculously to the site of Clarissa's grave, the prospect of seeing the region where her grandparents had spent the last days of their lives – and where her own mother had been born – lent the expedition a sense of personal pilgrimage that greatly appealed to her. She wondered why her mother had never felt the same urge to seek out her birthplace. How had Katherine lived so long without at least wanting to see the Valley, even if not to search for her mother's grave?

But the more she thought about it, the idea of Katherine, with her tweed skirts and neatly-permed hair, trudging through the African bush, was more than slightly incongruous. It was difficult to picture her mother anywhere but the familiar surroundings of her comfortable, restored cottage in Englefield Green, putting the kettle on, taking the dogs for a ramble in Windsor Great Park, or settling by the fire with one of her never-ending tapestries. As the familiar images flashed through her mind, she was suddenly swamped by a longing for her practical, down-to-earth presence. Katherine, whose outlook was always so eminently sane and sensible, whose focus on her two children had precluded any other intimate relationships since the day in 1943 when her young husband's plane was shot down in flames over Cologne.

Liz sat down and wrote her a long letter. And, inevitably, her thoughts turned to Alex and the letter in her handbag. He was still treating her defection to Africa as a temporary aberration: *Have fun, get a tan, come back soon. I miss you so much I don't go to our pub any more*, he had ended. He seemed to have forgotten their parting, and her determination to use her departure as a final break.

Alex. She was sitting in her favourite spot on the sleeping porch, overlooking the garden. Now she put the pen down, leaned back and closed her eyes. In the novelty of her new surroundings, she had been reasonably successful in pushing thoughts of him to the back of her mind, but the pressure of doing so had been slowly building up. Now she gave in, and allowed a score of painful, precious images to flood into her mind. Alex leaning over her desk to explain something, his blue eyes narrowed in concentration, the smell of him; Alex at the helm of *The Duchess* in his old navy sweater, shouting instructions as he steered the boat into a lock; Alex in a pub at the end of a day on the water, playing with her fingers, making love with his eyes.

Alex explaining patiently that while she mattered more than anyone else in the world, for the moment – with the children so young – he couldn't contemplate divorce.

On the radio, Julie London's husky, yearning voice crooned 'Cry me a River', one of his favourites. The old ache surged back, so deep that nothing could reach it, so strong that tears pricked her eyes. She blinked, pushed back her chair and went outside, calling to Barbara that she was taking Shumba for a walk.

On the way back, she decided to go out to the farm for the weekend, and when she returned to the house she phoned Nicholas. He sounded preoccupied.

"What's the matter?" she asked. "Is something wrong?"

"Just some labour hassles, nothing to worry about. Tell you about it when I see you."

She left straight from work, stopping at a cafe to pick up fresh bread. It was good to get out on the open country road again. The sun was setting but it was still light enough to enjoy the drive along a route that was becoming familiar. Here was the line of tall, ragged gum trees, here the road ran beside a beautiful dam surrounded by wooded hills, past a stall where you could buy fresh oranges. And here you turned off the strips on to the dirt track. When you reached the roadside store, closed up for the night now, you knew it was not far to the Mushana signpost. Now for the worst bit of track, although Nicholas had put the grader over it and it was marginally better than the first time she had come.

He was on the steps as her car climbed the hill from the dam, and the dogs galloped across the lawn to meet her.

"What was the trouble you mentioned the other night?" she asked when they were sitting out on the stoep.

"Lot of rubbish," he grumbled, opening a beer for her.

It appeared that the man Dendera who had been at the centre of the midnight incident, had not been content to let the matter drop. "He is spreading the word that Reta put *muti* in his beer that night. No one took any notice until his little girl got sick. She's in hospital now and they don't seem to know what's wrong, though they're treating her for malaria. Dendera says Reta is using witchcraft against him and his family."

"But why should anyone believe him?"

"I don't think they would have, if the child hadn't got sick. Like I said, they're superstitious."

"What are you going to do?"

"Nothing for the moment, I'm hoping it will blow over. I've talked to Luke, he's sticking by Reta, which is fortunate, because men are often quick to get rid of a wife who is suspected of anything like that.

"Trouble is, Moses says there's tension building up in the compound. I don't want to fire Dendera – he's a good driver and mechanic, but I told him this week that if there is any more trouble, he's out."

"Is witchcraft legal?"

"No, it's not. Usually these things blow up every now and then, and then fizzle out. It's understandable. In the old days, it was their way of dealing with anything they couldn't understand – illness, death, natural disasters. It may be against the law now, but you can't just stamp it out. It's part of their belief system."

"And the woman – Reta?"

"Swears she's innocent, of course. If the child hadn't got sick ..... but you just need one untoward event at the wrong time and something small can blow up into something big."

She saw the woman on Sunday morning as she walked the dogs down the dirt track past the compound. She was bending over a black pot set on a small fire, and when Liz lifted a hand in greeting, she flashed a smile and bobbed a half-curtsey.

Wanting to be friendly, Liz asked, "Are you better now?" and touched her own face to remind her of the midnight incident. Reta's eyes darkened and she turned away.

15

They called it the Elephant Road: the tortuous, fifty-mile highway linking the highveld with Kariba Gorge in the fiercely hot heart of the Zambezi Valley. From the crest of the escarpment, it zig-zags down through dense acacia forest into a heat-hazed wilderness that extends north to the great river – a vast silent world where lofty baobabs stand guard over a sea of mopani forest and dense scrub.

When the idea of harnessing the power of the river became an official government project, the first priority had been to lay a road to carry the heavy machinery needed to build the dam. At the time, the road from Salisbury ended about two hundred miles north of the city, on the crest of the Zambezi escarpment, at the tiny outpost of Makuti. Beyond, the only access to the river was down the old Hunters' Road, or along a few rough tracks used by prospectors or survey teams.

The Roads Department said it would take two years and up to a million pounds to run a road through that uncharted wilderness, figures heard with a snort of disbelief by outspoken Irrigation Department chief Jim Savory, one of the few in government who knew the area intimately. The road could be built for a third of that figure, in no more than a year, declared Savory. His department won the contract, and the sceptics rubbed their hands and waited for him to fail.

But he devised a strategy beautiful in its simplicity. Instead of using one of the existing routes, he would follow the well-worn tracks trodden by elephants for centuries past as they moved between the barren escarpment and fertile floodplains. He would build his road high on the hills, avoiding many of the rivers interlacing the route, and crossing others at levels where drifts could be used instead of costly bridges. It was 1955, and he pledged to have the job finished by December – an impossible deadline by most estimates.

With a dedicated young team fired by the challenge, he set out to clear a path for vehicles and machinery. To avoid hauling water, his reconnaissance team sank boreholes as they pushed and sweated slowly forward through dense thorn bush and head-high grass, while African scouts patrolled for lion, elephant, and buffalo. Tsetse flies plagued them by day and mosquitoes by night.

The close-knit crew of white, black and coloured men achieved impossible targets in searing heat and choking dust; when the relentless sun sank wearily below the tree line, they toiled on into the night by tractor headlights or the light of the moon. Living on a diet of impala meat, bully beef and beans, they quenched their never-ending thirst with gallons of beer and soft drink. Drawn together by months of isolation, the men developed a camaraderie forged by a determination to succeed for the satisfaction of having done it. Not that they thought of it that way. It was just bloody hard work. Dangerous too. One night, a herd of elephants silently materialised in their midst and the whole camp took to the trees, swearing and bumping into one another in the dark. On another occasion, men checking survey figures rounded a bend to be confronted by a pride of lion sprawled in the shade of a mopani. It was not unusual to find a cobra curled up in a sleeping bag, or a puff adder lying across the track, too lethargic to slither out of the way. It was just such an incident that gave one hilltop the name Puff Adder Ridge.

There were brief moments of relief: to stand at high noon under the outlet pipe of a water tanker for a few blissful moments; to pour a beer – even a warm one – down a parched gullet at the end of a long day. Rare moments of magic lightened the backbreaking toil: the primeval silhouette of a baobab, root-like arms outstretched to the sky, back-lit by an apricot sunset; or nights when the moon hung cool over an endless ocean of bush, and a leopard, with flanks silvered by moonlight, flickered through the shadowy trees, yellow eyes agleam.

Savory had two teams mapping the road, one working its way north, the other south. Shortly before they were due to meet halfway, the northern team reported their progress blocked by a chaotic jumble of hills through which there seemed no logical route. With a colleague, he slashed through dense undergrowth along an elephant path. On the crest of a ridge, the imperious roar of a lion halted them. They looked at each other and back-tracked, and the hastily-blazed trail became part of the road, christened Savory's Folly.

With heavy grey thunderheads massing on the horizon north of the river, the Elephant Road was completed by deadline, and celebrated with a memorable *braaivleis* at the halfway point.

Bouncing over the legendary road in a rattling government Land Rover, Liz was acutely, if uncomfortably, alive to the romance of its creation. She had heard the story from Derick, and was alert for the crude signs that told their own story: Buffalo Point, Rhino Nek, Razor Ridge. The bush was grey-brown and sere, and the blue smoke of fires hung heavy above the trees, mingling with the dust of passing vehicles. A kite circled in a rising thermal, and a troop of baboons occasionally careered across the road – past mounds of elephant droppings – with babies perched on adult backs or clinging upside-down to bellies. The heat was dense and suffocating, and swarms of insects splattered the dust-smeared windscreen. When trucks lumbered past, rattling with crates of beer, the dust billowing through the windows and cracks in the vehicle floor was so thick and choking the driver pulled off the road. As soon as they were stationary, clusters of tiny mopani flies danced around their heads, swarming about eyes and mouths in a frenzied search for moisture. Through the dust haze, the sun burned with a copper glow.

It was midday by the time the Land Rover reached the floodplain, and the desiccated jesse bush gave way to cool riverine greenery. Ian was waiting at the pre-arranged rendezvous on the river bank, and Liz climbed stiffly out of the Land Rover, wiping dust and sweat from her eyes.

Two khaki-uniformed Africans unloaded supplies and transferred them to the neat craft bobbing at anchor.

"We have to get moving," Ian handed her a warm bottle of lemonade. "We have a long way to go and a couple of stops along the way. Got a message from Chris, by the way. He might join us at the end of the week."

For a mighty river that cleaves the heart of Southern Africa for two thousand miles, the Zambezi's genesis is a remarkably inconspicuous trickle in a remote forest near the border between Northern Rhodesia and Angola. The stream gathers strength as it wanders aimlessly through verdant forests and dust-blown flats, fanning out into broad floodplains where life is paced to the rhythm of its seasonal inundations. Egyptian geese, herons and plovers find peaceful sanctuary here, and fishermen in *makoros* watch warily for the crocodiles and hippo that patrol the waters.

Flowing smoothly between widening banks, the river swells, fed by a score of tributaries, quickening to tumble over foaming rapids and sparkling cataracts, frothing and churning through deep dark gorges hung with velvet moss and emerald vines. Widening again, it filters through swamps, encircles floating islands of reeds and waterweed, until it reaches Kazangula, the meeting point of four countries – Northern and Southern Rhodesia, Bechuanaland and South West Africa. As the swamps evaporate, the Zambezi matures into a broad, sweeping waterway, more than half a mile wide; countless islands emerge from its glittering surface as it flows between banks of ilala palms towards its moment of supreme drama.

Watched by the stern stone figure of Livingstone, the passionate Scottish missionary who first relayed its wonders to the western world, the river plunges over the awesome precipice of the Victoria Falls, sheer cliffs formed by aeons of slow erosion. Billowing clouds of spray are flung high into the air, to drift like the smoke from an immense bushfire as the river thunders into the chasm below, a glistening world of tangled rainforest sheltering timid antelope and exotic birds. From this seething cauldron, it escapes, only to be imprisoned again, writhing in white-water fury through gorges scoured by restless waters over millions of years. Passion spent, it emerges as an indolent waterway sweeping through flat-topped hills, past scattered villages, until it meets a new obstacle – Kariba Gorge, lair of the river god Nyaminyami, where the white men are erecting a new monument to man's supremacy over nature.

Writhing through the narrow chasm, the river escapes once more, to flow on through the white-water of Cabora Bassa and into Portuguese East Africa. And here at last, broadening into a vast delta networked with islands and mangroves, its brown waters merge with the ultramarine blue of the Indian Ocean.

Although the heat on land had been intense, on the water – with the wind in her face – it was relatively cool as she clutched her broad-brimmed hat and shielded her eyes from the blinding glare. As the craft cut a white swathe across its glassy surface, the river flowed decorously past a reed-fringed shoreline. Swallows skimmed the sunlit surface and Egyptian geese clamoured overhead. It was Liz's first glimpse of Africa stripped of the accoutrements of 'civilisation', little changed from the wilderness through which Simon and Clarissa had wandered more than half a century before. This morning she had woken to the sound of traffic; within hours she had been transported to a realm where crocodiles basked on white sandbars and a elephant bull lumbered up a bank, water sluicing off its wrinkled grey hide. She was swept by a surging sense of freedom, of stepping into another world and another age.

After a time, Ian pulled in to the shore. They walked up the sand, criss-crossed with the prints of many animals, and sat in the shade, eating sandwiches and drinking warm Fanta under the watchful eye of an old buffalo bull, twitching his tail and tossing his massive head to rid himself of flies. When she related the story of Clarissa and Simon, Ian was disappointed she had so little factual information about the location of their campsite.

"If only you had more to go on," he told her, "I know this area well, but your description could fit a hundred spots along the river bank. The best we can do is ask at the *kraals* – it's the sort of thing that sometimes gets passed down in stories, from one generation to the next."

He told her that a number of *kraals* on the south bank had already been vacated and their occupants taken inland by truck. "We're calling in at one that's due to be moved soon. Then we'll head for the camp."

The *kraal* was a shabby group of thatched huts, some built on stilts. Dried fish hung outside the huts, a patch of desiccated mealies drooped behind them; chickens pecked listlessly, and a few figures lounged in the shade. "Wait by the water," Ian told her, "this won't take long, and you'll have plenty of time during the next few days for your interviews. But I will ask about the grave."

She walked to a small pool of shade and sat down to wait as he climbed the bank to meet an elderly man walking stiffly with a stick, and two younger men.

His business completed, Ian introduced the headman, who greeted her with grave courtesy. "He has no knowledge of any unknown grave," Ian said, "but says he will spread the word and send a message if he finds out anything."

The air was cooler when, an hour later, he steered towards the shore once more, along a narrow channel bordered by tall reeds and carpeted with drifts of waterlilies. On the bank, tents were clustered beneath mahogany trees, and two Africans slithered down the sand to meet them.

The camp was as clean and orderly as a military establishment. "We often have visitors, public servants, journalists sometimes, or mates slipping away for a weekend's fishing," Ian said as he led her to the guest tent.

It was big enough to stand up in, and held two mosquito-netted camp beds, a folding chair, and a paraffin lamp, candles and matches set on a small folding table.

After a mug of tea at a table beneath the tallest mahogany, Ian fetched two pairs of binoculars and led her along the river bank. It was a ritual they were to follow most evenings, walking along a well-defined track and pausing to watch animals coming down to the water to drink.

"For game viewing, you're here at a good time," he told her, as two elephants used their trunks to nudge their calves gently into the water, and others ambled slowly towards an island in midstream. "The inland pans and river beds are drying up, so the game congregates here until the rains come." His eyes never left the adult females, whose questing trunks tested the air. "Let's move. They're getting our scent and they're a bit edgy with their calves."

Further along the sandy track, a herd of impala drank nervously at the water's edge, pausing frequently to lift their heads and prick their ears; and as she watched through the binoculars, a group of zebra trooped down the bank. She turned to Ian with shining eyes. "It's wonderful," she breathed. He grinned.

On the way back to camp in the gathering darkness, the sound of splashing halted them above a secluded pool enclosed by reeds. Waterlilies bobbed as though disturbed from below; and a blacksmith plover tink-tinked over the water.

"What is it?" she whispered.

"Look, there." She strained to see. A pair of nostrils, two ears and a glistening black mound emerged through the carpet of lilies, and beside it, a miniature set of ears, nostrils and round pink back. "Mum and baby hippo," he said softly. "I thought at first the baby was caught in the reeds, but mum is there."

The calf looked like a bouncy rubber toy, she decided.

"The rest of the pod are somewhere else," said Ian in a low voice. "The female usually goes off alone to give birth. Males have been known to kill new arrivals."

"What about crocs?"

"A tasty snack that little one would make. Mum will have to keep her eyes skinned. All right, *mvuu*, we'll leave you in peace."

He grinned over his shoulder as they returned to the track. "That was a first for me too. I've never seen such a young calf before. That's why I love this place, every day is different."

In the camp, December the cook showed her to a grassed enclosure where the 'shower' was housed – a large bucket, attached to a branch and fitted with a watering rose. Washing away the dust of the day, she gazed through a network of branches at the stars while the warm water streamed down through her hair, over her breasts, and down her back. A breeze whispered across her skin, and she found it difficult to believe she was really here, in this magic place, beside Clarissa's river.

In clean shirt and slacks, damp hair slicked back, she joined Ian at the fire in the centre of the clearing. December was bent over two heavy black pots bubbling on the cooking fire. Ian opened a beer, and handed her a gin and tonic. "We don't really need the fire now, but it gets cool later, and keeps away the midgies," he explained.

Dinner was venison stew, spicy and delicious. While they ate, fires from small villages on the distant bank winked across the mirror surface of the river; now and then, the breeze carried the faint throb of drums, and she was suddenly conscious of their isolation, of the blackness of the forest. "I've never slept in the bush," she confided, making her voice casual. "Is there anything I ought to know?"

He grinned, leaned back in his camp chair and lit a cigarette. "Relax, Liz, you're quite safe. Occasionally elephants wander through, but they never bother us. Sometimes a honey badger comes looking for food, or hyena scavenging for scraps. If you hear them, keep your tent flap closed."

"Hyena?" She restrained a shiver, and they drifted into a companionable silence. After dinner, he poured a nightcap for them both, and the firelight was reflected in her glass as she sipped, listening to the night music: crickets, frogs, hippos grunting, nightbirds whistling. The river glimmered silver, moon-rippled, and she counted three shooting stars before her eyelids grew heavy and she said a reluctant goodnight.

When she lay down on the camp bed, extinguished the paraffin lamp and settled the mosquito net about her, she felt at once conflicting sensations of cosiness and imminent peril. Cosiness because the net enclosed her in a safe little cocoon, peril because of the sounds from beyond the canvas fabric separating her from the African night. Splashes from the river reminded her that the hippos could now be heaving their massive bodies out of the water and up the bank. The wind rustled the leaves overhead, an animal barked in the distance, and she recalled with chilling clarity a cocktail bar story of a hyena taking a chunk out of a camper's face while he slept.

Hyena. She remembered Ian's words. Crawling out from beneath the mosquito net, she made sure her tent flap was fastened, then arranged her suitcase, the table and folding chair on either side of her bed, and lay down again, feeling marginally more secure.

They were on the water shortly after dawn, and she quickly became familiar with Ian's routine. For the first two days they returned to camp after his work was done, but from the third day they moved upriver and stopped overnight at a temporary camp.

When they called at a *kraal*, the routine was always the same. They were met by a headman or a small delegation and, after complicated greetings, were led to a clearing among the thatched huts. There they would sit on low stools – often intricately carved – while Ian conferred with the elders on relocation plans.

Their questions focussed on practical matters. How would they survive without the floodplains on which to plant their annual crops? Some were skilled wood carvers: who would they sell their products to? Would their poultry survive the journey? How could they cross the water to visit relatives?

He was endlessly patient, lighting one cigarette from another, listening, explaining, pondering, while the men sucked on their long curved 'hubble-bubble' pipes fashioned from gourds.

Sometimes he would be called upon to arbitrate in some local dispute – which could be a lengthy and complex business involving tortuous explanations and long ruminative silences. During such discussions, time seemed to lose its meaning, it was as though the topic could be pored over for days, while they dissected, argued, weighed various points, and considered the issues from every angle.

Although the *kraals* were poor, primitive places, and many of the people were infected by disease, they were friendly and talkative, especially the men. A few women wore threadbare western dresses, but most were clad only in skirts of fringed animal hide. Necklets and bracelets of beads or small cowrie shells encircled their limbs, and some women plastered their hair and bodies with red ochre.

"Why do some have their front teeth missing?" she asked Ian.

"Some say it was meant to discourage raiding tribes from wanting to carry them off, others that it was a rite of passage to adulthood, like circumcision. Someone told me it was to make them more attractive to men. Couldn't quite see the logic behind that one. But not many do it any more."

Some of the men wore loin cloths, others tattered shorts. "The men have been to Salisbury or Bulawayo to earn money to pay their hut tax, so they've seen a bit of the world – if you can call Bulawayo the world," Ian told her. "The women have never been anywhere except across the river. They don't have to worry about border formalities, they come and go as they please."

If he finished his business during the morning, they would return to camp by midday, retiring after lunch to lie sweating in their tents through the drowsy hours of early afternoon. Later Ian would pound away at reports on an old portable typewriter, while Liz wrote up notes on her conversations with the tribespeople.

He went out of his way to find her men who spoke a little English, so that she could interview them herself. Sometimes his assistant Enos acted as interpreter. Talking to the shy, friendly people, she soon learned that it was the older ones who most dreaded the impending move. They avoided talking about, as though that might prevent it from becoming a reality. While a handful welcomed the promise of better facilities, most – particularly the young men – were vociferous in their opposition. But young men were in the minority; many of them had already left the river to find work in the south.

"The ANC have stirred them up, told them not to cooperate. They come from Salisbury and Bulawayo, and across the river. They're a damn nuisance and one of the reasons we're moving the people out as fast as we can," Ian told her one evening. "Most of them will be gone before the rains. We'll move the rest next year – it's impossible to do anything during the wet season."

"How far will they have to go?"

"It varies. Some will only have to move about 25 miles from where they are now, the furthest will be 150 miles. Most of them somewhere in between."

Gradually, she built up a picture of a people whose universe was inhabited by an array of supernatural beings – witches, sorcerers, powerful spirits both benign and evil, whose potency was unquestioned. Many were the spirits of ancestors who continued to wield enormous power long after they were dead. Among the congregation was the river god Nyaminyami, who took the form of a serpent and was enraged by the attempts of the white men to shackle the river.

Ian introduced her to a *sikatonga*, or spirit medium – a small, shrunken man with a few yellow teeth and a pendulous goitre on his neck. Through Enos, he told her the ancestral spirits were equally displeased at the building of the dam. "He say," translated Enos, "that the spirits want to stay in this place. If the people have to move, the spirits may be angry. If they angry they come and destroy the new crops."

"Is there nothing the people can do to satisfy the spirits?" she asked.

The old man contemplated the ground before replying, then launched into a lengthy and passionate dissertation. Enos summarised: "Some time they can do many things. They can kill chickens and make sacrifice, they can ask for pardon, but he does not know if the spirits will listen. He say the people have to wait and see. He will not go, he will stay and look after the spirits."

When she asked the old man about the river god, his face darkened as he stared across to the placid, sunlit water. Enos translated: "He say you must wait for the rains. Last year, Nyaminyami brought a very big flood, very big," Enos shook his head at the memory. "Next year, he say it will be a flood such as the white people have never seen."

At every *kraal*, Ian raised the subject of Clarissa's grave, but his questions were invariably met by the same response – blank stares and a slow shake of the head. But her days were so crammed with new sights and experiences that her lack of success did not dishearten her. Later, when she looked back on the interlude, she would see it as a defining moment, an experience which, subtly and imperceptibly, changed the direction of her life. At the time, it was simply a unique adventure into the wilderness with a companion she came to like and respect as much as anyone she had ever known.

One night by the fire, as hyena tittered from the forest and hippos grunted comfortably from the river, he spoke of his distaste for his task. "The hardest thing is to convince them that the dam is worthwhile – that some benefit will come out of it. They love the river, you see. It's no use telling them the dam is going to bring electricity to Salisbury and Bulawayo – why should they care? That it's going to bring jobs – they don't need work except to earn a little money to pay the hut tax. They've had no training for city life, when they go to town, a lot of them end up as bucket boys, poor buggers."

At Liz's blank expression, he explained: "A lot of houses still have outdoor toilets. The bucket boys have the delightful job of carting away the buckets. They are called *maZambezi* – the people from the Zambezi."

"So what do you tell them?"

He shrugged, tilting a beer bottle to his lips. "That it's going to happen and they have to make the best of it. We've taken a few from each *kraal* to see their new places, and some of the headmen up to Kariba to show them what's happening there." His cigarette glowed in the darkness. "I feel for them. I know the dam has to be built, and I can't help being excited by the scale of it. But that doesn't stop me from lying awake at night thinking about what we're doing to a lifestyle that has existed for thousands of years. It's always poor bloody people like them who pay the price for what we like to call progress."

He looked at her with a brooding expression. "Sorry, Liz. Shouldn't be boring you with all this."

"It's not boring at all. I want to learn all I can. And I can understand how you feel. It is a tragedy. But what about the animals? You can't move them."

"That's the other tragedy. It's going to displace thousands. The hope is that they will move inland of their own accord, as the water rises. Whether or not that will happen, I have no idea. If it doesn't......" He shrugged.

Despite the heat which grew more intense by the day, she became so absorbed by the people, the animals and birds that sometimes she barely noticed it. She had left her watch on her bedside table in town, but found after a couple of days that she had no need for it. She was even beginning to learn the names of different birds and antelope from Ian, who seemed familiar with every species, no matter how small or inconspicuous. She was charmed by the aerobatics of the lilac-breasted rollers, by sacred ibises pacing the bank as haughtily as fashion models in their black-and-white livery; even the marabou stork with its obscene, naked neck had a macabre appeal. On a steep bank eroded by floods into sandy cliffs, swarms of small birds with shimmering rose plumage hovered at the entrances to hundreds of tiny tunnels in the cliff face.

"The carmine bee-eaters have come back to nest." Ian picked up his camera: he was painstakingly recording each species with the ultimate idea of producing a book on the bird life of the Valley.

She developed a deep affection for the hippos lying half submerged in the water, grunting grumpily as they changed position. "It's the most comfortable sound," she remarked, but he was quick to disillusion her. "They cause more accidents than any other animal – they can move fast under water and overturn a boat with ease."

Sometimes they went inland, where tall kigelia trees dangled enormous sausage-like pods, and giant strangler figs embraced their host trees in suffocating, rope-like tentacles. As they left the floodplain, the lush green cathedral-like canopies of mahogany, ebony and tamarind disappeared, the earth became parched and dusty, the trees smaller, scrub-like and thorny, and gaunt baobabs loomed stark and prehistoric. Often the land was scorched by bushfires, and the grass crunched into charred fragments underfoot. Undulating waves of heat were intensified by smoke, mingling with dust and the high-pitched, incessant shrilling of cicadas.

Each day brought something new, and Ian was a natural teacher. He plucked the scented butterfly-shaped leaves of the mopani, showing her how they folded up in the midday heat to conserve moisture. "Elephant and impala love them – there's some kind of oil in them that make their teeth look as though they are chain-smokers," he would tell her with his slow smile.

One day, the hum of an engine disturbed the tranquillity of the floodplain, and they glimpsed a run-down pick-up truck through the trees. Ian swore under his breath. "Look's like the ANC have arrived, just to make life interesting."

The following morning, as they pulled into the bank at a large *kraal*, they were not welcomed by the usual delegation. In the clearing, the people were gathered together around two men who were getting into the truck they had seen the day before, and Liz caught her breath in surprise as it moved off.

"I've seen that man before," she told him. "In a restaurant in Salisbury."

"Paul Masimba? Don't worry, I know him," Ian said shortly. "He's the bane of my life at the moment."

The headman wore a sheepish expression as he began a rambling explanation in answer to Ian's questions. People milled around, the men arguing loudly, and Ian called them together and stood on a stool to address them.

His words were interrupted by hostile rumbles from the young men. Although Liz had no idea what was being said, their tones were all too clear. Ian was angry and patient in turns, he was heckled noisily, and at one point turned to her and told her to go down to the boat and wait, but she shook her head. After a while, the hostility ebbed, the arguments became less acrimonious.

Ian talked for more than two hours, mainly with the men – although one toothless old woman was furiously vocal. When at last he stepped down from the stool and came across to Liz, he rubbed his sleeve across a face beaded with sweat. "Bloody ANC. If they have to subvert us, they could at least tell the truth."

"What do you mean?"

"They tell these people not to move, that we are lying and there will be no dam. That even if the water rises, they will be safe. That's all old hat. Now they are handing out pieces of paper which are supposed to protect them. These are simple people, they believe what they are told. According to the headman, Masimba and his friend Sam Paradza – who is a nasty piece of work – have just done the same here."

He felt in his pocket. "Do you know what these magic pieces of paper are?" He held out a card. "ANC membership cards. And they have the nerve to make them pay for the bloody things – that was Paradza. I think I'll get this lot moved out next week."

As the boat skipped and bounced over the water and the wind whipped her hair, he said, "As we're in the vicinity, I want to show you something that's aggravating my problems."

He eased the craft towards the bank and cut the motor, and the throb of machinery drifted through the trees. Waves of dust surged towards them, and the roar of diesel engines mingled with a crescendo of others sounds – clattering, crashing, tearing sounds.

They entered a vast clearing where a straggling line of half a dozen gigantic yellow caterpillar tractors were at work. They were linked to one another by lengths of massive iron chains, attached to enormous steel balls that rolled over the earth like giant marbles. Like an advancing army, the cavalcade flattened everything in its path, bringing tall trees crashing to the ground with ear-splitting cracks and groans. Ahead of the vanguard, birds and small animals hurtled through the bush in panic – monkeys, a small antelope, tiny mouse-like creatures too small to identify. Clouds of dust mingled with smoke from fires lit by teams of black labourers burning off the debris lying in the wake of the machines.

"What are they doing?" she shouted above the clamour of engines and the crack of splintering wood.

Ian put his mouth close to her ear. "Clearing the land. When the dam is full, the government wants to develop a fishing industry. When a forest is drowned it doesn't rot away, it gets petrified – fossilised. The branches would interfere with fishing nets, so they're clearing as much forest as possible."

She shook her head, appalled by the destruction.

"Horrendous, isn't it? These machines can clear thirty acres an hour."

"Those magnificent trees..."

"See that baobab – some of them have been here thousands of years. They're sort of a symbol of the Valley. Do you know that the Africans say there's no such thing as a young baobab – they believe they were here since the beginning of time."

But for once Liz was not in the mood for tribal lore from Ian's encyclopaedic mind. "Can we go? I can't bear to watch."

That evening, she recalled a remark he had made earlier. "Why did you say that clearing the forest was giving you more problems?"

"Because the locals think the only reason for clearing a forest is to plant crops. Some ANC boys have already told them we're not building a dam, we just want to take away their land so we can use it ourselves. When they see those tractors," he shrugged, "it confirms what they've been told.

"And another thing. The Batonga believe some trees are inhabited by the spirits of their ancestors, so you can't just hack them down. There was a case recently involving a mahogany. This old guy, a *sikatonga*, stood in front of it and when a driver tried to move him, all the blacks threatened to walk off the job. In the end, they left the tree standing."

Two massive trucks were drawn up in a clearing beside the small shabby huts, and the occupants were loading their belongings into the vehicles under the supervision of the drivers.

They did not have much: small bundles wrapped in blankets, wooden stools, an assortment of black cooking pots, hubble-bubble pipes, sacks of grain and dried fish, poultry in reed baskets. Small naked children darted about, excited by the massive dusty vehicles, but their elders moved sullenly and in silence.

When the time came to climb aboard, they hung back, fearful and reluctant. The women muttered amongst themselves and huddled in a defensive group while Ian's assistants Enos and Bicycle talked to them patiently. The headman, a tall stooped figure with a face carved in grim ebony lines, argued heatedly with Ian, shaking his head and pounding the earth with his stick. "They not want to get into the truck," Enos told her. "Some of them have not seen a truck before. They want to walk. But it is too far."

It took half an hour, and the combined persuasive powers of Ian, Enos and Bicycle, to get the people to climb slowly and reluctantly into the back of the trucks, where the older men immediately sought comfort in their pipes. In the centre of the clearing, a skinny old woman with an impassive face stood immovable, with folded arms, a figure of implacable rebellion. After Enos and Bicycle had argued with her for several minutes, two younger women came down from the truck, took her arms and urged her towards it. Angrily, she shook off their hands and shouted at them. They drew back and waited. She stared contemptuously at Ian and Liz, the two assistants and the waiting people, and muttered something scathing under her breath. Finally, slowly and deliberately, she picked up a small bundle wrapped in a soiled fabric and hobbled with pathetic dignity to the vehicle.

Although Liz had brought along her camera, intending to photograph the departure, she found herself unable to use it. "That's why you will never make a real journalist," Alex had once told her matter-of-factly. Inwardly, she had to agree, for she could not condone intrusions into private moments of anguish such as this.

Now there was only the headman, leaning on his staff, silent tears staining his wrinkled cheeks as Ian patted his bony shoulder. "Come on, *madala,* time to go."

He looked at Ian's sombre face, turned away and walked in silence to the truck. The motors rumbled into life, the old woman began to wail and her chant was picked up by the other women. Slowly, the two vehicles rolled between the huts and out of the clearing down the track. A plume of dust spiralled upward through the tree canopy, and the wails were drowned in the roar of the engines that reverberated through the bush long after they had gone.

She took photographs of the silent, empty *kraal,* from which all life had suddenly drained away. Enos and Bicycle touched matches to the roofing, and within seconds the huts were crackling into flames. "Discourages them from trying to come back," Ian said in response to the question in her eyes. When the *kraal* had been reduced to charred logs and piles of smouldering ashes, he turned away. "Let's go." His voice was brusque and she followed him silently.

On the way back to the camp, he pulled in to the bank and they sat in the shade to eat their sandwiches. Afterwards, as they lay dozing, the sound of voices intruded on the heavy, somnolent silence. Liz plucked at Ian's sleeve: "It's that man – Paul Masimba."

He sat up quickly. They were standing by the water's edge, arguing – Masimba and a young woman, bare-breasted, slim hips encased in a skirt of animal hide. Ian's boat was moored behind a sandbar, and the couple had not realised they were not alone.

Ian stood up. "Good," he murmured, "got a bone to pick with him," and cleared his throat loudly.

Masimba and the woman started and turned. The men greeted each other curtly, and Ian introduced Liz. Masimba took her extended hand, but the girl only stared with apprehensive eyes and said nothing. She was slight, with high cheekbones and wide-set eyes.

Ian drew from his shirt pocket the card he had shown Liz, handing it to the African. "What are you playing at, Masimba?" he demanded. "Handing these out, feeding these people a lot of bullshit about witchcraft and magic?"

"What bullshit?" Masimba spoke aggressively.

"That," he pointed at the card. "I know what you're up to, you and Paradza. You'll do anything to stop them moving out, even telling them pieces of paper will protect them from the flood."

"And you want to take away their land. You have no right," retorted Masimba, "I have told no lies, only that if they stay you cannot make them go."

"That's not only damn stupid, it's bloody dangerous and you know it. Jesus, man, if they think they have some kind of divine protection, they might come back later. You could get them killed with your lies."

"I have told no lies....."

"Someone has. Look, man," said Ian more peaceably, "I don't like this business any more than you do, but – "

"Why are you doing it then? Why can't you leave them alone?"

"Because, dammit, the place is going to be under water," Ian said impatiently. "Whether you or I like it or not, it's going to happen. They have to go."

"And if they don't?"

They stared at each other, and when Ian spoke again, his voice was quiet. "You want to watch it, *shamwari*. If I catch you obstructing government business, you'll be in deep trouble."

"Oh yes?" Masimba shot back. "You have walked over us for so long you think you can do what you like. You've got all the best land already, isn't that enough? You've had it your way up to now, but things are changing."

"Is that a threat?"

"Think what you like," Masimba's voice was hard and contemptuous.

"I'm warning you, Masimba. Keep away. If you stir up trouble, people will only get hurt."

Masimba thrust the card back at him. "I will do what I have to do," he said curtly. Nodding abruptly at Liz, he turned and walked away. The woman followed, half running to keep up with him.

Ian rubbed his temple wearily as he watched them disappear into the trees. They are both doing what they have to do, she thought. Ian and Paul Masimba.

When they returned to the main camp the following afternoon, she felt as though she was coming home as she dumped her rucksack in her tent, and went to the table beneath the giant mahogany tree. December was already setting down a tray of tea, and complaining to Ian about a baboon that had been raiding the kitchen tent.

They were into their second cups when a vehicle sounded in the distance, and moments later a Land Rover drew up in a cloud of dust. Chris Rainier emerged, sweat-stained shirt clinging to his back, followed by a tall, slim man in immaculate creased khaki trousers.

"This is Robin Chase," Chris announced, "Brit photographer, I met him in Kariba. When I told him about fishing for tiger, he didn't believe me, so I brought him along. Hope that's OK, Ian. We've got some supplies – and a crate of beer," he added.

"More than welcome," Ian extended a hand to the newcomer.

"The truth is," said Robin Chase as they shook hands, "I thrashed him at darts in the pub the other night, and he wants to get his own back. Probably will too – the biggest fish I've ever landed is a rather smallish trout." He had a public school accent and the aristocratic looks and manner to match – smooth fair hair and a relaxed, assured demeanour.

"He comes from your neck of the woods, Pendennis," Chris informed Liz.

"Good," she smiled at Robin Chase, "when this man is around, I often need reinforcements."

Chris was staring at her. Long hours in the sun had tanned her arms and legs, her hair was uncombed and matted with dust, and her cheeks flushed from the day on the water. Wearing dirty khaki shorts and a yellow cotton shirt snagged by acacia thorns, she looked very different from the pale, svelte Londoner he had encountered in the Salisbury restaurant.

She stared back at him placidly. "What?"

"Nothing. Glad to see you've got rid of that pale, urban look you arrived with."

Chris's guest had brought along several bottles of South African wine, and Ian opened the first at the dinner table. Over a convivial meal, Robin explained he was covering the dam project for National Geographic, after which he would be flying down to South West Africa to accompany an expedition to the Skeleton Coast. He had a caustic humour, a fund of amusing anecdotes – most of them at his own expense – and a monumental capacity for alcohol. Already he had established a rapport with Chris, and Ian leaned back in his chair, listening with his slow smile as their arguments ranged from cricket and soccer to politics. When Liz mentioned the meeting with Paul Masimba, Chris listened intently.

"That guy is heading one way. What are you going to do?" he asked Ian.

"Keep an eye on him, call in the police if he gives any more trouble. He was with one of the local women. The Batonga don't like it when city guys play around with their women. There have been a few incidents recently."

"You'd better empty those *kraals* quick-smart," said Chris.

"We can't. Not all the land has been cleared yet, or roads and boreholes put in. Some of them have to wait till next year."

"Well, I wouldn't waste any time." Chris turned to Liz. "So how do you like bundu-bashing?" he quizzed her.

"I love it. Wish I could stay longer."

"Not scared of sleeping out in darkest Africa?"

"Well," she confessed, "there is one thing, but you'll laugh….."

"Go on," he reached for his glass.

"It's the hippo. When they come out at night to browse they use a path that runs through the trees over there. My nightmare is that one night they'll get panicked by something and charge through the camp. I have this vision of a hippo entangled in my tent ropes, galloping into the bush with the tent, and me inside, bouncing along behind him. You said you wouldn't laugh," she finished accusingly.

"How could I – at such a macabre picture?" But his eyes were brimming with mirth.

After dinner, as they sat around the fire and Robin uncorked another bottle of wine, Ian pushed back his chair. "Won't be a moment."

He disappeared in the direction of his Land Rover, and they heard him tinkering in the vehicle. Moments later, the strains of a Chopin prelude floated into the night, the melody falling like drops of silver into the darkness.

"All the comforts," murmured Robin.

"You have a gramophone?" Liz asked when Ian returned.

"A radiogram, I run it off the Land Rover battery. Don't use it all that often, because I enjoy the sounds of the night. The animals and birds make my music, but occasionally I like something different. Tonight, I'm just showing off."

Chopin was succeeded by Mozart and Cole Porter, by which time Robin was in full flight. He had been telling a story about a disastrous expedition to India; now he stood up and held a hand out to Liz. "Come on, let's show these colonials how to dance," he invited her.

"Here?" she protested, laughing.

"Why not?" He took her hand.

The ground was smooth and level, pounded hard by the long dry season and the passage of many feet, and Robin was a expert dancer. They found they had friends in common, but she decided not to mention Alex. She had not thought about him for nearly a week, and she did not want to break the spell of the river.

"Is this your first trip to Africa?" she asked.

"Yes, and it's living up to expectations. Tonight has a feeling of unreality," he added.

"How do you mean?"

"Well," he grinned, "here we are, on the banks of the great, grey greasy..... no, that's the Limpopo, isn't it? The crocodile-infested Zambezi, with wild animals all around us, dancing to Cole Porter and Frank Sinatra."

"It is a bit like a dream," she agreed, conscious, as they danced into the circle of lamplight, of Chris's eyes following her.

The music ended, and as they walked back to the fire, the cook emerged silently from the shadows and murmured something to Ian.

"What's up?" asked Chris lazily.

"Jumbo," Ian said. "Remember, Liz, I told you they sometimes come into camp. December always gets the wind up. It's all right," he added, "they're just browsing through."

"Browsing through?" Robin's voice had lost its lazy drawl. "What exactly does that entail, and what is the procedure?"

"Nothing. Just stay where you are."

"Don't you need a firearm at least, in case you have to defend us?"

Ian grinned and shook his head. They sat in silence, ears straining. Liz expected elephants to announce their arrival with a crashing in the undergrowth, but there was barely a rustle from the darkness beyond the firelight.

"They're feeding off the leaves," Chris told her.

"How many?"

"It varies," said Ian, "about half a dozen, sometimes more, sometimes less."

Now she could just make out shadowy forms moving among the trees, but still there was barely a sound. She felt exposed and vulnerable. "Shouldn't we go into one of the tents?" she whispered tentatively.

Chris's cigarette was a glowing point in the darkness. "The tents, Pendennis? An elephant would demolish a tent a lot quicker than your hippos."

"Well, what about the Land Rover? Wouldn't we be safer in that?"

"Not exactly," Ian was grinning too, "that's where they are right now. Next to the Land Rover."

"I have to confess I share the lady's concern," drawled Robin, emptying the dregs from the wine bottle into his glass. "What if they feel the urge to try this tree for dessert?"

"They won't. They know we're here."

A trickle of running water broke the silence, as though a tap had been turned on.

"Who's using the shower?" asked Liz in amazement, and Chris' laugh rang out.

"Sssh!" she turned on him. "You'll startle them!"

"Sorry," his shoulders were shaking. "That isn't the shower, thick one, it's a jumbo peeing."

"Jesus," Robin's voice was hushed and awed, "sounds like a ruddy waterfall."

"Quiet," said Ian in a low voice. An elephant had ambled soundlessly into the clearing and was standing beside her tent, fifteen yards from the fire. Of the dark ghostly form, the only features that were clear were gleaming ivories and a waving trunk probing the tent fabric very carefully as though testing it for flaws. Then the animal began to feed on the leaves of an overhanging branch.

Robin's journalistic instincts reasserted themselves. "Can I get my camera?" he asked in a loud whisper.

"Wouldn't advise it," murmured Ian, "he's a mite too close to your tent."

Despite the knot in her stomach and the thumping of her heart, Liz was suddenly alive in every cell to the thrill of the moment. Adrenalin raced through her veins, and after a few minutes her fear subsided and it began to seem almost natural to be sitting a few yards from an immense leathery, wrinkled hide, listening to the faint rumbling sounds emanating from the animal's stomach. She smiled to herself in the dark: did Clarissa get this close to an elephant? Did she feel the same thrill?

After a while, having scattered twigs and leaves on the ground around her tent, the elephant swung slowly round and, on noiseless feet, moved into deeper shadow to rejoin its companions. The dark shadowy bulks merged with the night. "And that, folks," said Ian as he stood up and stretched, "was the entertainment for this evening."

Next morning, while he finished off a report, Chris, Robin and Liz took the boat out fishing, though Robin spent more time using his camera than his rod. Liz was content to sit with the binoculars, testing her growing knowledge of water birds, watching the lines run taut as the tiger and vundu fought their predators. She mourned with Robin when a tiger snapped his line, and jeered when Chris, with infuriating smugness, landed a hefty vundu. But it was uncomfortably hot on the water, and after lunch she asked to be put ashore, leaving the men to fish on.

Today was her last day, and Ian accompanied her on a final walk in late afternoon, to see if the mother and baby hippo were still in the secluded channel. But the carpet of waterlilies was undisturbed.

When she emerged from her shower, Chris was stretched out in a chair absorbed in a book, and Robin – who had been boasting about his culinary skills – was preparing fish for dinner. She walked down the bank to watch the sunset. They were so brief, these flaring African sunsets. You had to catch and imprint their splendour on your memory, for they died almost as soon as they were born.

I haven't achieved a thing as far as Clarissa's grave is concerned – except, I suppose, eliminating the places we've visited, she reflected. But it's been worth it just to be here. And surrounded by eligible men, her feminine self mocked her. Yes, she replied, all except the one I want. Still, it was a pleasant novelty, after focussing her emotions on Alex for so long, to think about other men. Ian she was completely at ease with, they had talked late into the night on a range of subjects; but at no time had she felt sexually attracted to him, and at no time had he made any attempt to cross the line from friendship to intimacy. Maybe he had a girl friend; maybe, as she was his guest, he was simply being a gentleman. Robin was witty and charming, a flirt, who made her feel attractive and desirable. But not my type, she decided.

And Chris? Her feelings were decidedly ambivalent. He could infuriate her beyond measure, but she had to acknowledge it was he who had found her accommodation, and helped her in other ways – giving her lifts between Shangara and Salisbury before she had the car. During the weekend, he had baited her several times, but she was learning not to react so impulsively.

River and sky flamed crimson, and the water at her feet glimmered like silk. The only sounds were distant splashes as the silhouettes of two elephants waded towards an island in midstream. She wondered, not for the first time: why does beauty sometimes make you feel so sad?

She did not hear the approach of Chris until he stood beside her, in a clean shirt, hair slicked down from the shower, beer bottle in hand. "I was delegated to see if a croc had got you?"

He sat down on the bank. "The chefs send their compliments – dinner will be served in ten minutes."

"Thanks, I'm coming," she sighed but did not move.

"What? Have we managed to wear you out?"

"No. I just wish this week didn't have to end."

"Told you, didn't I? It gets to you." He offered her the beer bottle, and she took it from him and drank, wiping her mouth with her hand as she gave it back. "Funny thing," he mused, "is that sometimes you don't realise how much until you go away and leave it."

"Mmm, I think that's what happened to my grandmother when she went back to England."

She stared across the silent, darkening river, from which the crimson glow was fading. "This has been the best week of my life. I've never seen and learned so much in such a short time."

"Ian's a good chap." They sat in silence, watching the flicker of small fires on the distant bank. A black-and-white bird flew past on slow wing-beats. "Blacksmith plover," she said, pleased she had remembered the name.

He grinned and raised an eyebrow. "I'm impressed."

"I want to learn everything there is to know about this place," she said seriously. "I can't believe that it will all be drowned."

"Not all. There will still be hundreds of miles of river left. But I know what you mean."

From upriver another bird called, a piercing, exultant cry. She lifted her head. "And that?"

"Fish eagle." He pointed to a silhouette etched against the sky on the limb of a dead tree. "Stacks of them along here." He drank, and passed her the bottle again. "When I was working in London, and the weather was foul or I was stuck on a tube, I used to shut my eyes and think about this place."

"Have you been here often?"

"Not right here, further east – used to come with Dad and David during school holidays. David's a fanatical fisherman. We used to hunt too, here and in Portuguese East."

He stood up. "Come on, Pendennis, I smell fish."

She took his outstretched hand and as he pulled her up, a low, resonant roar echoed across the valley, a sound that seemed to penetrate deep into the innermost secret parts of her body and soul. Faraway, it seemed, and yet close. "What is it?" she whispered.

"Lion. Across the river."

"Lion." She shivered, half in fear, half in awe. He was still holding her hand, and as she felt in the gloom for the shoes she had slipped off when she sat down, she stumbled, and he put out his hand to steady her. She felt the warmth of his body through the fabric of his shirt, his breath feathered warmly against her cheek, and looking up she caught an unguarded expression of something like surprise in his eyes.

"My shoes," she murmured in confusion, and as she felt about, a sudden pain in the ball of her foot made her gasp.

"What are you doing?" His voice was exasperated as he released her and picked up her shoe while she hopped about on one foot.

"Something stung me!"

"Here – put this one on. Leave the other one off. Can't take you anywhere." He took her arm, and helped her up the bank. "Could be a scorpion," he added conversationally.

"A scorpion!"

"Place is alive with them. I'll get a torch and have a look at your foot."

December was laying the table, Robin and Ian were hovering over the fire. "We're doing a wine sauce, won't be a jiffy," Robin told them. He had a glass in his hand and was stirring something in a small pot.

She sat down in a camp chair in the light of a paraffin lamp.

"Don't touch," Chris ordered her. He fetched a torch and first aid kit, and squatted down in front of her, taking her foot in his hands. He switched on the torch. "Looks like one of those hairy caterpillars – must have left some hairs behind. Does it hurt if I do this?" and he ran a finger over the painful area.

"Yes!"

"OK, OK," he rummaged in the first aid kit and found some tweezers. "This could take a while."

Her face screwed up in anticipation. "Be gentle," she pleaded.

"Where's that British upper lip? Here, hold the torch." He held her foot firmly and began picking out the offending hairs, his hands deft and gentle. "Keep still," he muttered as she winced. "How can I see what I'm doing?"

He frowned in concentration, his thick hair still darkly wet from the shower, and she felt an unexpected impulse to run her fingers through it. She had the sudden sense that they were alone, the two of them, in the bright capsule of lamplight, quite separate from the rest of the camp. She watched his fingers, and the light gilding the hairs on his forearm. Tiny moths dropped on to the back of his blue shirt and crawled across his shoulders.

"There," he said finally, "I think I got them all out."

"Are you sure? It still hurts," she complained, trying to ignore the breathless sensation under her ribs induced by the warmth of his fingers.

"Should be something for that here." He rummaged in the box, found a small tube and rubbed ointment into the reddening area, covering it with a small piece of plaster. "There," he looked up, saw her watching him, and grinned mockingly. "All better now."

"Thank you," she said, but he did not move and he did not release his hold. Instead, his grip tightened; very deliberately, he ran his forefinger slowly along her foot, from her ankle down to her toes, gazing up at her with a small smile at the corners of his mouth, an unfathomable expression in his eyes. It was an odd, suspended moment.

"What are you two up to?" It was Ian's voice. "Grub's up."

"On our way." Unhurriedly, he picked up her sandal, slipped it on and fastened it carefully. Only then did he release her foot.

She stood up. "Thank you," she repeated, suddenly shy. He inclined his head without speaking, closed the first aid box, and they walked to the table together in silence.

The fish had been filleted, crumbed and fried, and arranged on a large platter decorated with cubes of tomato. Ian opened the last two bottles of Robin's wine. Starlight filtered through the canopy of leaves, and once again she had the feeling the small group was enclosed in a magic capsule of lamplight. Several times during the meal she caught Chris's eyes above his wineglass, watching her with the same expression she had seen earlier.

When she returned to Kariba the following day with Robin and Chris, the latter found a bed for her in the township with Dave and Joan Harvey, who ran the local service station. Unpacking her notebook, she spent the rest of the day in the company of a liaison officer, Jack Ross, touring the town and the dam site, interviewing engineers and labourers.

There was exciting copy here – the monumental scale of the project, the wild remote setting, and the human drama unfolding in the relocation of thousands of river dwellers.

Even the name Kariba had a mythic quality. "It comes from the word *kariwa*, which means a trap," Jack told her, explaining that the waters of the Zambezi, forced through the narrow neck of the gorge, were trapped in a turbulent whirlpool created by jagged rocks jutting from the riverbed. "If a boat is caught in the current it gets sucked down into the vortex by Nyaminyami, so the locals say. And no bodies have ever been recovered. Bit of folklore for you."

The locals avoided the area, but occasionally fashioned miniature dolls from sticks and seeds and plants, which they threw into the swirling waters to appease the deity. "Probably chucked the odd unwanted person in during the old days," he added.

Seven years earlier, a cyclone had rampaged through the Valley, swamping villages and sweeping away unknown numbers of inhabitants. Four young government employees were camped out in a hut on the banks. During the night, torrential rains unleashed a score of landslides, one of which hurtled down the side of the gorge and buried the camp. Only three of the four bodies were recovered.

In the gorge, she stood with Jack on the road bridge spanning the river below the construction site. It was fiercely hot, and the thud of machinery never ceased; trucks and bulldozers toiled up and down the roads scarring the forested flanks of the gorge; dust rose in swirling clouds, massive Blondin cables, strung from one bank to the other, shuttled buckets of cement; and Italian and African voices mingled as labourers, stripped to the waist, toiled on scaffolding on a vast, semi-circular structure rising in the centre of the river bed. Water flowed through gaps in a concrete wall extending from the north bank.

"That's the second coffer dam they're building now, in the middle there," Jack pointed. "The first was erected next to the north bank, and the first section of wall was built inside it. The river's low now, and it's been diverted to allow us to start on the second coffer dam. When it's complete, we start building the main wall inside it, and we'll be doing that right through the rains.

"We are crossing fingers we don't have floods like last season. We had to stop work, get all the machinery out, winch girders on to the piers of the coffer dam to strengthen it. This bridge was nearly washed away. It was a record flood, and the blacks say next season is going to be worse. Nyaminyami is not a happy river god."

Downstream was a second bridge, a suspension bridge, supported by steel piers. "Are these two bridges your only access to the north bank?"

"Yes, except for the Blondins – those cables up there. They can carry machinery and men. At the moment the men do shift work right through the night, to get as much done as possible before the rains. In a couple of months it'll be so hot they'll have to carry their tools in buckets of water."

As he reeled off statistics, Mario came up behind her, swept her up in a hug and ruffled her hair. "Lizi! I get your message. It is so good to see you. You are well? You look different. You have come to see my work, yes?"

"Yes, Mario." His skin was burnt almost mahogany, black hair closely cropped, eyes gleaming. He is truly beautiful, like a young god, she thought as she laughingly extricated herself from his embrace. He was still on duty, but arranged a rendezvous in the newly-completed hotel that evening.

Jack drove her back to the rapidly growing township of Kariba, home to a motley mix of engineers, labourers, adventurers, and drop-outs, a boisterous, youthful community where men sweated long hours in the blazing heat, and drank copiously at the day's end. "They keep the beer cool in the mortuary," Jack said.

Black labourers were housed in bachelor quarters in the nearby Mahombekombe township, domain of the shebeen queens Kariba Kate and Maria Whisky.

In the evening, she met Mario in the bar, surrounded by a group of fellow workers. Ian had told her that during the war, Italian prisoners had built a turreted hotel ("It is beautiful, like a castle") in the mist-shrouded mountains of the Vumba near Rhodesia's eastern border. But they had built it as captives. This project was a hundred times more ambitious, they had been selected because of their experience and expertise, and they were here to wipe away the stain of wartime memories.

Mario was beset by no ghosts of the past. He brimmed with enthusiasm for his work, though he complained about the heat and missed the pleasures of city life. There was not much to do during off-duty hours except drink or watch film shows in the open-air amphitheatre. "Of course, we have parties," he grinned, "many parties. And I have been fishing."

He was clearly popular, and not only with the men. Apart from the wives of the Italian labourers and engineers, and a handful of nurses, secretaries and typists, there were few women in Kariba, and those in the bar seemed to know him well.

Shouts of laughter emerged from a group at the far end of the counter; glancing across, she saw Robin Chase, glass in hand, eyes half-closed against the smoky atmosphere, relating one of his stories. Beside him, Chris leaned on the bar, a pretty girl with bobbed blonde hair at his side. He looked up and caught Liz's eye, lifting his glass in greeting.

Later in the evening, he came over with Robin, and she introduced them to Mario. "Come and join us," Robin suggested, but she declined.

"Thanks, but I'm beat. This is my last drink, then I'm for bed."

"Do you have a lift back to town?" Chris asked her.

"Yes, thanks."

"See you in Salisbury, then."

Mario's eyes followed them suspiciously. "This Chris – he is a friend?"

"Yes – the brother of the girl whose house I am living in."

"What he is doing here?"

She told him. "You like him?" he persisted.

She thought of the interlude the previous evening. "Sometimes."

"Come, I take you back."

But first he drove her down to the road bridge so that she could photograph the men working under brilliant spotlights where battalions of tiny flying insects whirled in a ceaseless dance.

"Look, Lizi," he put his arm around her shoulders and pointed. On the rocky ground below the scaffolding, the dark bulk of a large hippo plodded stolidly through the sand around the perimeter.

"That is Charlie," he told her, "he live in the river. Every night he come and look at our work."

When he dropped her at her door, he took her hand and kissed it. "Lizi, when I will see you again? You can come and write another story soon?"

"I don't think so, Mario, not for a while" she said regretfully.

"Then I will come to see you in Salisbury," he promised, his eyes warm.

After the hushed peace of Ian's camp, the sounds of civilisation – even on such a limited scale – seemed all the more intrusive, and she found it hard to sleep. For a long time, she lay listening to the laughter, Italian voices raised in song, the rhythmic thud of generators, and the beating of drums from the African township. Thinking about the Valley and the river, the animals and the people – black and white – who loved it.

16

Her lift back to Salisbury was in a delivery truck. To while away the hours in the heat of the cab on the long haul up the escarpment, she told the driver, Henry Horton – a beefy man with enormous thighs encased in tight khaki shorts – the story of Simon and Clarissa. So intrigued was he that when they reached the small country town of Sinoia, and she recalled it was where Simon was buried, he suggested she might like to take a look at his grave.

They found it without difficulty in the oldest part of the small country-town cemetery to which they were directed from the local hotel. On the plain headstone erected by Nicholas and Emma she could still make out the weathered inscription: *Simon Grant, died 1902, reunited with his beloved Clarissa.*

Henry wandered off discreetly to read tombstones, leaving Liz at the graveside, wondering how long it had been since anyone had come here to pay their respects to her grandfather. But it was impossible to think of Simon as anyone's grandfather; he had been in his forties when he died, and the figure shaped by her imagination from Nicholas's descriptions and Clarissa's diary would remain forever the dashing, dark-haired hero of a Victorian love story. One of many of his era who found themselves more at ease on the wide African veld than in the rigidly conventional society of his homeland.

Wishing she had some flowers, and promising herself to return one day, she pulled out a few weeds – the cemetery was well-kept and tidy – under the bright eyes of a toppie perched on a nearby tombstone. She was glad she had seen the wild river where Simon had wandered with Clarissa: it was much easier to imagine him there than in this hushed seclusion.

It was late afternoon when Henry's truck turned into the driveway of the Coles' Highlands home. As Shumba bounded down the steps to meet her, she realised with a surge of pleasure that it was good to be back, that her new lodgings were beginning to feel like home.

Later, as she sat on the stoep, giving Barbara and Derick an animated account of her expedition, the phone rang.

"It's for you, Liz," Barbara said, "long distance from England."

"Is it Mummy?" she asked anxiously. "There's nothing wrong?"

"No," said Barbara, "It's a man."

It was Alex, at his most charming and irresistible, despite the crackling line. Her heart somersaulted at the sound of his voice, and she struggled to keep her own light and chatty, laughing at his titbits of office gossip, asking about mutual friends, the latest London shows, mentioning her work and her trip to the Valley.

His voice deepened: "I feel as though part of me is missing," he complained. "When are you coming home?" and she felt the familiar conflicting emotions: the surge of yearning, the swamping tide of guilt. All at once, she was angry – not at him, but at herself. No damn it, she thought fiercely, I'm not going to let him spoil this week and the way I'm feeling. The line was fading, and she seized on it as an excuse. "Can't hear you, Alex, and I must go, anyway – Uncle Nicky has just arrived, he's waiting to take us out to dinner. Thanks for phoning," and she replaced the receiver, not before sensing the hurt in his voice.

But the damage had been done, and when she went back to the stoep she found it impossible to recapture her earlier effervescence. Her change of mood did not go unnoticed by Barbara, who said nothing until later, when they sat in the kitchen drinking coffee while Derick soaked in the bath with a novel.

"Tell me to shut up if I'm being a busybody, but that call from England did not make you very happy. Was he the reason you came out here?"

Until that moment, Liz had revealed only that she had broken off an unhappy relationship. Now, quite suddenly, she felt free to talk, particularly to Barbara. Not only was she far removed from Alex's world, but so eminently sane and down-to-earth, as she sat with her blue towelling dressing gown wrapped around her expanding belly.

Liz unburdened herself of the whole saga. How she had worked with the dark, intelligent features editor – fifteen years older than she – for six months before he had started inviting her for quick, snatched lunches; how the lunches had developed into drinks after work, then intimate corner-table dinners and, ultimately, stolen nights and occasional weekends on a houseboat on the Thames.

As she listened, it was not difficult for Barbara to read between the lines. Younger and more impressionable, Liz would, she guessed, have been easy prey in the practised hands of a man apparently dedicated to the indulgence of his appetites. All the clichés were there: the loveless marriage, misunderstood husband, promises of divorce, and inevitable, plausible excuses.

It had taken almost three years for her to accept that there never would be any divorce, that her lover was perfectly content with a status quo that satisfied his every need. Even then, she could not make the break.

The deciding factor had been an accidental meeting with Alex's wife, when she had dropped into the office unannounced during a shopping expedition to London. Face to face with Susan Stanton, the woman she had built up in her mind as a hard-faced, calculating shrew, Liz found herself shaking hands with a gentle, pretty woman, a little plump, a little harassed, with strands of grey in her dark hair, and devoted eyes for her wayward spouse.

With her were two boys – one tall, gangly and talkative (like Alex), the other freckled and rather serious. And as she watched them with their father, Liz's sense of self-disgust rose in her throat. She had excused herself quickly.

When she told him, a couple of weeks later, that she had booked a ticket for an extended working holiday in Africa, his consternation had been almost comical, and he had brought the full battery of his charm into play. But for once she had remained immovable, holding the image of the sad-eyed woman in her mind, and he had finally grinned crookedly and accepted her decision with apparent grace. "I think he was so sure of me he assumed I would be back within a few weeks," she said ruefully.

"How do you feel now?" asked Barbara.

"I still think about him a lot, still love him, though I don't have any illusions any more. Being away has let me see things more clearly." She fiddled with a teaspoon, "I miss him. We had wonderful times together. And he taught me a lot too – in my work, I mean."

"But he couldn't have been the first man in your life?"

"No, there were others, but he was different – so much older, for one thing. A friend, one of the few who knew about us, once told me he was a father figure, that I was trying to replace the dad I lost during the war. She could have been right, not that it made any difference. He made my day light up – in the beginning, anyway."

Barbara took her cup to the sink and stood looking out into the darkness, massaging the small of her back with both hands.

"Is your back worrying you?" asked Liz.

"Not really, it's just needs a good stretch every now and then. Look," she turned to look at Liz, "You don't need me to tell you that you did the right thing. What you need now is a gorgeous male to complete your rehabilitation."

Liz grinned, and her mood lightened. "I've been surrounded by men the past few days."

"So you have. What about this Mario? He sounds like just the antidote for a slightly battered heart."

"He's lovely," Liz admitted. "And he does wonders for my ego. But I won't see much of him – they keep him pretty busy."

"And Ian? He has a woman in his life, but I don't think it's going to come to anything."

She shook her head. "He's lovely too, but not in that way."

"It's that damn chemistry business. I swore I'd never marry a lawyer, and look at me. What about my brother? Don't tell me, he can be the most irritating guy. But I love him dearly, and you'd be a good influence on him."

Liz raised her eyebrows. "I don't think Chris would let anyone influence him – least of all me." She yawned and ran her fingers through her hair. "Don't worry about me. I'll go out to the farm next weekend. That will be distraction enough for the moment."

When she arrived at Mushana in the early evening, her uncle was out and Samuel informed her he had gone to see a neighbour. She was curled up on the sofa with a book when he returned, looking tired and harassed.

"Sorry I wasn't here to meet you, dear," he pecked her cheek abstractedly, "bit of a crisis on my hands. What about a drink? I need one."

He told her that while she was away Dendera, the man who had made the witchcraft allegations, had continued to spread rumours about Reta.

"I had warned him, so I fired him, had no option. Things seemed to be settling down after that, and I thought it would all blow over. And then, this week, all hell broke loose."

"What happened?"

Handing her a gin and tonic, he lowered himself into the armchair opposite with a glass of whisky. "You won't believe this. It was an antbear."

She stared at him, bemused. "An antbear?"

"I'd better explain." He lit a cigarette. "There are a few animals the blacks are hellishly superstitious about, and hyenas and antbears are high on the list. They say that witches ride around on hyenas and antbears at night, while they go about their business. It's all part of their mythology. The infuriating thing is that this particular animal was seen just outside the compound, close to Luke's hut, a week after Dendera left.

"It happened early one evening, and next morning Moses was at the kitchen door saying the whole compound was in a hell of a state. They're demanding Reta goes, and that the compound be moved to another site."

"Moved? The whole compound?"

"That's right. Because there's bad magic on it." He shook his head tiredly. "You can live in the bush for your whole life and never set eyes on an antbear. They dig tunnels all over the place, but you never catch them doing it. I've been here twenty-five years and never laid eyes on one. Now, at the most inopportune moment, the bloody thing has to appear on my doorstep."

"But why should they blame Reta?"

"Because they see it as proof that Dendera was right. She is a witch."

"What are you going to do?"

"I've just been over to see Tony Bell. He had some similar trouble a few years back, and I wanted to find out how he handled it. I'm buggered if I'm going to lose Luke, he's one of my best drivers. And I have no intention of moving the compound either."

"What does Tony Bell say?" Liz remembered meeting him: a small man with black hair and a neat moustache, who looked more like an accountant than a farmer.

"He called in an *nganga,* a witchdoctor, there's one in the reserve. Apparently this chap is well thought of locally, and he brought along his *mutis* and held some sort of a ceremony to exorcise the bad spirits. There were two women involved that time.

"Apparently it all worked out, so I've told Moses to send for this guy. He'll be here on Sunday. And I hope to Christ he can do something."

They were at breakfast the following morning when Chris Rainier arrived with Robin Chase. "David and Lillian are giving him a taste of colonial decadence," Chris said.

"Take a seat." Nicholas offered them toast and coffee, and they drew up chairs.

"We're going to get some venison," Chris told Nicholas. "Johnny Kruger has been keeping some impala on his land, but they've multiplied out of sight and have been getting into his vegie garden. Lilian likes a bit of venison, could you use some?"

Nicholas nodded vigorously, his mouth full of toast. "I'll take some, for sure. I'd come with you, only I promised to go over to Ngavi this morning. Why don't you go with them, Elizabeth?"

"You're going to shoot impala?" she said dubiously.

"Yes," said Chris. "Just a couple."

"Come with us," urged Robin.

"I don't think..." she began.

"I don't either," said Chris, an amused glint in his eyes. "It'll be too much for her sensibilities. She prefers her meat pre-packed."

She shot him a look of antagonism. "I'd love to come," she said deliberately, and he grinned sardonically as he poured coffee. Damn, she simmered, he's done it again.

They left the Land Rover on the farm road and walked through the *vlei* with their host Johnny Kruger, a thickset, good-natured bull of a man. He knew where the animals took shelter from the heat of the day, in a clump of trees by his dam, and led them to more than twenty impala, some grazing, others standing motionless in the violet shade, ears twitching occasionally.

During her time on the river, Liz had decided that impala – although they could not compete with kudu or sable for sheer majesty – were the prettiest of all the antelopes, with their tawny backs, striped rumps, slender legs and dark-tipped ears. Early one morning, she and Ian had watched a herd leaping joyously through a sea of feathery grass tinged with rose. Now she hung back behind the men, wishing she had not allowed Chris to needle her into coming. She did not want to see any of these charming, Bambi-like creatures reduced to haunches of venison.

Chris took the first shot, and as he lifted the gun stock to his shoulder and sighted along the barrel, she found herself whispering under her breath: run, little one, don't stand there, run for your life. A barbet trilled its strident alarm call, the shot crashed out, and the animal went down instantly, twitched briefly and was still. Then it was Robin's turn, Robin who had never shot anything bigger than a rabbit. His first shot missed. The herd was taking flight now, he fired again, and the animal faltered, but continued to stumble forward. A second shot brought it down, forelegs crumpling into the coppery grass. She felt sick.

"Not bad for a first go," said Kruger laconically. "Want to try, Liz?"

She shook her head violently and Chris looked at her sharply, "You all right? Not going to pass out on us, are you?"

Despite the sour taste of bile in her mouth, she glared at him defiantly. "I'm fine, thank you."

All the same, she was relieved when, having bagged an animal for himself, Kruger called it a day, and beckoned to two farm workers to carry the carcasses to the truck. "Keep you in biltong for a while," he said cheerfully.

On the way back to Mushana, with the meat packed in cardboard boxes in the back, Chris glanced at her as she sat beside him in the passenger seat.

"Turned your stomach, didn't it, Pendennis?" He spoke quite kindly.

"Yes, it did." Her nausea had evaporated, but she was still angry. "How can you do it – both of you? How can you kill so – so unfeelingly?"

"Primitive male instinct," said Robin cheerfully. He had been nervous about making a fool of himself. Now he was relieved and elated, pleased with his marksmanship. "It's in our blood. Hopeless cases."

"Such beautiful animals wandering free in the bush, not hurting anyone. How could you?" she repeated. "It's barbaric."

"Barbaric?" repeated Chris. "More barbaric than having their guts ripped out by a hyena, or their necks broken by a lion? Or being torn to pieces by wild dogs and eaten alive? Or caught in a wire snare?"

"There aren't any lion or hyena here."

"In the national parks there are. In their natural habitat they're surrounded by predators."

"That's different, that's part of nature."

"We're part of nature too."

"Guns aren't."

"You would prefer us to use bows and arrows, or our hands perhaps?" he said sarcastically, his eyes on the road.

She stared at him in exasperation. "I would prefer you not to wantonly kill beautiful animals."

"Why? It's a better way to go than being herded into an abattoir to be slaughtered, like cattle. This way, they die out in the wild. And it isn't wanton – though I don't deny I enjoy it. We're killing for the pot. The trouble with you," he continued calmly, "is that you are used to your meat sliced up on a butcher's tray. Which suits you because you don't have to see how it got that way."

He was doubly infuriating when he confounded her with logic. "It's not that at all....."

"Oh yes, it is," he said deliberately. "This is Africa. We've been hunting for thousands of years and beyond – it's what we do. If you don't like it, go back to England," he added without rancour.

"When you two have stopped squabbling," said Robin patiently, "d'you think we could stop at the hotel for a beer? This blood-sport has given me a hell of a thirst."

She glared at them both.

The *nganga* was a slight, hook-nosed man, with sunken eyes, prominent cheekbones and a deeply lined face. About his neck were strings of beads and copper wire, and his forearms were ringed in copper bangles; he wore a red band around his head and a blanket about his shoulders, over a skirt of animal tails.

Men, women and children were gathered in a semi-circle, watching the squatting figure in respectful silence as he opened a hessian sack and withdrew a Cobra floor polish tin and a number of other items, which he spread on the ground with deliberate ritualistic formality.

Luke and Reta stood slightly apart. Luke's pleasant round face was taut with anxiety, his wife stared in front of her with unseeing eyes, twisting her hands.

"What's happening?" Nicholas asked Moses.

"The woman will do a test," the foreman told him.

Nicholas frowned, "Not one of those boiling water jobs?" he barked.

"No. He is making *muti*. She will drink. If she is sick, it is all right. She is not a witch."

"That wasn't what I had in mind. I thought he was going to exorcise the spirits, clean the place up. Does she want to go through with this?" questioned Nicholas. "God knows what he'll put in it. Could be poison."

"She is willing. She ask to do it."

Muttering, Nicholas stumped over to Luke and Reta and spoke to them. The young woman nodded emphatically, her face set, dark eyes round and frightened.

The *nganga* picked up a gourd and poured some clear brown liquid into it from a Fanta bottle. Before him on a piece of cotton fabric, he had laid out small piles of leaves, seeds and some unidentifiable objects, including something that looked like dried meat.

He added small amounts from each pile to the gourd and stirred the contents with an animal horn. When it was ready, he stood up with it, muttering inaudibly. After standing motionless for a few moments, he turned to Reta and nodded.

Hesitantly, glancing at Luke, whose lips tightened, she took a deep, trembling breath and, lifting her chin, walked slowly towards the old man. He spoke a few words and handed her the gourd, gesturing to her to drink. A murmur ran through the gathering like a dry rustling breeze. A baby began to cry.

Reta seemed to shrink involuntarily within herself, staring about her like a trapped animal. The *nganga* watched impassively. Then, as though she had no thought but to get the ordeal over with, she lifted the gourd to her lips and closed her eyes. Liz could hear her convulsive swallowing as she drank almost greedily, not stopping until she had emptied it. Lowering it in shaking hands, gulping for breath, she stared at the *nganga*, and drops of liquid dribbled down her chin. She handed back the gourd, wiping her mouth with the back of her hand.

While she had been drinking, Luke had half-turned his head away; now his eyes, along with those of every onlooker, were fixed on her. The diviner placed the gourd on the ground beside him, and stood motionless, watching her without speaking.

She swallowed, and beads of moisture broke out on her face. Liz's heart thudded against her ribs; she and Nicholas glanced at each other. Seconds passed – strung out endlessly. A minute, and another. People began to shuffle their feet and murmur, Luke stared past his wife with set, blank face. Moses looked at the ground, drawing a pattern in the dust with his shoe. Nicholas was muttering: "Lot of bloody codswallop. Should never have allowed it."

The moments drew out. Although she stood beside the diviner, within feet of Moses and Samuel, and only a few paces from Luke, Reta was an infinitely lonely figure, facing the low, hostile murmurs of the crowd.

She began to move back, away from them. And then, as though racked by a sudden spasm, she clutched her abdomen and bent over. Her stomach began to heave, and she leaned forward and turned instinctively away from the now silent watchers. She stumbled, bent almost double, and gagged, spittle hanging from her lips. Luke put out a hand but did not move, her stomach heaved again and she began to retch. And a wave of whispers rustled through the onlookers. Liz closed her eyes and breathed a prayer of thanks.

When the violent retching had stopped, Liz took Nicholas' proffered handkerchief and went to the limp woman. With an arm about her trembling shoulders, she wiped Reta's sweating face and handed her the handkerchief. Their eyes met, the woman said nothing, but the hunted animal stare was gone. Reta looked past her and moved towards Luke; he was sweating heavily, and although he was not smiling, the tension had eased from his face.

As it had also eased among the crescent of onlookers, who began to chatter loudly amongst themselves.

Nicholas cleared his throat and wiped his face with his sleeve. He was quite pale himself. "Well, that was convincing enough. Some sort of an emetic the old boy must put in the brew," he muttered to Liz. "Now, what about that damned antbear?"

But the old man was already squatting, mixing another concoction in the gourd, using some of the items laid out on the square of fabric, and adding what looked like wings and body parts of insects from the Cobra polish tin. Once the potion had been mixed to his satisfaction, he rose once more, allowed the blanket to slide from his shoulders, and walked slowly and deliberately to the edge of the compound, the place where the antbear had been seen close to the surrounding trees. The people followed, forming another silent semi-circle, watching as he sprinkled the mixture into the dust, pacing slowly around the outermost three huts, chanting in a high, sing-song voice. Three times he circled the huts, then set the gourd on the ground and spoke to Nicholas.

"Those huts have to go," said her uncle philosophically, "well, I expect it's better than moving the whole box and dice."

The occupants carried out their belongings while the *nganga* built a small fire from grass, twigs and dead leaves. When it flickered into flames, he twisted grass stalks into a taper, lit it and touched the flame to the thatching of each hut in turn. A deep silence spread through the watchers as the rooftops crackled. The air was still, and as the smoke spiralled upwards, smudging the sky, it hung suspended above the compound. The slanting rays of the late afternoon sun shone through it, creating an eerie crimson haze that stained the roofs of the remaining huts and surrounding trees.

When the burning huts had collapsed into piles of smouldering timbers, Nicholas presented the *nganga* with his fee: a blanket and a five pound note, received with cupped hands. The ritual over, the old man became quite voluble as he spoke to the tall stooped white man.

"Is it all finished now?" Liz asked Nicholas' cook.

"Ya," Samuel nodded, glancing at Reta and Luke, who still stood apart from the crowd.

Nicholas limped across to Liz. "He's pleased with the payment, wants to know if there's anything else he can do. So I asked him if he could tell us where Clarissa's grave was."

She stared at him. "You did what?"

He grinned and looked sheepish. "Well, we haven't had much luck so far. What have we got to lose?"

"I think you've been too long in Africa," she said, still staring at him in disbelief.

"Maybe so, maybe so," he acknowledged peaceably, "but it's worth a try."

The diviner reached into his bag of animal hide, and withdrew a handful of small bleached bones, which he extended to Liz.

"What's this?" She shrank back, looking at Nicholas in alarm.

"*Hakata*. Bones. You must throw them because you are the grand-daughter," he explained.

"No chance. You do it, Uncle Nicky. It was your idea."

"Go on," he urged.

"But I'm not sure I want to." Drained by the tension of Reta's ordeal, she had seen enough witchcraft for one day. Hesitantly, she took the bones in her cupped hands. "What do I do?"

"Just throw them on the ground."

She obeyed, and the *nganga* squatted on his haunches, studying their configuration in the powdery red earth. Nicholas leaned forward, and Moses and Samuel squatted beside him. The sun was low, and brown smoke from the smouldering huts swirled around them. After a long silence, the diviner began to talk in the same singsong voice as before, his head swaying back and forward as he touched the bones one by one.

"What is he saying?" she asked sceptically.

"He sees water," Nicholas grinned crookedly. "Not entirely amazing as I told him the grave is near the Zambezi."

He said something to the old man, who ignored him and went on chanting.

"Near water," translated Nicholas, listening intently, "at a place where there are high rocks, and a tall tree. Well, that's going to be a huge help." His voice was sarcastic.

The diviner started to speak again, but now he was looking directly at Liz, and Nicholas leaned forward to hear. "He's talking about you."

She stepped back instinctively, then laughed. "Really? I suppose he's going to tell me how many husbands I'm going to have."

The high, chanting voice continued. The trees around the compound cast long shadows, and the sunset flared through the smoke haze, an almost theatrical backdrop to the hunched figure in his ragged, moth-eaten skirt of animal tails. She began to feel uneasy.

"He keeps on about water. Black water – and a tower falling – and a silver serpent," said Nicholas slowly. "He is warning that there is danger. When the tower falls – in black water, and the silver serpent twists. Now there's a riddle for you."

Prickles crawled up her spine, and she shook them away. "Danger for who?"

The *nganga* grunted, shook his head and muttered something. He began gathering up the bones.

"He can't say, only that he sees danger. Lot of rot," he said quickly, seeing her expression.

"Black water, a tower falling, a silver serpent," she repeated. She noticed Samuel and Moses murmuring, and staring at her. Nicholas cleared his throat and straightened, clearly feeling he had allowed things to go too far.

"Thank you, *madala*, that will be all," he said in his most brisk, British voice, and the old man inclined his head. Behind him, the sun burned crimson through the wisps of smoke still coiling skywards from the smouldering remains of the huts.

17

She bumped into the journalist Joe Guve at a press conference, and told him about the acrimonious meeting with Paul Masimba in the Valley.

"Stirring things up, is he?" said Guve with satisfaction. "Yes, he's pretty active with the ANC. He's been in Lusaka as well, working with them up there. I expect you know there are also Batonga on the north bank of the river. The government up there is much slower about moving them out, and he's hoping to have more success persuading them to stay put."

"A bit futile at this stage, isn't it?"

He shrugged. "I don't think he imagines for a moment he can stop the dam going ahead. But it catches the attention of the world press. That's worth something."

"He was with a woman," she told him.

"He generally is," Guve said dryly. "He has been given an official warning by the police, by the way. They've told him to keep away from the Batonga."

On her return home from work at the end of the week, an unfamiliar car was parked in the driveway, and Mario was in the sittingroom, charming a bemused Barbara. He had caught a lift into the city on a truck that was due to return with supplies on Monday.

"I have three nights," he told Liz gleefully as he rose to take her hands. "And I have a car which I borrow from a friend."

He took her to the Colony Restaurant for dinner. It was the first time they had ever spent an evening alone together, and she asked him about his family in Milan. His father was also an engineer, he told her, and he had one married and one single sister, both younger than himself.

"And do you have a girl friend in Milan?" Liz asked.

He hesitated. "There is a girl – my mother and father like for me to marry her," he admitted somewhat reluctantly, adding hastily, "but there is nothing at the moment between us. I tell my father it is too soon to think about. And you, Lizi," the warm, dark eyes looked into hers with intensity and he leaned across the table, "you have not met someone here? One of these Rhodesian men in khaki shorts?"

She laughed. "One or two, Mario, but I'm not involved with anyone," and was flattered by his evident pleasure in her reply.

"Except me," he teased. "*Benissimo*. Then we can have this weekend together, yes?"

"Well, I was going out to the farm tomorrow, just for one night. Why don't you come with me? My uncle will be happy to see you again. We can come back on Sunday afternoon."

It was agreed, and Barbara smiled her satisfaction as she waved them off the following day, declining Nicholas' invitation to join them.

"Please thank him," she told Liz. "Somehow, in my present condition, the thought of bouncing over his roads is less than appealing."

"You could have gone with them, darling," she said to Derick after they had left.

"No way, I'm not playing raspberry." He opened the Saturday paper.

"Gooseberry," she ruffled his hair in passing. "She's still recovering from that Don Juan in England – says she's not interested in him that way."

"Hmm," Derek sounded sceptical. "He doesn't look the type to let the grass grow under his feet. What do you think?"

"I think he's a charmer, and he has the most sexy cleft in his chin. I hope Liz allows herself to be charmed."

"What's wrong with your brother? Bit slow on the uptake?"

She sighed. "I've given up trying to understand my brother."

It was dusk on the dam, and the fish were biting. Her uncle was the second person that day to note, with a pleased inward smile, Mario's interest in Liz. The signs were difficult to miss: his hand lingering on hers as he helped bait her hook, the solicitous way he laid her jacket around her shoulders as they sat on the stoep later, and his eyes following her as she handed around coffee after dinner.

Very nice too, he thought. If young Rainier hasn't the brains... He turned to Liz. "We've been invited for the long weekend up to David and Lilian's cottage at Inyanga. Are you free? And perhaps Mario can join us? They've plenty of room."

"Lovely," replied Liz, but Mario shook his head regretfully. "I cannot get away again so soon."

On Sunday morning, Nicholas sent them over to the neighbouring farm. "They have tennis every Sunday, go and have a game. We can have a late lunch."

A dozen people were lounging in deckchairs on the lawn beside the tennis court when they arrived. Lilian gave Liz a motherly peck and greeted Mario with eyes bright with curiosity. On the court, Chris was partnering a dark willowy girl against David and an athletic-looking middle-aged woman with a horsy face. Lilian was not playing: immaculately coiffed, sheathed in one of her classically tailored linen dresses, she was absorbed in her role of country hostess. When Liz told her they had no tennis whites, she waved her hand airily, rattling her bracelets. "Doesn't matter at all, darling. You can go on after this lot. Have a drink in the meantime."

As soon as the older couple had left the court, Lilian sent them on. Chris introduced his partner, and Liz recognised the woman she had seen in the restaurant with him. Annabel Keightley's long black hair was tied back with a red ribbon, her shapely suntanned legs were encased in neat white shorts.

Liz took up her position with some hesitation: she had not lifted a racquet for several years, but she relaxed when it became obvious Annabel was no more than an average player herself. The set was dominated by the two men, and Liz and Mario went down six-four after Chris sent her a stinging shot that left her staring at him open-mouthed.

"Sorry, Mario," she apologised, "I let you down."

"Never," he replied, blowing her a kiss as he stood back to let her pass through the gate.

"Good game," Chris came up behind them and slapped the Italian on his back. "Hard luck, Pendennis." He grinned.

"That was not a gentlemanly shot," she told him, and Annabel glanced at him obliquely.

"This man is no gentleman," she murmured. Chris tapped her bottom with his racquet, and she giggled as she walked to the drinks' table.

Later, when the heat had driven everyone else into the shade of the wide stoep, Chris turned to Mario: "How about it?" and they went on to the court together.

Chris played cool, intelligent tennis, placing the balls with precision, his most effective weapons his service and strong cross-court shots. Mario was all verve and histrionics. Skidding from one side of the court to the other, he dived headlong in pursuit of impossible shots, and muttered Italian imprecations when he missed. He attacked the game, Liz decided, with all the energy he threw into living.

Though less proficient than his opponent, his speed and agility meant they were evenly matched, and neither retained the upper hand for long. With one game apiece, they settled down to a silent concentrated struggle under the noon sun; and by five games all, court-side chatter had died and all eyes were focused on the battle. Their shirts clung to their backs and Mario's hair was plastered damply against his forehead. In the final tussle, he took his opponent to deuce four times before succumbing to a ball placed with precise accuracy in the furthest corner of the court, inches from the back line.

Applause, cheers and whistles erupted as Mario, striking himself theatrically on the side of his head with his hand, bounded to the net to shake hands. Chris clapped him on the shoulder and they walked up the lawn together, breathing hard.

"He is too good, this man," Mario panted, shaking his head and flashing a grin at Liz.

"That was terrific." Chris wiped sweat from his eyes with his forearm.

Lilian bustled over. "You both deserve a long cold beer after that. Have you got one, Chris? Good. Come Mario, Castle or Lion?"

As Mario followed her, Chris reached for his beer, lowered himself to the grass beside Liz, and drank deeply.

"Well done," she said.

"Thanks, he's good. So, Pendennis, what have you been up to?"

"Nothing much. Work, mostly."

"No more shooting expeditions?" he asked smoothly.

"No," she said levelly, refusing to be drawn.

"Ah, but have you sampled the meat we gave Old Nick yet?"

She bit her lip in irritation. Only last night they had dined on roast haunch of venison, prepared in a herb marinade by Samuel. Mario – whose interest in food amounted almost to a passion – had been lavish with his compliments.

Noticing her discomfort, he raised his eyebrows and grinned broadly. "Go on – admit. You loved it."

"I hate you," she said resignedly.

He was still grinning when Mario returned, his expression wary as he noticed the interplay. But Liz turned to him immediately and patted the deckchair beside her invitingly.

"Sit down, Mario," she smiled brilliantly at him. "Well played. Where did you learn your tennis?"

He sat down. "I have English relatives. They are crazy about it, they play all the time. But you have no drink, Lizi," and he began to get up.

"Stay where you are, Mario, I'll get it." Chris stood up and looked down at her. "Gin and tonic, wasn't it?"

They drove back to the city in the evening, stopping for dinner at a small country hotel on the way home. She felt relaxed and lazy after the weekend in the sun; Mario was at his most lighthearted and entertaining, and when he walked her to the door of the back porch, she knew he was going to kiss her.

As he took her in his arms, Shumba arrived. Overjoyed at having his uneventful night enlivened, he thrust his wet nose between them, snuffling ecstatically and licking their hands and arms affectionately. Liz collapsed in giggles against the wall, but Mario's sense of romance was deeply offended. Looking around impatiently, he took her hand and led her down the steps and into the moonlit garden. "No," he said sternly to the dog, "stay." Shumba flattened his ears and sat down disconsolately.

"Where are we going?"

"Ssh. You will wake Barbara and Derick." He led her around the corner to the patio, where the night air was heavy with jasmine, and a cascade of scarlet bougainvillea formed a canopy of blossom. His aesthetic instincts satisfied, he pulled her into his arms and tilted her face towards his. "This is better, no?" he whispered, his mouth close to hers. She was laughing and he stopped her laughter with his lips. His mouth was warm and ardent, and when she finally pulled away from his embrace, the blossoms wheeled about her head, and his own eyes were unfocussed.

"Lizi, Lizi. You like me a little?" he murmured.

"I like you a lot...." she said breathlessly, and he kissed her again, on her eyes and ears, his hand moving to cup her breast. She pulled away, and he lifted his head.

"But I go too fast, no?" His face was so crestfallen that she laughed softly and touched his cheek. He covered her hand with his.

"A bit too fast," she whispered. "I must go in," and she made to break away. He caught her hand but she escaped and ran across the lawn, laughing. He was close behind her, and they were both giggling when they reached the steps.

Do I want this? she wondered as she tiptoed across the porch, and the sound of his car receded into the night. While I still ache for Alex? Do I want to start getting involved again so soon? And with Mario? She remembered the frankly admiring eyes of the women in the bar at Kariba, the approving feminine comments that followed his progress on the tennis court. He was too attractive, too charming.... Perhaps another Alex. No, he was not like that. Mario was as transparent as glass, he did not have the complex, manipulative mind of Alex.

And it felt good. To be wooed, flattered, enfolded in the warmth of his eyes, feeling like a desirable woman again without the crushing burden of guilt that had weighed her down for so long. She was smiling as she unzipped her dress.

Ian Coles telephoned. "Liz, listen. I've found a grave. Wait," he continued as she started to speak, "don't get your hopes up yet. There's nothing to say it is Clarissa's."

"But it might be. Where?" she asked eagerly.

"Further upriver than we went. I was taken to it by an old woman, she doesn't know who is buried there, only that it was a white. She's the oldest person in the *kraal*, slightly senile, but she swears the grave has been there as long as she remembers. No one else can tell me anything."

"What does it look like?"

"Nothing very much. Just a raised mound with a circle of stones around it, under a tall ebony, quite close to the river."

"A tall tree. Are there any rocks?"

"A couple. Why?"

"Never mind. How can we check it out?"

"Process of elimination I should think. I'll post you a map with the exact location marked. See if you can find a local history expert – through your paper or the National Archives. There could be some record of it somewhere."

"I'll get on to it tomorrow," she promised.

Finding an authority was not difficult. The historical society put her in touch with a well-known historian, and she visited him the following weekend, taking Ian's map with her.

A genial, balding man in his fifties, Jim Longman knew all about Clarissa and Emma and their walk. He was intrigued to meet her, and instantly agreed to help. "Leave the map with me, if you don't mind. There are a few sources I can check out. As you can imagine, scores of whites succumbed to various diseases while travelling through the Valley around the turn of the century. Hunters, prospectors, explorers. But this particular area was not quite so well frequented. Most of the traffic was further west on the Mpanda Mutenga road to Vic Falls. A regular Piccadilly Circus that was.

"I'll be in touch, but probably not for a couple of weeks. We have visitors from the UK and I won't have time till they leave."

She longed to say, "Oh please, can't you start tomorrow?" But she curbed her impatience.

The route to the Rainier's Inyanga cottage followed the main Salisbury-Umtali road, the same one Clarissa and Emma would have travelled by wagon when they left Umtali. Chris drove Nicholas and Liz in the Land Rover, turning off at the small farming village of Rusape, beyond which the rolling hills and granite kopjes became steeper and more rugged, and the roads progressively worse. Bracken and gorse carpeted the mountainside, and streams tumbled through valleys shaded by umbrella-shaped mountain acacias. It was dusk when they reached the cottage where David and Lilian were waiting.

"This is a cottage?" asked Liz in astonishment as she explored the four-bedroomed thatched house with its large wood-beamed sittingroom and enormous fireplace. Built on the side of a hill, it had no garden, just a steep track winding through grass down to a stream.

After dinner, the men spread fishing tackle across the sittingroom floor and began sorting flies, disentangling lines, trading hooks. "You're not going fishing tomorrow?" Lilian stated rather than asked, "Liz hasn't seen anything of Inyanga."

David and Nicholas glanced at each guiltily. "It's like this," said Nicholas. "We thought we'd try the stream down at the...."

"It's OK, Old Nick," Chris looked up from untangling a line. "I've been delegated to show her around while you go fishing."

"Delegated? You don't have to show me around," Liz protested, "I'm quite capable of taking the Land Rover....."

"I know," he interrupted, "totally independent and self-reliant. It's all arranged, Pendennis."

"But you want to fish too," she argued.

"I'll fish with the guys tomorrow, and you can go to Troutbeck with Lilian. On Sunday, we'll do the grand tour."

"Got some decent shoes on? Good, this is where we walk off Lilian's breakfast."

Having dropped Nicholas and David – loaded with rods, tackle and a picnic lunch – at a bend in the river a few miles from the house, Chris had taken a road that climbed through dense pine plantations and small holdings. He parked on the crest of a ridge.

A warm breeze sang through the pines in the valley below as they set off through a landscape so different from the highveld around Salisbury that it was almost like another country. Here the sense of space was even more exhilarating: rolling sweeps of moorland were mantled in bracken and gorse, starred with tiny flowers and threaded by icy streams.

Striding through the bracken in faded shorts, blue shirt and veldskoen, wearing a battered khaki hat and whistling 'Stardust', Chris too seemed different, more relaxed. They walked in silence until he stopped at some curious circular pits with stone walls and low entrances.

"Some people call them slave pits, which appeals to the tourists no end. But they were nothing of the sort, just places to keep cattle, protect them from lion and leopard and hyena."

"But was there a slave trade here?" asked Liz, walking around the perimeter of a low wall which reminded her of the ancient network that criss-crossed the moors in the north of England.

"Not much. Most of it was further north, from the Zambezi upwards, and around Lake Nyasa. The Portuguese were into it in a big way. Even though it was outlawed in the mid nineteenth century, it didn't really end until the early 1900s. David Livingstone and all that. Come on, we've got a lot of ground to cover before lunch."

Once, they paused in the shade of an acacia to watch a handsome kudu bull lead three cows across their path. The massive spiralling horns drew an admiring whistle from Chris, who aimed an imaginary rifle at the creature's head. "Make one hell of a trophy," he said, glancing sideways at his companion. She did not rise to the bait.

When the sun was high overhead, they returned to the Land Rover, drove up to an old hotel set on a hillside amid terraced gardens, and took a table by the window. Ravenously hungry after the fresh air and exercise, they both ordered roast beef and Yorkshire pudding.

"There's an experimental farm here," he told her. "They test different methods of fruit-growing." He stared out of the window. "It's a pity they haven't done anything in the line I'm interested in."

"What's that?"

"Well, I have an idea, but it's a long term thing. I have to be established before I try it out."

"Tell me your idea?"

"On one of the places I worked at in America, the owner kept wildlife on a section of his land – deer, buffalo, elk. Because they'd been shot out in most parts of the country, people used to pay to come and look at them. My idea – when I have my own land – is to use part of it as a private game reserve, let it go back to its natural state and bring in some wildlife."

"Could you make a living from that?"

"That's the risky bit, but I reckon the crops might subsidise it for a while. I would put up some lodges for people to stay in, might even try ranching wildlife, raising eland, kudu, whatever, for meat. They were here before cattle, and I could supply tourist outlets, and restaurants wanting to serve exotic local products." He gazed out over the terraces, locked in his dream.

"When is all this likely to happen?"

He grinned. "Not for a few years. I'll get the land when I've saved enough to borrow the rest. The old man might invest something, once he gets used to the idea."

As they were finishing their coffee, she said in surprise, "Do you realise we've spent a whole morning without arguing?"

He raised an eyebrow. "The day's not over. This was Cecil Rhodes' place, you know, used to be the homestead – though I don't imagine he would have had the time to come here very often. He lived mainly in the Cape, and died – I think – in a seafront cottage in Muizenberg. Brilliant chap," he offered.

"Yes. Pity he was so obsessed with money and power."

"No, he was obsessed with empire, with colouring the map pink. And the only way he could achieve it was with money and power. He was a visionary."

"He was a racist."

"He was a man of his time, you can't accuse him out of context. You can only judge someone like him in relation to his world and his time. Imperialism was the name of the game, it was not a dirty word. He happened to be better at it than anyone else. If he was a racist, why do Rhodes Scholarships disallow any discrimination on racial grounds? Besides, what about 'Equal rights for all civilised men'?"

"Huh?" she snorted. "As long as he was the one who decided who was civilised. He was a ruthless, greedy..."

"He ended the Matabele Rebellion," he interrupted smoothly. "He was the only person they would negotiate with, and it took guts, believe me, to go unarmed to the *indaba* and talk peace."

"No one said he didn't have guts...."

"The Matabele called him father. When he died, they carried his body up to the Matopos, and gave him the old Zulu salute, *Bayete*. In case you don't know, that's an honour they reserve for their chiefs."

"Much good it did them. They've been oppressed by his people ever since," she snapped.

He leaned back in his chair. "It never fails," he murmured.

She stared at him furiously, but he continued to grin, his eyes challenging her.

"You say these things just to annoy me," she accused him. "Whatever view I take, you take the opposite – on purpose. I don't even think you believe half the things you say."

"Who, me?" He lit a cigarette imperturbably. "Stop arguing and finish your coffee, I have something else to show you."

The Land Rover jolted up a steep winding dirt road, so badly rutted she had to cling to the dashboard to prevent her head hitting the roof as the wheels lurched through stone-studded potholes. In places, brushwood had been piled in ruts made by the churning wheels of vehicles that had come to grief. "The scenic route," he commented, his hands clamped on the wheel. On the summit, he eased the vehicle on to the grass.

She got out and walked to the edge. They were standing on the lip of an escarpment, but she felt as though she was on top of the world. Beneath her, the ground dropped away for hundreds of feet, small twisted trees and shrubs grew out of narrow fissures in the rock face, their roots clinging to precarious footholds; aloes sprouted at right angles to the granite, stabbing scarlet spears at the sky.

Far below, a ribbon of green punctuated by glints of silver marked the passage of a river twisting through a flat plain that extended to the horizon, broken in places by low hills. The only signs of habitation were the faint contour lines of cultivated terraces, and cleared areas signalling a *kraal* or village. Driven by a blustery breeze, scudding white clouds chased dark pools of shadow across the floor of the valley; to the north, they were piled in towering phalanxes, but to the east you could see forever, only a blue haze blurred distant details, making it impossible to see where the land ended and the sky began.

"The Honde Valley. And this is World's View – not the most original name," he said.

"It's incredible – beautiful. Makes you want to sing and shout. This is what God must feel like, when he looks down on his planet."

"Hot as hell. I went shooting there once."

"It looks so empty, feels like we're the only people in the world."

"It isn't, though. There's a lot of activity down there. Apart from the locals, some white farmers are starting to grow tea and fruit. We're almost at the border. That's Portuguese territory over there, and that river – the Honde – runs into the Pungwe."

"The Pungwe? Where Clarissa walked?"

"Not that bit. She would have crossed the border further south."

Liz walked closer to the edge and peered down the sheer rock face.

"Careful," he warned quickly, "the wind is strong." He came behind her and took her arm. "Careful," he said again. "It gets gusty."

Hair blowing across her face, she turned and grinned up at him, exhilarated by the view. "Afraid you're going to lose me?" she mocked provocatively.

He did not loosen his grasp. "Who would I argue with? Come back – you make me nervous."

"But you can't mind heights. You fly."

"I feel a lot safer in a plane. Come back, Pendennis," he insisted. His expression was serious, and she allowed him to draw her away from the edge, touched by his concern.

She sat down on the grass beside him. "It took Clarissa about two weeks. I suppose the country she walked through would be quite different now?" she ventured.

"Totally. There's a road through to Beira, well used by Rhodesians in search of beaches and peri peri prawns. And a railway as well."

"The road she followed went through Sarmento and Chimoio," said Liz. "I've checked it on the map. What would be along there now – farms, villages?"

"Yes. Run-down little dorps, sugar estates."

"It would be interesting....." she mused.

"What would?"

"To walk it."

"Walk it? What would you want to do that for?"

"I don't know. Just because..."

"The voice of female logic. Why because?"

She tried to explain. "To see what it felt like for them – as far as that's possible half a century later. As a kind of... I don't know... a recognition." And because I would like to do it. For me.

"Walk from Beira to Umtali. That is the most insane idea I have heard from you yet." He lay back in the grass, shading his eyes with his hand as he squinted up at her.

She was pursuing her thoughts, "It would make a terrific story. Retracing the steps of a pioneer, how the country has changed, how the people have changed – both black and white. That's National Geographic stuff. Why didn't I think of it before?"

"I give up." He pulled his hat over his eyes, and chewed on a piece of grass.

She stared towards the horizon, lost in imaginings, seeing herself doing it. After a while, she lay back on the grass behind him and filed the idea away in her mind. Watching a bateleur eagle, wingtips upturned, riding high thermals, she changed the subject, asked him about flying. "You really love it, don't you?"

"Mmm, you should try it." He spoke without opening his eyes; and she noticed the tips of his lashes were bleached by the sun. He explained the feeling of being unloosed from the earth, the sense of freedom, speed, the different perspective. "But it's more than that. You can see the shape of the land, the bones of it. Over the Zambezi Valley, you can follow the river for miles, and see both escarpments and all the game – jumbo, buffalo, rhino." His voice was lazy, relaxed. "Then there's the Great Dyke, a great mass of rock that runs all the way from Belingwe to Sipolilo. And when you fly over Vic Falls, you can see how, over millions of years, the falls have moved by eroding the rocks and creating a series of gorges. You can see the spray from miles away – like smoke. That's why they're called 'the smoke that thunders'."

"That's lovely." She looked at him in genuine surprise. "Why aren't you always as nice as this?"

He opened his eyes and they glinted with silent laughter. "I can never resist the chance of seeing you lose your temper," he admitted lazily.

After they had picked up the two anglers, he took a wide detour on the way back to the cottage, halting on a hill overlooking wooded peaks and valleys. There were beers in the back of the Land Rover, and he carried them a little way off the road to a point from which she could see, across the darkening valley, a narrow ribbon of silver cascading hundreds of feet through steep forested slopes.

"Pungwe Falls," David settled himself on a rock. Nicholas was wheezing loudly and Liz and Chris took his arms to help him up the last few yards.

"Pungwe – Clarissa's river?" said Liz, for the second time that day.

"The very one," agreed Nicholas. "It starts up here. Where's that beer, Chris? This old body needs sustenance." He eased himself down into a sitting position and leaned against a rock, pulling his cigarette pack from his pocket.

"So Clarissa saw the mouth of the Pungwe, where it joined the sea, and she followed it most of the way to Rhodesia," she mused. "And now, sixty odd years later, here I am – looking at the source. I like that," she said pensively, "it's fitting and rather poetic, don't you think?"

"Poetic? Here we go," Chris passed her a beer. "Would you like me to light a couple of candles?

"How long is it?" she persisted. "Is it a major river?"

"No, not like the Zambezi. A middle-sized river," David told her.

"Perhaps you'd like to walk to the source," said Chris with gentle sarcasm, "We could arrange a team of porters and a guide. He would wear a leopard skin band around his hat, of course."

David grinned, enjoying their banter.

"That won't be necessary," she replied. "Beira to Umtali will be quite sufficient."

"What's this?" Nicholas looked from one to the other.

"She wants to walk in the footsteps of her grandmother," Chris informed them.

"Not on your own, Elizabeth?" Nicholas said quickly.

She laughed. "Uncle Nicky, it's just an idea. I only got it a couple of hours ago."

"But when this one gets an idea, watch out," warned Chris.

"It's an intriguing thought," mused David, "a historic walk. Provided, as Nick says, you have someone who knows the bush to walk with you. What about you, Chris?" he suggested.

Chris raised a hand in protest. "Count me out. Pendennis would be at my throat in a couple of hours."

Liz grinned. "It wouldn't work, David. We're fundamentally incompatible."

"What about Russell?" asked David. "It's the sort of thing he would go for."

"Who's Russell?"

"Sort of a distant cousin. Doing an honours degree in science at the moment, and strong on flora and fauna," said Chris.

"His father's a game ranger," added David, "and he was brought up in the bush, learnt to track animals as a young lad. He's as much at home in the bush as any bushman. Took us hunting up Wankie way last year, and ran the most organised camp I have ever been in. He's done a lot of hunting in Portuguese East."

She listened with interest. "Perhaps I ought to meet this Russell. And I could ask Robin Chase to come along and take the photos."

Silence fell on the small group. She clasped her hands about her knees, her eyes following a bushbuck as it skittered through the scrub. Chris was looking through his binoculars at a kite suspended in the warm air; David sipped his beer and reflected on the afternoon's catch, pondering whether to try a different fly in the morning. Nicholas leaned back against the rock, and drew on his cigarette; he too was savouring the moment, and the day. At his last check-up, the doctor had told him that if he didn't stop smoking, ease up on the alcohol.... But then, old Penfold had been saying that for years. Borrowed time, he thought, I'm on borrowed time – but, by God, it's got a lot to recommend it.

The day after their return from Inyanga, she had a call from the historian Jim Longman.

"Sorry, Liz, but I don't think your search is over. It's not your grandmother's grave, I'm afraid."

"Oh." She absorbed the news. "Does that mean you've found out whose it is?"

"Yes. Well, I'm ninety-nine percent certain. There was a Jesuit priest operating in the area, he died in the Valley in 1901. He was buried under a tree close to the river in more or less the place marked on the map. So, yes, I'm pretty sure."

She thanked him, and put the phone down. Although deeply disappointed, some instinct had already warned her she would not find the grave so easily.

What next, she wondered. But she already knew: she would follow the trail Clarissa had walked. Even if it did not unearth any clues to the whereabouts of the grave (and she did not see how it could), doing it would bring her closer to Clarissa's life, and that was suddenly important.

It was a chance for her to do, for the first time in her life, something remotely adventurous. Despite growing up during the war, in a household without a father, her childhood had been sheltered and carefree. On leaving school, she had worked as a secretary in a law firm before taking the plunge into journalism through a job on a small weekly newspaper where she had learned her craft. Walking holidays in France and Italy, and brief relationships with a succession of callow young men, had been followed by a London job with a travel magazine. From there, she had moved to a large publishing house, and Alex had come into her life.

Compared with the images evoked by Clarissa's diary, her adult life until her arrival in Africa had been singularly unremarkable. While Clarissa had been trekking through the African bush, facing danger and saving lives, the best she had managed was a reasonably successful career and a shabby affair with someone else's husband.

She studied maps and reference books in the Queen Victoria Library and at the National Archives, marking the route taken by Clarissa. From the diary she had established that if the nurses had spent only one night at every campsite, they would have completed the trek in two weeks. Poring over old newspapers and books, old photos and letters, she soaked up everything she could find on Beira and Umtali in the 1890s, building up a picture of the first white men and women arriving in the country by wagon, their struggles to survive, the children they had buried. Once she found a faded photo taken at the Umtali Hospital in the 1890s; it showed two women in nurses' uniforms, but neither of them looked like Clarissa, and they were unnamed.

It was absorbing stuff, sometimes so absorbing that, after a couple of hours in a quiet corner of the Archives, she would look out of the window, past the scarlet aloes in the garden, and be half surprised to see cars speeding along a tarred road instead of wagons rumbling over a rutted track. The research aspect of journalism had always appealed to her: piecing together fragments of the past, following a trail to its source. History had been a favourite subject at school, and she still recalled the spine-tingling thrill of standing in the chapel at Windsor Castle, above the vaults containing the bones of Henry VIII.

The more she became immersed in the past, the more she wanted to know about the events that had shaped her grandparents' lives, like the rebellion of 1896. The year after Clarissa and Simon returned to Africa, both the Matabele and Mashona had turned on the settlers in sudden unexpected violence. In Mashonaland, scores of white families on outlying properties were hacked to death – women, children and babies as well as men.

She recalled Nicholas mentioning that Clarissa had been caught up in the rising.

What had he said? "I got the feeling something bad had happened, something she didn't want to talk about."

Hunting for clues, she paged through the harrowing stories of survivors: of savagely mutilated bodies, panic-stricken flights to the safety of the Fort Salisbury laager, a poignant account of a patrol in Matabeleland coming upon the bodies of two young girls, their blond tresses matted with dust and blood. But there was no mention of Clarissa, Simon or Shangara.

When she asked her editor for leave and explained her plans for the expedition, he agreed to allow her to write a feature story for the paper. Better still, through Robin Chase, an international travel magazine expressed an interest in a story for which he would take the photographs. Convinced her plans were not mere idle dreams, Chris introduced her to his cousin. "If you are set on this crazy idea, you need someone who knows what he's doing," he informed her.

With his quiet, almost scholarly manner, Russell Hemans listened intently as she spread her maps on Barbara's diningroom table and outlined her plan.

"There are probably roads all the way," she said, "but it looks as though, if we try to follow the exact route, there could be a few detours through the bush."

"Could be. A bit of bundu-bashing would be more interesting," his dark eyes were alight with interest. "I could pick up some plant specimens."

"You'll come then?"

He nodded cautiously. "Depending on when you were planning on going."

"Soon. September or October. Before the rains."

"September, my spring vac. It'll be getting hot but we can't leave it any later."

They agreed to catch a train to the coast, and start walking from Beira, not upriver as Clarissa and Emma had done. "It gets too complicated if we have to start looking at boat trips up the Pungwe," she decided.

Russell began jotting down a list of necessities: items ranging from tin-openers to snakebite kit, and Liz glanced at Chris, deep in conversation with Barbara, grateful that he had introduced this serious, efficient young man into her plan.

"Your worst problem will be your feet," Russell told her. "Get walking shoes now so they are worn in. Soak your feet in meths for a few nights before we leave – that will harden them up." He spent much of his free time at university walking in the mountains around Cape Town, he told her.

"Stay to dinner," Barbara urged the two men as they stood up to leave, but they declined. Russell was meeting his girlfriend, Chris had a date.

"Annabel?" Barbara asked.

"Mandy Johnson. You met her one weekend out at David's."

"Sometimes I worry about that man," mused Barbara as she stood with Liz, watching Chris's car disappear down the driveway.

"Why?"

"The women he dates," she said as they walked back to the house. "Have you noticed that he always goes for the same type – a bit hard and flashy and, I suspect, easy to get into bed. Annabel is a prime example, not that she isn't a nice enough girl," she added. "Mandy Johnson fits the mould too. He's careful to avoid serious involvement."

"You think so?"

"This goes way back. Tell you about it later, I must see about supper."

Derick was going out that evening to a meeting of the United Rhodesia Party. "We're trying to get electoral reform – more voting rights for blacks," he told Liz at dinner. She found him not only knowledgeable, but adept at explaining the complexities of African politics.

"We're a long way from perfect – but a hell of a lot better than South Africa," he said. "The Federation is committed to spend more on African health, education, agriculture, do away with discrimination. And to bring in a qualified franchise that will get some Africans into parliament."

"Qualified franchise?"

"You get to vote if you have a certain level of income, or education or property. Hell, we're about to open our first university, and it will be multi-racial – that's just the opposite of what the Nats are doing down south. They're trying to control where blacks can live, where they can eat, who they can marry, what kind of education they get.

"Trouble is, if we move too fast with reforms, we could frighten the hell out of our extremely conservative whites, particularly the farmers. If that happens, there's a danger we could start going the way of South Africa."

"What's the worst aspect of discrimination here?" she asked.

"The worst? Apart from them not having a vote, probably the Land Apportionment Act, which stops blacks from owning land in white areas. Parts of it have been rewritten and some of the worst bits taken out. There's still a long way to go, but at least hotels and restaurants and clubs are now multi-racial.

"These are things the British Government could have done, if they'd had any integrity. Even though we've had responsible government since way back, they still have control of anything relating to blacks. But they've done nothing. It was the same when they gave South Africa independence in the early part of the century. They did nothing to safeguard black voting rights."

"Do you have black people in parliament?"

"We have six in the Federal Parliament, and some in senior civil service posts. It's a start. Todd is pushing for a common voters' roll, but I don't know if he'll get it." Derick leaned forward intently. "This is a critical time, Liz. We have to make the right choices in the next couple of years. If we don't – *hokoyo*."

"What do you mean?"

"We're at a crossroads. We could go either way. If moderates like us win, and we start giving the blacks some say in running the country, we could have a future in a multi-racial society."

"And if not?"

He drew a finger across his throat. "One of these days – civil war." He got up from the table. "But not if I have anything to do with it, darling," he added with a grin, planting a kiss on Barbara's worried face. "I'm off."

She stared after him. "The more he gets involved, the more certain I am that he'll end up in politics."

"You were going to tell me about Chris," Liz prompted.

"Yes. Well, when we were in high school in Cape Town, Chris fell for a girl in his class – Elissa de Villiers. Lovely girl, popular, outgoing. They were both in the school tennis team, and Elissa lived a few blocks away in a rather run-down neighbourhood. Big family, she was the eldest of seven, and they were not well off. The father drank, and the mother worked like a slave. Chris and Elissa were a couple from the time they were fifteen. When we went on holiday to the Wild Coast, Mum and Dad always invited her along, so she was pretty much part of the family.

"One day, during their matric year, Elissa was hit by a car as she was cycling home from school." She shuddered. "I can still remember his face when he heard. He'd been playing rugby, and he took mum's car and went straight to the hospital. She died during the night, and probably just as well, poor sweet. Her head injuries were horrendous. If she had lived..." she shook her head.

"We were devastated. Mum had treated her as another daughter, Dad adored her, but Chris was hardest hit. They were such a beautiful couple together, Liz. You had to smile at them, they looked so good. He was totally in shock. Fortunately, matric exams were coming up, and I think that saved him. He withdrew totally, shut himself away with his books and his music. Wouldn't lift a racquet.

"He passed well, and went straight to university to get his law degree, like Dad. That had always been the plan, and although I knew he had reservations, he didn't raise a murmur of protest. But he was just going through the motions, it was as though all the lights had gone out. Wouldn't – or couldn't talk about it. He still finds it hard, even today.

"About halfway through his first year, I noticed the spark coming back. He started laughing and joking again, playing tennis. And dating. But he was never serious with girls. Plenty of girl friends but nearly always of a type. That was a long time ago, but he's still quick to back off if they show any sign of getting serious. There's a pattern, and it doesn't take a degree in psychology to work it out. He decided, maybe not even consciously, that he was never going to get hurt like that again."

"Have you ever talked to him about it?"

"I've tried. He just looks at me as though I've flipped my lid, and asks why I'm trying to marry him off. I'm not, I just think it's sad everything is so superficial with him."

"He seems perfectly fine to me, irritating sometimes, but fine. Don't worry about it, Bar. Personally, I think he has the right idea, avoiding complications of the heart."

"You would. Speaking of which, have you heard from Alex?"

"He phoned last week." The phone call had been a disaster; it had left her angry and shaking, furious with him and herself.

"Don't ask," she said now. "All I can say is that putting hundreds of miles between us was the wisest thing I ever did."

18

The alarm clock jangled, and she thrust out a hand to stop it, rolling out of bed in the same movement. Stumbling down the unfamiliar farmhouse passage to the bathroom, she heard Russell and Robin moving about in the adjoining room.

By the time they had downed a cup of coffee and picked up the neatly-wrapped packets of sandwiches left on the kitchen table by their hospitable hostess, dawn was breaking. Propping a thank-you note against a jug, they let themselves quietly out of the back door, and walked in silence down the farm track towards the road they had left the previous night, their shoes leaving dark imprints in the dew-laden grass.

Neither Robin nor Russell were early morning people. After being grunted at on successive dawns, she had learnt to avoid any conversation other than essential remarks for at least the first twenty minutes, until the coffee had worked its way through the bloodstream and social intercourse was a consideration.

Robin loped ahead to set up his camera and get a shot of Liz and Russell against the dawn sky. Once on the main strip road, they kept to the dusty verge and away from the jagged edges of narrow tarmac that ran in parallel lines to the horizon. Furrowed earth glowed red as the sun edged above the tree-line, and the grass was necklaced in spider webs glittering with dew. Ahead loomed the purple bulk of the border mountains. It was going to be another hot day.

Clarissa was right, this is the best time, decided Liz. It's not just the coolness, or the sunrise, it's the newness. The birds sound different, there are no cars, we have it all to ourselves. Most of all, it's the only time when I feel as though this might have been – in just the smallest degree – the way it was when Clarissa walked this way.

She was passionate in her desire to share that experience, but nothing had turned out as she had expected. It had started in Beira: in 1891, a few shacks on a beach beside a malarial swamp; in 1957, a busy port and holiday resort, surrounded by suburbs dense with bougainvillea, hibiscus and palm trees. The night before their departure they had dined on peri-peri prawns and drunk Mateus Rosé before returning to their beach chalets.

She had hoped that once they left the suburbs behind, things would be different. And they were, but not in the way she had anticipated. As she explained to Nicholas on the phone one night: "Nothing is more deflating than to set out on a grand adventure and have it reduced to a stroll through the countryside. Perhaps that's exaggerating, but I really did think that by following Clarissa's footsteps I'd be getting a real sense of her experiences. How naive. Clarissa walked on a bush track, we are walking most of the time on roads. They had to carry most of the supplies they needed, or shoot for the pot. We can stop at a store and buy a Fanta when we are thirsty, we are invited into farms or estates for the night.

"She was surrounded by danger and had to shoot a lion; apart from cattle and goats and birds, we have not seen any wildlife, except the occasional eagle. Our biggest danger is from mad Portuguese drivers." She laughed ruefully. "My big adventure."

It was difficult to get annoyed at the battered cars racing past at breakneck speed, their wheels churning up choking clouds of dust, because every other car immediately screeched to a halt, and reversed back to offer assistance. For the first few days, most drivers had stared in disbelief on hearing they were walking to Rhodesia. Now that they had been on the road for more than a week, news of their expedition had circulated on the bush telegraph, which operated with almost supernatural efficiency.

And it was from passing motorists that most of the hospitality was coming. If they were not able to offer beds, they contacted friends 'up the road', who appeared out of the blue as the sun was going down, and invariably refused to take 'no' for an answer.

We have not used our sleeping bags at all, she reflected, I don't know why we're bothering to cart them along. Everyone is so kind, why do I feel guilty? When she said as much to Robin, he was unsympathetic. "Search me. Why do you? Be grateful for any luxury we can get. Why sleep in the bush when we can have a bed and a liberal supply of beer?"

"But the idea was to walk in the footsteps of Clarissa and Emma, and they had to rough it. I was expecting to put up with some discomfort. It feels as though I'm cheating."

"Cheating?" Robin snorted. "From what you've told me, your grandmother and her friend weren't averse to accepting hospitality from the Portuguese. Didn't they spend several nights in beds?"

"That was different. They didn't have inner spring mattresses, and flush toilets and baths. They were sleeping on straw mattresses in mud huts with rats in the roof and lions prowling around outside. And it was only a couple of times, once when Emma was sick."

"The lions I can't help you with," said Robin. "Tell you what: if we get offered a room tonight, Russell and I will take it. You can sleep in the garden."

Some motorists stopped simply to wish them luck, offer cool drinks and snacks, and ask questions. It could be frustrating when they were making good progress to a pre-arranged target, but most of the time they welcomed the diversion, for the landscape of cultivated lands, straggly bush and small dusty towns, was monotonous.

The only people they encountered on foot were Africans from nearby farms or villages. Sometimes a whole family: the man followed by a woman with a bundle on her head and another on her back, trailing several children. Sometimes a party of chattering women, carrying bundles of kindling or baskets of maize cobs on their heads. While the children would stare or skip along beside Liz, and the men would raise their hands in salutes, and sometimes stop to pass the time of day, the women were shy and would drop their eyes until the trio had passed, giggling behind their fingers.

"Crazy whites walking when they could be driving," murmured Robin.

The only way in which she felt she was being tested was physically. Her shoulders ached from her rucksack, she was exhausted by the end of each day, and both she and Robin were suffering acutely from blisters. Every evening they treated and commiserated over each other's injuries.

In the distance loomed the same blue mountains Clarissa had written about, and they crossed the same rivers – dry, sandy beds at this time of the year. Otherwise, there was little to connect Clarissa's experience with her own.

And yet, the link was there, she consoled herself, in the simple fact that she was doing it. And occasionally, at the end of a long day, when the light was fading and the heat had made her a little light-headed, she could almost see the two women walking ahead of her, talking and laughing together, their long skirts swinging, hair coiled up inside their broad-brimmed hats. And Mukwasi with his toga flapping about his legs, and the line of porters behind.

She would still get good copy from the expedition, by focusing on the very differences that had dismayed her, by leavening her story with humour and weaving in selected extracts from the diary, and old photographs from the National Archives.

The long hours on the road gave her time to reflect on the past – and Alex, and as she grew in strength and vitality, she had the feeling of a burden easing. She thought about the future too. What did she want to do when she went back to England? Coming to Africa had marked the end of a stage in her life, she recognised that now. But what next? Back to the same kind of work? No, she enjoyed writing but she wanted to get away from the daily grind of deadlines. I don't know yet, she decided, but I don't need to go back until I'm ready.

She was enjoying the company of her companions. Apart from minor irritations, like Robin's habit of whistling the same tune over and over, they got on well as a threesome. Robin and Russell were opposite personalities: Russell quiet, reserved and efficient, spending his free time recording and drawing the specimens he was collecting along the way. Robin was easygoing about everything except his photography and equipment. An intriguing character, self-deprecating, assured, cynical but reticent about himself. Only after they had been on the road together for a week had he revealed he was divorced, and had a son of six who lived with his ex-wife in Surrey. As a freelance photographer, he had seen a lot of the world, and she suspected his cynical outlook was a form of defence.

He worked conscientiously, photographing her and Russell, the local inhabitants, the bush, homesteads; even the down-at-heel towns along the route offered a challenge. They were both artists in their own way: Robin with his camera, Russell with his intricate, meticulous drawings.

Like Ian Coles, Russell encouraged her to look at her surroundings in a new way. He gave her a magnifying glass and showed her insects camouflaged in the undergrowth, chameleons swaying on grass stems, the foam nests of tiny frogs.

Robin became equally fascinated by the miniature universe brought to life under the magnifying glass, and began experimenting with various lenses. "Well, I'm not likely to get an action shot of you and Russell fleeing an elephant," he commented when she found him prone in the dust, photographing a dung beetle struggling with a plum-sized ball of excrement.

Three days from their destination, she persuaded them to refuse further hospitality and camp instead. Later she was to remember those nights as the most memorable interludes on the walk, and even Robin and Russell, despite their complaints, were infected by her enthusiasm. The best moments came after a dinner of tinned spaghetti and tinned peaches, when they sat around the fire drinking coffee laced with brandy, and talking.

"This jaunt has been all very pleasant," Robin remarked on their last night, as they camped on a ridge overlooking a wooded valley, "but it hasn't brought you any closer to finding your grandmother's grave. Were you expecting it to?"

"Not seriously," she admitted. "I would have done it even if we had already found the grave."

"So, what's the next step?"

She hesitated. Ian had already given all the assistance he could. Was there any point in wandering aimlessly in the Zambezi Valley again without any new clues as to where to look? In all her research, she had never found the remotest indication that anyone else had known the location of the grave.

"I don't know," she confessed with a shrug. "Perhaps this is the end of the line."

The walk was to end in a small memorial garden commemorating the site of the first hospital built in the Umtali district. Before leaving Salisbury, Liz had contacted the local historical society, whose chairman had been instantly enthusiastic, and insisted on arranging a low-key reception to celebrate the completion of the expedition.

The sun was low by the time they located the small cemetery mentioned in the directions from the society president, and followed the track that wound around it, and up a kopje. As Robin sprinted ahead to photograph their arrival, she felt a glow of satisfaction. I've done it. Maybe not for their noble reasons, but I've run the distance.

The track curled upwards through parched woodland, between an avenue of jacarandas. Near the summit, several cars were parked and she recognised Nicholas' battered Land Rover. A few people stood in small groups. "Here they come," she heard someone say.

Throbbing feet and aching knees forgotten, she turned to Russell. "We can stop walking in about sixty seconds."

"Sorry, forgot to tell you," he said laconically. "We decided to carry on to Salisbury. Only another three hundred miles, and that's where Clarissa met Simon again, so it'll make better copy for the press." Grinning, he put his arm around her shoulders and together they walked towards the waiting group: her uncle leaning on his stick, Julius beside him, a couple of photographers, a group of men in suits and women in hats.

After the brief ceremony, Liz and Nicholas walked through a stone archway and down stone steps into a garden planted with scarlet aloes, flowering shrubs and trees, overlooking a valley. He showed her a small plaque, and she read the words: *On this spot, in the year 1891, nurses Clarissa Hamilton and Emma Clarke inaugurated Nursing Services in the Colony. 14 July 1891.*

He put his arm around her. "Clever girl. They would have been proud of you."

Later, in the lounge of the Cecil Hotel in Umtali, where Nicholas had taken rooms for them, he ordered champagne and they toasted their success. Then he sprung his news.

"I've been contacted through the Herald by a fellow who knew Clarissa and Simon."

She stared at him, speechless.

"His name is van Heerden. He's very old and sick, in a nursing home in Salisbury," he said slowly, relishing the impact of his words. "He'd read the advance piece in the paper about your walk. Used to be a hunter and prospector back in the early days and," he paused tantalisingly, "he not only knew Clarissa – and Emma – but camped in the Valley with her and Simon."

"Camped with them?" Her heart was thumping. "When?"

"From what I could gather, shortly before Clarissa died. He didn't want to talk on the phone – sounded very wheezy. He wants you to go and see him. He's a proper old Boer."

Jubilation surged through her as she picked up her champagne glass. "It feels as though I'm on the edge of fitting a missing piece into an enormous jigsaw puzzle. I can't believe it."

Robin raised his glass to her. "So the walk did help."

On her return to Salisbury, a bouquet of pink rosebuds was waiting on the hall table, with a congratulatory note from Alex. She had phoned her mother from Umtali, and Katherine, who knew nothing about the relationship, and regarded Alex simply as her daughter's friend and workmate, had passed on the news.

Beneath the smooth flow of words on the card, Liz sensed a carefully-concealed irritation. She had been gone for months now: when was she going to abandon this ridiculous charade?

But it was her own reaction that pleased her most. After the initial, automatic quickening of her heart that accompanied the sight of his handwriting, her pulse returned almost immediately to its normal, steady beat. A vague ache of regret remained, but it was no longer the old flaring pain. She stared at the card with a growing sense of elation.

"You know," she stroked Shumba's smooth head, "I do believe I have almost walked Alex Stanton out of my system."

"Heavenly." Barbara peered over her shoulder at the flowers. "Mario?"

"No. That rat in London," she replied cheerfully. "Pretty, aren't they? Let's put them in the sittingroom where we can all enjoy them."

"You don't sound particularly excited." Barbara looked at her with raised eyebrows.

"No." She grinned. "Isn't it wonderful?"

Her high spirits carried her through till the following morning, but when she phoned the nursing home, to ask if she might call on the old prospector, her hopes tumbled.

"I'm sorry," said the nurse on duty, "but Mr van Heerden had a heart attack the day before yesterday. He is back in hospital, in intensive care, and is not able to have visitors."

"How is he?" she asked anxiously.

"Comfortable," the voice said briskly. "Phone again in a few days, and we should be able to give you more news."

Her disappointment was so overwhelming it was impossible to concentrate on her work. He can't die before I've talked to him and found out what he knows, he mustn't, she thought, and was immediately appalled at her selfishness. During her lunch break, she went out and ordered some flowers to be sent to the hospital, with a note of good wishes. In the city street the heat hung heavy and oppressive. October weather – suicide month, with no rain likely for several weeks.

Two days later, when she entered the newsroom, an envelope was propped on her typewriter. Unfolding a sheet of notepaper covered in neat, upright handwriting, she read:

Dear Miss Pendennis,
I was interested to read about your walk in the newspaper. As you are

looking for information about your grandmother's grave, you may be interested to know that Emma Clarke is my mother.

She is in her late eighties, and very frail. Because of her health, I thought hard about whether to make contact with you, but I decided she would want me to do so.

She is living on the Transkei coast in South Africa, with an elderly woman friend who takes care of her. Although her short-term memory is not very good any more, and her eyesight is failing, where the past is concerned she is completely clear-headed.

Whether she can help with your search, I don't know, but I would be happy for you to contact me if you wish to pursue the matter.

Sincerely,
Margaret Payne.

Alive. Emma alive.

With racing heart, she reached for the phone book. When she dialled the number, a vague, cultivated and faintly worried female voice answered, and agreed to see her after work the same evening.

Margaret Payne lived a short way from the city centre in the old suburb of Avondale, opposite a school, in a white house set in immaculate gardens, with a gateway flanked by two tall palm trees. A small faded woman, with permed brown hair liberally threaded with grey, opened the door. Leading the way into a sittingroom where chintz furniture was draped in lace-edged protectors, she poured two glasses of sherry, gave one to Liz and sat down opposite her.

Setting her glass down, she clasped her hands and leaned forward.

"I don't know if I'm wasting your time, Miss Pendennis," she said in the same anxious tone she had used on the phone, "I wrote that note on the spur of the moment, after I had read the story. After I had posted it I wondered whether I had done the right thing."

"Oh, but you have," Liz assured her eagerly, "just to know Emma – your mother – is still alive, you have no idea how happy I am to hear it. Even if she can't help, I would very much like to make contact. She's another link with the past, you see. My great uncle, Nicholas Hamilton, was thrilled when I phoned him today."

"Uncle Nick!" her eyes widened, "I remember him from when I was a little girl. I never dreamed he was still alive. We used to go out with Mummy and stay on the farm in Shangara during school holidays. Is he still there?"

"Yes." Liz grinned. "Like your mother, he appears to be indestructible. Mrs Payne, could I get in touch with her?"

"Well, that's the trouble," she fiddled with her rings. "She can't write – her eyes are too bad, and she hates talking on the phone because she's a bit deaf. You could send a letter, which Julia would read to her."

"What if I went down there? You mentioned that she lives in the Transkei."

"Yes, a little seaside village – Port St Johns." She hesitated, "It's an awfully long way – three days by train or car. And even if you went to all that effort, you might find you've wasted your time and she can't help you at all." She took anxious, bird-like sips from her glass.

"I don't really expect her to give me any information about the grave that we don't already have," Liz explained. "We know your mother saw Simon just before he died, but anything he told her, she passed on to my uncle a long time ago."

"That's so," agreed Margaret Payne, "I remember her telling me. Well then, what do you expect?"

Liz sipped the excellent golden sherry. "I'm not sure. I just feel something might emerge if I could talk to her. I want to meet her. It's somehow become important to pull together the threads of Clarissa's life." She paused, searching for the right words, "It's just a thing I have to do, even if it means going down to South Africa. Would it be bad for her health to have me appear out of the blue?"

"On the contrary," said Margaret Payne slowly, "I think she would want to see you. She isn't going to last much longer, a year at the most, and she knows it as well as anyone. I've asked her a hundred times to come up here and let me look after her. But she loves that place. And she loves reminiscing about the old days. You being a writer, you could write a book about those two: the lives they led, the things they did."

"That's partly it," said Liz. "Uncle Nick suggested Clarissa's diary might be worth publishing, with some background detail. Your mother could definitely help with that."

"In that case," Margaret Payne leaned back in her chair, picked up her glass and relaxed for the first time since Liz's arrival, "I'll contact her. When would you want to go?"

"As soon as I can get away. I'll have to check with my boss," she winced at the prospect. "He will probably kill me – or fire me – for asking for more time off, but I've got to the point where I'll do it anyway."

When she returned home, Chris Rainier's car was in the driveway and he was at the front door, talking to the housemaid. It was the first time she had seen him since the walk.

He came down the steps to meet her. "Hi. I was going to invite myself for a meal, but Barb and Derick are having dinner with Derick's old folks. I don't suppose you were planning a three-course dinner?" he said hopefully.

"No," said Liz, "scrambled eggs was what I had in mind. Ekiniya is going off for the evening. Want to stay?"

"Scrambled eggs?" He wrinkled his nose. "I haven't eaten all day. Get in the car, I'll take you for a steak."

"All right."

He looked at her critically. "You look like a stick insect. Didn't you take food on your pioneering trek?"

"As little as possible. My pack was heavy enough without food. But we were very well fed en route. I think I just walked it all off."

"What have you done with your hair?" he grumbled, opening the passenger door for her.

"I had it cut," she ran her fingers through the short silky strands framing her face. "I thought it would be easier to manage while I was walking. But I'm thinking of keeping it this way. Why? Don't you like it?" She fluttered her eyelashes in mock flirtation.

"I preferred it the way it was."

"Yes, well, men usually do. Things don't always stay the way they were."

"Are we talking hair or life in general?"

"Both."

He glanced down at her profile beside him. "I guess it could be worse. Your neck isn't too bad."

"Gee, thanks."

He drove to a small suburban restaurant renowned for the quality of its steak, and ordered two T-bones without consulting her.

"Hold on a minute," she told him. "I might want something else. I want to look at the menu."

"Don't waste your time. Their steaks are famous."

"I'd like to look," she said firmly, and ordered curry, mainly to irritate him.

While they waited for their meal, she told him about Emma, and he became almost lyrical about the attractions of the Transkei coast. "We used to spend holidays in a fishing cottage," he concluded, and she suddenly remembered Barbara telling her about his teenage sweetheart.

"Yes, Barbara was saying you used to holiday there."

"That's right." He changed the subject. "When are you leaving?"

"Soon as I hear from Emma's daughter."

Margaret Payne phoned a couple of days later to say that Emma was expecting a visit, and her companion Julia Anderson was waiting to hear from Liz about her plans. As expected, her editor exploded at her request for more leave, but became a little calmer when she offered to write a follow-up story on her meeting with Emma. A meeting that had – she pointed out – been made possible by the newspaper report on her walk. "It's good human interest stuff *and* good public relations," she argued. "People will want to know that I've met Emma – and been put in touch with someone else who knew my grandmother – through the paper."

"Okay, okay," he said grudgingly. "You've made your point. Unpaid leave," he warned her. "I'm running a newspaper, not a charity. What about the old Boer?"

"He's still in intensive care. I've been phoning every day."

From the railway station she learnt that South African Railways only travelled as far as Umtata, the provincial capital of the Transkei. From there, she would have to make her own way. On Derick's maps the distances looked formidable, but he waved aside her concerns. "Port St John's is only a couple of hours further. Contact the old ducks. They'll organise transport from Umtata."

19

Derick lifted her suitcase on to the luggage rack. The compartment was a roomy, two-berth coupé, the other occupant a stout elderly woman in tweeds and sturdy, lace-up shoes.

The whistle blew, the engine hissed, and he pecked her cheek hastily – "Bye, Liz, good luck" – before rejoining Barbara, Nicholas and Chris on the platform. The train jerked and began to move, and she let the window down to lean out and wave. As the platform slowly receded and their figures grew smaller, she was assailed by an uncanny sense of a camera clicking, freezing the scene and the moment. It was not exactly *déjà vu*, but something very similar – something connected with the four people on the platform. As though some pre-ordained sequence of events was unfolding. How important are they in my life? she wondered, staring out of the window as the engine picked up speed and lights flashed past. Nicholas had always been part of her life, even though he was not often there, and now Barbara and Derick had begun to feel like a second family. Even Chris, despite his ability to irritate and arouse unsettling emotions.

She frowned. "All right, love?" asked her keen-eyed companion, taking a bundle of knitting from a tapestry bag. "Was that your boyfriend?"

"Oh, no," Liz smiled, "no, it was – nothing, just a funny feeling I had suddenly."

"Well, the dining car will be open soon. That should sort out any funny feelings," said her companion comfortably. "My name is Jean Stapleton, by the way." She chattered on while Liz took off her jacket and curled up beside the window, tucking her feet underneath her. Lights flashed past, Africans on bicycles in the orange glow of street lamps that gave the foliage of trees an oddly technicolour cast. The lights became fewer, until the blackness was broken only by the occasional glow from farmhouses and small villages, flickering fires in farm compounds or car headlights on the road running parallel with the train.

She felt her soul stretch itself luxuriously and relax. Since her return from the walk, she had been revelling in a new sense of freedom. The knowledge that she was no longer in thrall to Alex was wonderfully liberating, and she was beginning to realise how stultifying the relationship had been to her personally. How, without noticing, she had gradually tailored her life according to his demands. I stopped living my life, she now recognised, I became an appendage, fitting in with his schedules, adjusting my routine so that we could have time together. I'd stopped seeing most of my friends, stopped planning ahead for weekends or holidays, because I was waiting to hear his plans. He had only to twitch the thread and I dropped everything. My life was a tangle of lies and subterfuge, especially with Mum – because I couldn't bear the thought of her knowing. And because I was so dependent on him, I was losing confidence in myself. I never did things on my own any more – my things. I'd stopped being me.

Now I'm back, and Africa has done that. It changed Clarissa's life: although she came out here ostensibly to nurse, what she really wanted was something new and different. She was a romantic, she knew there had to be more to life. And me? I had to come to discover there was more to life than what I was running away from. And that it wasn't romantic at all, my affair – just rather degrading.

A surge of well-being flooded through her as she looked around the compartment for the first time, noticing the dark green padded upholstery, the narrow table that lifted to reveal a stainless steel hand basin underneath, photographic prints of the Victoria Falls and the Matopos – the site of Cecil Rhodes' grave – on the wood panelling above the seats.

She stared into the darkness, wondering what it would be like to meet Emma, what she might learn from her, until a cockney voice outside the cabin announced, 'First sitting', and she followed Jean Stapleton down the swaying passageway to the dining car.

Over a dinner of soup, roast pork and vegetables, followed by fruit salad, she found herself telling her companion the reason behind her trip. I'm beginning to sound like the ancient mariner, she thought. She was aware of standing outside the narrative, listening, realising quite suddenly that Clarissa's story would not be complete until her grave had been found; and that it was important, not just for Clarissa, but for herself, because Clarissa's story had become part of her own story.

She had not slept on a train since trips to Scotland during her childhood. Lying in the upper bunk while her companion snored gently below, she savoured forgotten pleasures: the comforting rocking motion, the rhythm of the wheels, the smell of soot and fresh night air, the feeling of being wrapped in warmth while the train rushed through the dark, the knowledge that she was once again on the road, exploring, tasting new experiences. Best of all, she loved that feeling.

When the train stopped with squealing brakes at lighted stations, shouts and laughter rang out, doors opened and closed, milk cans clanked. A female voice said in a headmistressy way, "Don't forget to put the dogs and the milk bottles out. I'll ring as soon as I get there." Then, with a long whistle and a lurch, they were moving again.

In the morning they changed trains at Bulawayo, and found seats together in another coupé. Although the first and second class carriages were not very full, Africans carrying suitcases and enormous bundles wrapped in sheeting crowded into the third class carriages – chattering women with babies tied to their backs and children clinging to their skirts, old men in army greatcoats, young men swaggering in brightly coloured shirts and sunglasses. They were on a South African

Railways train now, it was older, and the staff less friendly. Once beyond the wide, tree-lined avenues and colonial buildings of Bulawayo, the landscape flattened, the vegetation straggled into grey-brown scrub.

Crossing the border into Bechuanaland, the train rumbled through endless expanses of semi-desert punctuated by small, sun-baked villages. When it stopped at lonely stations, hawkers ran alongside the carriages waving fresh pawpaws, crude wood carvings of figures and animals, crocheted doilies. Small boys clamoured below the windows, shouting, "Pennies, pennies," and some of the passengers tossed coins on to the platform. A man held out the furry form of a night-ape with large frightened eyes. Liz alighted to stretch her legs and was immediately surrounded. She bought a pawpaw and passed it through the window to Jean, but even as she began to walk down the platform, the whistle blew and she had to swing herself quickly aboard as her companion's alarmed face peered out of the window. The train rushed on, through featureless thorn scrub, past dusty villages where skinny dogs barked and children waved, into a crimson and violet sunset that cloaked the stark landscape in brief dramatic beauty.

Late that night, alighting at a deserted station and walking away from the glow of the lights, she was awed by the multitude of stars overhead, the feeling that she only needed to put out her hand to touch the nearest constellation. It was cold, and an old black watchman in a balaclava and heavy coat, stamped his feet and held his hands over the crimson sparks floating into the darkness from a charcoal brazier. Then back to her bunk, to be rocked to the rhythm of the wheels, sleeping and waking and sleeping again, dreaming of Clarissa and Emma, and Simon, who was trying to tell her something.

In the morning, the landscape beyond the carriage window was changing, the towns were bigger and closer together. The notices at the stations were in Afrikaans and English, and on the toilet doors, the signs read *'blankes'* and *'nie blankes'* – 'whites' and 'non-whites'. She bought a daily paper and read of the preparatory hearings of the Treason Trial in the Johannesburg Drill Hall. Among the accused was the young black lawyer Nelson Mandela. She had been following the story with interest, and now she noticed that Mandela was born in the Transkei, her destination.

At the next station, her companion left the train, and her place was taken by a young university student with cropped hair and cinched waist, wearing skin-tight black jeans. A passionate opponent of apartheid, she had just taken part in a student demonstration. "We were protesting against the Treason Trials. It was fantastic," she enthused. "We wore our academic gowns and carried placards. The column stretched all the way down Grahamstown High Street. Everyone came out to watch – white and black."

"What did the black people think?" Liz asked.

"I don't know," admitted the student, sinking her teeth into an orange. "They just stood quietly."

She left the train a few stations on, and Liz had the compartment to herself until Umtata, where she took a taxi through wide streets lined with Victorian buildings to the hotel she had been directed to by Emma's companion. A message at the reception desk informed her she would be picked up by a Dr McCarthy at three-thirty, so she ordered a pot of tea while she waited in the lounge. He was twenty minutes late when he bundled in – an elderly, craggy-faced man in a faded khaki bushjacket and creased trousers.

"Mick McCarthy," he said in a voice that carried the lilt of an Irish brogue. "Apologies for keeping you waiting, but I've been undergoing torture at the dentist. Took a bit longer than expected, and I only hope I'm not dribbling – absolutely no control over my mouth at the moment."

If his appearance was dishevelled, his ancient black Austin was worse – pockmarked with rust and dented in a number of places. "Meet Gertie," he slapped the roof, "had her for twenty years, but she still gets us from A to B. I had some horse-feed in the back last week. Hope you won't be too uncomfortable."

He put her case into the boot, and cleared a space in front by throwing old magazines, a gumboot, a spanner and some parcels on to the back seat. She climbed in, and the car clattered out of town into a landscape of undulating brown hills sprinkled with neat mud huts and whitewashed stores. Small boys herded goats off the road as they passed, two men drove horned cattle through a dip tank; others, wrapped in blankets, on foot or on horseback, lifted hands in greeting.

The tarred road gave way to a dirt track that became steadily worse. Just as she was beginning to think the old vehicle could not sustain more punishment without disintegrating into a thousand clattering pieces, it wheezed up a steep incline to reveal, from the summit, a triangle of deep blue sea framed by the dark flanks of a ravine through which a wide river meandered.

Deep in late afternoon shadow, the road descended to the north bank of the river, and ran alongside it, beneath tall spreading trees festooned with tangled vines and lianas, where monkeys cavorted like trapeze artists. Behind the wall of greenery towered sheer cliffs encrusted with crimson, gold and creamy lichens. The river was a deep green until it met the ink-blue of the ocean in a surge of foam pounding jagged rocks.

The car grumbled into low gear to crawl uphill past whitewashed buildings, and on to a coast road flanked on one side by fishing cottages set in low windswept scrub, and on the seaward side by a rugged rock-strewn shoreline. The smell of seaweed and salt drifted through the window.

They stopped in front of a small white-washed cottage with a once-black corrugated iron roof now faded to grey. The front garden was a square of patchy lawn, intersected by a path bordered by daisy bushes and leading up to a narrow stoep.

The front door opened, and a tall, grey-haired woman in navy trousers and an old blue fisherman's jersey came down the steps, flicking a cigarette stub on to the grass. At her heels scampered a black and white terrier.

"Mike, you made it, heard you five minutes ago. Welcome, Elizabeth, you must be exhausted." She had a firm, masculine handshake. "I'm Julia," she added unnecessarily as the doctor wrestled the suitcase out of the boot.

"How's Emma keeping?" he asked as he carried it up the steps.

"Not too bad. Come in and say hullo."

He declined. "Better get back. You know Madge – can't relax until she knows Gertie has made it." He shook Liz's hand, and they watched as he coaxed the old car into breathless life once more.

Julia ushered her into a narrow entrance hall where the faded wallpaper was lined with framed photographs and prints. "We'll put your case in the back room, and then have a drink with Emma. What's your poison? I hope we have it. Here we are," and she opened a door into a small room, simply furnished. A cut-glass vase of flowers stood on the bedside table and the window opened on to the hillside.

"Not palatial, but I think you'll be quite comfy. Towels, cupboard here, couple of drawers cleared for you, and the bathroom is down the passage. Would you like a wash first?"

"Please."

When she emerged from the bathroom, Julia was waiting in the hall. "All right?" She laid her hand on Liz's arm, "Now, she can't see very well, she's a bit deaf, in fact, everything's starting to slow down, so we don't want to tire her too much."

She led the way into a room that could have been lifted out of an English country cottage. Dark beams supported the ceiling, the furniture was upholstered in chintz, horse brasses adorned the small fireplace and watercolour seascapes the walls. There was even a cushioned window seat, overlooking a view of rocky coastline. It was growing dark outside and the sound of pounding surf came clearly through the window.

In an armchair by the fireplace sat a small, upright figure so thin and fragile she seemed ready to crumble into dust at a touch. Her face was etched with a thousand fine lines that accentuated her high cheekbones; her dark eyes were faded but lively. Her white hair was coiled behind her head, and she wore a navy and white print dress ornamented with a silver brooch in the shape of a flame lily.

"Here she is, Em," said Julia briskly, raising her voice.

Emma held out her hands. "Elizabeth, welcome. Come close, my eyes are shocking." Her voice was soft and papery like the rustle of dry leaves. "Why," she smiled as she peered up at her and took her hands, "you're dark, you don't have

Clarissa's colouring at all. But of course, Simon was very dark. Sit down, dear, Julia will fix us a drink."

Liz perched on a low stool while Julia poured a sherry for Emma; she handed Liz a gin and tonic, the first taste of which made her gasp.

"Too heavy-handed? Sorry," said Julia. "Always do that. Here, have some more tonic."

Emma raised her glass with fingers that trembled slightly. "Here's cheers, dear," and immediately began to ply her with questions about her trip, her family, and the country north of the Limpopo that had once been her home. As she replied, Liz struggled to reconcile this wisp of a woman with the young, energetic companion of her grandmother's adventures.

"And Nick," Emma inquired. "How is the old reprobate? Still smoking himself to death?"

"Yes," Liz admitted with a grin. "He's a pack-a-day man. He sent his love," she added.

"Did he, indeed?" her voice was gently sarcastic. "A bit late for that now. Thirty years ago, it might have done me some good." Her face relaxed into a crooked grin that would become familiar over the next few days. She leaned forward and patted Liz's arm. "Don't tell me he hasn't told you I chased him for nearly ten years. It's quite true, I don't mind admitting it now. And I suppose I shouldn't be critical about one of the few men I've known who remained faithful to his wife – as far as I know, anyway. A rare breed," she added tartly, "particularly in Africa."

She leaned back in her chair, eyes glinting with laughter, but her breathing was laboured, and Julia stood up instantly. "Now Em, stop chattering, and take it easy, you'll have plenty of time over the next few days. Elizabeth, would you come and help me dish up dinner? It's not very exciting, just a casserole."

The mornings were warm and sunny, and while Emma sat enthroned on the tiny stoep, a blanket about her knees, Liz perched on the low stone wall overlooking the small garden and the sea, and asked all the questions she had been storing up since opening Clarissa's diary.

Through Emma's eyes she relived the trek from Mpandas, the encounter with Simon at Chimoio, their second meeting in Salisbury, Emma's wedding, the pursuit of Clarissa by Robert Hammond, and their departure for England. Emma told of her terror on the night of the lion attack, and her despair when Clarissa came close to death in Umtali. As her daughter had said, her mind was very clear on the past.

When Liz mentioned Clarissa's grave, Emma stared out beyond the rocks to where the wind tossed the spray into a fine mist, her brow furrowed in concentration. But she had nothing new to add.

"It wasn't a priority at the time, as you can imagine," she reminded Liz gently. "I was distraught over Clarissa, and Simon was so ill he could barely speak when

I got to him. We both knew he was dying, and he was suffering dreadful guilt for not having brought Clarissa back to Salisbury sooner. It was agonising to see. He was also desperate to make sure the baby would be looked after, that I get in touch with Nicholas. He was sinking fast, there wasn't much time to talk."

"Did you ask where she was buried?"

"Yes, I did, but what he told me you already know. Surely her diary would have given you some clue...."

"No," Liz interrupted her. "The diary ended before she went back to Africa with Simon."

Emma stared at her. "Not that one, dear, the other one."

"There isn't another one," said Liz in perplexity. "There's only one diary."

"Oh, no, Elizabeth," Emma said firmly, "of course there was another diary. But surely," she stared at Liz, "surely it must have been among the belongings that came back from the Valley with Simon – the trunk that Nicholas took back to England."

"No," Liz's heart was pounding. "No, there was nothing like that. Uncle Nicky would have told me. Are you saying she kept a second diary after she went back to Rhodesia?"

"But of course," Emma's voice was assured. "I saw it several times when she came to stay – she used to visit me sometimes when Simon went off on one of his expeditions. It had become a habit, writing her diary – she never bothered much in England, said there was nothing to write about there. But as soon as she came back, she started again. Didn't write every day, of course, but I think she kept it up faithfully."

"Another diary?" Liz's mind was in a tumult. "Would she have taken it into the Valley?"

"I'm sure she would." Emma was silent for a moment, thinking back. "I wonder why it wasn't amongst her things. Must have got lost. Because if she had left it on the farm, Nicholas would have found it."

Liz rubbed her forehead, her thoughts racing. "He definitely didn't, and if it was left at the campsite, it's lost now, for sure. I suppose in the panic of the moment, Simon could have left things behind."

"I suppose so," Emma shook her head, "how infuriating. Simon never mentioned it, and I didn't think to ask. We had other matters on our minds." Gulls screeched from the rocks and she stared out over the sea, preoccupied by old memories. Liz's mind seethed at this unexpected revelation, but she did not pursue the subject. She would think about it later.

"What about other people they might have met in the Valley, who might know where they went?" She remembered the old prospector, and when she mentioned his name, Emma nodded.

"Hennie. Yes, I remember him from Mpandas, but I never knew he met them in the Valley. As for others," she shook her head. "Not that I remember."

Heeding Julia's warning, Liz tried to ration her questions. In the afternoons, while Emma rested, she would accompany the other woman into the small village of Port St Johns to help with the shopping, or go for walks on the hills or along the shore. North of the line of cottages a long white beach extended to a rugged bluff where native cattle grazed on the edge of a sheer cliff. In the early morning and evening, fishermen gathered on the rocks in front of the cottages, and Julia took her out one evening and lent her a rod. Although the only thing she accomplished was to lose her bait several times, it was exhilarating to stand on the wet rocks with the spray breaking around her, feeling the tug of the waves on her line.

After dinner that evening, she asked Emma what happened to Clarissa during the Mashona rising. "My uncle seems to think she had some sort of bad experience."

"It was one thing she never talked about. Frank and I were in South Africa at the time, and I didn't see her more than a couple of times during the last few years of her life. What she did tell me was that she lost her first baby during the rising, but when I asked about it, she said she couldn't remember what had happened. She seemed to have blanked it out. That was when she started the clinic for the locals, and children especially."

"When was the last time you saw her?"

"About six months before she died, after we came back to Salisbury. She had got her old sparkle back, thank God. She was amazingly resilient. I was so relieved I didn't want to pry into painful territory." Her face darkened. "There were things that happened in those years that were better forgotten. Now," she turned away from her memories, "tell me, why do you think your mother never had any interest in the country she was born in?"

"Uncle Nicky thinks it was because of losing both parents there. Perhaps some kind of sub-conscious memory made it impossible for her to feel any love for Africa."

"Perhaps. She certainly wouldn't have survived if it hadn't been for the young wife of Simon's tracker. You know about that – that she breast-fed Kathy. What a dear baby, she hardly made a sound while I was looking after her." She paused. "Does she ever talk about Simon and Clarissa?"

"Oh, yes, she liked to tell me the story. But to her, Uncle Nicky and Aunt Felicity were her parents. Mum is very practical. If it was me, I would never have rested until I'd found Clarissa's grave."

"I can see that." Emma's eyes met hers and they both laughed.

"The Wild Coast – the name is just right," Liz remarked to Julia, gazing around her at the rugged landscape, the sheer cliffs dropping hundreds of feet to jagged rocks pounded by waves. They were sitting on a windswept vantage point, drinking coffee from a thermos. Emma was resting and Julia had suggested a drive up the coast.

"Yes, we love it, it's so peaceful. You'd never think it was the scene of a horrible tragedy not all that long ago," said Julia. A high school teacher before her retirement, she had an encyclopaedic knowledge of local history, and Liz was enthralled by her stories. "Tell me," she said now, cupping her mug, her hair tossed by the sea breeze.

"Just over a hundred years ago, the Boers were spreading east and the Xhosa were expanding west. They met at the Fish River, and there was a lot of cattle raiding and violence, so the British settled English immigrants along the border as a buffer between them. But the violence continued, and both groups became more and more frustrated. The Xhosa were desperate to get rid of the whites who had stopped their natural expansion. I don't suppose you've had any experience of African superstition?" she asked Liz.

"A little." Briefly Liz told the story of Reta, and Julia nodded.

"Imagine that situation magnified a hundredfold," she said. "Along came a young spirit medium, who had a vision. It was a bizarre story, but what it amounted to was that Russians from Crimea – the Crimean War was in the news – would ride into the country to save her people from the white settlers. To meet the conditions of the vision, the people had to make a sacrifice: they had to destroy all their cattle and crops. Then, on a certain day, a great wind would come and drive the whites into the sea.

"The local missionaries tried to stop them, but the people slaughtered thousands of cattle and burned their crops to the ground. When the day came, of course, nothing happened. Hundreds of starving people fled across the river and settlers took many of them in, but thousands died in the famine that followed."

"This is true – not just a legend?" Liz asked in disbelief.

"This really happened, only about forty years before your grandmother and Emma came to Africa."

"They wouldn't be as easily taken in today, would they?" asked Liz, awed by the magnitude of the tragedy.

"Possibly not. Not the educated ones, but most of them still live much the same lives as in the nineteenth century. And the strange thing," she added, "is that it sometimes rubs off on the whites. I knew of a man whose son disappeared about ten years ago. When he had all but given up hope of finding him, he consulted a witchdoctor."

"Did they find him?"

"They found his body. You hear a lot about black culture being destroyed by white influence. What people forget is that it works both ways. Several farmers I know call in rainmakers when they are suffering from drought."

Liz remembered Nicholas asking the old diviner about Clarissa's grave. When she told Julia, the older woman nodded. "That's exactly what I mean."

The day before her departure, Liz asked a question she had been reluctant to put to Emma. Why, she wondered, had she waited so long? Was it because she was afraid to hear the answer?

"Clarissa's marriage to Simon – was it happy, or do you think she ever regretted not marrying Robert Hammond?"

Emma looked at her in surprise. "Clarissa wasn't one for regrets. She and Simon were the most self-contained couple I ever knew. You know, although I was the one who encouraged him to go back to England and find her, I didn't really approve of him as husband material. I only did it because I knew how she felt. I was convinced that after a few years, when the gloss had worn off, he would lose interest, take off into the blue again, dump her in England, probably bringing up a family on her own. That's the type he was, or so I thought.

"Well, I was wrong. Frank and I used to say they would be content on a desert island as long as they were together. Mind you, I always wondered what would have happened if they had both lived. I was afraid Simon might have been jealous of the baby, because it would have meant Clarissa having someone else to think about. He was used to having her undivided attention, and he could be quite selfish. I was afraid their unique relationship would be spoilt, and it meant a lot to me, because by then my own marriage had become difficult. But I could always look at them, the strength of their love. And I wanted that to last."

"And it did?" Liz persisted.

"To the end. If she hadn't died, I think Simon might have fought back and recovered, but to be hit both by her death and blackwater in the space of a couple of weeks – it was too much."

She was silent, but after a few moments she turned to Liz with a faint smile. "I suppose a young thing like you would think it was a tragic ending."

"Oh yes," Liz said fervently, "the saddest thing ever."

"Of course, to die young is always sad and wasteful. But when I look back, it doesn't seem so terribly tragic any more, except for Kathy, of course, and she seems to have survived perfectly well. But for them: they never grew old, they were never disillusioned by each other. To stop loving, that's the worst tragedy. Those two had more happiness than millions of crabby couples who live to sour old age together."

"Is that possible?" Liz said doubtfully. "They had so little time."

Emma nodded. "If you could ask Clarissa whether she would do it again, I know exactly what her answer would be."

When Liz was packed and waiting for her lift back to Umtata, Emma handed her a little box containing a small wood carving of an impala. "They were always my favourite animals. Clarissa gave it to me in Salisbury the week before my wedding. It's no work of art, but it has sentimental value. I'd like you to have it."

"Thank you." Liz bent and kissed her cheek, and Emma reached for a handkerchief. "Tell that uncle of yours it's time he gave up smoking. And send him my love," she added, a glint of laughter in her faded eyes.

20

The first rains swept through the city, pelting the jacarandas along Moffat Street until the fallen blooms formed purple carpets on the red earth. Clouds of steam rose from tarred roads, gutters overflowed, and Liz savoured for the first time the rich, heady, indescribable smell of the thirsty earth drinking in moisture after the long dry months. The city streets and buildings shone clean and new, and people stood in their gardens, lifting their faces, letting the rain stream down over their bodies, as though receiving a benediction.

"The rain spirits are pleased," Barbara's housemaid told her.

Across the country, rivulets of muddy water trickled into parched, cracked riverbeds, turning powdery dust into thick chocolate mud. Far away to the north, towering thunderheads fed the sprawling network of rivers and streams that flowed into the Zambezi. Hundreds of miles upstream of Kariba Gorge, on the Barotse plains, fishermen in scattered villages smiled as mountainous rain clouds released their burdens, and the broad river that provided their living began slowly to spread across the plains.

Immediately on her return, Liz telephoned the nursing home to inquire about the old prospector. Half expecting to hear he had died during her absence, she was overjoyed to learn he was out of danger and well enough to have visitors.

She drove to a quiet tree-lined street in one of the older suburbs north of the city centre. The nursing home was a rambling building roofed in faded red corrugated iron, with a broad, pillared stoep and cream plastered walls, stained russet close to ground level where years of torrential rains had spattered red soil.

In the cool antiseptic interior, she was led down a corridor and through a screen door at the end. It opened on to a stoep, where a number of beds and wheelchairs had been trundled outside to allow their occupants to enjoy the afternoon sunlight.

"Mr van Heerden, you have a visitor," said the young nurse, touching the shoulder of a bulky figure in a wheelchair.

Sharp grey eyes looked up at her from a face wreathed in lines and leathery with age. The blanket around his legs and lower body did not conceal his enormous bulk and massive belly. His liver-spotted skin was dark, not merely through years of burning sun but in a way that hinted at mixed blood in his ancestry. His head was almost bald and the little remaining hair grew thinly behind his ears. A couple of teeth were missing, and the balance were stained by a lifetime of smoking. Purple veins criss-crossed the prominent nose, and his eyes regarded her with shrewd humour.

"How do you do, Mr van Heerden." She was hesitant as she extended her hand and he took it in his gnarled and shaking one, "Thank you for seeing me. I hope you don't mind me coming?"

"*Ag*, no, girlie, take a seat. There's a chair over there. Bring it here so I can have a good look at you." He spoke with a guttural accent in a voice gravelly with age, and his breathing was slow and laboured.

"I'm sorry you've not been well," she said diffidently, as she carried the chair across to the wheelchair and sat down, "I hope you're on the mend."

"On the mend?" He chuckled asthmatically. "Fact is I'm on the way out – it's just taking a blerry long time. Thought this attack was curtains, but they pulled me through. Blerry miracle, this old ticker – given me eighty-seven good years, but it's about to call it quits."

"I'm sorry," she said uncertainly. "You were a hunter, weren't you? You must have known the country during the most exciting times?"

"*Ja*. Reckon I've lived more than most men in three lifetimes," he agreed, "never thought I'd end up in a place like this. Would have been nice to *kaak* it out in the bush, or hooked into a vundu on the Zambezi. But that's life, not so?"

With his leathery skin, he reminded her of an old bull elephant who had roamed countless miles across the brown earth of Africa, forged a thousand rivers and seen a thousand suns rise and set.

"So, you looking for your grandmother's grave?" he studied her face intently. "Man, but you do look a bit like her, come to think of it. She was only two bricks and a tickey high, and her hair was much lighter, but round the eyes – *ja*, there's something."

"Is there?" She was pleased. "You knew them both – her and Simon?"

"*Ag*, yes, but it was her I met first, with her friend. Down in Portuguese East, just before they started to trek to Umtali. I drew a map for them – I had done the trip twice by then – hauling ivory. Must have done it another three times after that, though the last two times the railway was running so my kaffirs didn't have to carry the stuff."

"But you met her again in the Zambezi Valley. Is that right?" asked Liz.

"*Ja*. She was married then and out to here," he held both hands six inches above his swelling belly, "and they were about to go back to Salisbury before the baby came."

"That would have been just before she died." Liz leaned forward, her heart thumping. "Did you ever see her grave?"

"*Ag*, no, girlie, I never went back there, didn't even know she was dead until I heard from a *shamwari* in a pub in Umtali a couple of years later. But that time in the Valley, I stayed with them a couple of days. They had a *lekker* camp near the water, that's where she would be buried. If you find the camp site, you'll find the grave. True's God."

"My uncle tried," she explained, "and I've done a bit of looking. Could you find it again after all this time?"

"For sure I could find it." Her pulse leapt. "Trouble is, my Valley days are finished, I'll never get out of this chair again." His eyes brooded unseeingly past the wheelchairs on the lawn. "But," he brightened, "reckon I could tell you where to go. You got some paper?"

"Right here." She withdrew a pad and pen from her handbag.

"Just pull up that small table. OK. When I found them I was following the river with a couple of kaffirs carrying the ivory. Here's the river," and he drew a line, "west to east. Kariba Gorge is about here, and the Sanyati comes in here. The camp was roughly here, on a channel that ran into the Zambezi – didn't have a name.

"If you went upriver in a boat and turned into the channel, they were on the east bank, like so, where it made a kind of lagoon. There were two big figs – here and here – and acacias back here."

"You remember it so well?" Liz was watching intently.

"*Ja*," he grinned ironically, "things that happened sixty years ago I remember like it was today. It's yesterday I have trouble with."

"You wouldn't have any idea where in the camp the grave would be?"

"I been thinking about it. There was a place she liked, close by, she showed it to me. She used to write her diary there."

She stared at him. "So there was another diary?" she murmured.

"Another? Don't know about another, but she had this little book, and she used to sit under this mahogany tree near some rocks – a kopje. It was high up, and she could watch animals coming down to the water to drink. I remember she used to leave the diary in a bag in an old hollow tree – said she had a few things nicked from the camp, so she kept it there. Said it was safe from the weather."

He was silent for a moment or two, lost in thought. "*Ja*, that's right, the rocks were some kind of holy place for the local blacks. An old chief was buried in a cave in the kopje and so they steered clear of it, and she knew her stuff would be safe. Did your family ever get that bag?"

She shook her head, and he grinned. "Funny if it was still there, hey? In the tree?"

She stared at him. "But it couldn't be, could it?"

"Not blerry likely, girlie. Couple of floods, rain, wind, no. Still, can't hurt to look, hey?" His breathing was becoming more and more laboured. "Get a boat, go up the river from Kariba – about two hours maybe, and look for this little channel. It's hard to see till you're on top of it – makes a dog leg, then runs into a kind of lagoon. The kopje was about here," he jabbed the pen at a point on the map.

He paused, frowning. "There was something about the rocks," he shook his head, "can't remember. Never mind, I reckon Simon would have buried her up there near the mahogany, looking down at the river." He smiled reminiscently. "She was a nice little lady. Small, with a *lekker* smile. Those two, they were quite happy on their own with their kaffirs."

"What were they doing?"

"Having a look, going up river by dugout. He was doing some hunting, mostly for the pot. And some prospecting, but didn't have any luck. She went along, fishing, shooting too, small stuff – buck, geese, things like that. Sad they both died, hey?" His breathing was becoming stertorous.

"Look," she said hastily, "I don't want to take up too much time. You must be tired." She studied the map. "So the best way to get there is by river, is that right? Not by road."

"There would've been a track, but I didn't use it. I just carried on down the river after I left them." He slapped his thigh. "I remember what it was about those rocks. The big one on top of the kopje, that you could see from the lagoon, it looked like it had been split down the centre. Round, but a clean cut right through, so you could see the sky. Like if you cut an apple in half. *Ja*, you look for that – a split rock."

"A split rock," she repeated, trying to recall whether she had seen anything similar on her boat trip with Ian.

"Here," he held the map out to her, and grinned. "Funny thing, eh, I gave a map to your grandmother to help her find her way, and here I am, giving you a map to find her grave."

"Yes, indeed." She stared down at it before folding it carefully and putting it in her bag, "It is strange."

"Come back and tell me if you find it, hey? If I'm still here, that is." His eyes were suddenly very tired.

"It's a deal, Mr van Heerden," she took the trembling hand. "Thank you very much for your help."

"*Ag*, just call me Hennie."

She hesitated. "Sometime, when you're feeling better, I'd like to come and talk to you about your experiences, Hennie. You must have seen so much, when it was all wild and unspoiled."

"That's for sure," he stared out over the garden, "I been from the Cape through to East Africa – Lake Victoria, Dar, the Congo, and here. The ivory in Rhodesia was never as big as in Kenya, but it was good quality. Could tell you a few stories. Mind you, if you wanted to know what it was really like, you should've been around to talk to my *oupa*."

He leaned towards her, his watery eyes gleaming. "Know what he told me once," his gravelly voice sank almost to a whisper. "He once saw a herd of springbok so big he rode for a day before he reached the end of it. A whole day," his voice was awed. "Packed together – like sheep, he said – like a river. Springbok – far as your eye could see. True's God." He leaned back in his wheelchair, "Man," he said softly, "that would have been a *lekker* sight."

Lying in bed, with the rain drumming on the iron roof, she went over in her mind the trip upriver, scouring her memory for any recollection of the place described by Hennie van Heerden and, in particular, the unusual rock formation. We must have passed it, she thought, it's not that far from Kariba. But it struck no chord. She tried to contact Ian, but he was away on leave in South Africa, and she had to wait three weeks before she could talk to him.

His response was immediate. "'Strewth," he said slowly, "I think I know it."

She tried to speak calmly. "Are you sure?"

"Either that or something very similar."

"We never stopped there?"

"No, because the people had already been moved. They were one of the first groups to go. The headman is a nice old guy – I remember because he was so cut up about leaving. He even showed me the cave – if that's the one, and explained why he didn't want to move his people away from it."

"You know where it is?" After waiting so long, she could hardly believe it was happening so easily.

"No problem. If it's the place I'm thinking of, I can take you there. But not for a few months. The roads are impassable now the rains have set in."

"What about by river?"

"Yes, we could do that. But I can't get away for a couple of months anyway."

To be so close..... She remembered Clarissa's second diary and told him about it. "D'you think there's a remote chance it could still be there?"

He laughed. "Never. It would never have survived sixty odd rainy seasons. Tell you what," he was thinking out loud. "I'll be going to the new settlement to see how they're getting on. I'll talk to old Musa, ask him whether he knows anything about it – and the grave."

"Would you?"

"No trouble." He paused, and his tone changed. "Look, Liz. I know you're frustrated as hell that you can't go down there straight away, but..."

"It's all right," she interrupted. "I couldn't anyway. I'd be fired if I asked for more time off right now. Besides, I'd be afraid to go off upriver on my own."

"Good. Then you'll just have to be patient. Because I don't want you doing anything stupid – especially in this weather." His voice was serious.

She sighed. "I've waited this long, I guess I can wait a bit longer."

But it wasn't easy. At work, she would find herself staring into space, fingers motionless on the typewriter keys, unable to concentrate. To be so tantalisingly close....

When he contacted her again, two weeks later, she could barely restrain herself. "Did you see the headman?"

"Yes. And it is the right place. He doesn't know anything about the grave." Her heart dropped. "My bet is it's so overgrown he could have walked past it every day without seeing it. But listen, Liz. He knows where the diary is."

She hardly dared believe what she was hearing. "You mean it's still there?"

"Yes. Well, we have to be talking about the same thing. It's hardly likely there are other books lying around in the Zambezi Valley."

"Of course not. It has to be....."

"Before you get too excited," he said quickly, "there's a slight problem. Old Musa is adamant the diary is one of the ancestral relics of his clan. He found it close to the cave where an old chief was buried and he's convinced it belonged to the old boy. So he's been guarding it with his life. Only person he told was the local *sikatonga* who he consulted about what to do with it when they were moved.

"Apparently, the *sikatonga* said nothing should be moved. Everything should be left with the chief's remains, mainly because he is convinced the dam wall is going to collapse anyway. So it's still there."

"Still there..... Did he say where exactly?"

"That's the tricky bit," Ian's voice became rueful. "He refuses to say."

"Refuses?"

"Because he says it belongs to the old chief. I argued with him but he's stubborn as hell. Finally, when I had just about given up hope, he relented a little. Said if we produced some kind of proof, he might reconsider."

"Proof?" She was silent for a moment. "What about if we showed him the first diary?"

"I thought of that. But he came up with his own idea. The diary is apparently in a bag, but there's something else in there too. Something else that Musa also considers the property of the chief."

"Something else?"

"Yes. So the deal is: if you can tell him what it is, he'll be convinced we aren't pulling a fast one, and tell us where the bag is. He was so damn pleased with his idea that I couldn't budge him. I don't want to play the heavy – he's been through enough with the move."

"Something else – something Clarissa kept with the diary. Ian, I haven't the faintest idea," her voice was despairing. "How could I possibly know?"

"Well," he said cheerfully, "you've got plenty of time to think about it. We can't hope to get down there for several months. I've got my own boat now, by the way, bought it off a guy at Kariba, so we can go together."

She rang Nicholas immediately, but he was as mystified as she. "Think hard, Uncle Nicky," she pleaded. "It could be something you've forgotten."

"That's more than likely," his voice was wry. "There's a hell of a lot I've forgotten – could fill a book with it." He was silent for a moment. "Why don't you come out this weekend and read the diary again? Now you know what you're looking for, you might find something. I'm going fishing with Chris and Robin on Saturday, but we'll be back on Sunday morning."

She left town after work on Friday evening. She knew the road by heart now, nursing her car over the potholes, slowing down to avoid rabbits scampering in the beam of her headlights. Most of all, she loved arriving at night, seeing the house lights winking in the distance as she drove past the dam and up the hill.

Nicholas was on the stoep having a beer with a neighbour, talking politics. The ANC had been re-launched in Southern Rhodesia, with Joshua Nkomo as its new president, as predicted by Joe Guve.

"That's OK," Nicholas was saying, "Nkomo's not as militant as some of the others."

"It's not OK," growled Hilton James, a square-jawed, sandy-haired man with a ruddy complexion. She didn't like him. The first time she had encountered him, he had been loudly abusing his labourers as they loaded grain on to the back of his pick-up truck.

"They mustn't let the ANC get organised," he said now. "We'll start having the kind of trouble they're having down south: blowing up power stations and such like. And now Todd wants to give them the vote – one roll for whites and blacks." His tone was outraged.

"He's still going to keep the franchise requirements," Nicholas pointed out, "they'll have to have a certain level of education, income and property before they can vote – as we have now."

"Ya, but he'll drop the level way down to get them on the roll. Mark my words, he'll have to – at the moment, only about four hundred kaffirs qualify. It's the thin end of the wedge, the road to chaos," he warned darkly.

"Twaddle. Todd is strong on law and order. He just recognises that we have to start giving them a bigger say in government. It's a pity people like you prefer to keep your heads in the sand."

"A bigger say?" James thumped the table with his fist. "How can they have a bigger say when they don't know the first thing about democracy? Nick, man, you are *penga*."

She recalled a conversation earlier in the week, when she had dropped in at the cramped, shabby offices in Pioneer Street where the magazine, Zimbabwe Dawn, was published. Hunched over his typewriter, surrounded by unwashed coffee cups and overflowing ashtrays, Joe Guve had listened patiently to her questions.

"In South Africa ANC people are being charged with treason. Here, it has only just been re-launched. Why are people here so far behind? Why are things so different?"

"It's just a matter of degree. South Africa has been strengthening its anti-black laws ever since Malan and the Nats got in. Here, Federation is supposed to be moving in the opposite direction – towards partnership."

"Equal rights for all civilised men," murmured Liz. "Not women, I notice."

He grinned. "Figure of speech. We've not had as much rabid discrimination as in South Africa, and Federation is supposed to be getting rid of some aspects. Supposed is the operative word: I'll believe it when I see it." He tilted his chair back and lit a cigarette from a crumpled pack of Star. "As to the ANC, it has been operating a lot longer down there, so they're more organised, and Mandela and his friends have done a lot to rev things up. Up here, although it's been around a long time, it's been totally inactive. Now they're starting to get their act together."

She came back to the present. Nicholas was still arguing good-humouredly, and she sensed the two men were revisiting familiar territory. They had done this countless times over the years, over countless tankards of Lion, as the sun dipped behind tall tassels of maize on broad acres of russet earth. Two old Africa hands, each with his own implacably-held opinions on how to solve the intractable problems gathering like thunderclouds on the horizon.

"It's a ritual," her uncle confirmed later. "About once a year he has to find out whether I've come to my senses yet, or whether I'm still what he calls a half-baked, kaffir-loving liberal."

The fishermen went off early on Saturday morning, and the dogs followed her around the house, glad of her company. When she curled up on the sofa with the diary, they thrust wet noses in her lap, begging for a walk. "Not now, later," she told them.

But, although she re-read the diary from cover to cover, when the men returned on Sunday morning, she had to shake her head and confess she was no nearer to an answer.

A clue was to come from an unexpected quarter. They had driven over to the Rainiers' farm for afternoon tea on the stoep, and Lilian was chattering about friends who had retired to Tunbridge Wells after a lifetime in Africa.

"Can't imagine why they did it – try the granadilla cake, darling," she passed Liz the plate, her rings glittering in the sunlight. "They've never stopped regretting the move. Whenever we go to see them, they weep into their gins about the msasas, the animals, the sunsets. Don't they, David?"

"Mmm," said David. "Last time we were there, I was wondering what I'd miss most if we ever had to leave. Decided it would be the smell of the bush after rain."

"The sound of a Heuglin's robin," offered Nicholas – it was his favourite bird.

"Hippos grunting," said Liz, thinking of her Zambezi trip.

"You're all way out," said Chris. "It's the call of the fish eagle."

"Fish eagle?" said Liz. "Didn't I see one on the Zambezi?"

"You would have been hard put to miss them," said David.

Something stirred on the fringes of her consciousness, a faint, elusive chord, and she frowned, staring unseeingly up at the scented flowers of a frangipani tree near the stoep. "Fish eagle....."

"Big fellow, white head, dark body," offered David.

Chris was watching her. "What?"

"Nothing. It just.... made me think of something."

But what? The conversation moved on but the nagging hint of a memory tugged at her brain, and returned to perplex her at intervals on the drive back to the farm. It's something just out of reach, something I have to remember, she thought, as she packed the diary in her suitcase that evening.

"Go back and see the old boy in the nursing home," Nicholas suggested as she climbed into the car, discouraged by her lack of success.

"That's an idea." She cheered up. "If he knew about the diary, he just might have seen whatever the other thing was."

But when she called in at the nursing home on her way home from work the following day, the plump, pretty nurse who had greeted her the first time looked at her in dismay.

"I'm sorry, Miss Pendennis, I'm afraid old Mr van Heerden passed away a couple of weeks ago. Did you not know?"

"No," Liz stared at her, shocked. "No, I didn't. Two weeks ago?"

"Yes. You're not a relative are you?"

"No, just a friend. Was it – very sudden?"

"Well, it was his heart. Sudden, but not unexpected, if you know what I mean. He knew he didn't have long. I'm sorry you didn't hear about it. Is there anything I can do?"

"No, thank you. It's all right, just a bit of a shock. I had hoped to see him again. Thank you," and she walked slowly back to her car.

Impelled by a sudden sense of urgency, she phoned Port St Johns that evening. Emma was bedridden again, Julia told her. "Nothing to worry about – just a touch of 'flu. I'm keeping her quiet."

"Could you ask her something?" Liz explained about the bag and the unknown object, and she promised to pass on the message.

"Could it be a piece of jewellery? Something given to her by Simon?" suggested Julia, who relished a mystery.

"I don't think so. My mother has Clarissa's rings, and a few other valuables that they had left with the bank before they went down to the Valley."

"The line is very bad, Liz. I can hardly hear you, but I'll let you know if she remembers anything."

Later, unable to sleep, she stared wide-eyed into the darkness, trying to remember her conversations with Emma, whether she had ever said anything about fish eagles.

Fish eagles. She sat up in bed, suddenly alert. The diary – perhaps that was the source of the nagging memory. Switching on her bedside lamp, she fetched it from her cupboard, and climbed back into bed with it.

She flipped through the pages, skimming the words. And as she did so, she had a sudden certainty that what she was looking for was near the end; it was something Clarissa had written while she was in England. She turned to the back of the book, searching.

Yes. There it was. On the second last page: *I feel as though, every minute I am away from Africa, I am missing something. We are both exiles, the fish eagle and I. We both want to go home.*

The fish eagle and I, she repeated, mystified. What does it mean? What is she talking about? What fish eagle? Page by page, she searched back through the diary for more clues. Clarissa did not mention the bird anywhere else. But then, there were many gaps, many periods when she had not written. The fish eagle and I – the words hammered in her mind, and she sank back against her pillows, pounding her brow with a fist in sheer frustration. Swarms of flying ants and brown beetles, attracted by the lamp, fluttered on the bedclothes and the wall behind her head. Switching off the light, she lay down and stared into the darkness.

After work the following evening, a few days before Christmas, she phoned Port St Johns again, but could not get through. Over a crackling line, the operator told her there had been storms up and down the coast and the lines were down.

On the day before New Year's Eve, Mario appeared on the Coles' doorstep with a sheaf of yellow roses for Liz, and chocolates for Barbara. Ebullient as ever, he told them over tea on the patio that he had a couple of days' leave, and was staying in town with his Italian friends.

"We go dancing tomorrow night – New Year's Eve. Yes, Lizi?" he urged. "You are not – *come si dice*- booked out?"

Liz laughed. "No," she agreed, "I'm definitely not booked out." She had been invited to a house party by someone at work, but had not committed herself. "Yes, all right, Mario, let's go dancing."

"You and Derick, you will come too, Barbara?" Mario asked.

"Thank you Mario, but I don't think so. I can't go dancing like this," protested Barbara, "I feel like a mountain. You go off and have a good time."

"You can, of course, come," Mario urged, "you must come, tell her, Lizi. She must come with Derick."

"Come on, Barb," said Liz, "wear that black lace top you wore the other night. It looked lovely."

"It's getting too small for me now, and everyone will be looking slinky and glamorous. No, I don't think so, I feel so dowdy, waddling around like a great duck."

"Barbara," Mario's eyes were dark and warm, "you not speak like that. Your baby comes soon, yes?"

She nodded. "Two weeks if it's on time."

"This is wonderful," he leaned towards her earnestly. "You are so funny, you people, you think you are ugly when you are having baby. You are beautiful, like Madonna, and I am proud to dance with you. You come, yes?"

Barbara looked at him helplessly. "Mario, you are practically irresistible. All right, we come – if Derick agrees. I won't have another chance for a long time, God knows. Shall we ask Chris and Annabel to join us later? They're having dinner with people in town, but they might come afterwards."

Derick, who abhorred dancing, was less enthusiastic. "Do we have to, Bar? You know I loathe New Year's Eve – paper hats, streamers, all that forced jollity. Why can't we have a *braai* in the garden?"

"Tell him, Liz," Barbara sighed in exasperation.

"Because you can have a *braai* any night of the year, Derick, and this is probably your last chance to go out dancing and enjoy yourselves without worrying about baby-sitters, and bottles and that sort of thing," she said persuasively.

"Thank goodness for small mercies," he grumbled. "All right, if I can still fit into my dinner jacket."

Privately, Liz had her doubts about how Barbara's reserved, intellectual husband would hit it off with the effervescent Mario. But she needn't have worried. No sooner were they seated at the dinner table at Highlands Park Hotel than the two men discovered a mutual love of Italian opera. Before the first round of drinks had arrived they were deep in a passionate argument about the relative merits of Verdi and Puccini. Outside, thunder crashed, and the rain drummed on the tin roof of the old hotel.

During dinner, the conversation turned to progress on the dam, and once again they found a shared fascination.

"You have started work on the foundations inside the main coffer dam, haven't you?" Derick asked.

"Yes, it goes well."

"You're expecting floods again, aren't you?" queried Barbara, sipping orange juice.

"*Si*," said Mario. "Maybe more big than last year," and he shrugged expressively. "This is what everyone say. Already, there has been much rain."

"If you get heavy flooding, could the coffer dam go?" asked Derick, attacking his steak.

"It will not happen," Mario assured him, "we have made it too strong."

"You will be careful, won't you, Mario?" said Liz.

"Not to worry, Lizi," his eyes laughed at her, "nothing will happen to me. We dance, yes?"

He led her on to the already crowded floor, and Barbara looked across at her husband and held out a hand. "Come on, lover, we can still manage cheek to cheek if I suck in hard."

Liz had not been able to indulge her love of dancing over the past few years: it would have been too public an activity for her and Alex to enjoy. Tonight, she was making up for lost opportunities. The band was lively, the female vocalist sang with earthy exuberance, and she danced with both Mario and Derick, who was giving a fairly credible performance of a man enjoying himself.

She was leaving the dance floor shortly before midnight, hand in hand with Mario and out of breath from a boisterous rhumba, when Chris arrived, his arm about Annabel's waist. Greeting them breezily, he kissed his sister lightly on the top of her head.

She stared at him in amazement. "How many drinks have you had, CJ?" she asked severely. "I can't remember the last time you kissed me."

He grinned, pulling a chair out for Annabel. "We killed a bottle of red at dinner," he admitted, sitting down and looking around for a waiter. "Derick," he looked with mock concern at his brother-in-law. "I hope you haven't been wearing my sister out. I know how crazy you are about dancing, and I don't want the family heir delivered on the dance floor."

The band had started playing again, and Mario rose to ask Barbara for a dance. Derick led Annabel on to the floor, and Chris looked across the table at Liz with a quizzical expression. "Looks like that leaves us, Pendennis. How about it?"

"So gallant an offer – how could I refuse?" she countered as he rose and took her arm.

"Looking good tonight," he said, gazing approvingly at her filmy white dress with its narrow halter strap and swirling skirt.

"Thank you, Chris, I'm feeling good."

He did not dance like Mario, who tended either to whirl her energetically around the floor or clasp her in a tight embrace and shuffle on the spot. Chris was a relaxed, almost careless dancer, but he had an innate sense of rhythm; he held her lightly but firmly and hummed softly under his breath. "Is Robin still around?" she asked.

"No, he's down south, doing a couple of stories, then back to the UK for an exhibition. But he's coming back in a few weeks."

The band was playing a selection of Cole Porter, and she gave herself up to the pleasure of the music. "Reminds me of the river. Remember Ian's radiogram?" and she smiled at the memory.

"Mmm."

She looked up at him appraisingly. "You dance quite well."

He grinned down at her. "We colonials do learn skills other than hunting, shooting and fishing."

"In fact, we dance well together," she continued, ignoring his remark.

"Life is full of surprises."

The song ended and the band swung into another of her favourites – a haunting Rodgers and Hart number. His arm tightened almost imperceptibly about her waist, and she felt his body against her. The top of his chin was touching her hair, and she floated away on the music. His hand slid up her back and she felt it warm on the bare skin above the fabric of her dress. Without thinking, almost automatically, she moved closer in his arms, and felt his thighs warm and hard against her legs.

The song ended, and as they moved apart, the bandleader began the countdown to New Year. "Ten, nine, eight, seven…." The others joined them, the chimes sounded, and Mario laughed in confusion as they initiated him into the Auld Lang Syne tradition.

It's just like England, Liz thought, as paper streamers rained down. I could be at a party in London. Mario's arms were around her, and he was whispering, "Happy New Year, Lizi," and kissing her ardently, and she laughed and hugged him. Everyone began kissing everyone else, and throwing streamers, and she hugged Barbara and Derick and half a dozen strange men doing the rounds with alcoholic enthusiasm. Caught up in the general atmosphere of bonhomie, she had just been released from the embrace of a man with a prickly ginger moustache, who claimed to be Derick's closest friend, when Chris stood before her. She smiled and opened her arms expansively – and a little tipsily – to include him in her swelling impulse of goodwill towards the human race.

"Happy New Year, Pendennis." He drew her to him and his arms went around her. It started off like all the other friendly, pseudo-passionate embraces of the evening, but somewhere along the way it changed, his hands on her waist tightened, and it was not at all like the other kisses, not even like Mario's ardent embrace.

It was quite different. And when he released her, his grey-green eyes were deep with the strange, almost watchful expression they had held that night in the Valley. They stood together, still clasping hands; he started to say something, and she knew instinctively that he was going to toss the moment away with a flippant comment.

And she did not want him to: she wanted him to kiss her again. Barbara's words flashed through her mind: "Everything always has to be on a superficial level with him. If someone could just penetrate that barrier he always throws up..."

On a sudden impulse, she drew his face down and kissed him, long and deeply, tasting brandy on his lips. His arms slid around her again and his mouth moved, parting her lips – and it was wonderful. And this time, when he lifted his head and they drew apart, he said "Wow, Pendennis," very softly, and continued to hold her. And she murmured, "Happy New Year, Rainier," demurely, and a little breathlessly.

Then Barbara was beside her, touching her arm. "Liz, the witching hour has struck. I've got to get Derick home before he turns back into a frog." And he slowly released her, and she turned to Barbara, and the moment was gone.

She danced again with Mario, and when Chris and Annabel left soon afterwards, his goodbye was as casual as ever, and she was left with a feeling of having been cheated.

The rain had stopped by the time Mario took her home. It was past three o'clock, so she was surprised to see all the lights on. There was no one in the sittingroom, only Barbara's wrap flung carelessly over the back of the sofa. But as she went into the hall, Derick appeared, still in his dinner jacket, his face pale, dark hair falling over his brow.

He grinned nervously. "It's all happening. Barbara started having pains on the way home – and her waters have just broken. All very sudden. Looks like your dancing did the job, Mario." He ran his fingers through his hair.

"*Dio!*" Mario's eyes were startled. "She is all right, Barbara?"

"I think so, just getting changed. I've phoned the hospital to let them know we're on our way." He opened the drinks cabinet and poured Scotch into a glass with shaking hands, downing it in two gulps.

"That's better," he gasped. "How about you two?"

"No thanks. I'll go to Barbara," said Liz.

"Do, I'm sure she could use some help. Here, Mario, help yourself."

Barbara stood in the bedroom fastening the buttons on one of her daytime maternity dresses. The black lace top was lying on the floor, and Shumba sat beside it, watching his mistress with a deeply furrowed brow. Barbara looked up with a calm smile. "Hi there."

"Are you all right? Are you getting bad pains?"

"Don't panic – Derick was bad enough. I'm fine. My suitcase is there. Could you just get my toothbrush? Oh, and there's a bottle of Arpège on the dressing table. Throw that in too, would you. Stop looking at me like that, Liz. I'm all right, truly. Oops," and she paused and straightened, her hand on her belly, "here comes another one."

Mario took the case out to the car, where Derick waited with the engine running, drumming his fingers on the wheel.

"Mario," Barbara smiled, biting her lip as he helped her carefully into the passenger seat, "I'll be forever grateful to you. Thanks to the dancing, I'm getting rid of this bump a couple of weeks sooner than I expected."

"You are not angry?" he asked cautiously.

"I'm delighted." She leaned out and patted his hand, and he kissed her impulsively on both cheeks.

"God be with you," he said fervently.

Derick gunned the engine, and narrowly avoided the stone gatepost as he swung the car on to the road.

Jonathan Rainier Coles was born at eleven o'clock the following morning. Mother and child were both reported well according to a dazed and bleary-eyed Derick, and Mario accompanied Liz to the nursing home that evening before returning to Kariba.

"We have to pretend you are a father," she warned. "They don't allow stray men in at this stage – especially men who have precipitated the birth by violent dancing with the mother."

Surrounded by flowers, Barbara's face against the piled pillows was pale and tired, and her short blonde hair hung limply, but her eyes glowed and she greeted them with a broad smile. Derick perched on the bed beside her, holding her hand.

"So, proud father," teased Liz, "you are not sorry any longer that Barbara got pregnant before she was supposed to?"

"Sorry? Have you seen him yet? Excuse us for a minute, darling."

And he led them down to the nursery, where they pressed their noses against the glass to stare at the diminutive sleeping form of his son, visible only as a dark fuzz of hair and a tiny red fist emerging from a blanket.

Mario murmured Italian endearments, Derick beamed foolishly, and Liz put an arm around both men and hugged them. As they stood together, Chris loomed behind them, clapping Derick on the shoulder.

"How did you get past the dragon on the door?" asked Derick, "My wife already has two husbands visiting her."

"Told her I was her favourite brother and I have to leave for the States tomorrow morning. Won't be back for two years. You could hear the violins. Joke," he said as Liz stared at him in momentary alarm. "Congratulations, old son. Now, which one of these is my nephew?" He peered over their shoulders at the row of identical bassinets. "Don't tell me, the bald one with the prizefighter's nose."

He turned to Mario. "Just heard the news on the radio. Looks like the Zambezi is going to flood any time now."

21

The new year swept in on a torrent of rain. Away beyond the country's northern borders, it was normal for the Zambezi waters to spread across the vast Barotse plains. In an unusually wet year, a few huts might be washed away, a few people drowned.

This year was different. Huts, people, animals – entire villages – were swept away in flash floods that swamped forests and transformed hillocks into islands where crocodiles glided soundlessly between the sodden rooftops of drowning settlements. The swelling brown tide surged down into Southern Rhodesia, and still the rains fell, and still the Zambezi continued to rise, bursting its banks, even flowing back up its own tributaries.

At Kariba, tension mounted as flood warnings poured in from remote stations upstream and people began to talk about another record season. The experts had described last year's floods as an event that happened once in a hundred years. Now it looked as though they were about to be proved wrong.

She phoned Mario. He had hoped to get a few days' leave, but was too busy working with teams strengthening the coffer dam wall to withstand new pressures. One of the piers supporting the road bridge below the construction site had collapsed, halting road traffic between the north and south banks.

"And the suspension bridge?" she asked.

"It is still holding."

"Are you worried about the wall?"

"No," he assured her, "we build it to take much pressure. This is a good chance to show how strong we make it."

Every day brought news of rising water levels, each one heightening her growing frustration. What if the floodwater reached the grave? After surviving for more than half a century, suppose the diary was swept away before she could reach it?

And then, one evening, Julia telephoned. "I've got Emma right here. She has something to tell you. You'll have to speak up – her deafness is worse but she wants to tell you herself."

"Hullo, Elizabeth." Despite the thunderstorm rumbling overhead, Liz sensed the suppressed excitement in the soft, dry voice.

"Emma, how are you?"

"Creaking along, dear. Listen, I remembered last night. I was thinking about the walk, and suddenly it came back to me. Can't think how I had forgotten."

"Yes?" Liz strained to hear above the growling thunder.

"The fish eagle – Simon gave it to Lissa at Chimoio."

"Simon gave her a fish eagle?" repeated Liz blankly.

"Not a real one – a carving."

"She never mentioned it in the diary."

"She was probably too busy looking after me – it happened when I was ill. She used to keep it on the mantelpiece at Mushana, but she could have taken it with her, because she loved it. She told me once it was the fish eagle that brought him back to her. It was very special to her."

Of course. *"The fish eagle and I – we want to go home."* The final link. It had to be.

She closed her eyes, and leaned against the wall. "Thank you, Emma, thank you."

But when she contacted Ian with the news, he told her he would not be visiting the resettlement area for two weeks. She was in limbo again, waiting. At work, there was plenty to occupy her mind; after work, she played tennis, went for walks, and helped Barbara with the baby, but the days dragged, and as flood reports continued to pour in, her anxiety and frustration mounted.

But when at last Ian contacted her again, his voice was triumphant. "I've seen him, and you're right. It was the fish eagle."

Jubilation swept through her. "He believes us? That the bag belongs to Clarissa?"

"Yes. Poor old guy was a bit stunned, but he came round quickly. In fact, I think in the end he was relieved it was no longer his responsibility."

"Did he tell you where it is now?"

"Yes. On a ledge inside the entrance to the cave, on the left. But don't worry about that. When the rains are over, I'll show you."

When the rains are over... That wouldn't be until the end of March. "Do we have to wait that long?" she pleaded.

"'It's only a couple of months."

"But the floods, Ian. Suppose the diary is washed away?"

"Liz, it's survived half a century. It will last a few weeks more."

She said nothing, but she was assailed by a burning sense of urgency. Suppose he's wrong? Suppose it is a record flood, one that reaches levels never seen before. "Worse than last year, that's what they're saying. It's going to be a mother of a flood," she had been told only a couple of days ago by a South African journalist at the Press Club.

Without Ian, how could she find the bag? He had a power boat at Kariba, but she could not ask to use that – she knew what his answer would be. There were other boat owners, however, locals who knew the river well, including the Harveys, the couple who ran the service station. If she went up to Kariba, surely she could persuade someone to take her up the river.

Her chance came a week later, when a recording station near the Angolan border reported a massive build-up of water on the floodplains. On the strength of her feature story on the relocation of the Batonga, Liz's editor called her in and told her to go up to the dam site and report on the situation.

"See if you can wangle a seat on one of the official flights. And come back straight away," Humphrey Allen told her. "The airport could close down in a few days."

"I'll get on a flight right away," she said jubilantly.

She consulted Chris, who was flying a BBC television crew up to Kariba. "Yes, there's a spare seat – day after tomorrow," he told her laconically.

It was the first time she had flown with him, and she was impressed by the unflurried competence with which he handled the Cessna as it bucked and heaved in the turbulent air. As he began the descent to the airstrip, heavy cloud banks brooded low along the massifs of the northern escarpment beyond the river, and the forest below was a deep green. Pools of water gleamed on the airstrip in the intermittent sunshine.

"You're not going to do anything crazy while you're here," Chris instructed rather than asked her as she climbed out of the aircraft.

"What do you mean?" She tried to look blank.

"You know exactly what I mean, Pendennis." He looked at her intently. "This is no time for Girls' Own Adventure stuff – like going up rivers looking for graves. Get your story and go back to town."

He was reading her mind again, and she was disconcerted and annoyed. She tried to laugh it off.

"Don't worry about me. Thanks for the ride." She picked up her case, but could feel his eyes following her across the airstrip.

The scene in the gorge had changed dramatically since her last visit. The river was no longer the lazy green serpent she had cruised with Ian; it was an angry brown python, a creature of mythic power, writhing furiously through the narrow gorge and pounding at the ramparts of the circular coffer dam in which the central foundations of the wall were rising. The section of wall on the north bank was much higher now; it had the crenellated appearance of castle ramparts, and brown water gushed between the gaps in its concrete face.

As the river hurled tons of debris against the pilings, the bloated carcasses of buffalo, antelope, cattle and goats floated past; huge branches, whole trees and tangled masses of undergrowth were swept beneath the swaying suspension bridge on which she stood with the television crew.

The roar was so deafening it was difficult to talk, and the small party was silent, awed by the display of surging power. Awed – and exhilarated, because there was something magnificent about it, thought Liz as she stared, mesmerised by the spectacle, and the fact that men still continued to work on the scaffolding inside the coffer dam.

"Do you expect it to get worse?" she asked Jack Ross, the liaison officer.

"From the reports from upriver, yes. The main floods still haven't arrived. We have teams working around the clock to strengthen the wall," he told her, as a massive truck was winched across the water by one of the Blondin cables.

She found a bed once again with Dave and Joan Harvey, and met up with Mario in the hotel bar that night. Retiring to a relatively quiet corner, he told her he had spent most of the previous night in the gorge; he was unshaven and his eyes were red-rimmed with tiredness.

"How can you go on working inside the coffer dam when it's so dangerous?" she asked.

He shrugged. "The walls are strong, and we have to keep going as long as we can. You know, Lizi," he confided, "we were laughing when the Africans tell us this story about the river god – Nyaminyami – is a good name, *si*? They say he is angry, that he will make a flood because the white people want to stop the river. We were laughing," he repeated sheepishly, "now we do not laugh so much."

She recalled the words of the old *sikatonga* she had interviewed – "A flood such as the white people have never seen," and felt prickles of unease.

The following morning, Mario took her to a religious service in the carpentry shop near the dam site, where black and white men bowed their heads and prayed to St Joseph, patron saint of carpenters, for protection from the fury of the river. Then they went back to work in drenching rain, winching massive girders on to the main piers of the wall to strengthen it against the pressure of thousands of gallons of water ripping into the river bank, gouging out massive chunks of earth and unleashing small landslides.

"We are going to have to watch this river," Impresit's chief engineer told the media, only half jokingly, "it looks as though it knows exactly what we are up to."

In the night she was woken several times by rain pounding on the tin roof of the Harvey's small prefabricated house. In the morning, the air strip was declared waterlogged. "Looks like we're stuck," said Chris, who was due to fly back later in the day.

She rejoiced silently, and immediately plunged into a trough of fear. Now that she was free to do what she had hoped to do, her courage ebbed and left her prey to a thousand fears. She was afraid of taking on the river in its present savage, unpredictable mood. In this type of situation, Mario had told her, a thunderstorm on the escarpment could bring any one of a dozen tributaries roaring into the Zambezi without warning, and already the water was afloat with debris capable of holing a boat.

She stalled, using the rain as an excuse, and spent the day interviewing Impresit officials and Italian and African labourers, and phoned another report through to

Salisbury. By the end of the day the river had crept two feet higher on the upstream wall of the coffer dam, and most of the heavy machinery had been removed from its interior. Now the teams concentrated their efforts on erecting scaffolding on the upstream wall.

"We have to put sandbags to keep the water out," said Mario as she stood with him on the suspension bridge in the rain, awed by the rush of power beneath her feet. The swaying deck felt as frail as matchsticks and she clung to the railings, but his eyes were dancing. "It is something to see, no, Lizi? So much power!"

"Come away, Mario," she begged, but he laughed at her fear as he stared in fascination at the pounding foam.

"Please, Mario," she repeated. And he grinned, and took her hand and ran with her across the deck to the bank.

As they walked into the hotel she noticed, across the road, a familiar figure in conversation with two men. She had not seen him since that day on the river bank with Ian Coles, but she was sure it was Paul Masimba. "Do you know that man?" she asked Mario, but he shook his head.

In the pub that night, an engineer told them that the Sanyati, a tributary upstream of the gorge, had broken its banks, flooding small riverside *kraals* and sending their inhabitants to higher ground. But by the following morning the rain had stopped, and construction teams were back on the scaffolding in the coffer dam, seemingly unconcerned by the brown waves lashing the upstream side of the wall, or the knowledge that only a few inches of concrete prevented them from being swept into the cauldron below.

The clouds parted, the sun shone through. If I don't do it soon, I'll lose the chance, she told herself, and went in search of Dave Harvey, who listened to her request with a dubious expression on his cherubic face.

"I don't like it, Liz," he frowned, "I can't get away now, and it's not the best idea in this weather, with the river like this. How far did you want to go?"

"Just a little way," she said quickly. "For a couple of hours."

"Not on your own?"

"No, I'm going to ask Mario if he can get time off."

"Well," he was still reluctant, "all right, but only if Mario goes."

But when she located Mario, he was too busy. Chris was nowhere to be found, and she was forced once again, with something like relief, to abandon the idea for the moment. In the pub that night, she spied Robin Chase, who had arrived on the last flight before the airstrip had closed. When she told him of the possibility of photographing villagers displaced by the floods, he immediately agreed to go with her.

"Lizi, you cannot do this," said Mario, when he heard. "I will not let you. It is too dangerous. This river is like an angry animal, you do not know what it will do next. Wait a little – three, four more days."

"We'll only be gone a few hours," she told him. "I have to try, Mario. If I don't, I might never get another chance."

When he had exhausted all his arguments, and was convinced she would not change her mind, he took his St Christopher medal and looped the chain around her neck.

"It is my good luck," he told her, "it will help bring you back safely. Be careful, Lizi, please you will not do something stupid." His eyes were more serious than she had ever seen them.

Next morning, when he heard that Robin would accompany her, Dave agreed to let her take the boat, but she was immediately confronted by another setback. The Blondins were going into action, lifting the last of the heavy equipment from inside the coffer dam. There was a chance for some dramatic shots, and Robin did not want to miss the opportunity.

"Sorry Liz. Leave it for today," he suggested. "I'll go with you tomorrow, promise."

She was evasive, replying that she would try to find someone else. Chris – where was he? When she asked around, she was told he had gone with a team to help dig out some heavy machinery stuck in the mud beyond the settlement.

The sky was blue, and the river – a-sparkle in the sunlight – looked infinitely less malevolent than the previous day. But would she manage on her own? She remembered Clarissa's quotation: *Our doubts are traitors...,* and made up her mind. I'll go out for a couple of hours, see how far I get, she decided. If I haven't found anything by three, I'll come back and wait for Robin to come tomorrow. Just a recce.

Into a rucksack she packed a windcheater, a plastic wrap to protect the diary, torch, lemonade, apples, biscuits, and a thermos of coffee.

The river surged and strained beneath the hull as the small boat negotiated floating trees, rotting vegetation, unidentifiable carcasses. The sun shone intermittently through jaunty white clouds, a flock of sacred ibis winged overhead, and her spirits rose. She steered close to the bank, except where streams flowed fast to join the mainstream. Abandoned *kraals* were already half submerged, and at one she glimpsed people still leaving, their belongings balanced on their heads.

It was difficult to guide the boat through floating debris and watch the shore for the landmark she was seeking, and she was shaken by the number of crocodiles basking on the bank or sliding into the river at the sound of the engine.

Whenever she spied a channel through the reeds, she turned the boat into it, searching for Hennie van Heerden's landmarks – the lagoon, the kopje, the distinctive rocks, the tall tree.

Watching a sixteen-foot crocodile slide into the water, she re-affirmed her original decision – to be back in Kariba by five. That meant she had to turn around if she had found nothing by three: she reasoned that it would take her far less time to return downstream.

The sun still shone benignly, and it was hot. But in the north a ridge of dark thunderclouds massed, and she turned her eyes away. Half an hour later, the rain began, so heavily she was forced to pull in to the bank, shelter under a tree and bale with an old tin until the downpour eased, and she edged out into the current again.

It was tiring and frustrating having to explore every channel, however unpromising. Tired and disheartened, she ate an apple and some biscuits; it was three o'clock, and thunderclouds leaned on the hills. Five minutes more, she told herself.

The boat had almost passed it when she glimpsed the narrow slanted opening, almost completely hidden by tall reeds. As she passed through the gap she thought she had entered nothing more than a small inlet, and was already taking the craft around in a circle to withdraw when she spotted another narrow channel.

Easing the prow through the second gap, her pulse quickened. She was in a lagoon, where the water was already lapping the trunks of tall mopani trees that had once stood high on the banks. The lagoon was shaped like a dog leg, and the far end was hidden around a bend. Acutely conscious of the darkening sky and the hushed, expectant atmosphere, her stomach constricted as she steered the boat towards it.

A low kopje, more tumbled rocks than earth, jutted into a silent backwater carpeted in purple water hyacinth and the trailing golden flowers Ian called Zambezi sweetpea. Halfway up the kopje, on a grassy knoll, a mahogany tree was swathed in tangled vines and creepers. The summit of the kopje was capped by a granite boulder silhouetted against the sky. It had the appearance of having been split at an angle by a giant's axe.

With thudding heart, she cut the motor and drifted to the bank. Small fish leapt in the silence, white egrets erupted from the mopanis, and the wind ruffled the surface of the pool. Beaching the boat, she made it fast with a rope looped around a tree trunk, her fingers fumbling clumsily with the knot, oblivious now to the thunder that rumbled like distant artillery.

She climbed the bank, pushing through the undergrowth. The ground was wet and she had to grasp clumps of grass and hold on to rocks to stop slipping. Even before she reached the knoll, she could see, beyond the mahogany, the opening of a cave – a dark triangle framed by two slabs of granite and protected by a low stone wall.

A small, blurred shape scuttled into the darkness of the cave, a bird erupted from the undergrowth and she followed its flight to where the granite reared skyward, its weathered surface a tapestry of russet and gold lichens swathed by the roots of a tree growing out of a crevice.

The smell of damp, rotting vegetation hung in the air, and the trunk of the ancient mahogany had the appearance of being carved from the same granite as the rocks behind it. She walked through the grass to the low stone wall. Overhead the rock leaned outward forming a natural shelter, protecting the cool, dim interior.

A few yards into the cave was a ledge level with her head and as she ran her fingers along it, they touched and closed over something. Her legs were suddenly weak – she had not expected it to be so easy. Moving back into the light, she sat down and opened the leather pouch.

The binding of the diary was dusty and mildewed, the edges of some pages had rotted or been eaten away, but it was intact, the handwriting was quite clear, and she breathed a prayer of thanks. A folded sheet of paper slipped out, and she picked it up and looked at it in wonderment – a letter from Nicholas, dated January 1897. And a photograph, faded and dog-eared, Emma and Clarissa in nurses' uniforms, in front of a thatched building. The mud had come off the wall in places, revealing the wooden poles underneath.

Reaching into the bag, she withdrew the stone carving. It was quite small, no bigger than her hand, and even to her inexpert eye, a work of art. She wanted desperately to sit and gloat over her finds, to read the diary, but she saw with a shock that it was four o'clock. Hurriedly, she replaced the diary and carving in the bag, and hugged it briefly before putting it in the rucksack.

Between the entrance to the cave and the tree was a tangle of grass and small shrubs. She began to look for the grave, pacing slowly up and down, patiently quartering the area, looking for a cairn, a raised mound. But, after a few minutes, she remembered the old prospector's words, "He would have buried her overlooking the lagoon."

She should be looking on the river side of the tree. There, the ground was even more overgrown, but after only a few minutes she tripped and almost fell as her foot struck against stone. Scrabbling through the grass, she felt rocks, and very carefully – so as not to dislodge them – she began pulling out the enveloping grass and vines. Because the ground was sodden, they came out relatively easily, and there it was – a cairn of stones about eighteen inches high. Nothing else, no cross. But she knew this was Clarissa's grave, and she sat back on her heels, laughing and crying.

Found you at last – knew I would. You knew too, didn't you? Funny, I can't think of you as my grandmother – not at all. Maybe because you never had a chance to grow old, but it's more than that. It feels as though I've found a very old, precious friend.

Lightning flickered in the north and the sky had darkened, but she barely noticed as she set about tidying the grave. Her hands were stained and scratched by the time she had cleared a space of about a yard around the cairn. As she worked, she talked quietly, half to herself, half to Clarissa. When she was satisfied, she made a rough cross from two sturdy sticks, and tied them with bark stripped from a nearby tree, as she had seen the Batonga doing when repairing their huts.

Setting the cross in position on the cairn, she secured it with stones and, using pebbles, wrote CLARISSA on the cleared ground on the north side of the grave. As she could not remember exactly when her grandmother was born, she added '1902 RIP' beneath the name.

It was starting to rain when she went down to the river to gather water lilies, yellow sweet pea and small white flowers that were growing on the bank. She laid them at the foot of the cairn: "From me, from Nicholas, from Simon, and from your daughter." Tears pricked her eyes, and she blinked them away as she sat back on her heels and surveyed her handiwork.

"It's the best I can do," she spoke out loud, "because I have to get back. I know that you're not down there, anyway – it feels much more as though you're here beside me. Or else away in the bush with Simon. But it looks pretty, and Nicholas said you liked things to look pretty."

The rain was falling harder, and she seized the rucksack and ran to the shelter of the cave, scrambling over the wall as the skies opened to release the kind of deluge she had now become familiar with.

Only this time it did not stop. Two hours later, with the sun gone and the light fading, she confronted the realisation that she would not make it back to Kariba that night. The sense of exultation that had swept her along since the discovery of the grave was fast ebbing, to be replaced by rising panic. On top of her own predicament, she knew that people would be starting to notice her absence. In an agony of indecision, she paced the small sheltered space at the entrance to the cave. Should she start back, pull into a bank when it became too dark, and wait until morning? Or stay where she was? When the rain showed no sign of abating, she decided to stay put. At least she would be dry and relatively warm.

Night fell swiftly, but it was not at all like the magic nightfalls she had shared with Ian on this river, when the sunset glow had burnished the water and the stars had emerged like scattered diamonds. This was an enveloping blackness, unrelieved by moon or stars, and as the hours passed, a gusting wind rattled the branches overhead.

With the torch, she went down to the river to check on the boat, and found in a locker an almost empty box of matches and an old jersey. The boat was too heavy to drag any further up the bank. The water lapping the hull was black, and the words of the old *nganga* suddenly came back to her: black water, and something else – a tower falling, and a silver snake. Don't get hysterical, Pendennis, she told herself.

With the matches, she lit a small fire in the cave entrance, more to keep up her spirits than for warmth. But there was not much dry wood around, and it went out after a while.

She did not venture further into the interior: cold dank air issued from the darkness, and little scrabbling noises, and the shadowy forms of bats swooped silently past her head. She was very hungry, so she ate some biscuits and the second apple, and finished the little coffee left in the thermos, trying to suppress the waves of panic that flooded through her.

There was time a-plenty for self-recriminations now. Her mother had once told her: "You shape events to suit your whims, see what you want to see, and shut your eyes to anything you don't want to see." It was true. She had done it with Alex, thrusting the fact of his wife and children to the back of her mind. Now she had done it again, ignoring warnings and, in all likelihood, putting at risk those who would undoubtedly come in search of her.

But if I hadn't, I would never have found the grave – and the diary. If I had listened to them. Whatever happens, I can't regret that.

Thunder rolled ceaselessly, and lightning flashes illuminated the branches that creaked and groaned in the gusting wind. It was the sort of night for witches to ride abroad on their hyena steeds. She switched on the torch and played the beam deeper into the cave – and stifled an involuntary scream.

The beam had picked up, on a broad flat ledge, scattered bones and a skull, whose empty eye sockets stared blankly at her. Well, of course, she told her pounding heart, the old chief – he was buried here, Ian told me about it, it's him. Breathing more easily, she went closer. Some of the bones had been gnawed by animals; alongside them were gourds – the type used for carrying water – and two pipes, and a few clay pots.

Rubbing her arms against a sudden chill, she went back to the entrance and sat down under the rocky overhang. She took the diary from the bag and began to read by torchlight.

Clarissa had started it shortly before her wedding, Her handwriting was bold and forward-slanting, her mood lighthearted and happy as she wrote about honeymooning at Great Zimbabwe, the mysterious ruins in the south of the country. Liz riffled through the pages, turning to the back, wondering whether she had written anything during the last few days of her life. She found the name Hennie van Heerden two pages from the end. After he had left the camp, she spoke of packing up, of looking forward to returning to the farm and preparing for the baby. It was getting hot now:

The animals are coming back from the south, to find water. We will be gone soon, but we will bring the baby back when it is old enough, to learn to fish and hunt. But Simon doesn't love hunting the way he used to. He won't shoot elephants any more, and talks instead of protecting the game, setting up reserves and parks – like the new Kruger Park. I'm glad. He says we should....

There the writing ended, as though she had been interrupted. There were no more entries, just a series of blank pages. No clues as to how the end had come.

Remembering Clarissa's silence over the incident which had led to her losing her first baby, Liz leafed back through the mildewed pages. Had she perhaps written about the event she had been unable to talk about?

She found the year 1896 and a number of entries that made no mention of any unrest. After a brief account of a visit from Emma, there was a blank space, and then, on a new page, an entry in a different ink, dated two years later. So she had apparently stopped writing her diary after the Mashona Rebellion and had not picked up her pen for two years.

Under the new date was the explanation:

For a long time I could not remember what happened, but recently it started coming back in flashes, like nightmares, and now I remember it all. Writing it down will be hard, but I must try to do it, to face those memories. The terrible things that happened during that time are as much part of Africa as all the fine, beautiful things that I love.

When I heard from old Viljoen that killings had started in Matabeleland, Simon and Jerry were away in the hills, hunting for the table. Old Viljoen was not worried, and assured me the trouble would never spread to Mashonaland. When I went next door to Kombora, Peter and Nell did not seem worried either.

But a few days later, the day before Simon was due back, all the boys disappeared, and Mukwasi and I were left alone....

Mukwasi urged her to leave.

"Why?" she demanded. "Did the boys say anything before they ran away?"

"They not speak to me, but I hear them talk. They say that the Matabele have come, they want the men to fight. We must go. The 'nkos would not like you to stay here."

"Just wait, Mukwasi, I have to think."

She tried to busy herself in the kitchen while she decided what to do. Simon should be back either today or tomorrow, but suppose he was delayed? I'll go to Peter and Nell just for tonight, she decided. She told Mukwasi to get the horses ready, packed a small bag, took the Holland from the rack in the sittingroom, and left a note on the kitchen table for Simon. It was mid-afternoon.

Mukwasi was waiting outside with the horses, an axe thrust through his waistband. She ordered the dogs to stay, and they watched disconsolately from the front stoep.

It took nearly an hour to ride to Kombora. As a rule, she would have passed at least half a dozen people on the track; today it was empty, and she frowned, feeling the first stirrings of alarm.

The approach to the homestead, which was set on a small hill, was a long winding wagon track between tall grass. She liked coming to Peter and Nell's – it was linked in her mind with riding through the bush with Simon to see his land for the first time.

Peter's dogs did not bound down the road to greet her as they usually did; they were met instead by a heavy, oppressive silence. To her suddenly sensitive antennae, it seemed as though even the birds had stopped singing. Mukwasi, usually talkative, was silent too, watchful eyes quartering the long grass on either side of the track.

Still she was not overly alarmed. Peter had probably taken the dogs out hunting, the whole family could be visiting a neighbour. But, as they rounded the last bend in the road, something made her rein in her horse and gesture to Mukwasi to do the same. Something about the silence.

They left the tethered animals and walked up the road together without speaking. But for the eerie silence and the absence of life, everything looked quite normal. They passed the small orchard of trees planted by Peter, and the memorial she had helped Jamie build for his dog. Washing hung limp on the line behind the house, and a yellow ball lay on the grass.

Mukwasi muttered under his breath, but Clarissa ignored him. "It doesn't look as though there is anyone here," she said briskly. "They must have gone out – probably to see old Viljoen. I don't see the wagon or the dogs."

But as she spoke, she saw something else, on the ground near the front stoep. It was blue and red, and Mukwasi saw it at the same time, and hissed between his teeth.

"What is it?" she whispered. Her stomach contracted and her heart knocked against her ribs as she walked slowly toward it.

Peter lay face down, his hair matted and sticky. His head had been smashed by heavy blows, his body slashed again and again, and his blue shirt was stained with dark reddish-brown patches. On the ground nearby, the barrel of his gun was smeared with blood and strands of hair and tissue.

She knelt, feeling for a pulse. She knew there could be none, but felt for it nevertheless. Mukwasi went past her, and she registered with her numbed brain that he was standing over the bodies of three black men sprawled only yards away. Peter must have brought them down before he was overpowered.

It was difficult to get to her feet on legs suddenly so weak. She did not want to look any further, but she called shakily to Mukwasi and he turned to her in silence, taking the axe from his belt, and following her stumbling steps to the house.

On the cement floor of the stoep, Nell's baby lay in a pool of red, like a broken doll smashed by a bad-tempered child. A short distance away, her face streaked with a dark stickiness, was Nell, face upwards, eyes staring, one leg twisted at a grotesque angle beneath her. Her skirt had been ripped away, there was blood on her thighs, and one hand was flung outwards as though reaching for something.

Clarissa was aware of a strange moaning sound, and she looked around her before realising it was her own voice. She swayed forward and stumbled past the broken bodies. Jamie, where was Jamie? Maybe he had got away. Please God, not him too. Let him be all right.

His Labrador lay beneath the msasa tree outside the kitchen, disembowelled, its neck broken. She stared about her wildly, whispering his name, afraid to shout. There was something in the tree, and she moved towards it stiffly, as though her limbs had turned to wood.

The boy's limp body dangled from a fork in the tree. His torso had been slashed almost in two. Her legs gave way then, and she crumpled to her knees. "Sorry, madam, sorry," Mukwasi's hushed and shaking voice whispered.

She held out her hand to him, and he helped her to her feet. "We go now," he hissed urgently. "They come back."

"Help me get him down," she spoke thickly, as though her tongue was swollen. Her vision kept clouding over with a red film, bile rose in her throat and she swallowed it down, struggling to hold on to her consciousness. "He would want to be with his mother. We must put him with his mother. I'll get something to..."

She forced herself past the bodies on the stoep, and stumbled through to the bedroom where she found a blanket. Together they brought down the bloody, shattered form, wrapped it in the blanket and carried it to the stoep where they laid it down beside Nell.

"We go now," Mukwasi said urgently.

She looked at him, frowning, as though she was not seeing clearly. "More blankets, sheets, we must cover them. I'll go. Go and see if the horses are alive." Her mouth felt strange, and she had trouble shaping the words, but he turned and went.

Moving stiffly, she went back to the bedroom, and put the gun down on the bed while she stripped off the blankets and took them outside. One blanket she wrapped around the baby, laying it gently beside Nell; with the other she covered them both. "There now," she whispered, still speaking thickly. "There now."

Footsteps padded behind her and she rose unsteadily. "Mukwasi," she said, turning.

It was not Mukwasi. He was much shorter, and his eyes were wild. Behind him were three more men, with assegais and axes.

"No!" She screamed, but he seized her arm, yanked her to the floor and dragged her, struggling, past the bodies of Nell and the children, down the stone steps. The men were whooping and shouting, and she struggled and tried to pull her legs up to protect her belly. He held her by her hair, and pulled her to her feet, and she screamed again, pleading, "No, no, please, my baby, my baby. Don't hurt me..."

She was flung to the ground again, and he raised his assegai and she rolled onto her side, cowering and whimpering.

A shrill, blood-curdling yell exploded, and her attackers turned as the figure of Mukwasi raced towards them, axe raised high. He was shouting as he came, "Run, madam, run! Go, go, go."

Her attackers were caught off balance. Now they surged towards him, and she stumbled to her feet, screaming. As they closed in, his eyes were bright and wild, and still he shouted, "Run, madam, run..." His axe cleaved into the skull of her first attacker, whose yell of fury changed to a gurgle as he stumbled to his knees. The axe rose again, assegais flashed, and the screaming shrilled to a crescendo. But above it all, Mukwasi's voice: "Save your child! Run! Mukwasi will kill the jackals ..."

She ran. Stumbling, tripping, falling, whimpering and panting, without direction. She was in long grass, trees whipped past her vision, and the shouts and screams followed her, Mukwasi's voice above all. Her skirt caught and ripped and she tripped and fell down and got up and kept running, the blood pounding in her head, her breath coming in sobbing gasps.

The gun – she had left it on the bed. But, if she could get it, she could – . No, I can't go back. My baby. But Mukwasi. Maybe it's not too late. Every nerve screamed at her to keep running, to save herself. Not to think about Mukwasi...

She stopped, turned, forcing herself back, blocking all thought but the need to get the gun. The shouting had stopped, but even before she reached the edge of the bush she could smell the smoke. Staying under cover of the trees, she crept close enough to see that the thatching was on fire. Two figures tossed lighted branches on to the roof of a shed, and Peter's horses screamed from the stables. The figures ran swiftly away into the trees.

She stumbled to the back of the house, but the roof was already collapsing inwards with a roar of flames. There was no way she could reach the Holland. Her pulse pounded in her ears as she crept around the side to the front of the house.

Beyond the forms of Peter and the men he had killed, two more bodies lay sprawled and bloodied. Beyond them, Mukwasi.

He was horribly mutilated and bleeding, intestines bulged from a massive stomach wound, and his face had been slashed open from the side of his mouth to his ear. He lay on his side, his legs drawn up.

She knelt and whispered his name. He opened his eyes and tried to speak. His face was grey and shrunken. "Don't move," she whispered. "It's all right, old friend. They've gone. It's all right..." Her throat constricted.

He was trying to say something. "How many I kill?" he finally mumbled, his broken face contorting with the effort.

"Two," she whispered. "You killed two. Don't try to talk."

He coughed painfully, and blood trickled through broken teeth. "Two," his mouth twisted into a grimace that was meant to be a smile. "Is good. You go now."

"No!"

"Yes.... you go ....." He tried to say more, but could not. There was nothing she could do for him, so she took his hand and held it tightly. Until his rasping breathing faltered, and stopped.

As she bowed over his body, the screams of the horses intensified, and she forced herself to her feet again and stumbled towards the stables. They were roofed in tin, and slower to burn than the house. One of the horses broke out as she approached, and galloped past her, whinnying in terror. She unlatched the doors and the remaining two erupted past her, eyes blazing.

Renewed shouts echoed from the south, the direction the two attackers had taken. Perhaps they would come back to loot whatever had escaped the fire, or to search for her. Stumbling over the hem of her skirt, she paused by Peter's body, but his gun was gone, they had taken it.

She made for the trees, uncertain which way to go. She wanted desperately to go home, but it could be the next target. The shouting was louder and closer, giving strength to her limbs. She found a track and followed it through the trees, but bile welled up in her throat, and she stopped, and retched violently, clinging to a msasa trunk for support. She had to go home – Simon might come back early. He might not know what was happening.

The sun had gone, dying in a crimson smoke haze, and as she stumbled on she forced her shocked mind to think. She would go back to the farm but not to the house. She would hide on the kopje and watch for Simon.

Having the semblance of a plan helped a little. Although she was on an unfamiliar path, she knew she was heading in the right direction. But her mind reeled with shock, and trees looming out of the dusk became the figures of crazed warriors, rocks became crouching figures. I must keep calm for the baby, she muttered to herself.

With a sob of relief, she reached the road to the farm. As it was now dark, she risked following it, staying under the cover of trees. She was stumbling in exhaustion, her mouth was parched, dry lips caked with dust, legs weak and trembling.

When the outline of the farmhouse loomed ahead, she crept through the grass in a wide arc around the garden. There was no sound, no movement. The moon was rising and she could see the house quite clearly, but she dared not approach it, and she crouched behind rocks, shivering with cold and terror. Feet padded towards her, and she suppressed a scream; then the dogs were beside her, licking, making comforting, snuffling sounds, and she hugged them to her.

Much later, a raging thirst drove her out of cover. She had to get water. Using trees and outbuildings to provide meagre cover, she crept to the back door, followed by the dogs, and eased it open. Inside, she felt the illusion of safety in the familiar surroundings of her kitchen – the pots and pans, the still-warm stove, the soup she had made that afternoon. But she knew it was an illusion. Gulping water, she splashed her face, seized a wrap and some blankets from the bedroom, and went back up the kopje with the dogs.

Her teeth were chattering. She wrapped herself in the blankets and curled up on the ground, huddling against a still-warm rock, alert for voices. The dogs lay beside her, and the warmth of their bodies was immensely comforting.

As soon as she closed her eyes, the dreadful images of the afternoon unfolded in her mind, repeating themselves over and over, until at last she sank into a restless, haunted half-sleep, to be woken with a start by distant screams. She sat up, heart pounding, and the sounds came again – blood-chilling screams that made her scalp crawl. The dogs sat up and growled, and she quickly quieted them.

But the sounds came no closer, and the long night dragged on. Sometimes she dozed fitfully, her dreams peopled by shrieking phantoms and she would wake shivering, and pull the blankets closer about her shoulders, and hold her breath, listening, listening. And then she would close her eyes in exhaustion and the images would rise once more – the broken, bloodied bodies of Peter, Nell, the children. And Mukwasi.

It was shouting that woke her again. Someone was calling her name, and for a moment she thought she was back on Elderbrook and it was her father's voice. The dogs sprinted off and she sat up, dazed, and saw that it was morning, cloudy but bright, and the voice that called – with desperate urgency – was Simon's.

Thank God, she whispered. All the horror of the previous day surged back, and she crawled out of her hiding place, feeling weak and sick. Unsteadily, clutching a blanket about her shoulders, she stumbled down through the trees and into the garden. Her face was scratched, her hair matted with grass and leaves, her dress torn and stained with blood and dust.

He came through the kitchen door at a run, shouting her name as the dogs bounded towards him. In the doorway behind him was Jerry.

"Here, Simon!" she gasped. "Here!"

His face was smudged with dirt and very pale beneath his tan, his hair was unkempt, his shirt torn in several places. He caught her in his arms, and when she saw the terror in his eyes turn to relief, she tried to smile. But instead, she began to shiver uncontrollably and to cry, and he held her tightly, murmuring into her hair. As she touched his cheek with her fingers, she realised he was crying too.

"It's all right," she whispered. "I'm all right – they didn't hurt me."

"I thought you were dead." He took her face in shaking hands, laid his forehead against hers, and closed his eyes. "When we heard – and we went to the Ashtons and saw what they had done – and Mukwasi. When I saw him, I thought I would find you too. I looked everywhere... and you weren't there... and I didn't know what to do....Thank God," he buried his face in her neck. "Thank God."

Inside the house, she washed her face and hands. Simon had regained his composure, and a kind of steely calm.

"We can't stay, we have to get into town." He slotted ammunition into his belt, while Jerry checked the rifles. "Get water bottles."

But even as she filled them, the smell of smoke and the sound of crackling grass penetrated the kitchen.

"They must have seen us coming," muttered Jerry.

"They're going to burn us out," she whispered.

"No, they're not. We're getting out now," said Simon sharply.

"My horse," she remembered suddenly, "it's still at Peter's."

"No – I found it. They're hitched up outside the stoep."

She filled the bottles with fumbling hands. Jerry strapped on his ammunition belt, picked up his rifle. "I'll bring the horses," he said, and Simon opened the door a slit.

"Now!" he hissed, and Jerry darted past him, crouching low. The smell of smoke was stronger.

"Take this," Simon handed her a rifle, and she could hear Jerry outside with the horses. Simon opened the door again, they slipped out and mounted, swiftly and silently. Smoke swirled towards the house, but she could see no figures yet.

"Keep your head down, my darling, stay just behind me," he said rapidly. "The smoke will help us."

Moments later, flames leapt skywards and she was galloping through the smoke behind Simon, Jerry in the rear. Crouched low over their horses' necks, they covered the first hundred yards without mishap, but as they hurtled down the track it turned sharply to wind through granite outcrops, and they had to slow their pace.

She heard a yell, a startled grunt behind her, and twisted her head to look back. Jerry's horse reared and plunged, and he pitched forward, and slid sideways out of the saddle. As he fell, she saw a spear embedded deep in his back, and his attacker, crouching in long grass. Screaming, she tugged at the reins, and Simon wheeled around and fired at the crouching figure.

As she slid out of the saddle, another warrior pounded through the grass towards her. He had a gun, not a spear. With shaking hands, she fired, and he staggered, and sank to his knees with a howl. Behind her, Simon's rifle crashed out.

Silence. She reached the still form in the grass, fell to her knees, Simon panting behind her. Jerry lay face down, arms spread-eagled as though pinned to the ground by the blade that protruded starkly from the dark spreading patch on his shirt. His head was turned to the side, and his eyes stared with a look of frozen surprise. With fingers that would not stop shaking, she felt his throat for a pulse. She could feel nothing but did not know whether her shaking fingers were at fault, so she tried again.

There was no pulse. She looked up at Simon and shook her head; his eyes darkened, but he only took her hand and pulled her to her feet.

"Leave him," his voice was abrupt. He took the weapon from Jerry's hand, and together they remounted, urging the sweating horses forward.

Ahead was a broad expanse of open grassland. There was no cover. "Make for the gap in the trees," he shouted to her. "Don't ride straight, zigzag. Go! I'll be behind you."

The pounding of hooves merged with the blood pounding in her ears, and the shouts of their pursuers. A spear flashed past her, the horse stumbled, regained its footing and galloped on. Simon was behind her, shouting, "Zigzag, zigzag," and she tried to obey, swerving dangerously from left to right.

The belt of trees lay ahead. Out of the corner of her eye, she saw men running, one crouching to take aim, and her horse lurched and stumbled again, and she thought: this time it has been hit. But again it regained its footing and she dug her heels into its flanks.

And now they were among the trees, they had to slow down, and the shouts were dying away, and there was just the panting of her breath and the horses blowing heavily.

"Are you all right?" he was shouting, and she saw blood on his sleeve.

"Your arm!"

"It's nothing. Don't stop," he panted, "there'll be more. And they have guns."

They pushed the horses on. For a while there was no attack, but then they came to a valley, the track narrowed, and the shooting began again. And terror welled up in her stomach. And the nightmare was not over.

They made it through into the open, the horses lathered in sweat. Numbed by the accumulation of horrors, she tried desperately to focus only on the next mile, the next river to cross. When we get to the next kopje, she kept telling herself, we will be safe, there will be no more.

But there was nowhere safe. They galloped past silent, empty *kraals*, burnt-out homesteads, some still smoking. Once they saw African women and some children, who fled at the sight of them. Hour after hour, they pushed south, keeping under cover of the trees, alert for ambush, dazed with exhaustion.

Towards nightfall her vision started to blur, and she began to see things that were not there: figures that leapt and danced, dissolving as she approached, shimmering mirages and flickering fires. She swayed forward in the saddle, and he was beside her in the gloom, tireless, urging, shouting, shaking her into alertness when she laid her head down on her horse's neck, wanting only to sleep.

It was almost dark when they reached the scattered dwellings – empty now – that signalled the outskirts of Fort Salisbury. And then they were riding down the centre of the deserted town, deep in shadow, past shops and hotels, locked and shuttered. From the darkness, pickets called, "Stop! Who goes there?" and she heard, as though from far away, Simon's shouted reply.

Barbed wire emplacements loomed, and sandbags, and then they were inside the laager, in a shouting throng of people, and she slid from the saddle, and someone caught her as she fell.

Their son was born the following afternoon, two months ahead of time. They named him Nicholas, and he lived for two days.

> *A few days later, when the trouble had died down, Simon and some men went out to the Ashton's to see if they could recover any bodies,* Clarissa wrote. *Nell, Jamie and the baby had been lost in the fire, but they were able to give Peter a proper burial. Jerry was buried at Mushana, and we put up a headstone. He was our good friend. He had never married, Africa was his life.*
> Simon brought Mukwasi's body back to the farm too. We buried him under the big msasa tree down by the river, where he liked to fish in the evening. I still miss him.*

Liz closed the diary. The torch battery was fading and she switched it off, and the night was blacker still, lit only by jagged blue forks of lightning. Rain fell in sheets beyond the rock overhang, and she wrapped the jersey around her, besieged by ghosts of the past, brought to life on the yellowing pages. She was swamped by loneliness, an aching yearning for the comforting presence of another human being, someone to talk to, to dissipate the terrible images evoked by Clarissa's words.

After a while she drifted into an uneasy slumber, and woke later to the growl of thunder, the crash of a tree falling. She fell asleep again, dreamed she was being chased by unseen pursuers, that she was trapped in a tangle of weeds and vines, and unable to struggle free.

When she woke, to a swelling chorus of birdsong, a large black beetle was crawling up her arm. It was daylight, a weak, grey dawn, raindrops glittered on the leaves of vines overhanging the cave. She was cold, stiff and hungry, but the phantoms of the night had evaporated, and she climbed over the rock wall and clambered down the bank to the river.

She stared about her with unbelieving eyes. The landscape of the previous afternoon had vanished. Entirely. Gone was the lagoon, gone the channel she had passed through. They had merged to become one with a vast brown lake that slapped against the lower branches of trees whose trunks had yesterday been above the waterline.

Of the boat there was no sign.

22

Slipping and sliding along the bank, through rivulets of muddy water gushing into the river, she searched downstream for half an hour – but the boat was gone.

Waves of panic washed over her. She would never make it back now, there was no way to cross the many tributaries and flooded streams she had passed the previous day. No, don't panic, she told herself fiercely as she went back to the cave. At least three people, five counting the Harveys, knew where she was heading; someone would come and look for her today. Maybe they'll find the boat, she thought suddenly, and think I've drowned. No, don't think about that. *Our doubts are traitors.* Someone will come. I'm not lost – and at least I won't die of thirst. It was a feeble attempt at humour, but she felt a little better.

With a rush of guilt, she remembered Dave Harvey's instructions: she had ignored them, and now his boat was gone. Selfish, she told herself bitterly, selfish and stupid. But she had the diary. Surely that was important too? And she had found the grave. Trying to calm her racing mind, she drank the remainder of the lemonade, ate three biscuits and noted that there were half a dozen left. She was very hungry.

Staring unseeingly into the cave, beyond the gaping glare of the old chief's empty eye sockets, her attention was caught by a scuffle from the shadowy interior. Idly, she picked up the torch and switched it on.

In the dying beam, something dark and bulky loomed in the far corner, against the rock face. She went closer, and the beam picked up the dusty folds of a canvas tarpaulin draped in cobwebs. A small creature – a mouse, perhaps – scuttled into the dank, musty blackness and metallic lizards gleamed in the torch light. Gingerly she lifted a corner of the canvas. Underneath were wooden crates, nailed up. They carried no labels, only stamped figures and letters. Swept by an unreasoning sense of disquiet, she dropped the tarpaulin and retreated to the entrance. She had enough on her mind, she did not need any more complications.

Checking that Clarissa's pouch was safely stowed away, she picked up the rucksack, scrambled over the stone wall, and went to the grave.

Although the flowers had wilted under the onslaught of the storm, the cross and the lettering were intact. "I wonder if you ever did the brainless things I sometimes do," she said aloud. "But it was worth it. Whatever happens, I'm glad I found the place where you were happy with Simon."

She followed the new waterline: a litter of leaves, branches, rotting maize stalks, and small, damp, furry corpses washed up by the floodwater. To distract her overactive brain from her plight, she turned her thoughts to the crates in the cave. What did they contain, who had left them there? How long had they been there? Her imagination threw up a host of fanciful possibilities: the river was a border after all, they could contain any kind of contraband, probably something quite harmless like whisky. But she found it hard to shrug off her instinctive sense of unease.

The rising water had erased any tracks that might have existed, and the undergrowth was dense and tangled. Her sneakers were soaked, her slacks drenched from ankle to knee. Heavy rain clouds brooded low over the water. But at least it was not raining.

She climbed a low kopje to get a better view, and in the faint hope of spotting the boat. But there was nothing – only water and half-submerged trees where cormorants perched, drying their outspread wings. She ate a biscuit, cupped her hands to drink river water, and walked on, uncomfortably conscious that she was unlikely to find an inhabited village. Those she had seen the previous day had either been empty or were in the process of being abandoned.

By early afternoon her legs were heavy, and she climbed a small hillock, propped her rucksack against a tree and settled against it, closing her eyes. If a boat came, she would hear it.

When she woke, damp and cold, the void in her stomach was a yawning emptiness. It had started to drizzle and she got stiffly to her feet.

Hell's teeth, she thought, staring about her. The knoll was now an island, surrounded by fast-flowing brown water. There was just one place, ten to fifteen yards wide, where grass tips emerged from the water and it looked shallow enough to cross. Then, as she rolled up her slacks, a movement on the opposite bank made her glance up. A crocodile slid without a sound or a splash into the water. She had not even noticed its presence.

Retreating up the bank with thudding heart, she scanned the water, but it was so muddied she could see nothing. Only a pied kingfisher, diving down from an overhanging branch and emerging with a small silver fish in its beak.

The river was rising, she could not stay here. Tossing stones into the brown depths, she waited for any reaction, and as she did so, she heard a shout.

Two men were walking down the bank she was trying to reach. With a start, she recognised Paul Masimba. They both stared at her. "Hi," he called.

"Hullo," she replied, feeling a little foolish.

She explained about the crocodile, and Masimba nodded. He picked up stones and flung them into the water, watching the widening ripples. "Come now. We will make a noise and keep watch."

She stayed where she was, unconvinced.

"Come on," he shouted. His companion tossed stones into the water, and Masimba began to sing loudly. Hesitantly, she waded in, feeling cautiously for each step. How deep was it? It was not just crocs, it was the diary she was concerned about. Masimba and his companion lobbed sticks and stones into the water on either side of her, and Masimba continued his shouting song. But the water was getting deeper. When it reached almost to her waist, she took off the rucksack and balanced it on her head. The current tugged at her legs, and every obstacle that brushed against them sent new waves of panic through her. But Masimba shouted encouragement and waded in to extend a hand to her.

"Thank you," she said breathlessly as he helped her up the bank, a puzzled frown of half-recognition on his face.

She reminded him of their last meeting, and he nodded slowly. "Ah yes," his face cleared. "The DO's friend."

He introduced his companion, Sam Paradza, the man she had seen leaving the Batonga *kraal* with him. Paradza nodded without speaking, his eyes flat and expressionless.

"What are you doing here?" Masimba asked.

As she explained briefly, some inner caution stopped her from mentioning her discovery in the cave. "When I woke up this morning, the boat was gone," she concluded.

"You had a boat?" Paradza glanced sharply at her.

"Yes, but it was washed away in the night. You haven't seen it, have you?" They shook their heads.

"And you? What are you doing here?" she asked.

"We have business," Paradza said curtly. As though embarrassed by his abruptness, Masimba was more forthcoming. "We have friends up the river. We have to see if they need help."

"Oh." She hesitated. "How did you get here?"

"In a pick-up. It got stuck, so we can't offer you a lift. You are trying to get back to Kariba?"

She nodded. "I'm sure my friends will come and look for me." She tried to sound confident.

"I hope they come soon," Masimba said. "We will be coming back this way later today. Look out for us." He hesitated. "I have to meet someone about five miles from here – that way," he pointed downstream. "If you see her, will you tell her I will be there this afternoon. Tell her we have been held up."

"The woman you were with last year?"

He nodded. Paradza said something and Masimba answered him shortly and turned back to Liz.

"Her name is Elina. Tell her to wait. Tell her I will come." He spoke with careful emphasis.

"Yes, all right. Thanks for your help. Goodbye."

"Good luck," he said. Paradza nodded, but said nothing.

As they walked away, Masimba turned to wave. Although she had taken an instinctive dislike to his companion, she felt a renewed sense of isolation as they disappeared into the trees.

Ian had told her it was impossible to bring a vehicle down during the rains. What was so urgent the two men had risked it? And how could they help relatives without a vehicle? Her thoughts flew once more to the crates, and Paradza's abrupt manner, and she laughed at her own too-vivid imagination. The River of Adventure, she jeered, you read too much Enid Blyton in your youth. But, if the pair were connected with the crates, it would have been logical for them to want to check that they were not threatened by the floodwater.

She walked for hours, wading through streams, scrambling through undergrowth. The heat was leaden, and her shirt clung to her back as she entered an abandoned, half-submerged *kraal* where brown water ran into low doorways, and the rain-soaked thatching had collapsed between crumbling walls. The rain had stopped for the moment, and steam swirled up from the streaming earth. Her stomach was hollow with hunger, and her legs were tired.

A troop of guinea fowl chittered noisily, metallic helmets bright against the damp earth. If I had a gun, she mused, I might be able to shoot one. Roast guinea fowl. And then she thought of Chris, and grinned wryly, remembering their argument about hunting.

A party of red-billed hornbills pecked in the mud, and the air was a-flutter with birds swooping in pursuit of swarms of flying ants erupting in iridescent clouds from holes in the ground. She came to another *kraal*, but this one was on higher ground and a few huts were still above the waterline. There was no one around, but maybe she would find some food. Mealies perhaps.

As she dragged herself tiredly up the bank, her ears caught a faint sound. An animal? She stopped and listened. No, not an animal, more like a baby crying. Her heart leapt: could there still be people here? The sound came from a small hut near the trees.

"Hullo!" she called. Raindrops dripped from the eaves, and she called again and waited, and the small mewling sound came once more. Then, as she walked closer to the hut, she heard another sound – someone moaning.

Stooping, she went through the low doorway. The hut was windowless and it was several moments before her eyes adjusted to the gloom. On the floor was a woman, lying on a blanket. Beside her, loosely wrapped, was a very small baby.

The woman lifted her head weakly, and gasped incoherently before sinking back on the blanket. Liz dropped to her knees.

The haggard creature on the blanket bore little resemblance to the lithe, glowing-skinned woman she had seen on the river bank with Paul Masimba. "Elina?" she asked tentatively.

The woman stared at her and nodded.

"I have seen Paul Masimba," Liz spoke the words slowly and carefully, and the dark eyes gleamed briefly.

"Masimba?" Elina's voice was a thread.

"Yes. I saw him today, back that way," she pointed upstream. "He is coming. Coming soon." She thought the woman understood because she smiled weakly, licked her dry lips and tried to clear her throat. "Masimba," she whispered again.

"I'll get some water," Liz put her hand on the woman's thigh to reassure her, and felt a wet stickiness. In the torchlight she saw that it was blood. The woman's skirt was stained darkly, and Liz looked from her to the baby with dawning comprehension.

Hesitantly, she picked up the tiny bundle, unwrapped the crocheted blanket and saw the crudely-severed cord. With fingers that shook, she wrapped the baby up again, laid it down by the mother, doing her best to smile reassuringly.

In a bundle on the pounded earth floor, she found another blanket. She laid it over Elina and did her best to staunch the bleeding with clothing from the bundle.

"I'll get water," she said shakily, and took her thermos down to the river. When she returned, she lifted Elina's head and helped her to take a few sips. The woman sank back immediately and closed her eyes. "Masimba," she murmured in a cloudy voice.

"When was the baby born?" Liz asked, but her eyelids only fluttered, and she moaned again.

The baby began to cry, its eyes opened and Elina reached up and tried to undo the button on her blouse. It's hungry, she probably hasn't fed it yet, Liz thought.

"Let me help you." She lifted the baby to its mother's breast, but although it made small sucking sounds, it did not drink. Supporting Elina's head against her own shoulder, she tried again, and finally the baby began to suck at the nipple. But it seemed almost as weak as its mother, and after a short time it stopped drinking.

The woman sagged heavily against her and Liz eased her down. Holding the baby in her arms, she sat down beside her, and fought back renewed surges of panic. She needs help. It must have been a difficult birth. But what can I do?

Restless, she stood up and walked outside with the baby, shushing it gently. The rain was holding off, but the western sky was an angry, bruised crimson riven by towering grey thunderheads. A hadeda ibis flapped heavily away to the north, uttering its long, doleful cry. Fetching the thermos, she dipped her finger in the water and held it to the baby's lips. The baby sucked automatically and Liz dipped her finger in the water again. After several minutes the baby fell asleep, and she went back into the hut and laid it down beside its mother. Elina had not moved, and her breathing was fast and shallow.

Where was Masimba? If only he would come, he might know of a nearby village where they could get help. She sat down outside the hut and ate the last few biscuits. Scrabbling in the bottom of the rucksack she found a half-eaten apple she had been chewing on when she had discovered the channel leading to the grave site. She ate that too, but it did little to fill the void. She thought yearningly of a cup of tea as she walked to the water's edge and stared down the river, the colour of pewter in the deepening gloom.

Darkness fell swiftly, and the long night began. She did her best to make the sick woman comfortable, keep her warm, and give her water whenever she surfaced. When the baby woke, she fed it water from her finger. As the hours dragged by, Elina floated in and out of consciousness, and by midnight she had become delirious and no longer recognised Liz. When Liz tried to help her to feed the child she simply stared at it, mumbling incoherently through dry lips.

Thunder rolled intermittently, rain leaked through the thatching, and as the minutes ticked by, she thought that never in her life had she felt so helpless. Again and again, she went down to the water's edge to stare into the darkness. It was difficult to imagine anyone coming to look for her in the dark, but the faint hope prompted her to maintain a vigil.

Once, above the rain and thunder, she heard the imperious roar of a lion from across the water. Once, she thought she saw the sinuous gold and black silhouette of a leopard slipping between the barred tree-shadows, but it was gone so quickly she was not sure. She went back inside, and crouched by the motionless, grey-faced figure on the blanket.

The rain stopped, and a snuffling sound from outside brought her cautiously to the door with thudding heart and tightened throat. In the shadowy clearing, a pale half-moon gilded the sloping shoulders of a hyena. It limped off at the sight of her, and minutes later she heard its eerie, gibbering cackle.

It was almost dawn when Elina stopped breathing. Liz felt for a pulse on her throat and wrist, and held her hand to the slack mouth, but there was no breath of life. Pulling the blanket gently over the dead woman's head, she picked up the baby, sat down in the doorway and stared unseeingly at the first rays of light glimmering on the river. Her mind was drained and numb. After a while she leaned against the mud wall and fell asleep.

When she awoke, dizzy with hunger, the baby was crying, and she fed it a little water in the same way as she had done the previous night. Its cry was weaker now, and it stopped sucking her fingers after a few minutes. It was a sweet baby, a boy, with tiny fists, a small button nose and a soft fuzz of hair. Liz looked down at it compassionately. Poor little thing, if she waited much longer for Masimba, she was sure it would not survive. There was something more than hunger wrong with it.

He would probably come during the day, but she dared not wait, she had to move on with the baby in the hope of finding help.

How to let him know? There was paper in the diary but nothing to write with. Finally, she wrote a message in the wet earth outside the hut with a stick. She scraped the letters deep and large, and hoped he would arrive before they were obliterated by rain. She could not think of anything else to do.

Before leaving, she searched through Elina's belongings and found half a mealie cob which she ate hungrily. Then she wrapped the baby securely, and put it inside her windcheater.

Remembering the hyena, she searched the compound and found the remains of a grass fence still partially intact. This she dragged to the hut and propped against the doorway as a makeshift barrier.

Then she set off downstream, conscious of the small warm body in the windcheater. Yesterday, her concern had been as much for the trouble her disappearance would cause in Kariba as for her own predicament. Now she was frightened, both for the baby and herself. She felt weak, and her head was pounding.

But, after walking for a few minutes, the weakness began to dissipate. The sun warmed her spirits as well as her body, and the activity took the chill from her bones. When the baby cried she gave it water, and as she walked she sang to it, all the songs she had every learned: lullabies, songs from musical shows, love songs, songs she had forgotten she had ever known. A troop of baboons fossicking for insects watched her as she passed.

After a couple of hours, she began to tire, and stopped singing. Sometimes she waded through streams running into the river; she did not know how far she had come, only that the baby was not crying as often as before. She woke it up and made it take more water from her finger; it was not sucking, so she tried dribbling drops into its small pursed mouth, but it choked and she panicked, thumping it on the back until it stopped spluttering and started to breathe normally again.

She walked until the trees began to quiver and then to dance before her eyes, and she sat on the ground and leaned against a tree.

She dreamed Simon had come looking for her in a boat, and woke up, heart thumping, convinced she had heard a motor. But when she looked out across the water, there was still nothing and no one.

Except for an eagle, perched motionless on the topmost branch of a tall dead tree emerging from the swirling river. The bird gazed with imperious eyes over the water, and as she watched, it flung back its snowy head and called – a wild yelping cry that pierced the heavy air. Moments later, the call was echoed upriver, and suddenly she recognised it. "Clarissa's bird," she whispered, "it's a fish eagle."

The eagle spread its immense wings and flapped lazily over the water, and she watched until it was out of sight.

When she tried to feed the baby again, it took only a few drops; the small mouth drooped, and Liz bit her lip and hugged the tiny form fiercely. Just a little longer, baby, she pleaded as she stood up and walked on.

She found a dugout canoe, a *makoro*, floating in the shallows, but the current whipped it away before she could reach it, and tears of rage and frustration welled in her eyes.

It was dark now, and a strong wind had blown up. So that, when the sound came, it merged into the gusting of the wind and the roar of water, and she kept walking doggedly, telling herself it was just her imagination. But the sound became louder and she stopped, held her breath, and listened.

And then she saw a light, and now the throb of a motor carried to her clearly on the wind. Stumbling down the bank to the water's edge, she shouted as she felt for the torch in her rucksack. With fumbling fingers, she flicked it on. The batteries were almost dead, only the faintest orange glow emerged, but she held it high and waved it, shouting, "Here! Over here! Over here!"

For an eternity, there was no reply. And then a voice floated across the dark water. "Liz! Is that you?"

"Yes! Yes! Over here!" But her voice was carried away on the wind. Frantically she waved the torch again, but the batteries had died, there was nothing, and she yelled in frustration, "Here, over here!"

The sound of the engine faded. But the light was coming nearer, and she hugged the slight, limp form in her arms. "They've come, baby, they've come!"

The dark hulk of the prow slid up the bank and she ran to meet it, shading her eyes against the light. A figure dropped lightly to the ground and came towards her at a run. Chris.

"Are you all right?" His voice was taut.

"Yes, yes. Chris, thank God you've come........." She got no further, because he seized her arms. He was shaking her, and his eyes were blazing.

"What the hell did you think you were doing? You've got half the bloody population of Kariba out looking for you. Going off without telling anyone, taking Dave's boat – he's been shitting himself worrying about you. We found the boat about two hours ago. When you weren't there, we thought ... Jesus Christ, woman, what did you think you were doing?" he shouted.

Stunned, she struggled to wrench herself free. Robin appeared behind him with a torch, clapping him on the shoulder: "Hey, Chris, take it easy."

Still struggling, she gasped, "Be careful – the baby," and he released her so suddenly she almost fell. They both stared at her.

"Baby?" stuttered Chris, but she was already unzipping her jacket to reveal the small black head inside.

"What the hell....?" said Robin slowly.

In a few words, she blurted out her story. "It's barely alive," she finished, an edge of desperation in her voice. "We have to get help for it quickly."

"Come on, then," Chris' voice was brusque. "Give me that," he indicated her rucksack and she shrugged it off her shoulders.

On board, he handed her a thick jersey and pair of corduroy trousers. "You're cold. Put these on." Robin took the baby and wrapped it in another jersey while she pulled the trousers on over her own, and the jersey over her jacket. The warmth of the dry clothes was so comforting that hot tears started to her eyes. She blinked them back and held out her arms for the baby.

Robin was frowning uncertainly. "Liz, it's so cold, are you sure it's...?"

Taking it quickly, she laid her cheek close to the small mouth, and felt an infinitesimal puff of breath. "Still alive," she whispered. "Hurry, please hurry."

Robin held the spotlight, Chris took the wheel and the motor sputtered into life. The wind was colder now, the water dark and choppy as she stood in the prow between them. Even with the powerful torch, it was difficult to see, and no one spoke for several minutes as Chris navigated through the maze of floating debris.

"Did you find the grave?" he asked abruptly, his eyes intent on the water.

"Yes." Her voice was subdued, and he glanced at her quickly.

"And the diary?"

"Yes."

"Clever girl," said Robin. "Where is it?"

"Here," she patted her rucksack.

It was raining again, hard, cold needles that stung her face, and she turned her back to it, shielding the baby. Beside her, Chris was silent, hands clamped on the wheel, narrowed eyes scanning the water, steering a way through branches and tangled undergrowth. It was impossible to see the bank, impossible to see beyond a few yards of black water. In a trance of tiredness, she cradled the baby, staring through the rain into the blackness, willing the boat to go faster.

She did not know how long they had been travelling when a thud juddered through the craft. As she stumbled against Chris, he swore and swung the wheel hard.

Robin flashed the torch beam downwards, and she saw the glint of water near her feet. "It's coming in – we've got a leak."

"How bad?" Chris asked.

"Not good." Robin rummaged in a locker, and found a cup and an empty tin. He handed her the cup and they bailed furiously. But the water was coming in faster now, faster than they could get rid of it, it was over their ankles, and Robin swore in frustration. "It's no good, head for the bank," he shouted. "We've got to get out."

"Bloody hell!" Chris swung the wheel over. Half-submerged trees loomed ahead, he cut back the motor, and eased the craft between them. The hull scraped against wood, they were in shallow water now, but the boat was still filling, water swirling about her feet, needles of rain on her face.

"I'm going over," shouted Robin, letting himself over the side into the water. Chris edged the boat behind him, and the hull grated against something hard. Robin was in water up to his armpits, holding the torch. "Give me the baby," he shouted.

She gave it to him, and he waded slowly towards the bank.

"Come on!" Chris was holding a hand out to her. "Get out! I'll take the bag. Hurry!"

She climbed on to the side of the boat and jumped in. The water was warm after the cold spears of rain. Although her feet just touched the ground, it was easier to swim, and she struck out towards Robin's voice and the torchlight. Even so close to land, the current was strong and underwater branches ripped at her legs. She looked back: Chris was behind her, the rucksack on his shoulder. Ahead, she could just make out Robin's dripping form, wading out of the water and up the bank.

Something caught hold of her ankle and held it fast. Remembering the crocodile, she screamed and began to struggle, wrenching to free herself. Then she realised her ankle was stuck in the fork of a branch. Chris was behind her, pushing her forward. She tugged again.

"My foot! It's caught!" she gasped, and he dived. His hands gripped her legs, feeling down to her feet, seizing her ankle, twisting it. And then her foot was free and he was surfacing beside her, sucking in air, gasping for breath.

Robin splashed towards her and took her hand, pulling her out of the water and up the bank. Chris collapsed on the ground beside her. She looked around wildly. "The baby! Where's the baby?"

"It's okay. Right there," Robin pointed, "under that tree. Where's the bloody rucksack?"

"Christ, I dropped it." Chris plunged back into the water while Robin played the beam over the surface.

The rucksack was floating in the shallows, caught against a projecting branch. As he waded up the bank, Chris opened it and undid the plastic wrapper.

"One diary – intact," he said. His hair was plastered to his head, and he looked exhausted, but he was grinning. She slumped against a tree, weak with relief.

"And one baby," said Robin, placing it in her arms. She felt its face, the faint warmth emanating from the soft skin. Still alive.

"The boat!" she muttered in horror, "that's the second in two days."

Robin shone the torch on the water. The boat had settled in the mud, its prow still visible.

"It's okay, it's only Ian's," said Chris, and they began to giggle hysterically.

Half an hour later, a man in a truck picked them up on the outskirts of Kariba and gave them a lift to the hospital. It was almost midnight. The Scottish night nurse shook her head when she saw the baby, and took it swiftly away. When she returned, her face was grave.

"You mustn't expect too much," she said. "He's such a wee lad, and so weak. We'll do what we can." She saw Liz's expression. "Still, babies are amazingly resilient. If he's still alive tomorrow...." she paused. "Now, let's have a look at you."

Afterwards, Chris drove her back to the Harveys' in the nurse's car. The hospital had wanted to keep her overnight to treat her for shock, but she had refused.

He drew up in front of the house. "Go and get some sleep, or that Scottish dragon will have both our scalps," he said. "How are you feeling?"

"Fine." She felt tired, emotionally drained, and suddenly embarrassed. "Thank you. For coming. I'm sorry – that I caused so much trouble."

"It's okay." His voice was tired too, but he reached out his hand and smoothed the damp hair out of her eyes. "Forget it. Just don't do it again....ever. Now go, get out of those wet clothes."

Joan Harvey was in the kitchen stirring a cup of coffee. She stared at Liz as though she was an apparition, and then came across and hugged her.

"Thank God you're all right. We were so worried."

"The boat – ," Liz flushed with embarrassment and remorse. "I think it's all right, Joan, it was washed away, but Chris and Robin found it. We can go back and fetch it."

"It's you we were worried about," said Joan reproachfully. "Now all I need is for Dave to come back."

"He didn't come after me, did he?" She felt worse than ever.

"No. He's down at the wall. The river's coming up fast and they're trying to save the suspension bridge. He went down to help. I couldn't sleep."

Liz stared at her. "Mario will be there."

"Yes. They need all the help they can get. Want a coffee?"

"No, thanks, we had some at the hospital." She felt a sudden urgent need to find Mario. "Have you got the car here?"

"Yes." Joan looked at her. "Shall we go down?" Liz nodded.

The scene in the gorge was a drama in monochrome, floodlit by arc lights on the bank. The river had swamped the coffer dam, churning white foam as it plunged over the wall and thundered into the maelstrom below. The road that had once skirted the south bank was under water, and sections of the bank had been gouged out and washed downstream. Teams of people were clearing debris.

Below the coffer dam, on the swaying deck of the suspension bridge, more than a dozen small figures worked with oxy-acetylene torches and giant cutters on the braces that held the structure firm.

"What are they doing?" Liz asked an onlooker.

"Cutting it free so they can winch it up higher – away from the water," he shouted over the roar of the river.

The bridge looked frighteningly insubstantial, and her heart thudded against her ribs as she recognised Mario among the figures on its jerking deck. Her fingers closed on his St Christopher medal inside her shirt. Please be careful, Mario, she prayed.

The men on the bridge worked calmly and methodically, never pausing to look at the tumbling foam surging beneath their feet. The wind was rising, and the bridge jerked as the stays were cut away, throwing the men against the protective wire netting sides.

Above the roar of water, she heard another sound – a creaking, metallic sound. She strained her ears, but it was gone. She fixed her eyes on Mario, and a minute later it came again, the shriek of steel breaking, and this time a murmur rippled through the onlookers, and someone shouted, "Look! It's moving!"

Floodwater surged up the north bank on the far side of the river, tearing at the earth between the bank and the foundations of the tall steel pier supporting the bridge.

"It's going!" someone yelled.

Intent on their work, the men on the bridge had not noticed. But the watchers on the bank shouted at them and started to run towards the bridge, waving their arms. "It's going! Come back, get back!"

The steel column moved again, tilting slowly over towards the river, and the centre of the bridge dipped a few feet lower and jerked, flinging the men to the deck.

The bridge was moving now – slowly, like a giant silver snake against the blackness of the water. And suddenly she heard the words, as clear as a voice in her head: *When the black water comes, the tower falls and the silver serpent twists.*

She tried to speak, but the words would not come. She tried to move, but her feet were frozen. She was trapped in a nightmare. The men on the bridge had stopped working, they stared towards the steel tower, dropped their tools and began to run. Back along the heaving, bucking deck towards the bank and the shouting onlookers.

Her voice came back, and she pushed her way through the watchers and stumbled down the bank, screaming, "Mario! Come back!"

Dave Harvey was instantly beside her, seizing her arm, "No, Liz! Keep back! They're coming," and as she shouted at him furiously and tried to struggle free, she saw Chris and Robin among the first to reach the bridge.

Chris got there first. As he mounted it, the tower on the far bank swayed once more, and the centre of the bridge sank lower and waves swamped its deck. But there were no men there, they were already struggling up towards the bank, slipping and sliding as the waves leapt towards them from below.

The supporting cables strained and groaned, but the two nearest men had reached Chris's outstretched hand. He dragged one and then the other to safety.

Again the tower swayed, and the bridge shuddered along its entire length. Several men lost their balance and were flung backwards, but they struggled to their feet and kept coming. Now some onlookers had formed a human chain to help the struggling men up the bucking deck to safety. Chris was at the head of the chain, reaching for the advancing men and passing them back along the line.

Now there were only five still on the bridge, and Mario was second from the end. Three were scrambling to safety. The last man – the one behind Mario – slipped, and as the bridge dipped lower he began to slide back into the water. His mouth was open and Liz knew he was screaming for help although she could not hear above the roar of the river and the groaning cables and creaking tower.

But Mario heard, and turned, and went back, and seized the man's outstretched hand as he slid into the water surging over the deck. Then the tower leaned hard over towards the river and began very slowly, and with a kind of ponderous dignity, to slide into the water.

As Liz broke away from Dave Harvey, Chris began to move down the sloping deck towards Mario and the other man. As he did so, the bridge tore free of its north bank moorings and snaked high into the air as though it was a living being writhing in spasms of pain. The cables began to snap one by one, and the whole structure seemed to convulse, but incredibly the three figures still clung to the heaving deck.

One of the main cables snapped with a report like gun fire, and the freed end of the bridge was flung high into the air as though it was made of matchwood. Mario and his companion were hurled upwards, arms flailing, and then they began to tumble – over and over and over, plummeting down until they plunged into the surging black water and disappeared.

She tried to whisper his name, but no sound would come. All around her on the bank a stunned hush had fallen. She stared into the blackness, as the bridge twisted and writhed and thrashed at the water, arching its broken back as it began to break up.

And then she saw that Chris was gone too, and movement came back into her legs, and she stumbled down the bank. Two figures had been thrown into the water, two – not three. She pushed through the crowd at the end of the bridge.

And she saw him. He was in the water, clinging to the wreckage of the sinking bridge, about twenty yards from where it was attached to the south bank tower. He was struggling to grapple his way back to the bank, but the water dragged at his clothes, and when the bridge dipped under the water, he went down too, and disappeared. His head emerged again, and he dragged himself up the deck. Someone pushed past her with a rope, and began making it fast to the pier. Robin was there, throwing the rope towards Chris, but the waves whipped it away. They pulled it in and he threw it again. But the same thing happened, and Chris went under.

Not him too, her mind screamed. Again the rope was thrown out and this time he grabbed it.

Slowly, painfully slowly, as the river dragged at his clothes, they hauled him in. Hands reached out to help him scramble out of the roaring water. Robin was there, helping him up the bank.

She pushed her way through to him, and he saw her as she came and clung to him with cold, shaking hands. And he put his arms around her and held her shuddering body. He was breathing in hard, painful gasps. "I'm sorry," he muttered against her hair.

"I thought you'd gone. I thought you'd gone, too," she whispered, and his arms tightened as he stared over her head into the blackness, his eyes bleak.

She pressed her face hard against his warm, wet body. Warm and alive, he was warm and alive. But Mario was gone.

"We have to do something! Mario… Can't we do something?" Her teeth were chattering with cold and shock, her voice rose hysterically and she tried to break away, to go back to the water, to look for him. But Chris held her and spoke gently, although his voice was unsteady and she could feel him shaking.

"Liz. Liz. There's nothing we can do – nothing you can do. He's gone. They've both gone. I'm sorry."

A man near her muttered in a stunned whisper, "Poor buggers – didn't stand a chance."

Lifting her head, she stared out to where the broken bridge still writhed in its dying convulsions. "Can't we go and look – get a boat, a plane – something, anything?"

He shook his head. "Tomorrow, when it's light. We'll go and look."

The bodies of Mario and his colleague were found two days later, several miles down river. Mario's body was flown back to his family in Italy, but a memorial service was held at the dam site. Several hundred people attended – Mario had made many friends among colleagues, Italian and African labourers, and the local community. At the end of the simple ceremony, a group of black workers sang a praise song, paying tribute to his courage in going to the aid of his companion.

Already the floodwater was subsiding, flights to Salisbury were operating once more, and work had resumed on the wall. He's gone, but everything carries on, just as before, thought Liz. Almost as if nothing had happened.

Before she returned to the city she was visited by a sombre Paul Masimba. He had reached the *kraal* a few hours after she had left, and found her message and his dead sweetheart.

"I'm so sorry – sorry I couldn't help her," Liz told him. "I tried, but I think she was dying when I found her. She had lost so much blood."

He looked away, and shook his head. "It was my fault," he said dully. "I said I would come the day before. Maybe if......," he shrugged. "Thank you for taking the child, for getting him to the hospital."

"He's going to be all right, isn't he? I saw him yesterday." It was the one bright point she could fix her mind on at this moment.

"Yes, he will be all right." He smiled briefly.

She learned that he had met Elina during his ANC activities along the river. She had become pregnant, and because she was married (her husband was working in Salisbury) she had been too frightened to tell anyone. Masimba had arranged to meet her on the river and take her back to the city with him. She was waiting for him when the baby was born.

Liz did not mention the crates in the cave. She had passed the information to the police at Kariba when she reported Elina's death, and they had found the two men, and brought them back. But there was no evidence to link them to her discovery.

The police were going upriver the following day to check out the contents of the cave.

"There was a similar find further along," the officer told her. "Arms, Russian made. AK47s."

"What would they be for?" she asked.

He shrugged. "A lot of blacks are against Federation."

Her feelings towards Paul Masimba were hopelessly confused. She felt instinctively that if there was an arms cache, he would have something to do with it. She had no idea what its purpose was, but she liked him. They had helped each other and that had forged a bond between them.

Before leaving, he promised to keep in touch and let her know about the baby's progress.

"How will you manage?" she asked.

"My mother in Salisbury will look after him."

Chris was to fly Impresit officials to the city later in the day, and she was to leave on the regular flight the following day. He called in at the Harveys' before he left.

"Are you all right?" he asked.

She looked away from his intense gaze. She felt drained of all feeling but a profound aching sadness for Mario, for the loss of his infectious vitality, his irrepressible zest for living.

"Yes," she said flatly. "I'm fine."

"What are your plans?"

"Go back to Salisbury, work on the diaries. There's a publisher in Johannesburg, a contact of Derick's. I've spoken to him on the phone, and he's interested in seeing them. If he likes the look of them, I will do the editing, and add background material to fill the gaps. I'll stay in Salisbury till I've finished, and then go back to England."

"Had enough of Africa?" His voice was casual, but he still looked at her with that odd intensity.

"You could say that." She stared out of the window at the grey day. It was raining again, but softly, and quietly, as though the fury of the past weeks had been spent. She thrust her hands deep into the pockets of her jacket, and felt something metallic.

It was Mario's St Christopher medallion on its silver chain, and she drew it out and held it in her hand. "I should have given it back to him. It was his good luck charm, you know." She ran the chain through her fingers. "He lent it to me – and I had all the luck. His ran out, didn't it?"

"Stop that. Don't talk like an idiot," he said sharply. "It was nobody's fault."

She blinked, and grinned wearily at him.

"I know." She sighed, and dropped it back in her pocket. "Sorry. What about you? There won't be much flying work up here once the wall's finished."

"I have to go down south right away. Had a message from Mum – the old man has had a stroke. He's on the mend but I must go, in case. Barbara will try to get down soon, with the baby, but Mum needs me. I've got a few things to settle as well."

"I'm sorry about your father," she said slowly. "I hope he'll be all right."

"Thanks. Look, I have to go. But..." he came and put his hand on her arm. "I wanted to be sure you were all right." He paused. "I know what it's like for you just now – how you feel."

She stared at him, desolate at the thought that he too would be gone. It was all ending. "I didn't...," she began, and then stopped. "Have a safe trip."

He nodded. "Take care," he said, and turned and went out into the rain.

23

Ten months later

Sunlight glimmered through the stained glass windows of the small circular church on the hill overlooking Kariba Dam. Named after St Barbara, patron saint of builders, it was dedicated to the memory of the scores of men who had died, through accident or illness, during the building of the wall. In the centre of the white stone floor, the altar on its raised dais was dominated by a statue of the Virgin; set around the perimeter were the sculpted figures of St Barbara, St Joseph, St Catherine of Siena, and St George of England.

As the service drew to a close, and the voices of the choir of African children soared in heart-stirring harmony, Liz decided Mario – with his passion for music – would have approved. The ceremony had been simple and moving, and when the final benediction had been pronounced, she threaded her way through the large congregation in search of his family, who had flown from Italy for the occasion.

She was not sure how she would recognise them, but as soon as she spotted the tall thickset figure with the cleft in his chin, she knew he had to be Mario's father. His wife was small and plump, and with them was a voluptuous young woman who must be Mario's sister, Renata.

Liz introduced herself, and Adriana Pallivera looked at her with her son's dark, expressive eyes, now red-rimmed. "You are Mario's good friend. I know, he write to me about you. Lizi," and she took Liz's hand in both of her own and held it tightly.

For the second time that day, she had to blink away tears. "I was lucky to know him, Mrs Pallivera, even for such a short time. You can be proud of him."

Adriana Pallivera nodded, unable to speak. To give her time, Liz turned to her husband, who smiled Mario's irresistible smile as he kissed her on both cheeks. "We are proud, yes, but... we are also lonely without him to make us laugh."

His daughter put her arm around him and squeezed his shoulders. She said something in Italian, and he touched her cheek affectionately.

Liz drew from her pocket the St Christopher medallion, and held it out to Mario's mother. "Mario lent this to me. I'm sure he would want you to have it."

Adriana Pallivera's eyes brimmed over again as her fingers closed over the medallion. "I give to him for his birthday," she murmured. For a long moment she was silent, looking down at it. Then, with a small shake of her head, she took Liz's hand, and gave it back to her. "You keep. No, *grazie*," as Liz began to protest. "He give to you. Mario like for you to keep. Is better, *si*? I have many of his things."

Liz lingered with them for a few minutes. Mario's father told her they had been shown around the dam during the morning, had walked on the wall, and were returning to Salisbury later in the day. Before saying goodbye, she promised to visit them in Milan when next she was in Europe.

The crowd was dispersing, and she climbed into the borrowed car and drove up to a lookout point with a panoramic view over the new lake.

It was a warm, golden afternoon, the air champagne-fresh. Leaning on the bonnet, she stared across the expanse of shining water. Funny, she thought, I didn't expect it to be blue – more green or brown, like the river, but it's as blue as the sea. Behind the beautiful, sweeping curve of the massive concrete wall, the spreading waters had already obliterated all trace of the original shoreline, shaping a new landscape bordered by hills shrouded in a blue-grey summer haze.

Already hundreds of trees – half submerged by water – were drowning, their branches still green with foliage, and alive with cormorants, darters, kingfishers. On the glassy surface of the lake, the crests of kopjes had created a myriad of small islands, and although she could not see them from here, she knew they sheltered a multitude of animals and birds trapped by the rising water. A new drama was about to unfold.

She recalled a story about an old, half-blind diviner who had refused to be moved from a hill overlooking the water, believing his duty lay in staying to protect the river spirits. Even after the waters had begun to spread, he stubbornly stood his ground, and it was not until the hill had shrunk to an islet a few yards across, that he had reluctantly boarded a rescue boat.

How strange and sad, she mused, that underneath all that water are the places where we walked, where people and animals lived for thousands of years. All the little huts – the ones that weren't burned down, are they still standing? With water running through the doorways, through the mealie patches, over the graves, and into the dark vine-shrouded caves and the secret, sacred places of the people? Ian's camp beneath the mahoganies, where we listened to Mozart and Sinatra, the channel where we found the baby hippo.

And Clarissa's grave, and all the places where she and Simon had walked, laughed, made love, and been happy. All drowned.

What was it André Coyne, the French civil engineer had said when the final gap in the dam wall had been sealed? "We are proud of what we have created, but there is also the feeling that something has been destroyed."

Indeed. And what of the river god? Had he at last conceded defeat, or was he biding his time in the cool green, shadowy depths of the gorge? He had already exacted a price in lives – Mario's among them. But was it enough, or would he – perhaps years from today – emerge from his subterranean lair to take his revenge on the arrogant white race that had violated his stronghold and subjugated a mighty river?

Memories of the world beneath the waters drifted through her mind. And images of Mario – although now, at last, the pain of his death had begun to ease and she could think of him with a smile, and a sense of gratitude that he had come into her life, even if for such a brief time.

Climbing back into the car, she drove to the hotel to meet the journalist who had offered her a lift back to Salisbury. In a few days she would fly to London. The book – an edited version of the diaries, with background material added by herself (with help from Nicholas) – was finally in the hands of the printers.

She found the journalist in the bar. He raised his glass and slid off the stool, swallowing the last inch of beer. His eyes were slightly bloodshot, his lips rimmed with foam. I won't go unless he lets me drive, she decided. While he was collecting his bags she went back to the foyer to get the suitcase she had left at the reception desk.

A familiar figure leaned on the desk, talking to the receptionist, who looked up and nodded in her direction. He turned, and she saw that it was Chris. He strode across the foyer to her.

He had been away in South Africa for almost a year, during the dark months following Mario's death; and because she had spent the past few weeks in Johannesburg, working with her publisher, she had not seen him since his return. He looked thinner, but tanned and well, and she stared at him in a tumult of surprise and pleasure.

"Pendennis, you're an elusive woman. I was hoping you wouldn't have left yet."

"Chris – what are you doing here?"

"Rush job – so they called on me. Old Nick told me you were here. I'm about to fly back with an empty plane. Like a ride?"

"Wonderful – my lift has been in the bar most of the afternoon. I'll go and tell him."

The journalist was philosophical at the prospect of losing her company on the long haul back to the city. She rejoined Chris and he picked up her case. "Is this all? Let's go, I've got Dave's car. He'll pick it up later."

"How is your father?" she asked as he put her case in the boot.

"A lot better. He had a second attack after I arrived, and it was touch and go for a while, but he's picking up now. His heart has been damaged, so he has to be careful, had to give up work, but we're a tough breed. They're planning to come up here in a couple of months for a holiday."

"And you?" she asked. "What are you going to do now that there's no more flying?"

"There's a new exercise started, rescuing wildlife trapped by the water. Sounds like the kind of work I'd enjoy. Russell is involved, he's with the Game Department now, and I know the guy who's running the operation – Rupert Fothergill. There'll be some flying to locate the game, and in between I can help with the rescue work.

Old Nick is thinking about letting us use his plane. I'm looking for sponsors to cover the fuel and costs."

She was pleased. "Good. I was worrying about the animals this afternoon. I'm glad something is being done."

"A drop in the bucket, but still...." He was silent for a moment, then – "And you?" he asked abruptly. "I hear you're about to leave?"

"Yes. On Thursday."

"So?" His eyes were intent on the road. "It's all over between you and Africa. Back to civilisation and British weather."

She grinned wryly. "I'm not looking forward to that. I think my blood's thinned out."

"What'll you do? Have a reunion with the heavy charmer on the magazine?"

"You're way out of date, Chris, in more ways than one," she said lightly, "it was over with him a long time ago." She looked at him in perplexity. "But didn't Barbara tell you?"

"Tell me what? I only got back a couple of days ago. Haven't seen her yet."

"I'm just going over for a holiday, and to see my mother. I'll be coming back in a couple of months."

"Coming back?" She sensed a stillness in him. They had reached the small airport, and he switched off the motor and turned to look at her directly. "Last time I saw you, you couldn't wait to get out of here."

"I know." She gazed out across the runway into the trees. "I did feel that way, after Mario – and that poor woman. But then....."

"Yes?"

"It had something to do with the book. Working with the diaries, filling in the gaps, putting a shape to Clarissa's life – it made me see things more clearly."

"See what more clearly?" His eyes, almost pure green in this light, were intent and serious.

"Just things. Clarissa – how after she lost the baby, put all her energy into starting a clinic for the local Africans, how much she did to help the children. She turned her tragedy into something good. And how she savoured every moment of her time with Simon, no matter how short it was. I've learned something – about living. And I want to come back. I've been blooded, like Clarissa. This is my place too now."

He was silent. "Anyway," she said decisively, "if there's going to be an animal rescue programme, I ought to be around to write about it. Besides, whatever money the book makes, I would like to use for something Clarissa would approve of. And from what you've been telling me, putting it towards a rescue operation in her valley fits the bill perfectly."

"Well, well," his voice was quiet, "so it got to you after all."

"You said that once before. If you say 'I told you so...'"

"Wouldn't dream of it. But if you're planning to cover the rescue program, let's have some balanced journalism, none of that bleeding-heart bullshit about cuddly animals." His voice was teasing, but the expression in his eyes reminded her of the night on the river bank a long time ago.

She would not allow him to take refuge in flippancy. "Are you glad I'm coming back?" she asked impulsively, surprised at her own frankness. But, until half an hour ago, she had lost hope of seeing him before her departure, and now there were things she had to know.

He reached out and laid his hand on her cheek. His fingers, warm and sure, ran gently down her neck, over her shoulder and down her bare arm. Lifting her hand to his lips, he kissed the inside of her wrist, and then the back of her hand. "I'm very glad."

He smiled into her eyes, then his voice became matter-of-fact. "We'd better move if we are to get back before dark."

While she climbed into the aircraft and strapped herself in, he stowed her suitcase and went over to the airport building to take care of officialdom. Then he was back, running through the pre-flight checks before guiding the Cessna to the end of the runway. She remembered hippos wading through pools of rainwater on the old airstrip, now under water, then they were off the ground, climbing smoothly and swiftly into the glittering blue air.

Away in the north, the clouds were massed grey battalions on the march, and thunderstorms, split by shafts of sunlight, poured dark curtains of rain on the hills. But in the south the sky was a clear, tranquil blue.

"Show you a bird's eye view of the finished product," he said, taking the craft in a wide circle over the town on its seven hills. The arches of the small white church slipped away behind them, the wings tilted and they swooped down, to glide over the pale crescent of the dam wall and the shadowy gorge below. Then up, up, up, and the wooded hills slid away beneath their wings and they were drifting over the shining sheet of water.

"Look," he pointed to beyond the port wing. A fish eagle glided below them, its shadow winging across the waters of its vast new domain. She smiled. It was a good omen.

"Tell you what," he said. "There's a new Italian place in the avenues. They make roast fillet like you have never tasted. When we get to town, I'll pick up a bottle of red. And over dinner, I'll tell you how glad I am." Their eyes met. "Will that do?" he asked.

She smiled, wriggled down in the passenger seat and tightened her belt. "That will do very well."

He banked, and turned the plane's silver nose towards the south, to follow the pale ribbon of the Elephant Road as it twisted through the hazy wilderness of the Valley towards the blue escarpment and the high plateau beyond.

GLOSSARY

Boma	Enclosure, fence
Braai, braaivleis	Barbecue
Hokoyo!	Look out!
Impi	Matabele regiment
Induna	Commander of a Matabele regiment
Kraal	Small village
Kanjan?	How are you?
Kurumidza	Quickly, hurry
Limbo	Fabric
Madala	Old man
Makoro	Dugout canoe
Mukiwa	White man
Muti	Medicine or magic potions
Mvuu	Hippo
Nganga	Witchdoctor
'Nkos	Sir
Nyama	Meat, game
Penga	Crazy
Shamwari	Friend
Shumba	Lion
Sikatonga	Diviner
Vlei	Low-lying grassland